MU
WATER

Inspired by a true story, Neil Watson's rather unusual debut
novel is set in Wivenhoe and Yorkshire. Characteristically, Neil
didn't want to take the conventional route when creating the
cast populating *Muddy Water*. So he developed a scheme dubbed
'Cash for Characters', whereby a number of people (and even a
cat) donated money to charity for the chance to see their names in
print. Although appearing in name only, and not actually enjoying
or suffering the fate of Neil's imagined characters, this generous
group of people donated a considerable amount of money to
MIND, The Royal British Legion and The Royal National Lifeboat
Institution for the opportunity to see themselves in the pages of
this book. Listed in order of appearance, they are:

Hatty Palmerstone

Chris Dickinson

Anna Hennings

Mark 'The Praying Mantis'

Andy Stollery

Lesley Fretwell (aka Alberta Louise Baudet)

Fiona O'Brien-Smith

Baci the cat (owned by Lisa Lord)

Helen Durrant-Green (Helen the Hairdresser)

'West Ham' John

Alfie The Barber

David Anderson

First published 2015 by Hornet Books
Text © Neil Watson 2015
This work © Hornet Books Ltd
Paperback ISBN: 978-0-9934-3530-0

Editor: David Roberts
Illustrations © Laura Watson
Proof reading: The Destiny Angels (Janet Roberts and Jane Watson)
Cover design and photo: David Roberts
Front cover artwork: Pat Gibbon

Hornet Books
Ground Floor, 2B Vantage Park, Washingley Road,
Huntingdon, PE29 6SR

info@hornetbooks.com

MUDDY WATER

Neil Watson

Hornet

MUDDY
WATER

Leslie Markland is a loner who winds up living on a barge with his little dog Harry on a muddy Essex estuary at Wivenhoe. Cruelly denied his share of a substantial inheritance by his less than loving father, Leslie sets out to gain revenge by creating an heir to his former home on the Markland Estate in Yorkshire. But just when Leslie is tantalisingly close to securing his revenge, his plan unravels when a damaging climax to the story sends him to prison. Leslie has plenty of time on his hands to contemplate his actions. Was he morally right to do what he did? How could the events that unfolded as a consequence ever create a happy ending? As his time spent at Her Majesty's pleasure drags on, Leslie puts pen to paper and tells his story.

CHAPTER 1

Discretion Guaranteed

"That whole embarrassing episode makes me really cringe"

Leslie Markland

One cold, damp day in 1996 I found myself wandering around Mayfair in London, with an hour or so to spare before my appointment with Miss Pinchbeck. "Discretion guaranteed" was the slogan on the letterhead that first attracted my attention. Another positive was the fact that her agency was the only one of its kind I could find. I daresay that there were others, but you have to remember that those were the days before the internet had really got going. It wasn't like it is nowadays. If you type 'sperm donor' or 'surrogacy' into Google you would get half a million results in less than a second. But in 1996 it was much more complicated than that.

Since the reading of the will my brother gloated and did nothing but constantly remind me about how I'd always played second fiddle to him in the eyes of Father, how I'd lost out and how he had become a winner. He even suggested that it was because of me that our mother eventually upped and left. Well, I knew that last part wasn't true, but the other things he said certainly hit home. They hurt, because at the time I suppose he was correct – I had indeed lost out.

I'll explain later about the will and why I did what I did, but for now I'll just say I couldn't let my father get away with his final insult to me, whatever reasons he had for disinheriting me. And as for my brother, well, I wasn't going to allow him to keep his smug smile on his face for any longer than I could help it.

Walking up the steps to Miss Pinchbeck's Angelpride agency I pressed the white ceramic door bell. I almost wanted the bell not to work so that I had an excuse for not entering through the dark blue heavy door with its shiny brass fittings. But alas, it did ring very loudly and soon after it was opened by a very well-dressed tall, elegant woman with immaculately brushed hair.

"Miss Pinchbeck?" I enquired, nervously.

"No," came the reply, in a distinctly Scandinavian accent. "I am Silvie, Miss Pinchbeck's personal, how do you say, assistant. You have to be Mister Markland. Thank you so much for being punctual. Miss Pinchbeck is expecting you. Come in, please, and take a seat while I inform her of your arrival."

I followed her in and sat down on the only seat in the room, a very sumptuous leather sofa large enough for four people. I sank into it and took in my surroundings, all very plush and tidy, with large pictures of happy, smiling babies dotted around the walls.

Oh goodness, what on earth am I doing here, I thought. I was about to get up and beat a hasty retreat into the safety of the Mayfair streets when the Scandinavian girl reappeared.

"Miss Pinchbeck is looking forward to welcoming you now Mister Markland. Please come with me," she said quietly in that curiously attractive sing-song accent that Scandinavians possess.

Follow her I did, down the corridor and into an office, much smaller than the room I had been waiting in. As I entered the room I smelled cigarette smoke as strong as in any working man's pub. There were piles of books stacked on the book case in front of me. More piles of manila foolscap folders were on the chair in the corner of the room. On the desk, which was deep and had a black leather inset, there were more folders, and various photographs strewn across the surface. Behind the desk sat Miss Pinchbeck.

"Good morning Mr. Markland, or please, can I call you Leslie?" she began, and without waiting for a reply she continued, "I'm Miss Pinchbeck. It's so good to meet you and thank you for coming. Welcome to Angelpride. We are so glad you could take time out of your schedule to visit us. But of course you must have many questions you want to ask, and ask them you must, and answer them we must, ha ha ha. But before we begin there are several formalities we have to go through to ensure that we are both singing from the same hymn sheet, so to speak - ha ha ha - and then we can get down to business."

I didn't like her already. The smoke-filled room didn't help matters, and her cackly laugh made things worse. She was painfully thin with wiry grey hair and boney hands with long fingers. No nail varnish, I noticed, and no rings either.

But in for a penny, in for a pound, I thought. Besides, it was too late to back out now. I was here, after all, and at great expense as well. The Fiat was having yet another of its uncooperative periods and was being repaired again by Phil at the garage. So I'd had to make my trip to London by train and then walk in the rain to Curzon Street. The rail fare certainly hadn't been cheap.

I may as well go through these 'formalities' and then see what happens, I'd thought. Besides, I had become so bitter and angry about my father's will and I was desperate to do something about it. I hoped that, despite Miss Pinchbeck's less than attractive appearance and heavy smoking, she would at least be empathetic towards my situation and give me a chance. Of course she would - I had money in my pocket.

So we got down to business.

"Mister Markland: Sorry, Leslie, ha ha ha... You know it's not really for me to explain the importance of what we're discussing here. We're talking about a child's life, and you know, aha, that a child doesn't stay cute and young forever. One day it will grow up and will have his or her own feelings, and with that your feelings will evolve like you have never felt before."

Unprepared for this extraordinary lecture, I once again looked at the door, getting ready for a quick exit. But something kept me there. It was a certain vulnerability that I could sense in Miss Pinchbeck herself. Maybe she had personal experiences of her own - a similar scenario to my own perhaps? I didn't know, and I didn't want to know - instead I decided to allow her to pry into my world.

As if she could read my thoughts, she said: "Leslie, I am going to be deadly serious now, if you will allow me. Have you thought good and hard about the reasons why you are here? Why you want to create a life? Why you want to bring a child into this world? If you can look me in the eye and tell me straight that you have thought this through and that your reasons are honourable, then I will help you all I can. But if not, then the fee for my time today is £200, and I will ask Silvie to show you the way out."

I hadn't been expecting to have to reach into the depths of my conscience and question my own ethics. Up to that point I'd only been out to gain revenge against my late father and my brother. Not to be wrestling with deep thoughts about babies and life and reasoning and honour. Thankfully it was still day-time and I hadn't had the opportunity to allow the power of an evening's nice full-bodied glass of Merlot to influence my reaction to Miss Pinchbeck's scrutiny.

———————

Just as I'm getting to the important part of my visit to Miss Pinchbeck's clinic I'm abruptly brought back firmly to the here and now as I squat on my uncomfortably-hard prison issue chair, while writing my story and reflecting on that day 18 years ago.

"Exercise time you ugly lot!"

It's now six in the evening and as regular as clockwork, Rodney the Roof comes round to churn us inmates out into the quadrangle for our H&R - health and recreation. So, I'll have to leave my writing for now and pick up again in an hour or so. Twenty minutes of fresh air, twenty minutes of ablutions, and twenty minutes to gobble down whatever's on this evening's haute cuisine menu, and then I'll be back here in the sanctuary of my 12 foot by 10 cell I call home. Oh, and just in case you're wondering why we call him Rodney the Roof...it's on account that he found himself stuck up there on the roof of one of the outbuildings rescuing his precious adopted wild tabby cat that somehow found its way in here. Someone must have 'accidentally' knocked away Rodney's ladder, and there he was stuck all night until the following morning's warden discovered him, cold and wet and shat upon by the pigeons. Poor Rodney – he's never been quite the same since.

When I return to pick up my pen again perhaps I'll describe where and how this whole story started and then more about the awful time I had in Miss Pinchbeck's Angelpride Agency. That whole embarrassing episode makes me really cringe and I can hardly bring myself to recount it, but I will.

"Come on. Come on. It's now or never," shouted Rodney the Roof, at the top of his voice. I guess I'd better go now before it's too late. I don't want to miss my exercise.

CHAPTER 2

Growing Up

"I admit to preferring him dead rather than alive"

Leslie Markland

To explain how I ended up at Miss Pinchbeck's agency in Mayfair I need to take you right back to where my story begins. One, on the face of it, comparatively trivial incident I remember well is a good place to start.

The motorbike was a little too heavy for me to control, especially on our Yorkshire country roads. But he kept egging me on to go faster, and so I did just that. As I turned the corner and began scaling the hill in front of me I could feel the start of the rain that had been threatening all afternoon. My father's truck was in front of me and I was close behind. I could almost hear the old bastard cursing me for being too far behind him. I'll show him, I thought. With that, I opened up the throttle and came closer and closer until I could take him on the bend. There was no one coming and the coast was clear, but no sooner had I shot ahead of the old man I hit a pothole that caused me to swerve. I thought I was pretty good on the Triumph – after all, I'd been riding it ever since I'd passed my test – but I suppose I was just a tad over-confident.

The front wheel began to skid on the loose stones where tarmac should have been. I held the handlebars as hard as I could, but try as I might they were just too much for me. The rear wheel slipped from side to side and before I knew it I was holding on for dear life. Why do we do that? Hold on to something that you know in your brain is not stable – and yet you think it's going to save you the tighter you cling on: Well, no it doesn't.

Next thing I knew I was lying in a muddy puddle at the side of the road, soaked to the skin, with a deep graze on my left leg and something that hurt badly around my temple. My father's truck trundled past me as I lay there in a daze. Surely, I thought, it wouldn't be long before he'd reverse back to help me.

Eventually I did hear the sound of his truck approaching. It was a very distinctive sound – sort of a whine from the engine that was like the number 22 bus that went to town on Mondays, Wednesdays and Fridays combined with that of an old tractor that had seen better days. No matter. It was help, it was coming my way, and my father would take care of me and get me back home.

"That'll teach you to ride that thing like a bloody maniac, son," he bellowed above the noise of his truck. "I'll see you at the house. Your mother will have the dinner on the table at seven, so don't be late, or you'll have me to answer to."

And with that he stepped on the accelerator and drove off again, without even checking to see if I'd broken any bones. I could have been gravely wounded for all he knew, and he didn't give a damn. What an utter, utter sod.

Bedraggled, cold and hurting, I did my best to hold back the tears I felt were welling up inside me, just in case someone passing might see me. But of course no one would see. No one would be coming along this lonesome stretch of road, certainly not in the early evening. Of course not: they'd all be cosy, inside their homes, watching *Crossroads* in front of the fire.

What the heck was I doing anyway, trying to show off to my dad just how much I could beat him on the road? He didn't care less whether I was faster than him or not. So why on earth did it matter to me?

If it had been Stanley who had come a cropper on his bike, all hell would have broken loose. The old man would have danced around, flapping his arms with concern. Probably would have even gone and called for an ambulance and told them it was an emergency.

I don't know what Stanley had that I didn't, but it sure wasn't any skill in anything. Lazy with it, too: 'Stanlazy' was my name for him. I didn't actually dislike him, because he'd always been good to me while we were growing up together. So even though Stanley was my younger brother by three years, I still felt as though he were looked up to by his lordship as some wonderful person on a pedestal. And then there was the question of the girlfriends he used to bring home. They were always pretty, always had interesting things to talk about, and always seemed to be just the right type of girl in my parents' eyes. Just because I wasn't interested in girlfriends didn't mean that I was gay or anything. I just wasn't interested. It was as simple as that, but perhaps that was why my father looked up to Stan and down on me. I guess it may have been a kind of survival instinct, from his point of view. You don't follow? Well let me explain.

You see, my father was proud of his title Lord Markland. Maybe that fact went a long way towards explaining his behaviour towards me. He wanted to ensure his title would continue to be passed down to the next generation and beyond - and he could probably sense that I was unlikely to continue the family estate into the next generation and beyond on account of my seemingly celibate ways.

Anyway, I digress. Perhaps I should explain how I got home after my motorbike fall. Well, I managed, but not without a struggle. I must have broken something on the kick-start so all I could do was to push the bike in the pouring rain and hope that some passer-by would stop and help.

No such luck. In the end, the weight of the bike got the better of me and I had to abandon it and continue the remaining mile or so on foot at a steady pace so as not to be late for Mother's supper. I made it just in time, cold to the bone, wet and in pain.

"What kept you son?" laughed Father as I wearily walked in through the back door. "That'll teach you for showing off on a bike you can't handle," continued Stan. My mother kept quiet as she dished up the potatoes.

That's how life was back then. And now here I am, stuck inside these four walls that make up my temporary home, if that's what you can call a prison cell. I suppose it would have been a lot worse years ago, but thanks to bills of reform for this and that and various European Parliament directives for human rights, some may say that we've never had it so good. The room that I'm locked up in is comfortable and warm. The bed is not hotel standard but wouldn't go amiss in a reasonable B&B. I've got a TV in the corner for which I don't have to pay the license fee, and I get fed three times a day. Okay, so I have to work my chores, but if I keep my head down and just get on with them, nobody really bothers me. The best thing is that I have a desk in my room and an endless supply of paper on which to write these words.

And writing is what keeps me sane. I suppose you could say that telling you my story is my redemption for what happened as a consequence of my trying to right a wrong.

It was all because of that damned will that my father made. Looking back now I can see how one event led to another, but if someone had told me the same story I simply wouldn't have believed them. Ever heard the word entailment?

My father had died of bronchitis that turned to pneumonia that finally led to the heart attack that finished him off. He'd been ill for a while but carried on smoking his pipe, thinking that it was a more healthy way to smoke. What an idiot. It served him right - it wasn't rocket science to work out the correlation between smoking and dying.

"Look here, son," he would say, "I've managed to survive this long without the likes of you telling me what I shouldn't do. Do yourself a favour and mind your own bloody business."

I felt divided. Despite despising him as I did, part of me still wanted him to keep living for the sake of my mother, who, let's face it, had been his wife. Eventually, as it turned out, I discovered she couldn't stand him any more than I could and she decided to leave. But at the time I admit to preferring the thought of him dead rather than alive. And for wanting someone dead I do feel terribly guilty.

CHAPTER 3

The Getaway Car

"I tossed Jim straight out the window"

Leslie Markland

B ack in the days when I had my old Triumph bike, the one that I'd come a cropper on all those years ago, I kept it in tip-top condition, cleaning it and maintaining it religiously. It was worth a bob or two and when I began to think I should move away, my thoughts turned to getting a car, and of course Father and Stanley were full of sarcastic advice.

"You want to get a good old British car, Son. For someone of your calibre, something like a Ford Anglia or an Austin 1100" was the sort of advice Father would dish out for free.

"Or you could get a Mini - there's nowt much room for shagging the birds in mind - but then that wouldn't bother queers like you," would be my brother's contribution to the discussion.

"I'm not queer" I'd retort. "I'm just busy with other plans."

"Oh, yeah, what plans are they? Setting the world to rights? Well no one's listening, especially to you," Stanley would say. And so it went on and on and on.

"I'm going to get a car, I'll show you, and I'm getting as far away from you lot as I can," I remember shouting.

It was true that I couldn't wait to get away from my father and brother - but my mother was a different matter. I didn't want to cause her pain or heartache and after all, she was the innocent party as the feud between the men of the house continued to grow. She kept her head down and carried on dishing up the potatoes, so to speak.

And I've got to tell you, I didn't want any old boring car like an Anglia or Mini, or anything else British for that matter. I wanted something a little out of the ordinary, something that would help me gain some self-esteem. God knows, I was in need of some self-esteem back then. It was being thrashed out of me at every opportunity by my father. Why he picked on me to quite the extent he did I didn't know. The funny thing was, with all the jibes that Stanley gave me about me being gay, I was beginning to see some small signs in *him* that were, how would you say, somewhat effeminate. For one thing he never kept a girlfriend for longer than a few dates and I could never work out why. He'd stand in front of his mirror, quiffing his hair for far longer than was necessary. Whereas I just put a comb through mine for two seconds and it was done, he would continue going over and over the same patch, adjusting it until it was just how he wanted it. And then there was his 'purse'. He loved it and was proud of it, all leather and soft with a little clasp on the top to hold the coins in tightly so they wouldn't rattle around inside. It was a bit girlie if you ask me, but when I made a disparaging remark about it one day he blew his top.

"What do you know about anything, you big tosser? This is a Pierre Cardin. This is quality. But then you wouldn't know anything about that, would you?" he shouted, before whacking me around the head with it. I learned to keep my thoughts to myself after that.

Stanley did teach me something useful. It was that I shouldn't be afraid of going against the norm, and not being afraid to be different. So for him it was having a Cardin wallet-purse, for me it was my Fiat Sport, my first car.

Every Friday I would grab *The Yorkshire Post* before anyone else did as it hit the doormat, turn to the back pages and scour the lines of classified car adverts. I gazed past the Austins, the Fords, the Hillmans and the Talbots, instead focusing on the Renaults, the Citroens, the Dafs and the Fiats. One morning a particular heading caught my eye.

"Fiat 124 Sport Coupe: Low mileage: One Owner: Red."

I chuckled to myself as I imagined a 'red owner'. I promptly telephoned the number and arranged to go and see the car in Pontefract. I had a job on the following day, fitting some guttering at an office in Leeds, and it would take me half an hour or so to take the bike along the M62 to the seller's house in Eastbourne View after work. The car sounded just perfect for me and I couldn't wait to view it.

With the final guttering clip firmly in place, I raced south to Lofthouse and east along the motorway eagerly anticipating owning a red sports car. I could smell the freedom that having a car would give me and I hoped that it would be what I was looking for. I knew the Fiat 124 well, but only the saloon version that a friend had in mustard yellow. It was ugly and square, but I'd also seen a few of the sports versions around town, and they were in another league. If I got one, it would certainly shut up Stanley and my father for once. When I arrived at Mr. Sandeford's drive, I spotted several beauties parked neatly here and there in various stages of renovation. There was a blue Reliant Scimitar with a door missing, a Jensen Interceptor all polished but with no bumpers, several Jags up on jacks, and there in the corner of the garden was the red Coupe. My heart skipped a beat as I drew closer, and despite the cracked windscreen I knew I had to have it. I hadn't expected Mr. Sandeford to be a trader, but it didn't matter to me as I promised to part company with £690 of my hard-earned cash and suggested I'd return at the weekend to collect the car as long as I could get a lift from someone.

I could barely understand what Mr. Sandeford was saying in his broad Yorkshire accent: "By 'eck lad…why don't thee take it now?" he quizzed me, keen to seal the deal before I had second thoughts. He caught me hesitating as I glanced at the Triumph. "Thee can leave the bike here and I'll take it off thee hands for…" He ran his hands over it, looked it up and down, and felt the saddle. "…Shall we say 200 quid? No, I'll tell thee what, I'll give thee two twenty towards the Fiat and I'll let thee have the spare parts in that box over yonder. They must be worth a hundred quid if not more. Now I can't be fairer than that, can I, lad? Oh, and there's a few tapes in't footwell pocket as well."

Well, I couldn't say no to Mr. Sandeford's generous offer, could I? So we shook hands and I waved out the window to him as I drove off in my new acquisition.

I could plan to leave the Markland Estate in earnest, now that I had a car to keep my few possessions in – just some clothes, boots and tools. I may even need to sleep rough in the car a couple of nights, I remember thinking, but I didn't care. And as for money, I was sure that wherever I ended up, I'd find some odd jobs like painting and fixing things, maybe even a spot of light brickwork and suchlike.

I vividly remember the swell of excitement I felt when I neared the motorway. At last I would be free of the verbal bullying I'd suffered on the estate. Note that I didn't call it 'home'. Home is a place of comfort, and my new sports car was more like a home to me than the pile of bricks that Father was so proud of.

Despite the occasional miss-firing every so often, I was very happy with my new 'home' and I was sure I could fix that little problem by tinkering with the carburettor later. No matter for now, I thought, as I turned the knob of the Javelin radio. No sound came out but I imagined that would be just a loose connection and nothing major. And it wasn't until it began to rain that I understood why there was a stick with a half a potato on the end of it protruding from underneath the passenger seat. It was an old trick to lean your arm out the window and wipe the screen with the flat part of the potato that worked as a water-repellant wiper.

Ah, yes, although I'd begun to realise I'd been sold a pup, I was already in love with my car.

On the plus side, there was an eight-track cartridge player already fitted - all the rage back then - with several tapes tucked in the front pocket. I pulled the car over and shuffled through them until I came across *Jonathan Livingstone Seagull* by Neil Diamond, and I pushed it in the slot. Having read the book by Richard Bach, I recall recognising a certain similarity between the bird and me – both of us breaking free from our surroundings. After listening to a couple of songs, I stopped the car again and rummaged further in the compartment. There was Curved Air and Deep Purple. Great. The Eagles. Not bad. Oh dear - I found Jim Reeves' *Moonlight and Roses* lurking among the collection too. I'm ashamed to say that, without considering how environmentally unfriendly it was, I tossed Jim straight out the window. But then, oh my goodness, I pulled out *Nilsson Schmilsson*. My mother had first turned me on to Harry Nilsson by playing that record over and over, and here was the album in my very own car. At that discovery, I promptly forgave the Fiat, which incidentally I'd named Alfonso - Alfonso The Fiat - for whatever shortcomings it had or would develop in future.

I had quite a passion for music – except anything by Jim Reeves. That was who my father always played during lunchtime on Sundays. After we'd sat down in silence at the table and Mother had finished dishing up, he would start the record player in the teak radiogram and we'd all have to listen without interrupting. It was only after he'd left the table for a smoke that I could put on the Light Programme for *Round The Horn*. Julian and Sandy were my favourites, with Kenneth Williams as Sandy making me laugh until tears poured down my cheeks. Those brief moments were the only ones I can remember with any happiness on the Markland Estate.

CHAPTER 4

Cross Country

"And the strange thing was, I rather liked it"

Stanley Markland (1970)

I could sense right from the word go that Father had more of a soft spot for me than for my elder brother, but when I was younger I couldn't understand why. Father later disclosed to me that he'd wanted Leslie to be born a girl, making me even more confused. It didn't make sense as I thought he wanted his first child to become a male heir for all his property. He said that a daughter had been predicted by Aunty May. She wasn't my real Aunt - she was more like an aunty to the whole estate, doing kind errands to all. Well, apparently she did this thing, you see, where she got Mother to lay on the table and dangled a gold ring above her bulge. "There you are," she'd said, "You're carrying a baby girl in there." And they believed her: so much so that they got all the clothes bought ready for a girl. When the time came, they were convinced as sure as night follows day that a pretty little baby girl was being brought into the world. And of course it wasn't. It was a boy. Mother didn't mind

- she was grateful to have a healthy child born to her. But not Father. He could hardly bring himself to even look at the boy, or so I'm led to believe by Aunty May.

While we were growing up on the Markland Estate, I'd sometimes look out for my brother when Father was on the warpath. He did scare me with his temper, although it was never directed at me, only at Leslie, and quite often at Mother too. Sometimes I could walk into the kitchen with Mother at the stove and him at the table, and I could just sense the bad atmosphere and that something was up. It was never that way with me, mind you. Father would be cussing and threatening what he'd do to the boy when he came back from school, and it was all that Mother could do to calm him down. She didn't want any trouble, but I suppose she was caught between the devil and the dealer, if you get my meaning. She carried an awful feeling of guilt, having given birth to a son and not the daughter that her husband had been eagerly anticipating. For years I couldn't work out why he carried on like that. You'd think he'd have wanted a boy first - especially when it came to passing on his precious estate. He carried his reasons with him to the grave and it was only many years later that I eventually discovered the truth.

On one occasion I came home from school and could hear shouting going on even before I got to the back garden path. It wasn't only shouting. There was the sound of Leslie screaming and crying as Father set about him with his belt. I sneaked in the door and ran upstairs to my bedroom before I could be spotted. I played with my trains and sang to myself until the fracas died down.

"You good for nothing so and so," I remember Father hollering. And then he let go. As quick as lightening my brother ran up the stairs to his room, going past mine and slamming his door behind him. In that split second, when I caught a glimpse of him dashing to his sanctuary, I saw the look of unhappiness in his expression and his eyes red from crying.

I think I must have been seven or eight by then, with Leslie being three years my senior. I knew that I should have followed him into his room to console him - but I didn't. Instead I went downstairs where Father was going about his business at his desk, sorting out some papers and doing what grown-ups did. He was still red-faced with anger from whatever it was that Leslie had done to upset him. He looked up at me.

"Ah, there you are, my boy. Come here and give your Pa a cuddle and tell me what you've been up to at school," he said. "What have you learned today? Anything interesting?"

I liked his attention, and his interest in my school day made me feel special and important.

Franklin House was a private school for boys. It was run strictly by the masters and prefects, who strutted around the corridors in their mortar boards and gowns. There were only two mistresses - Miss Duxbridge, and Mrs. Buxton who taught maths. It was the beginning of the new year term, and Leslie had now moved on to his new school. It's fair to say that Leslie, although not thick by any means, was somewhat 'academically challenged', and as a consequence he flunked his Eleven Plus. So instead of going on up to Ashley Grammar, he had to settle for Cromedale, the new comprehensive school set up to replace the former secondary modern. This was a real source of embarrassment for Father, who faced unspoken ridicule by some of the tenants on the estate - especially those whose own offspring would be entering Ashley. How could it possibly be, he fumed, that mere farmhands and foresters could have kids cleverer than his own? I later worked out that it was this episode that had sent Father into a frenzy on that day when Leslie was belted.

Thankfully for Father, and me, I created no such problem. I not only excelled in nearly all the subjects, I had no difficulty in producing homework on time, usually getting 8's and 9's from the masters and mistresses. The only area where aptitude was definitely lacking was in games, and I would find any excuse to get off football, rugby and cricket. These lessons were ruled like iron by the prefects who relished their bullying roles. Mr. Vickers the P.E. master had delegated responsibility to them, while he stayed in his office until the last minute, smoking on his ebony pipe until it was time to go outside and onto the playing fields.

Usually at school, if I kept my head down and got on with my studies, and was attentive in class answering when I was spoken to, I managed to keep out of trouble. But there was one prefect, Philip Mennotsy, who relished his ability to bully, without repercussion. He was one of Mr. Vickers' chosen few, selected to get us smaller boys out on the pitch ready to play football when his pipe had been finished. Mennotsy was horrible, and had particularly sadistic tendencies towards me and two or three of the other boys, whose soccer ability was as equally lacking as mine. He was tall and built like a brick, and he wasn't to be messed with. He enjoyed ordering us to run around the edge of the playing field until we were puffed out, and would also order us to do sit-ups and press-ups until we were nearly at the point of throwing-up. Then he'd make us do it all again, laughing out loud and threatening us with physical harm if we didn't comply. One games period during my last year at Franklin House I decided that enough was enough and that I would rather go on cross-country running exercises - a new option that Mr. Vickers had introduced so that he didn't have to put up with boys like me who had no interest in his stupid soccer lesson.

Mennotsy was still Mr. Vickers' right-hand man, in charge of preparing the other boys for the football match and getting them in line ready for each team captain to pick their players. I was instructed by him to go off on my cross-country run, along with three other boys of my age who had a similar dislike of football.

"And I want to see you sweating like a pig by the time you're back in the showers, Markland," Mennotsy shouted after me as I set off on the five mile course around the adjoining woodland.

I actually rather enjoyed going on these runs and I had no trouble in working up a sweat. My return to the school building coincided with the football game ending and the whole class of 31 boys piling into the changing rooms. First into the showers meant first out, and almost certain pain from the towel-whipping that was customary on these occasions from the others. Whoever stepped out of the shower first would have to run past the other boys and their line of fire. They would wet the end of their towels and flick them at the 'first-outers' with a deafening crack as the wet cloth hit the backs of the victims' legs. To avoid this torment, the logical answer was to shower later - but I didn't know what was worse. You see, the showers were hot at the beginning, and that was the reward to offset the towel-flicking. Gradually the water temperature became lower and lower as the hot water ran out until it was near freezing. Mennotsy would stand around making sure that everyone took their shower, and I usually caught him peering round the wall to spy on me and the other boys washing. It could have been my imagination but, although I suffered my fair share of grief from him, over time his shouting appeared to decrease. Was I mistaken in thinking that he'd taken to standing between me and the towel-flickers so that they couldn't get a swipe at me? Surely it couldn't be that Philip Mennotsy was actually becoming, well, nicer to me?

Then one Wednesday's games lesson I had my answer to that question. I went off on my cross-country run with nine of the other boys, while the other 22 from the class played football. As usual, we would settle into our groups based on our natural running speeds, and as usual I would end up alongside Michael, Gary and Malcolm. The others in the group were fatter and slower than us. By now I was taking this running business more seriously and decided to put a sprint on, distancing myself from the others. What was the point, I was beginning to realise, in wasting time by going for nothing much more than a fast walk? Having decided to put some effort in and do a proper run, it wasn't long before I was on my own, jumping over tree stumps, splashing through the mud and maneuvering around the wet path that wove itself around the small lake. Enjoying this, I ran faster and faster until I inevitably slipped and lost my balance.

Crack! My leg crumpled under me and I fell to the ground in agony. I'd not known pain like that before, and I couldn't move. I had to lay there in the wet mud until the others caught up. When they eventually arrived, they managed to get me up with my arms around the shoulders of Michael on one side and Gary on the other. Both of them dragged me to a nearby clearing on the edge of the woods. We could see the school building about half a mile away, but there was no way I could make it that far unaided.

"You three stay here," said Malcolm, "and I'll go back to school and get some help."

For what seemed like an eternity, I lay on the cold ground, feeling dizzy. I must have passed out, as the next thing I remembered was looking up at Mennotsy towering over me.

"Come on, up you get Markland, we'd better get you back and get you warm and seen by Nurse Strick."

But I couldn't get up. The pain was too great, and my leg buckled under me when I tried.

"Okay then, I'm going to have to carry you," reasoned Mennotsy and with that he picked me up and threw me over his shoulder as if he were a fireman rescuing me from a burning building, and proceeded to carry me all the way back to school.

Once there he deposited me in Mr. Vickers' office and onto the physio bed against the far wall. But instead of going off in search of Nurse Strick's professional expertise, after closing the door he stayed to take matters into his own hands.

"Firstly, we'd better get these damp things off you, or else you'll catch a death," he said. "Lift your arms up so that I can pull your shirt over your head. Good. Now lie back on the bed and let's remove these muddy shorts from you."

My head was beginning to spin, and not just from the pain from my throbbing foot. I was also becoming light-headed as I realised that Philip Mennotsy's hand was brushing against the front of my pants a little longer than necessary.

And the strange thing was, I rather liked it.

CHAPTER 5

Entailment

"We'll be alright, won't we Harry?"

Leslie Markland

F ather had died in 1995. His funeral had been a basic affair. There weren't that many attendees. The vicar did his best to say the right words that wouldn't upset anyone, but there were no eulogies and no stories told of what a wonderful man my father was: Hardly surprising in my opinion. Were there any tears shed? I didn't see any. Those present were there more out of a sense of duty than love. There were several in attendance from the houses on the Markland Estate - probably thinking they ought to make an appearance to ensure their tenancies would be renewed when the time came. We all returned to the Manor house after the church service to eat sandwiches that had been made the day before by Phyllis, the cleaner-come-housekeeper, who was dragged in on her day off to help out.

Entailment? I was about to find out what the word meant the hard way.

A few days after the funeral I had an appointment with Mr. Ainsworth. Roger Ainsworth had been the family solicitor for as long as I can remember.

My father first came into contact with Mr. Ainsworth on an occasion when he supposedly needed to evict one of his tenants for non-payment of rent. Mr. Ainsworth was able to draw the matter to a successful conclusion, and ever since then he'd been my father's solicitor of choice. Over the years they socialised as well, thanks to a common interest in clay pigeon shooting. One day my father organised a shoot on the estate and several local acquaintances and businessmen were invited, including Roger Ainsworth himself. I must have been four or five years old at the time and that was the first occasion I can remember meeting him.

I still recall to this day having a feeling of warmth and calm coming over me when on one occasion he'd come to the house for drinks in the parlour. Unlike Father, he showed interest in me as he walked through the kitchen where I had been drawing some pictures of racing cars in my exercise book, and he leaned over my shoulder to take a closer look.

"That must be Emmerson Fittipaldi's Lotus if I'm not mistaken, young man. You know Leslie, if you draw the wheel that's nearest to you just a little larger than the one behind, that will give you what's called perspective, and it'll make your picture look even better."

I couldn't believe that any grown-up would actually take the trouble to look at what I was drawing, let alone help me to improve my art technique. And the fact he recognised my favourite Grand Prix car made me sit up and take notice of him all the more. In the years that followed I became more and more enamoured with him. He was a real kindly sort of man, and I came to respect him like no one before - or since, for that matter.

According to my father, Roger Ainsworth always wore a bright cravat and exquisite shirts that he had tailor-made for him in London's Jermyn Street.

"You see Son, if you did a proper job like Mr. Ainsworth, you could afford to dress yourself respectably like he does."

He never took account of the fact that I actually did alright as a general handyman and painter. There was always someone wanting something doing that they couldn't or wouldn't do themselves. But there I go complaining about my father again. Well, he's six feet under now, and there I was waiting for Mr. Ainsworth to take me through the contents of the will. My brother Stanley was already there, sitting in a green, leather-backed armchair and drinking coffee from a Wedgewood cup.

"Ay up Leslie. Good of you to show up," Stanley said scornfully as he sank back into his chair. Of course he'd have a pop at me at the first opportunity, but I dismissed him.

"What's the problem? I'm not late, it's you who's early - I guessed you'd be here before me, so you could try to weasel out some titbit of information from Mr. Ainsworth before I got here."

"Gentlemen, please," responded Mr. Ainsworth. "Can we have a little decorum here? I've known you both since you were born, and I'm sure you know by now that I like to conduct these kind of proceedings with dignity. After all, your father has passed away and we should have respect for the way in which he chose to do things, although a little unusually, uh hum, in my opinion, but nevertheless, uh hum, we'll do things, uh hum, properly while you are in my office. Is that understood?"

"Now, would either of you care for a cigarette or a cigar?" Mr. Ainsworth went on. He made it quite clear he wouldn't stand for any nonsense in his firm, and I felt like I'd been ticked off for something I hadn't done. I looked up and noticed a drawing pin still stuck in the window frame with nothing attached. My mind glazed over as I wondered what had been hanging from it previously and why it was still there. Maybe some office Christmas party where it held up a paper chain. Did they leave it there deliberately, ready for next Christmas, or had they simply forgotten to remove it?

"Leslie! Please pay attention," continued Mr. Ainsworth. "This is very, uh hum, important and it is essential that you and your brother fully understand the consequences of your late father's wishes. When you're quite ready I will begin to, uh hum, explain."

And that was when I learned about entailment.

When Mr. Ainsworth leant back in his swivel chair I knew that he was being serious and he required the complete attention from us both. I had presumed that my brother and I were going to become the beneficiaries of our father's estate, and I was keen to hear the fine details.

"Uh, hum, Gentlemen. Thank you for coming. As you know, I have been doing business with your father for many years, and have seen you both grow up. It is my duty as the Estate's lawyer, and also as a family friend, to see that your father's last will and testament will be disclosed to you in a manner in which you fully understand and appreciate."

Without lifting his head, he raised his eyes at us and peered over his gold-rimmed spectacles. Come on, come on, I thought, let's get on with this. But I decided to sit patiently and let him continue at his own preferred pace.

"Now, I have to say, uh hum, that I have seen many, many wills in my time at Ainsworth & Stephens, and I dare say that my son Brian will see many more, especially when he takes over from me as senior partner when I retire, which is going to happen in due course. In all the years doing this work, I can't say I recall seeing anything like this one, and whilst being completely within the law, it is however, uh hum, somewhat irregular. I want you gentlemen to absorb what I'm going to say very carefully."

"For goodness sake, get to the bloody point," Stanley muttered just loud enough for me to hear, but too softly to reach Roger's ears.

"On your father's estate, as you probably are aware, there are 12 individual tenanted houses, with each one commanding a rent which is fair for this day and age, and at current market rates. The income from these is moderately good. In addition, there is also Markland Hall, which was divided up some years previously into six individual flats. These are rented out to retired workers from your father's farmstead at a rate below market value. They could of course fetch more on the open market, but your father expressly wished for those tenants to remain in place for as long as they chose, and at the rents laid down in the ledger. It was his way of thanking those men for their loyalty towards him on the farm. And then of course there is the farm itself, a not insubstantial 150 acres. Since your father ceased maintaining the fields and cowsheds himself and decided to lease the land to a handful of local farmers, all he has had to do, uh hum, was to sit back and count the revenue. The farmers pay the estate an annual rent, plus a percentage of the revenue generated when their produce goes to market. That rate is currently 2.5%, which may not sound much, but in fact it is running into many thousands of pounds."

I had no idea that my father had been such a business man. I just saw him as a grumpy bad-tempered, tweed jacket-wearing old so-and-so who had a chip on his shoulder when it came to me. I had hoped that he would have mellowed in his old age when it came to divvying up the proceeds of his fortune. Of course it would have been nice to have some money to my name, that goes without saying. Who wouldn't have liked that? I dreamed of affording a decent car for a start. I'd still have a Fiat Sport, but I would find a good one that didn't break down every few minutes. Or perhaps even treat myself to something grander. Maybe an Alfa, or, oh my goodness, maybe even a Maseratti, or, or...a Ferr-.

"Please, Master Leslie. Please can I have your attention? You appear to be miles away." I apologised, and he continued.

"Thank you, Leslie. Now, as I was saying, with the Markland Estate comes certain maintenance responsibilities, especially the upkeep of the Manor House. That old house needs a lot of looking after, and that can be expensive. So, your father has made a provision in his will that the funds in his bank deposit account are to be used solely for that purpose. If the roof leaks, if the gutters fall down, if the windows become rotten - that kind of thing - then Mr. Tibbs can be called upon to fix them as and when necessary, and you are not to worry about how Mr. Tibbs will be paid. There are sufficient funds to cover such costs."

"But," Mr. Ainsworth plodded on, "I am sure you are wondering where you yourselves come in to all these, uh hum, arrangements of your late father's affairs."

Well, yes, that's a fair summation, I thought. Please, Roger, just get to the point.

He must have read my mind. "I am now going to get to the point. The main crux, uh hum, of the matter, so to speak…"

At last, thank goodness. My brother and I sat slightly more upright than previously.

"Your father decided, for his own reasons whatever they were, to use the law of what's called entailment. Entailment is not uncommon, and examples can be found going back centuries, where a landowner may wish for his estate to be left to his eldest son. He may wish to entail his property to his male offspring, thus limiting the inheritance to specific heirs and therefore continuing the estate or property in the deceased's name. Take Jane Austen's *Pride and Prejudice* for instance…"

Oh no, he's off again, I thought to myself as I shifted around uncomfortably in my chair and found myself focusing once again on the drawing pin stuck in the window.

He droned on. "…where the Bennets only had one daughter, so the entailment was broadened to include Mr. Collins, who was a distant cousin of Mr. Bennet…"

"Mr. Ainsworth," interrupted Stanley, abruptly. "Jane Austin is all very interesting, but we didn't come here today for a lesson in English literature. What exactly has all this got to do with us? Please can we get straight on to our inheritance?"

Although I was somewhat embarrassed by my brother's tone, I admit that I too was glad of his somewhat impolite intervention.

"Patience, Master Stanley, is a virtue that clearly you do not possess. If you can summon some patience, I was just coming to, uh hum, your inheritance". And now it was Mr. Ainsworth's turn to shuffle uncomfortably in his seat.

"Very well, Master Stanley, I'll come to the conclusion. Your father has left the bulk of his estate to your children. That's not to say that you don't stand to gain anything - you will in time, and you will immediately begin to receive some rental income from the flats in Markland Hall. Each of you brothers shall receive the rent from three of the six dwellings - but you must also keep those properties in good repair from the proceeds of those rents."

"But, you said Mr. Tibbs had been provided for to look after those things, didn't you?" I asked.

I had come to this meeting, hoping against hope that my father had finally decided to let down his mean facade and allow me to see that all along he actually did love and care for me. But there I was faced with looking after three flats on behalf of elderly tenants who could live there for the rest of their lives, paying under-market rents. And the part about my children hadn't yet sunk in - I couldn't have heard Mr. Ainsworth correctly on that point.

"No, Master Leslie, I said that the cost of maintenance of the Manor would be covered by the funds in the deposit account. Now, have you digested what I said about your children being entailed?" I was beginning to become somewhat irritated by him calling me Master and not Mister. After all, I was old enough to be driving my own car now, not still drawing one on a sketch-pad in the kitchen.

"You see," Mr. Ainsworth continued, "your father has left his estate, and the bulk of income being generated from it, to his grandchildren, and half of this income will be held in trust for them until they reach the ages of 18 for any grandsons, and 21 for any granddaughters. When the grandchildren come of age, they will benefit from the whole of that income, but until then, their parents - that's you two brothers, uh hum, will receive the other half of the income."

All of a sudden the reality of the situation hit me like a ton of bricks.

"But Mr. Ainsworth, it may have escaped your notice that I don't have any children." My voice grew softer as the consequences of Mr. Ainsworth's statement were beginning to sink in. I couldn't help noticing the expression on Stanley's face, as the significance of Mr. Ainsworth's words also sunk in for him. My brother and his wife Constance had twin daughters, Sophie and Hilary, who were nearing their first birthday. My father had doted on them, the proud grandfather that he was, and I had seen the happy glint in his eyes when they were around him. During that weekend when I came up from Essex to the Manor House for the girls' naming ceremony, despite all my father's unpleasantness towards me, I had been pleased to see him looking so content. I'm not sure whether he knew he was ill by that time, but whatever. He was certainly in sound mind, and he knew exactly what he was doing when he wrote his will. So, in effect, the old bastard had finally turned the screw of hatred on me by cutting me out from his estate's inheritance, except for a couple of hundred pounds a month rent from a few flats. As I said earlier, and I'll tell you again, it wasn't about the money. Not really. Even now, as I sit writing this account all these years later, I can feel my cheeks reddening with rage once more when I consider my father's final callous actions towards me.

There were, of course, formalities that needed to be conducted during the rest of the meeting with Mr. Ainsworth that day. Documents had to be signed, and papers had to be photocopied. Mr. Ainsworth's secretary, the formidable Mrs. Harris, came in and out of that room on at least four occasions, each time with some folder or other. I could see that Mr. Ainsworth was himself upset about the circumstances, and empathised with my sentiments that an unjust conclusion had been decreed by his old friend, my father. Of course, there was nothing he could do and no words that he could say to change my feelings of betrayal.

Meanwhile, my brother was pretending to be sorry for me, but I could see the hint of a wry smile at the edge of his mouth as he tried to conceal his excitement about what had occurred moments earlier. I calculated, even with my somewhat poor mathematical skills, that he would be receiving something in the region of £7,000, maybe even £8,000, inflation-linked every month for the next 17 or so years. He would be able to give up his job, if he wanted. He'd be able to travel anywhere in the world, to buy that new car I had dreamed of. He could be lazy if he wished - and truly live up to my nickname of him - Stanlazy. I thought back to the old days when we were growing up and he would sometimes look out for me when I was secretly smoking out the back to escape doing my mother's chores. I wondered if he'd be looking out for me now. Somehow I doubted it.

The contents of that will were the catalyst for the chain of events that followed. In essence it cut me off from any benefit, simply down to the fact that I had no children. My brother Stanley, however, did. At least he did have back then, but I'll come to what happened to them later on.

You could say that those two girls are why I'm here, and you have to believe me when I tell you that the reason I'm now in prison had nothing to do with the money.

So, you may wonder what I did after the meeting finally ended that day. I shook hands with Mr. Ainsworth and said goodbye to him. It wasn't his fault that I felt as low as I did. I even felt sorry for him, as it couldn't have been terribly easy for the man. Despite all his waffling on about Jane Austen, and his nervous 'uh hums', he was a decent man. Age was catching up with him, and I knew he would be very happy to be away from all this legal business, to go fly-fishing on the River Aire, or, to practicie his beloved clay-pigeon shooting.

My brother tried to console me as we left the Ainsworth & Stephens office. He invited me back to have dinner with Constance and the girls, but I declined. I didn't know how I would react to seeing those two little girls, still babies. They had no idea what their future held, but I knew it was a brighter one - or at least more affluent - than my own. Instead I conjured up enough bravado to look Stanley in the eye and shake his hand goodbye.

"No hard feelings, old chap," he said, with a barely concealed expression of false remorse. I couldn't answer him in case my voice broke down, and as the dark clouds above began to create drizzle, I walked away in the opposite direction, towards my clapped out old Fiat.

My head was in a daze. I needed to go away somewhere and think everything through. But actually there wasn't much to think about. It was plain and simple. I had no children. I hadn't even had any relationship with a woman before or ever been interested in that sort of thing. It simply wasn't going to happen, and I guessed my father knew it. I was never going to be wealthy. But it wasn't about the money, as I kept saying to myself. It was more about the pain of knowing once and for all what my father had thought of me. Now there could be no doubt.

As I dawdled slowly along the pavement, I heard the little patter of feet scampering behind me. By now the drizzle had turned to rain, and I wasn't wearing a coat. The side streets of some northern towns can be very gloomy and depressing, and I wanted to get away from there and back to Essex, where I felt much more at home, as quickly as possible. I looked behind me to see the source of the noise following me. There, bedraggled and forlorn, was the sweetest little terrier you could imagine. I stopped to take a closer look. The small dog gazed up at me, its brown matted hair dripping wet, with its head turned to one side and ears pricked up, as if waiting for me to say something. Examination revealed no collar and no name-tag.

Seeing the little animal must be a boy, I bent down and quietly asked him, "Hello little fellow: Where are you heading?" Instinctively I wanted to strike up a conversation with my new-found friend. The dog twisted his head the other side this time, and as I turned to continue walking, he followed me.

I crossed the road, recognising that I was nearing the spot where I'd left the car. I didn't know how those little legs could keep up with me, but they certainly did.

"Go on boy - I've got to go now," I commanded half-heartedly, as I pointed for him to go the other way. He didn't take any notice of me. I continued walking toward my Fiat Sport in the far corner of the car park next to a red Ford Escort and a white Vauxhall Cavalier. The little chap followed. As I turned the key and opened the driver's door, I glanced back to say goodbye to my furry friend, but as quick as a flash, the dog leapt in and jumped over the front seat into the back where he promptly laid down and began to lick himself dry.

"Come on, you can't stay there," I reluctantly told him. But then, a flash of inspiration came over me. Oh yes he can, I reasoned. I looked around to make sure no one had seen the little mite jumping in through the door, but the car park was thankfully empty. I got in behind the wheel, started the engine and drove into the downhill cobbled road, now lit by the street lights that had just come on.

Adjusting the rear view mirror, I could see the dog's reflection, and as I did so it also looked at me with, if I wasn't mistaken, a knowing glint in his eyes. If only I could have some of that sparkle, I thought. I rummaged around in the footwell pocket until I found my best eight-track cartridge - *Nilsson Schmilsson* - and slotted it into the player. The last song of the album came on, 'I'll Never Leave You' - one of my favourites by Harry. It was a sad song and it suited my mood perfectly, but as I glanced up at the mirror again and saw the dog catching my eye for a second time, I felt a wave of love for this poor little helpless creature that I instinctively named.

"We'll be alright, won't we boy? We'll be alright, won't we Harry?"

CHAPTER 6

My Master and Me

"And believe me, I knew exactly how to play cute!"

Harry (1995)

Dogs can be more intelligent than you humans may think. It wasn't by accident that I decided to leap into the back of that dark blue car. Besides, it was drizzling and my coat was getting wet and bedraggled. But there was something about the man. I felt he needed help. There was definitely pain. I felt his pain. But mostly I was simply cold and the rear seat of his car felt warm.

He thought he was clever, naming me Harry after his favourite singer. He thought there was some connection. I humoured him.

As we travelled south that night, he needed to stop for a break, not before time I can tell you. I was nearly at bursting point myself, and was about to wet the seat. "Shall we take a break here Harry?" he asked as he looked at me in his rear view mirror, almost expecting me to reply. He knew I instinctively understood what he'd asked. I sat up on the seat and his eyes met mine in the reflection of the mirror, my little head twisting to the left with both ears lifted. I'd never really known what it was like to have a close human friend, but I could tell that was all about to change. He pulled in to the parking area of a large building next to the road and opened the door. The tall light posts dotted around the car park shone down upon us, and the cool air made him feel chilly, although I was nice and warm with my furry, fluffy coat. I shifted my head to the other side as if waiting for his permission for me to jump out. He released the lever to tilt the seat forward and yet still I sat there, cross-legged. We'd only just met and I didn't know whether he was going to hit me. "Come on Harry. Let's go and get us a drink and something to eat," he said. And with that I leapt out and impatiently waited by his side as he locked the door. But I couldn't hold out any longer, so I darted off to the nearest tree. Ten minutes later and we both had some food in front of us, with a coffee for him and water for me. He had no difficulty in obtaining a suitable bowl and plate for me because the girls at the self-serve counters fell over themselves in attending to my every need. And believe me, I knew exactly how to play cute! I could quickly obtain more human girlfriends than he'd had hot dinners. At least I think that's the expression you humans sometimes use.

Satisfied, rested, fed and watered, we set off again for the last leg of the journey to a boat that was to become my new home.

CHAPTER 7

Meeting George

"I could do with another Ovaltine, if you wouldn't mind"

Roger Ainsworth (1964)

During the last five years or so I had become a family friend of George and Iris Markland. It hadn't been intentional, but I suppose I quite liked them both and they always made me feel very welcome – and I enjoyed seeing the boys, especially young Leslie. When I took over the law firm from Mr. Fawcett with my partner Philip Stephens I thought I'd be working for the rest of my career on house sales, with a smattering of employment issues concerning the Leyland truck factory over in Lancashire. I was generally content with my lot, albeit I have to admit, a little bored. I welcomed some excitement in my working day, something to get the old grey matter ticking over.

Our firm's account was healthy enough and our offices were relatively plush and comfortable, The wily old man, Mr. Fawcett, had deviously begun using funds from his firm's client account and was being investigated by The Law Society. So when we'd heard through the grapevine that Fawcett was to be struck off, we were able to make our move and take over the firm with some money we borrowed from the bank. Of course, as the old firm had previously conveyed properties for many local families, it stood to reason that as Fawcett & Co. held the respective deeds in the firm's archives then any new business involving those properties should now come our way. I'd heard of Mr. George Markland. Who around the area hadn't? But I'd never had cause to meet the man until that summer's day five years ago when my secretary announced his unexpected arrival in the reception area.

Normally, Philip and I would see our clients by prior appointment and we would either visit the premises of Leyland's, or individual clients would come to our office, usually on a Friday, to sign a contract of sale ready for exchange the following week. So, to discover that Mr. George Markland of the Markland Estate wanted to see me personally certainly raised my curiosity.

Without usually being rude or impolite, I would make it common policy when our new receptionist Hatty advised us of the arrival of a client to keep them waiting in reception for two or three minutes before asking them to be shown in to my office. It was our little way of keeping an air of authority about the place - showing the clients who was boss, so to speak.

Hatty Palmerstone had been with us nearly six months by then, and jolly good she was too. Very efficient. Very competent at her job, and I daresay in another six months if she carried on the way she'd been going, we would pay for her to go on college-leave so she could get some qualifications under her belt. That way she would be able to carry out more profitable duties on the firm's behalf and hopefully earn herself a small pay rise as well. She deserved it, after all. But we couldn't afford to get ahead of ourselves and we would just have to continue with how things were for the time being.

As well as being a rather excellent tea and coffee maker, she was very pleasant to look at, with her formal attire and appropriate hair-style. She made a good first impression when people came in to our small but neat reception area, and today was no exception when Mr. George Markland called to see me.

"Mr. Ainsworth," Hatty announced. "We have Mr. Markland of the Markland Estate waiting in reception. He says he doesn't have an appointment but would appreciate a few minutes of your time, if you are not too inconvenienced."

Hatty spoke with a confidence that was quite a pleasure to listen to. Yes, we would definitely be promoting her as soon as we were able, I remember thinking.

"Thank you Hatty. I wonder what he may want," I pondered. "This could be interesting. Please show him in straight away. No three minute wait on this occasion. And ask him whether he'd like tea or coffee please, and I'll have my usual if you don't mind, Hatty. Oh, and I think we'll have the biscuits today please, and bring two of the china plates please - the Willow pattern ones."

A minute later Mr. Markland was sitting opposite me at my desk, and as if by magic Hatty reappeared within what seemed only seconds with a tray containing tea for him and Ovaltine for me - and an array of Peek Freans custard creams and shortcakes. Mr. Markland ate one of the custard creams as he added two spoons of sugar to his tea, and stirred it slowly clockwise as if contemplating the importance of his actions.

"Mr. Ainsworth, it's good of you to see me like this without an appointment and I must tell you how much I appreciate that. I like a man who doesn't mind breaking away from his routine from time to time in order to accommodate me. As you are no doubt aware, I own the Markland Estate a few miles east of here and I occasionally need the services of a good local lawyer."

Markland's stocky figure would certainly benefit from losing a few excess pounds from his midriff I thought, and his double chin looked dark with a five o'clock shadow even at that hour of the morning. Despite his rather pompous manner, his deep yet precise voice drew me in.

"You have built yourself quite a reputation, you know," he continued, "and I thought I'd call by and introduce myself."

"Well, that's very kind of you, Sir, and I'm glad that you did," I replied as respectfully as I felt to be appropriate. "Please, take another biscuit. Is there anything in particular I can help you with?", I enquired, trying to sound casual while excited at the potential of some lucrative new business.

"All rather mundane, I'm afraid but, nonetheless, it is important to keep on top of all legal matters fastidiously, wouldn't you say? And of course sometimes affairs can be of a confidential nature, and I need someone who I can trust implicitly to keep things close to their chest, as it were. Can you keep things close to your chest, Mr. Ainsworth?" he asked while looking me straight in the eye.

"Mr. Markland, confidentiality is a fundamental principle of the solicitor-client relationship. Of course solicitors require all the relevant facts from their client in order to give the best possible service." I was now in full flow in response. "And what's more, Mr. Markland, a solicitor's promise of confidentiality continues after the death of the client. So you can rest assured, Sir, that whatever you disclose to me or my partner Philip Stephens, your business will remain just that - *your* business."

"That's what I wanted to hear, Roger. May I call you Roger?" he quickly added. "I have a feeling that we will both be on first name terms before too long. Now, in the meantime I must finish my tea and take my leave as I have a lot of pressing errands to fulfil this afternoon. I do have one small particular matter that I'd like you to handle for me. It's of a somewhat delicate nature, I have to say, which is why I wanted to meet with you in person to ensure that your firm is able to provide the service I need in this particular instance. I'll bid you good day for now but I wondered if you might call at the Manor House tomorrow morning at ten o'clock?"

And with that, Mr. Markland stood up, held out his hand for me to shake, and before I knew it he'd seen himself out and was gone.

I sat back in my chair, which I'd just had delivered from Selfridges of London, together with a similar one for Philip. They had been rather expensive, but we both decided that considering the amount of time they would be accommodating our posteriors, it was an investment well worth the money.

A delicate matter? Confidentiality? What on earth was that all about, I wondered. If it had been anyone else, basically asking me whether I could keep a secret, I would have been deeply offended and would have shown them the door there and then. But to have the chance of doing some business with the Markland Estate, I felt it was prudent of me to play the game and dance to the man's tune.

Before tackling my next appointment I decided to find out some more about George Markland and the Markland Estate, and dialed Hatty's extension.

"Hatty, would you see if you can find any references to the Markland Estate in the cellar in our records, in case Mr. Fawcett ever had any dealings with the estate in the past? I feel sure he must have done. Then, be a wonder and pop up to the town library to see if there are any books or documents on the history of the place. But before you do that, I think you'd better postpone the appointments I have made for tomorrow morning: Thank you Hatty. Oh, and I could do with another Ovaltine, if you wouldn't mind, my dear."

"Right you are, Mr. Ainsworth. I know that at 9.30 you have Mr. Davis coming in about the Parkland Avenue semi-detatched, and at 11.15 you're meant to be at Leyland's for their new working hours contracts. I can telephone Mr. Davis and ask him to come in half an hour earlier, and I'll see if Mr. Stephens can take your place at Leyland's."

Replacing the receiver in its cradle, I made another mental note to financially reward Hatty Palmerstone just as soon as the firm could.

My Ovaltine arrived and Hatty removed the cups and Willow-pattern plates from the recent meeting with George Markland. "It's all arranged for tomorrow morning, Mr. Ainsworth. There were a couple of files in the cellar concerning one of the cottages on the Markland Estate". She placed the manila foolscap folders on my desk and I noticed how musty they smelled.

"Excellent Hatty": I thanked her as she informed me she was now going off to the library. "Please leave anything you find on my desk and I'll have a read through in the morning. I'm thinking of going early today as I have a feeling that tomorrow may be quite a heavy old session. Have a good evening Hatty. I'll see you in the morning."

I drank my Ovaltine and remembered to take my cup to the kitchen when I'd finished. There was nothing worse, I thought, than assuming other members of staff would collect up my dirty cups as a matter of course. And Hatty was a lawyer's protégé, not a skivvy, and deserved to be treated properly. If truth be told, I have to say I had rather a soft spot for the girl.

Picking up the manila files, I carried them out to the car, climbed in to my newly purchased light blue Ford Corsair and drove the six and a half miles home. I ran a bath and poured myself a Johnny Walker. As the bath was filling I glanced through the Markland Estate folders. There was nothing in them that was particularly unusual or interesting - just normal property things like tenancy agreements and general bills.

One such agreement concerned a Mr. Chris Dickinson, who was one of the farm worker tenants, and his tenancy of a two-up, two-down cottage was on the south-east corner of the estate, near the mill. This estate must be quite something, I thought, for it to have its own water mill. I was looking forward to visiting it for the first time in the morning.

Damnation! I'd let the bathwater run until the water was coming out cold. Luckily it didn't lower the temperature too much to spoil my enjoyment. I lay back with my tumbler of whisky in hand, with a feeling that something interesting was going to present itself tomorrow. I stared up at the ceiling and noticed how the paint was peeling in the corner. It occurred to me that I needn't be concerned with such things once Ainsworth & Stephens had become firmly established in a few years and proper funds had begun to flow in. I'd be able to simply call in the decorators. Perhaps the name of Ainsworth & Company sounded even better. Uh hum.

The following morning I awoke earlier than usual, and got up, eagerly anticipating the day ahead. I was convinced that something interesting would come out of my meeting at ten o'clock, but I had no idea what. I made myself my usual cup of Ovaltine - God I love that drink – and made two slices of toast with a thick scraping of butter on each. My old grandmother, bless her, used to tell me there was no point in having toast unless you can have real butter. None of this new-fangled margarine for me, no thank you. I washed my face with my flannel, brushed my teeth and did my ablutions before the drive to the office to meet Mr. F. Davis about his Parkland Avenue house. Although it was just another conveyancing job, I never lost sight of the fact that it was conveyancing that paid our rent and rates, our wages, electricity and telephone bills. Where would Hatty and Philip be without such an income? Where indeed would I be either? But that morning I couldn't help my mind wandering to the next job in hand at the Markland Estate. After arriving at the office and greeting my client as I walked past him in the reception area, I sat Mr. Davis down and got him to sign the relevant documents that Hatty had so efficiently prepared and left on my desk. Then it was time to leave for my trip to the Markland Estate.

I drove carefully like I normally do in the Corsair, and pressed the push-button radio that was set into the dashboard. The newsreader on the Home Service was giving out the main headlines - something about Prince Edward being christened - but I wasn't paying much attention. I pushed the next button in time to catch the last few notes of a Russ Conway tune being played on the Light Programme. Turning the knob to 'off', I drove the last few miles with just the sound of the car's engine.

I'd often driven past the entrance to the Markland Estate. There was a huge wooden gate, at least ten feet high, set back from the road a few yards. I pulled up to it and wondered how I should continue my journey. To the left of the gate was a bright red pillar box. It looked as though it was polished every single day, with the embossed letters 'GR' standing out proudly. I knew from my formal education that those letters meant George Rex, the 'Rex' being Latin for King. So the letter box must have been installed sometime between 1910 and 1936. How many significant changes had occurred within those walls of the estate since then, I wondered. Was I about to become a part in yet another? As I sat in the car a man appeared through a small door set within the gate, and he asked if I was Mr. Ainsworth. When I confirmed that I was he stepped back through the small door and closed it, then pulled open the large gate so that I could drive through. "Mr. Markland is expecting you, Sir. Please follow the gravel drive to the front of the Manor and someone will take you to Mr. Markland's office."

I drove for a few minutes along a tree-lined lane and over a small bridge crossing a stream that flowed into a small lake to the right of the property. The large house was predominantly built of sandstone brick, with the main door at one end under an enormous porch, flanked by beige painted sash windows, which was about the size of my living room. As I approached the house I could see a glass-topped annex at one end, housing who knew what - a pool perhaps, or a collection of plants? The lawn was beautifully kept and plants and ornamental trees that I didn't know the names of grew from stone pots surrounding the house walls. I'll admit, I was feeling slightly envious that Markland actually lived here - it was idyllic. No, let me correct that. It wasn't envy I was experiencing as I gazed beyond the lake to the view of the rolling hills in the distance. I realised it was more of an aspirational emotion as I pulled the handbrake of the car up and stepped out, crunching the shingle underfoot. Walking to the front door, I was able to see the path sweep downhill to an oak-timbered outbuilding with four large red painted doors side by side. Parked outside was a maroon Bentley Continental. The Continental in my opinion was, and still is, one of the finest motorcars ever manufactured in this country: So much classier than a Rolls. Wealth with taste. I wondered if I would ever get to drive one during my lifetime.

I looked at my watch and refocused on the task in front of me. Five to ten: Good, I was on time. Punctuality had always been very important to me. It is so discourteous to be late and I don't appreciate that discourtesy shown to me. I knew somehow that Mr. Markland also shared such sentiment. At that moment I spotted another vehicle coming towards me from across the field beyond the red-doored outbuilding that I assumed was the garage. I recognised the unmistakable shape of a Land Rover and the dark green body was muddy and scuffed. As it sped closer I saw that it had a number of dents across the front of it, and one of the headlamps was missing. The man behind the wheel was Mr. Markland himself. It skidded to a halt a few feet from me and he got out, his arm outstretched towards me.

"Roger: I'm just in time, thank goodness. I hate to be late for an appointment," he said in a very abrupt tone. "And especially as you have clearly gone out of your way to be here punctually. I would imagine you had to move a few things around in your busy schedule and I have to thank you for that. Now, come, come, let's go inside and get Mrs. Adams to fix us a couple of coffees - or indeed I can ask her if we have any Ovaltine. I noticed you had a preference for that yesterday and I'm sure we must have some in the pantry. No, no, I've changed my mind – let's have a whisky, eh?" I had no time to answer before he went on. "There's always something to be done on the farm, you know. That's where I've just come from: some business over at one of the cottages that needed, er, my undivided attention."

Did I notice a certain look in his eye as he told me this? I couldn't be sure. But there, he did it again for certain this time, as well as giving me a wry smile, as if to tease me with his own private joke. I didn't get the joke but I was itching to understand what it was about.

I followed Markland as we went up the stone steps and through the heavy front door. Inside, the entrance hall was dark and formal with a sweeping wooden staircase to the left and a door to the right. This he opened and beckoned me to follow him into the room, which I presumed was his office. There was a library of books from floor to ceiling against one wall, and one of those ladders on wheels that you see in movies propped up at one end. The ceiling was at least ten feet high and had cast coving all the way round. There was a desk in front of the window that looked out to the lake I'd seen as I'd driven up. He didn't sit at his desk though. Instead he sat on the Chesterfield sofa in front of the marble fireplace, and he invited me to sit on an identical one, opposite him.

I tried not to stare at him, but it was impossible not to. He had a commanding air about him, with rugged features and extremely thick, black, slightly curly hair. He was wearing a brown tweed suit, perfectly fitted for his somewhat tubby form, with a white handkerchief folded neatly and sticking out of his top pocket. I'd have to admit that I was carrying a bit of extra weight myself - probably due to too many of Hatty's ham and mustard sandwiches in the office, or indeed those marvellous pork pies they do at The George Hotel - but I would say that Mr. George Markland, Lord of the Manor, could have done with losing a few pounds. 'Stocky' would have been my description: stocky, and *cocky*. But then, as I looked around at my surroundings, I concluded that he had plenty to be cocky about. I liked the man, but I couldn't be sure whether it was because of him, or because of *who* he was. I decided it was best to like him for his own sake. "See the good in everyone if you can", my old mother used to say, bless her, and I tried to always take her advice. What I saw in Markland was an abrupt businessman who didn't suffer fools gladly, but who also had a certain vulnerability lurking beneath the surface and beneath his robust facade.

He stood up and walked over to a dark wood cabinet upon which there was a half-full decanter. "Try this, Roger. I think you may rather like it," he offered. "It's a pure malt from a dear chap I know on Bute. I invested a few guineas in his distillery, and now he sends me several bottles of the stuff every month or so. His family have been making it for centuries, and this particular one is 30 years old. Can you imagine that? I hope you like it."

I did like his whisky, despite it being so early in the morning for me to be drinking anything stronger than my usual Ovaltine. But I was on his patch, so I may as well enjoy his offering, I thought.

"Roger, I'm now going to come straight to the point." Markland began, as he sank back into the sofa. "I want your help, but it's important for you to understand the need for complete discretion and confidentiality on your part. And of course we discussed that yesterday, didn't we, but as long as we're clear on that, we should get along just fine."

Good, I thought. Even though I was thoroughly enjoying his Scotch, I was impatient to discover why he particularly wanted my services. Despite feeling somewhat light-headed already, I leaned forward attentively.

"It was no accident that I came by your office yesterday," he began. "I am aware that, as I'm sure you are too by now, that your firm holds the legal documents for one of our tenanted cottages, in which one of my farm workers, a certain Chris Dickinson, resides."

Then his tone changed. "I want him out, and I want him out straight away. I have my reasons," he continued. "Every month he is a day or two late with his rent, as are nearly all my tenants and I usually choose to turn a blind eye. Until now that is. If I can use it as a reason to evict our Mr. Dickinson, that's what I want to do."

He paused for a moment before forcefully concluding his little speech.

"I know that he has some rights, but I also know that since some changes in the law a few years back, it should be easier for me to kick him out without too much of a fight. I want him off my land and far away for good, but without any reprisals that may come back and bite me in the future. I'm prepared to compensate him to the tune of three months' wages if he leaves voluntarily. But if he kicks up a stink, I want him dealt with by the law of his tenancy agreement. You'll see in the documents that it stipulates the due date of each month's rent. You can use that as a way to make him see sense if you have to, although I doubt that you'll need to with the spineless rascal."

I sat back against the leather upright. So this was what it was all about: a simple tenancy disagreement, with a smattering of employment law thrown in for good measure. It all sounded simple enough to me, and nothing that I couldn't handle with ease. But why all this larking around? Why the need for me to come all the way here today when he could have told me all this yesterday? Why the lecture on confidentiality? And why the whisky? I didn't mind that part, especially as my head was now enjoyably spinning, and my tongue was now looser than it had been only a few short moments ago.

"That all sounds like a matter my firm can handle for you George. You don't mind me calling you George, do you?" I began. "Of course we can do this for you, and it would be a pleasure to also deal with all your other legal matters concerning the Markland Estate. But please tell me what on earth has this Mr. Dickinson done to get you so worked up? You needn't be concerned about telling me if you don't wish to, but please remember what I said yesterday." Two could play at this game, I thought, as the whisky helped me push home my point. "Solicitors require all the relevant facts from their client in order to give the best possible service."

"Right you are then, Roger. Right you are," he responded. "It's about a woman, you see. Her name is Iris Lament and she resides in one of the tied cottages over on the other side of the field you saw me driving across from earlier. She lives with her old father, who's retired now. A good mechanic he's been, looking after our tractors for many years. The thing is I can't get enough of Iris. She has this way about her see …well, you know what I mean. You're a man of the world."

I wasn't sure that I did know what he meant, until he spelt it out for me.

"She'd been carrying on with Dickinson before she saw sense and realised I could offer her much more than he can. And now she's told me that I'm going to be the father of her child. Can you believe that, Roger? I don't want any scandal around here and I don't want to bring any shame on old Mr. Lament, so we are to be married very soon. She says it's only early days of her pregnancy yet and we are going to have a small service in the chapel up on the hill on the far side of the estate before her bump becomes too large. To be honest Roger, between you and me, she is already showing, but with the right frock no one will tell. You will be invited of course, and if you can handle this affair for me then I'm sure it will mark the beginnings of a very long and prosperous relationship between Ainsworth & Stephens and the Markland Estate. But be clear on one thing, my Iris is not to be distracted by what's gone on previously in her life. I want rid of Dickinson, and I want rid of him now."

All that was five years ago now, when the newly-married Iris Markland gave birth to a lovely, healthy boy in February, 1959. The baby was called Leslie Valentine Markland, first and middle names chosen by Iris's husband, George Valentine Markland.

CHAPTER 8

Lord of The Manor

"Any man in my situation would have done the same. Wouldn't they?"

George Markland (1962)

I'm not proud of what I did, but then again she had it coming to her for making such a fool of me. We were married in late 1958 soon after I had that meeting with Ainsworth. I liked Roger and I knew that he would be competent in carrying out my little 'business' request concerning the tied cottage on the land. I also knew that he was ambitious for his career. I had the money and he had the ambition, so it was a perfect match.

Any man in my situation would have lost their temper, wouldn't they? After all, it was only a natural reaction when I found out that Iris was already pregnant with another man's child. In hindsight I should have put two and two together much sooner, but I was blinded by love at the time. Was it love, or was it lust? I'm not sure. She seduced me with her come-to-bed eyes, her provocative air, and her flirty nature. I didn't mean to hit her, but it was her own fault, wasn't it? I'm not normally a violent man. Whether she'll forgive me or not for my actions I don't know.

Nonetheless, we carry on with business as usual for the sake of the Markland Estate and of course my good family name.

That man Dickinson saw sense when he upped and went. Yes, I paid him to go, and Ainsworth did a good job in putting forward the legal arguments about the breach of his tenancy agreement, but if he'd had any real guts he would have stayed put to fight his corner. Iris didn't seem to be that bothered. She wanted to be married to me and at the time I genuinely believed that the child inside her was mine. But when it was born only six months after the wedding and I thought it was premature, the doctors said otherwise.

I had a reputation to uphold and it wasn't conducive to the smooth running of the Markland Estate to allow a scandal to occur and become public knowledge. Albeit unwittingly, Iris had made a fool of me and I could not forgive her for that. But as far as all and sundry were concerned, Leslie Valentine Markland was my son, and only Iris and I knew the truth that he wasn't. Oh, and of course Roger Ainsworth, but I knew he could keep a secret. For him there was too much at stake if he didn't.

I even gave the bastard son a middle name and the outside world would merely see that as the continuation of a fine Markland family tradition. That said, when I was at school I was teased incessantly because of that stupid middle name which had belonged to my father and some of his forefathers. To be honest, it didn't do me too much harm, and perhaps it won't do too much harm to Leslie in the long run. Whether it does or whether it doesn't, I dare say I couldn't really care less.

Leslie was born in February of that year. He wasn't mine and there was nothing I could do about that. I wanted him and Iris to leave, but so soon after the wedding would have raised too many eyebrows and I'm sure that damage would be done to the farm business with all the ensuing gossip that was bound to have followed. It was for the best that we carried on as one happy family, even though we were not. I swore to

Iris that I would never again lay the back of my hand against her, and I did mean it at the time, honest to God I did.

When I first put two and two together, having worked out the due date against the times when we'd first fornicated, I was pretty shaken. There was no way that the child could have been mine. Initially Iris tried to convince me that I was mistaken, but I'm not stupid, am I? After things calmed down following my outburst we called in that woman who runs the Post Office in the village, who says she can predict whether a baby will be a boy or girl. All she did was come over to the house one evening and get Iris to lay across the dining room table on some cushions. The woman, known locally as Aunty May, stood over her with Iris's wedding ring tied to some black thread and dangled it above her stomach. What a load of mumbo jumbo, I originally thought. I couldn't believe I was falling for it. But I was so convinced by May's sincerity that I ended up believing her prediction. I suppose it was because I wanted to.

I remember my beloved grandfather, my namesake George Valentine Markland, with great fondness. Over and over he would tell me all about the history of the Markland Estate and how the first boy born in each generation would become the future Lord of the Manor. I never tired of hearing that story. "George", he used to bargain with me, "George, if you roll me a cigarette in my special machine and lick the paper to seal it, I'll tell you again how your great, great grandfather came to build our home from a single field of grain and a lot of sweat and toil."

Yes, I loved my Granddad and I loved his story telling, especially the part where I would one day end up owning everything, as I do now. For the sake of my forefathers it was so terribly important that I should continue this fine family tradition, the tradition of passing the estate on to the first male born in each generation. Naturally, any girls born would also benefit and be looked after generously, but it was the first boy who would become the future Lord of the Manor. With that in mind, there was no way I wanted 'our' first child to be male, the child that Iris had conceived with Dickinson.

"Iris, you are most definitely having a girl," said the post-mistress grandly, and the relief I felt was so strong that it was like a physical feeling I'd never experienced before. Before she was born we'd decided to call her Lesley, a name that was very popular at the time, and I even found myself quite looking forward to her arrival.

All I needed to do was simply get rid of that spineless Dickinson fellow, pretend the baby girl was mine and keep popping away at Iris until she eventually gave me my very own true-blood male heir to my property and fortune. Even during her pregnancy, Iris was still pretty playful after a bit of coaxing, and it was never a hardship for me to give her a right seeing to whenever the mood took me. I figured that once she gave birth to 'our' daughter it would only be a matter of course before she'd fall pregnant again, preferably with a boy next time round.

But for now and for the sake of appearances, I planned to bring the baby Lesley up as my own. No one would be any the wiser, and I would allow Iris's deception with Dickinson's child to be forgiven and forgotten. The problem with my plan was that the stupid post-mistress was completely wrong with her prediction. Iris didn't have a girl after all.

I wasn't present at the birth. With more important business to attend to that day, firstly at the bank and then over at the livestock market, I combined a meeting with one of the auctioneers over a spot of lunch at the club I visited regularly in Leeds. It was a bit of a spit and sawdust place and not really to my taste, but the women that flaunted themselves around were good on the eye, and I hadn't had much in the way of gentlemen's pleasure that week. The auctioneer took his leave, and I stayed around a while to go into the back room they set aside for me with one of the tarts.

Then I finished the day off nicely with a couple of whiskies before driving back to the Manor House to see how things were going with Iris and to see whether she'd had 'our' daughter by then.

When I arrived, the midwife greeted me on the gravel path outside the front door. She looked uneasy.

"Congratulations Sir. Everything has gone well. Your wife has given birth to a very healthy six and a half pound baby. She is asleep now, your wife that is. But the baby is wide awake in the nursery, and you can see him now if you like, Sir."

I don't recall how many whiskies I downed following those few words from the midwife. My mixture of emotions was complex. Anger: definitely, betrayal: certainly, hurt: yes, disbelief: of course, and fear of the future: perhaps. Without even seeing the newborn, I knew straight away we wouldn't be getting along too well. Not now. Not ever.

I dashed up the stairs to where Iris was sleeping and stormed into the room. "How could you do this to me?" I yelled at her, my voice so shrill it was like a scream. Without control, and with the whisky to blame, I stormed over to her bed and before she had barely woken I slapped her face with the back of my hand. Any man in my situation would have done the same. Wouldn't they?

No, I wasn't proud of what I did that day. After I'd calmed down, I quietly said she could call her bastard son the name of Leslie instead of Lesley, as I knew she'd got used to the sound of it by then. She was shocked and probably frightened and didn't say a word. As for me, I was beyond caring what its bloody name was.

CHAPTER 9

A Ticket to London

"Basically, I was sexy and I knew it"

Silvie Tosgiev (1995)

I had known Liz Pinchbeck for a few years now, having met her while she was on a cruise holiday travelling from Oslo to Hamburg. Employed as a medical assistant, I had a job working on the ship taking care of passengers needing first aid. Operating out of the sickbay, I would help with ailments like sea sickness in bad weather, headaches on mornings after nights of ballroom dancing, and diarrhea, especially for the older passengers not used to eating so much of our beautiful Scandinavian herring.

A few hours into one trip, the liner was navigating a course through the most magnificent fjords with high green mountains on both sides. Peering out of the porthole, I was mesmerised by the whole scenic beauty of the vista, while I waited for my next patient to knock at my door.

That patient was to be a tall thin lady in her forties or fifties, clearly in pain as she stepped over the threshold and walked into the cabin with a limp.

"I think I've broken my ankle going down the ship's stairs," she wheezed as she slumped onto the trolley bed.

"You mean the ship's *ladders*, Madam," I corrected her in a jovial tone. "I doubt that the ankle will be broken because if it were you would not have been able to walk in here. Let me take a look at your foot to see what I can do to help you."

I gently manipulated her foot, giving it a mild massage as I moved it from side to side. My training at college in Uppsala had paid off, although those days seemed like a long time ago now. I'd alleviated some of my patient's pain by some skillful massage around her swollen ankle, and I was able to advise with confidence that my visitor had in fact no broken bones.

"Okay, there we are now," I reassured her. "It is fortunately nothing more than a sprain which will, I am certain, become less painful from now on. It would be a good idea to keep this compression bandage around it for a couple of days, and if you wish you can come back for another massage later today. I will be on my shift again after six this evening, or if you want to come earlier my other colleague will see you. Now, please, I need to write down a few, how you say, details in the ship's medical log."

And that's when I became officially acquainted with Liz Pinchbeck from Curzon Street in Mayfair, London.

Before getting my job on the cruise ship I had decided to leave the family home in Stockholm and travel around just to see what life threw at me. Having completed my three year studies to become a registered physiotherapist, and thanks to generous financial support from my parents, I was able to take a year off to travel the world - well the world of Scandinavia at least - exploring Sweden, Finland and Norway, as well as brief trips across to Denmark and Northern Germany. But London had always been my, how you say, end goal, and I had been determined to find my way there one day. Carnaby Street, Soho, The Ritz, Mayfair, Piccadilly Circus: all these glamorous places I'd seen on imported TV programmes that had set my heart racing, especially Soho.

Uppsala, being Sweden's fourth largest city and only 70 kilometres north of Stockholm, had its fair share of excitement while I was a student there, and I particularly enjoyed the nightlife. I was an after-dark person much more than a morning girl. Quite often I would finish my day at college and head straight out to the bars for my favourite drink - Carnegie Porter. While my fellow student girlfriends preferred white wine or vodka, I just couldn't get enough of that beer, and boy, it was good. Luckily for me it was easy to obtain anywhere when I moved on from the bars and into the clubs. I wouldn't venture into the clubs before midnight unless I was wanting a quiet evening to myself, as they would be virtually empty until then, giving me little chance of meeting anyone for sex.

Sex was, and still is, an addiction for me as much as that glorious dark beer. I got the taste for both before beginning college, while ensuring I kept my 'extra curricular' activities secret from my parents. They would, what's the expression in your English, 'have had a fit' if they had known their only daughter had lost her virginity just two weeks after her thirteenth birthday, drunk on Carnegie Porter.

Naturally, I'd had conversations with my girlfriends about their sexual experiences, and without exception they all grumbled about their first time going with a boy, but that certainly hadn't been my personal recollection - I totally loved it. Johan had also been a virgin like me, which I found to be all the more exciting. I taught him what my body enjoyed. Despite his inexperienced fumblings I found him very endearing, and since then I have always loved the thrill of initiating, how you say, a boy's transformation into manhood.

During my days at nursing college I took my studies very seriously, but there was also a side benefit to those classes. It was a legitimate way in which to explore the sensation of physical touch while allowing myself to be caressed by others. Little did my fellow students realise how turned on I was by their practicing hands. It was the same sensation, the same feeling of light-headiness that I got from dancing to a slow song at Studio K and pulling a man so close that I could feel his hardness against me, with everyone else being oblivious to what was happening in my personal space. Watching his surprised expression was an absolute delight as he quickly fell under my sexual spell. "Press yourself against me," I would whisper in his ear.

I never wanted to be paid money to go with a man. That would have made me cheap, although I had many opportunities to make a lot of krona. It was okay to be wined and dined, and if I was treated to a gift of perfume, jewellry or expensive clothes then I would have been rude to refuse, and I did not want to cause any offence. I also was not searching for a long-term relationship, because I was perfectly content with my own company and with the way my life was developing.

What did I have going for me in my favour? Well, I had my qualification in physio, so I could become independent financially if I wanted. I had my good health, and I had my looks. I would not say I was beautiful, but I was aware of my attractiveness to others, and in fact I enjoyed the thrill of showing off my body when I knew others liked to see it. Slightly above average height, I was around one metre seventy-five, and weighed just over seventy kilos, which was perfect for my frame. I looked after myself with regular running and exercise, so my stomach was flat and my limbs were firm but not unnaturally muscular for a girl. My natural hair colour was blond, like many Swedes, but I sometimes liked to dye it dark brown, black, or even red, grown long and tied into pig-tails. Without being boastful, I would say that my best assets were my breasts. Not large by any means, but I was pleased with their firmness and the way my nipples pointed directly forwards giving the appearance of being permanently erect, even when wearing a bra, although I usually preferred not to wear one. Basically, I was sexy and I knew it.

Sometimes, purely for the excitement of doing so, I would just stand around inside Hoffner's Sizzle Haus on the Reeperbahn for a moment, flaunting what I had and observing the looks on the young men who were, I liked to imagine, trying without success to prevent their erections from showing in their jeans. Hoffner's was a human supermarket with an entrance one end and exit the other and several pillars in between where prostitutes and punters would mingle around inside together. These were mostly punters visiting the red light district for a stag weekend and the working girls were desperate to earn their nightly quota to keep their pimps happy. While these poor girls would have to negotiate their rates face to face with the punters, I was privileged enough not to have to. Never more than sexual teasing on my part, those evenings at the Sizzle Haus taught me that with my body, facial looks and sultry eye contact I had power, and it was a power that I could use to maybe help me get to where I most wanted to be - London.

Liz Pinchbeck did come back to the sickbay later that evening, but I don't think her swollen ankle was the real reason for her return. Of course I gave her foot another massage, and made sure her bandage was replaced tightly, for which Ms. Pinchbeck was grateful enough to offer me a drink in the bar after I had finished my shift at nine.

"It would be nice for us to get to know each other a little better," she said. "You could be exactly the woman I'm looking for, and you have a good character, I can tell."

More than mildly curious after she left the medical cabin, I impatiently waited for the remaining couple of hours to tick past on the wall clock. What did the lady mean? Get to know me better? Good character? What was she was looking for? Did she want a sexual liaison with me? For me, nearly everything in life revolved around sex, and so I assumed the same applied to everyone else, but of course that was not necessarily true.

Nine o'clock arrived more slowly than I had wanted, with only one other patient's visit to help pass the time. I dished out some constipation tablets to the charming old man who informed me he was on his 50th wedding anniversary treat, handed over my rota paperwork to my replacement, and went up on deck to one of the bars, intriguingly named

The Ship's Allure, where Miss Pinchbeck was already waiting.

"Ah, greetings Miss Silvie," she called out. There was a bottle of Carniege Porter already on the table next to Miss Pinchbeck's glass of white wine.

"How did you know?" I asked, my eyes raised quizzically at her, glancing at the beer.

"Please don't be concerned Miss Silvie - it's just that I couldn't help noticing you relaxing at one of the other bars last night. You are, how can I say, rather striking, and it appeared that the old Carniege was your tipple of choice, ha ha." What an unusual cackley laugh Miss Pinchbeck had, I observed, as I poured the drink into the empty glass that was next to her already full one.

Putting the thought to one side for the moment that she might be stalking me, I began with an enquiry about her swollen ankle. She assured me I had done a superb job in alleviating her pain and that she was very grateful to me.

"I believe," she said, "that the massage you did on my foot did wonders and you seem to have a knack of making me feel comfortable in your presence." Pleased as I was to hear this I still wondered where this was leading. Was she coming on to me? I was about to find out as she continued.

"After I have finished this mini-holiday and have spent a couple of days doing a little sight-seeing around Hamburg, I will be flying back to London and I was wondering if you might be interested in coming with me. You see, I have been searching for an assistant for a new enterprise that I'm starting up, and I have a hunch, my dear, that you could be exactly the woman I am looking for."

There, she said it again - 'the woman I am looking for' - and this time I had the opportunity to ask her what she meant. She drew a deep wheezy breath and began her explanation.

"Miss Silvie, I have recognised that there are a number of circumstances where a child, a baby, is lacking from a family unit, and with advances in science coming on in leaps and bounds over the past few years, what previously would have been completely impossible is now possible. With modern science we are now legally and physically able to enable childless couples to conceive a child whereas previously that was not the case. You see, I never had any children of my own - I am not and have never been in a relationship with a man in the normal sense, and alas my body is now too old for that to happen. Had there been a possibility of having my own baby without going about it in the usual way I would have leapt at the chance of having that fulfilment. And not only that, I would have been prepared to spend a lot of money to do so. I am guessing, Miss Silvie, that I am not the only one. I believe there is an opportunity to enable and help women and men to make their dreams of becoming parents come true, and of course we could make a good living for ourselves in the process. I am talking specifically Miss Silvie, about you coming to work with me in London at my Angelpride agency."

My initial reaction to all this was negative. I thought this lady was 'galen' as we would say in Sweden - a little crazy. But she was worth listening to. She did appear to be genuinely sincere about her plans. And here she was practically offering me a job in London. I would dismiss my immediate thoughts, be more open minded to what she wanted to tell me, and remain in the Ship's Allure with Miss Pinchbeck a little longer.

"I am sure you must think me somewhat, ha ha, unconventional," she said as she made a circular motion with her right forefinger around the side of her temple. Her finger was long and bony and her nails were plain. How different the two of us were, I noticed, as I looked down at the bright red varnish that I liked to wear. She also wore no jewellry, unlike me. No earrings, no necklace and no rings. But her blouse and skirt were of the highest quality and must have cost a fortune, and I began imagining me wearing London fashion bought from places that I had only read about in the style magazines I picked up on the cruise ship.

I then observed more closely her pale green Burberry handbag. That was snakeskin, wasn't it? I'd seen one like that costing more than six thousand krona.

I sat up more attentively and leaned forward to meet her eyes at my level, deciding to play hard to get.

"But Miss Pinchbeck, I have a job here on the cruise ship that I enjoy. I also get to meet interesting people, people just like you certainly, and I like making their acquaintance. In fact I have everything I need here, plus, I could never afford to live in London. I have read it is one of the most expensive capital cities in the world. And also, I do not have a clue about what you would want me to do at your agency."

"Miss Silvie," she began, "sometimes we have to follow our hearts and take leaps into the unknown. I know what I am setting out to do is perhaps unusual to say the least, but if I am able to bring some happiness to a few people along the way, I will be content with myself. I cannot do it on my own and I would like you to help me. I have a good feeling about you. Please allay your fears about money and the high cost of London living. I have my own place in Mayfair that is where my Angelpride business is to be located, but there is also an apartment I own nearby in Curzon Place that you can live in - rent-free. I will reward you handsomely - certainly enough for you to afford your own Christian Louboutins" she said as she caught me staring at her designer shoes when she stood up to get us both another drink.

While she was attracting the attention of the barman I mulled over the prospect of working with this lady. Even though I was still none the wiser about my actual job role, here was my golden ticket to live in London and to meet all those beautiful English men. What was more, it appeared I would have the ability to enjoy their adult company whenever it suited me...

I would go to London, I decided.

CHAPTER 10

The Consultation

"I instinctively knew that I would be helping this man"

Part One: Silvie Tosgiev (1996)

Almost a year had gone by since that first encounter with Liz Pinchbeck on the cruise liner, and I am now enjoying London living, especially as I have the advantage of rent-free accommodation in a prime location. It's all I'd ever dreamed of, thanks to Liz keeping her word. I admit to having been suspicious and doubtful to begin with since usually people I meet are full of verbal promises that very often do not come close to reality. But I am the kind of girl who doesn't mind taking a leap of faith occasionally and on this occasion I am so glad I did.

My job is like no other. It is very satisfying, in more ways than one, and extremely interesting. Of course Liz is the driving force at her Angelpride agency: 'Where Parents' Dreams CAN Come True,' according to the letter heading. Liz meets with clients in her office to discuss their situation and then works tirelessly to find a match for them. You see, although she is running Angelpride as a business and is undoubtedly making a good profit from it, I am convinced that she has her heart actually in the right place, and genuinely cares for those people engaging the services of the agency. Some are so desperate to become parents that they will pay anything for the chance to either father a child with a surrogate mother, or, in a woman's case become pregnant without having intercourse with a man.

For the time being, I am taking care of the day-to-day running of the place, taking calls from clients, booking their appointments, and meeting and greeting them when they arrive. It has not been unusual for women and men to come from long distances - even from abroad - for a chance to have a baby. Mostly we are dealing with heterosexual couples who for some reason cannot conceive naturally. In some situations the man's sperm count may be too low and as a couple they do not mind for the woman to use the sperm of another man with whom they already are friends.

Personally I would not like to have someone else's child if I were in a loving relationship with my boyfriend or husband. But people do, and that is their business for their own reasons.

Who am I to judge what is right or wrong when something so crucial to them is at stake? There are other scenarios, of course. For example, if a lesbian couple wants a child together, but does not care to have a man in their lives to make it happen, Angelpride endeavours to find the ideal sperm donor for them.

We are also experiencing a growing trend of gay men couples who are desperate to become fathers, especially now that the world is more tolerant towards homosexual relationships. Twenty years ago it would have been almost unthinkable for men in this situation to openly talk about this kind of activity, and back then who would have thought that this scenario would eventually happen today? I think that Liz is happy that she can play a significant and important role in these sometimes very delicate family issues, and why not? If I were charging a basic fee of over £5,000 per client and a further £5,000 upon successful conclusion, I would be equally happy!

One of the more uncommon ways in which Angelpride could also help was in the donation of sperm anonymously, from a man to a surrogate mother. This was indeed the case with Leslie Valentine Markland.

The internet was developing and changing rapidly in 1996, and I could see that Liz was deploying it to her full advantage. She would use it not only to introduce her services to potential clients but she would also use it as a tool to help find potential donor and surrogate candidates. She had equipped the office with the latest dial-up technology, and within minutes was able to search for what she was looking for on the World Wide Web. She had done her research well, and despite there being no advertising by similar agencies, she knew where to find what she wanted by using certain key words and phrases. I found this all very fascinating, and it was one of the areas Liz said I could become involved in after I had worked there for a while. But for the time being I continued to look after the routine issues of the business.

My job could be satisfying in more ways than one. When we require a sperm sample for sending off to the lab for tests, our male clients need to be relaxed enough to perform what they came into Angelpride to perform. After they have had their initial interview with Liz, I would take them into a comfortable room, leave them alone and they usually emerge ten or fifteen minutes later with an embarrassed grin on their face and a sample pot in their hand. This is all very well when a man is visiting us with his wife, girlfriend or gay partner, but occasionally they are single and on their own, and could do with a little, how would you say, encouragement. I think that maybe you can guess what I mean when I say that giving that encouragement, as part of my job, is a challenge I readily accept.

Now I am not suggesting that this happens every day. But we are catering for, I would say, four or five male clients each week, and of those perhaps one would benefit from a little assistance from me. To begin with I would try to make them feel comfortable on their own. Although there are no windows, the private room is very pleasant and relaxing to be in, with soft green colours on the walls. Liz had given me the task of creating that perfect environment.

"Silvie, I would like you to take care of our Function Room and its facilities please, ha ha," she had requested, laughing at her little joke as she regarded my confused expression. It wasn't until she explained what function the room would be used for that I got her meaning. And when she went on to explain how it would be *my* room, I don't mind admitting that a tingle of excitement ran through me.

A week after I had been given that task, the room was ready. I had found an excellent father and son firm who did a great decorating job for me, even arranging for the new carpet to be fitted. Then I went in search of the right furnishings, a luxurious double bed being the priority, the sort being what I imagined you might find in a top Paris hotel. Lighting was key to setting the right mood and so I chose an arc lamp by Floss. Not the cheapest by any means, but Liz had told me "not to worry about the cost" and I'd always admired those steel arcs embedded into marble blocks so heavy that they needed two men to carry them. Sure, I could have bought an imitation but that just wouldn't have been right, would it? Next I went in search of some original art to adorn the walls and I chose a set of three nudes, very tastefully drawn in black charcoal. With an antique wooden chair in one corner and a low Italian soft leather sofa in the other, my Function Room was complete and ready for action. Of course it wasn't actually called 'The Function Room' – the name on the door simply read 'Private'. And to complete the spend Liz also suggested I buy myself an Angelpride clinic uniform. She even said I should take a whole day out in Oxford Street to find just the right outfit.

"Just don't get anything too tarty," she advised. "Get something tasteful, but arousing and sexy at the same time."

Well, I didn't need any prompting, as shopping was my second favourite pastime, after sex. I bought two sets of everything I chose. A black pencil skirt, some black tights with a dark seem up the back, and some black shoes with a heel of five centimetres. For the top half I chose a silk white blouse and one of those new push-up bras that were all the rage at the time that helped to make my small cleavage somewhat larger than it really was. With the top three buttons left open, and with the bright red tantilising silk scarf around my neck I dare to say that I was quite, how do you say, the pretty picture.

I had no idea back at the beginning that Liz had this extra kind of role in mind for me. I can't honestly say how I would have reacted had I been aware of the whole concept of the service I was expected to provide. With mixed feelings, I guess the thought of doing an excellent job to boost Angelpride's business in this exciting way was irresistible.

However, we were in our relative early days of the agency when I opened our front door to greet Leslie Markland for his initial consultation with Liz Pinchbeck, and my services offered were limited to what Liz and I would come to refer to as 'Level Two'. This second level, where my 'special help' might be required had a basic rule applied to it. There was to be strictly no physical contact between client and Angelpride staff.

Leslie Markland was certainly fine looking. His fair, thick hair was brushed sideways across his head, cut short and neat. Now that I am becoming familiar with these English measurements I would say that his height was approximately five feet and ten inches, his build was slim and, because of his hair colour, he could have passed for being Swedish and wouldn't have looked out of place back home in Uppsala. The most striking thing about him was his eyes - not the dark brown colour of them - but the unmistakable story I thought they told of sadness and vulnerability. I instinctively knew that I would be helping this man, and that I would welcome the chance to do so.

Taking him into the waiting area, I left him there looking a little uneasy until Liz told me she was ready to meet him. On this occasion she said

I could sit in on the consultation as part of my training. I was to only listen and not make any comments. She had promised that in the future it was probable that I would be able to become more involved in the proceedings, but for now this was to be only a 'listen and learn' exercise.

Liz's office was filled with her cigarette smoke as usual as I opened the door and beckoned Mr. Markland in. I had tried a few times to tell her that her nicotine habit was neither good for her or her clients, but she took no notice. Mr. Markland took a seat opposite Liz's desk, while I sat in the corner, with my Filofax in hand ready to take notes and observe how Liz operated. She appeared to give the poor man a small lecture on the ethics of what he wanted to do, but she also seemed keen to understand the reasons behind why he was there.

"So Mr. Markland, please tell us why you are keen to father a child with a surrogate mother with whom you have no acquaintance?" Before he could answer Liz hurriedly continued. "I have to say it is a somewhat irregular situation. Usually our clients are already in a relationship and they have difficulty in conceiving, or they are perhaps in a single-sex relationship, obviously making things somewhat problematic. But in your case I can see that we are in a somewhat different area altogether."

Part Two: Leslie Markland

"I just wanted to get this over and done with, get out and go home"

Back from my prison exercises and evening dinner, I now have 60 minutes in which to continue my story. Long enough, I think, to put down in words what happened during that embarrassing episode in Mayfair.

Unsurprisingly, Elizabeth Pinchbeck had asked me to explain why I wanted to have a child so badly with a surrogate mother. I decided to tell her the truth, but perhaps not completely the whole truth.

I wasn't sure of the ethics involved at Angelpride but I imagined that the large sum of money I was willing to hand over would smooth the way. Explaining, quite honestly, that this was something I had to do to make amends with my late father, I described the ancestral convention of my family. As his eldest son but without any children of my own for him to bequeath his estate to, I had let him down. I told her that I felt responsible for him passing away a dissatisfied and unfulfilled old man and I wanted - no, needed - to make it better.

"But there's also another reason, Miss Pinchbeck..."

I went on as earnestly as possible, glancing down at a letter-heading that lay on her desk, "...You see, Miss Pinchbeck, if with your help I could also enable someone's parental dreams to come true, I would be very happy. And of course, as my family's business could well afford the best possible education for that child, he or she wouldn't want for anything."

There! Judging by the dreamy expression on the lady's face, I think I nailed it.

"That's very noble of you, Mr. Markland," Miss Pinchbeck said as she recovered her composure and peered at me over her reading spectacles. "I appreciate your answer to my question, but I can't understand why you don't wish to be associated with the potential surrogate mother of your child. Based on the letter you wrote to us, that is in fact the case, isn't it? Are you not, or are you not likely to be, in a relationship with a woman who can bear you the son or daughter that you are craving?"

I feared that this question was going to come and that eventually I may have to explain to Miss Pinchbeck why it was out of the question for me to have sex, or even admit that I was still a virgin at 36. I was embarrassed at the very thought of it. I'd convinced myself that I needn't ever put myself through the humiliation of having sex with another human being. Explaining that it was all down to trauma inflicted on me by my father, would have been one way to answer her. But that wouldn't have been the real truth. I most definitely didn't want to disclose such personal details to Miss Pinchbeck, especially with her assistant also in the same room. You see, my problems with the opposite sex all began with a girlfriend in my teenage years. Already I'm stretching the truth.

I'm kidding myself that she was my girlfriend. She was really Stanley's girlfriend. Gwen was very flirtatious and didn't mind at all catching my eye when she walked around the house wearing a skimpy t-shirt and no bra. Stanley seemed to enjoy showing her off to me - I guess so that he could tease me later about how much more mature and macho he was than me. But he wasn't macho at all. To use the now thankfully outdated expression, I thought he was a right queer at the time.

One evening Gwen came round for a date with Stanley to go to the latest *Dirty Harry* film, *The Enforcer*, at the pictures. Stanley went off upstairs to have a bath and spend the usual half an hour combing his hair. While he was gone, Gwen went straight for me and made a grab for my trousers. Surprised to say the least, I backed away: I didn't know what to do. If Stan had caught me even near her he would have blown his top. Undaunted, she then did it again.

"Come on big boy," she whispered. "Why don't you show me what you've got down there? It must be bigger than your brother's and he never gets it up anyway."

And with that she began stroking me through the material in a way that I couldn't quite believe. It made me dizzy, and I liked it. But I was dreading what may be happening next - and it did. Before I knew fully what was going on, she unzipped my flies and undid the top button of my jeans. Gwen was clearly well used to doing this sort of thing, as it only took her two seconds to reach in and pull out my erection. But then just as quickly, she began to laugh at what she saw down there. I had always been concerned about my curved penis, but I had never previously had a girlfriend to confirm or deny that it was unusual. I felt my face go redder and redder. And the more blushed I became, the more she laughed at me. My erection disappeared more quickly than it arrived and I ran away up to my room to get as far away from her laughing face as possible. Tears filling my bloodshot eyes as I slammed the door behind me, I threw myself on to my bed and sobbed silently until I had no more tears left. What was the matter with me, I wondered? Why was I like this? I gave myself an examination like I had done many times previously and couldn't avoid the truth. My penis was odd-shaped. It was bent. It was tiny. It was a disaster and I believed then that I would never want to show it to another girl. Not Gwen for sure. Not anybody. I didn't want to feel that kind of humiliation ever again. I sobbed again, this time not so silently.

"Leslie, what on earth is the matter, darling?" called out my mother from the other side of my bedroom door. If I thought the trauma of my first sexual encounter was over, I was mistaken.

"Nothing Mum, it's nothing," I stammered. The door opened slowly and she poked her head round, and saw me crying. I didn't want her to enter my bedroom, but strangely at the same time I did. So I didn't protest when she came and sat on the bed next to me and asked what was wrong. To begin with I clammed up, but eventually she relaxed me, allowing me to drop my guard. Should I be talking to my mother about this, I asked myself, about something so personal, as I slowly and softly told her about what had just happened.

"Not a word to Stanley about what went on between you and Gwen," she warned, frowning a little. "He'd never live it down, having his older brother being flirted with by his girlfriend. But then again, he's probably confused about his sexuality anyway. As a mother, I can tell that he's not as straight as he'd like us to believe. But there's nothing unusual about you, my boy. Trust me."

And with that she held me in her arms and cradled my head against her bosom. I never recalled her having done that before apart from when I was around three or four years old and I'd fallen off the swings in the park and grazed my knees. It was a warm, comforting feeling, but one I wasn't used to. I pressed my head tighter to her, and at the same time felt myself becoming slightly aroused. No, surely this could not be happening, and yet it was.

My head began to swim as I wrestled with my conscience. What was really messing with my mind was that my mother seemed to know what was occurring and yet didn't attempt to stop it.

In a sudden rush, I jerked away and leapt up. Even in my confused state I was able to recognise what was right and what was wrong, and this was most definitely wrong.

So, there were two good reasons, I'd told myself, for forgetting about sex forever. I had a deformed penis and secondly, God forbid, could I have been developing an alarming fancy for my own mother? Totally disgusted with myself and riddled with guilt, I never wanted to risk having those terrible thoughts ever again. I loved my mother, but I knew I had to keep my distance from her in case... well in case anything like that ever happened again. If it did, I felt sure I'd have to kill myself.

So since that episode with Gwen and my mother, I had managed to avoid the whole business of sex, preferring instead to occupy my mind with other joys, such as cars, music and my work. Having said all this, I knew enough about the birds and the bees to understand that I'd need to give a sperm sample for the agency if I were to ever produce an heir to my father's fortune. And in doing so I would have to... well you know. But I wasn't sure I'd be able to do even that.

Swiftly bringing myself back from the recollection of that day with Gwen and my mother, I told Miss Pinchbeck that I was simply too busy to have a woman in my life, and I couldn't see myself having any kind of meaningful relationship in the foreseeable future.

I explained to Miss Pinchbeck how I wished to support the child financially from a distance, while remaining anonymous, unless the child later wished to trace me. During its early years, simply knowing of its existence would be enough for me. The child's details, along with the name and address of the surrogate mother, would be kept safely at my family's solicitors, Ainsworth & Co. My plan was that Ainsworth's firm would be keeping an eye on the mother's whereabouts and would make sure that the child received enough money from me for a good education, as well as anything else it needed.

Fortunately, Miss Pinchbeck didn't pursue the question of why a 'normal' relationship was not possible for me. Instead she began quizzing me on how I would be paying, whether by cheque or cash. Somehow the knowledge that this was, at the end of the day, a monetary transaction made me feel somewhat exonerated. It was almost like going to one of the auctions I liked to attend. I imagined the Scandinavian woman sitting in the corner bringing down the gavel and calling out 'Sold to that man in the leather jacket.'

"Alright, very well, Mr. Markland, we will see what we can do, but please don't be expecting an instant result. We may get a number of potential matches for you, and I'm fairly confident that we'll eventually be able to score a bullseye for you, ha ha."

Her cackle irritated me, but it was too late now to change my mind as I handed over a thick wad of 50 pound notes - a novelty to see in those days as they'd only been in circulation a while. She thanked me and handed me a receipt, while at the same time indicating that I should go with her assistant, who she now properly introduced as 'Miss Silvie Tosgiev.'

"Of course Mr. Markland, we are going to need a sample from you," she continued, "so we can send it off to our associate laboratory that we use to ascertain the quality of your, er, seed, ha ha."

The moment I had been dreading had arrived and I felt cold with fear.

"Please follow Miss Tosgiev to our private room, and afterwards she will show you out. That will be all that we can do for today, and we will then be in touch with you as soon as we have some results back from the lab. Assuming that your, er, stock is all working well, ha ha, we will ask you to supply more of the same when we find the right potential candidate for you. And then when we do, we will be requiring another similar payment upon pregnancy at six weeks, and then another immediately after birth. But you know all this already, of course from the literature we sent you."

Actually, I hadn't realised there were in fact two further payments to be made, but money wasn't on my mind at that point. My thoughts were totally consumed by the worry of having to perform an act that was so alien to me, and I was even more worried that I wouldn't be able to produce any results at all.

We shook hands, said goodbye, and I followed Miss Tosgiev down a corridor and through a door marked 'PRIVATE' as she stood aside while I looked anxiously around.

"Don't be so nervous, Mr. Markland," she began, smiling reassuringly. "This is a perfectly normal procedure and nothing to worry about. We have several things here to help stimulate you to climax. There are magazines in the rack and plenty of VHS tapes there on the shelf. There must me something there that will cater for your interests. Here, let me turn on the television for you." She did have a calming nature about her, and as she glided past me she seemed to intentionally brush her hand next to mine. Her voice was soft and calming. Despite my embarrassment, I noticed for the first time just how very beautiful she was: Slim, with fair blond hair in pig-tails, bright red nail varnish on her fingers, matching her red silk scarf, subtle makeup that made her eyes look bright and attentive, and dressed well in a black skirt, black tights and white blouse. Then my embarrassment returned, as she instructed me.

"The most important thing, Mr. Markland, is that you aim squarely into this pot. We want to keep as much as you can manage, and we certainly do not want to waste any of your valuable commodity," she said as she handed me a glass jar the size that I buy my Robertson's Golden Shred marmalade in.

Oh my goodness, oh my goodness, oh my goodness. What am I doing here? I thought. I composed myself to conceal the panic, but I am sure Miss Tosgiev sensed something was wrong.

"If you have any difficulties, Mr. Markland," she said, matter of factly, "please simply press this buzzer and I will come to assist you with proceedings."

What!? What did she mean, help me with proceedings, I questioned under my breath as she slipped out of the room, closing the door behind her. At last, I was left alone in private to do what I'd come to do.

The room was relaxing, warm and cozy, as I lay on the bed and picked up a *Penthouse* magazine from the rack next to it. I flicked through the pages looking at pictures of naked large-breasted women in poses that made me shudder with embarrassment. Nothing stirred where I knew it was supposed to. I tried reading one of the articles - a story about how Nina had a secret rendezvous with her husband's best friend John and she was satisfied by him so much that she begged him for more and more. I had hoped that the written word would do better than the graphic pictures, but still there was no reaction down where it mattered. Oh goodness, what was I to do? I picked up one of the video cassettes and put it in the JVC player, sat back on the bed and waited for *Riding Miss Daisy* to begin. A lady gets into an old American car and she beckons her black chauffeur to join her on the back seat. She becomes naked all of a sudden and calls out in ecstasy as her driver touches her underneath her handbag. No, this complete and utter rubbish certainly wasn't going to help me produce any results.

Beginning to think I was a lost cause, I remembered Miss Tosgiev's words about her assistance. By this time my head was in such a whirl that I felt drunk, giddy, and I no longer cared what was to happen. I just wanted to get this over and done with, get out and go home.

Part Three: Silvie Tosgiev
"That will do just fine"

I was in my office going through some documents relating to other cases when the buzzer on the wall went off. Leslie Markland had been in the Function Room for a good 20 minutes and I had begun to wonder what was keeping him. The buzzer indicated that maybe he had finished. Or was he, perhaps, requiring my help? If that was the case I wouldn't have minded one little bit, I remember thinking. In fact, if I were honest, it was what I had been hoping for.

It didn't surprise me that this handsome looking man might be requiring some assistance. Right from the beginning he'd appeared to be extremely nervous, especially as we entered 'my' room, and he looked like, how do you say, a rabbit in the headlight? I do love your funny

English expressions. It wasn't until several months later that Leslie confessed that this had been his first sexual experience ever - or at least one with anyone that he was prepared to tell me about.

Putting my pen down, I went to the room and knocked at the door before going in. He was distraught. The sample jar was on the table, unused. His face was bright pink and the television was showing a snowy screen and a tape was ejected from the machine. There was a discarded magazine on the floor.

"I'm so sorry Miss Tosgiev, but I simply can't do this. It just isn't happening for me and I'm afraid I'm wasting everyone's time," he said in a low, quiet whisper.

"There, there, Leslie. I hope you don't mind me calling you by your first name," I responded, trying to put him at ease. "Now relax, and let us see if we can get things, er, back on track for you." This was the sort of thing I enjoyed most. It was the challenge to turn a man on so that they would become putty in my hands and I could take complete control. Bearing in mind our strict Angelpride rule of no physical contact, I set to and began to see how I could assist this shy embarrassed man to achieve what he needed to.

"I see you have tried visual stimulation but without success. That's perfectly normal Leslie and nothing to get upset about," I reassured him. "I have a feeling that I know what I can do for you. Do you mind if I show you?" With a shocked expression, and realising his long uncomfortable silence, he then hastily nodded once. With that I sat on the bed next to him and began talking to him softly into his ear, saying all the erotic words I could think of that might get him stimulated, even throwing some Swedish ones in for good measure. It was no matter that he didn't know their precise translation. I told him how good looking he was and how excited he made me feel, which in fact wasn't too far from the truth. Pulling a chair from beside the wall I repositioned myself and sat cross legged in front of him and leaned forward to tease him with my soft voice, while at the same time allowing him a glimpse down the top of my blouse - just enough so that he could clearly see my firm but small breasts poking over my new push-up bra. I could feel my nipples becoming harder, and I glanced up at Leslie's eyes to see that he had noticed as well. Even if he thought my behaviour was a little, er, unethical, he didn't seem to put up much resistance. He appeared to calm down, looking like he was in some kind of trance. I gently told him how the thought of his sexy body was making my panties wet, and this definitely seemed to do the trick. My skirt was short enough for it to ride up my legs as I sat there opposite him, and it was perfectly obvious that he was staring straight at my red knickers that I'd bought the previous morning from Pretty Polly in Oxford Street. I still had my sensational Christian Louboutins on, as I knew that some men also liked shoes to be worn in the bedroom. Yes, my efforts definitely seemed to be working now, and I could feel, how would you say, a certain frisson of electrical energy between us. He was ready…

"Would you like me to stay and help to hold the sample jar for you Leslie?" I asked tentatively, as I could see from the bulge in his trousers that my tactics were now working very successfully. I hoped he would let me stay, but I didn't want to lose sight of the main reason he was here. The production of a sample for the lab test was of paramount importance over and above any pleasure that I was privately experiencing. I prayed he would not be shy in letting me see him in action. The poor man couldn't answer, but his eyes said it all and so I held the open jar strategically placed to capture his sperm as he stimulated himself to a climax, while I whispered more words of encouragement. I really liked this man, and I don't mind telling you that I was myself very turned on by now, and it was not at all easy to adhere to the 'no-touching' rule of Level Two.

Unable to actually see just how much he'd produced, when he withdrew from the jar and collapsed back on the bed, I quickly screwed the lid on and held the vessel up to the light to examine its plentiful content.

"Well done Leslie," I said abruptly. "That will do nicely. That will do just fine."

CHAPTER 11

Planning Application

"I know that love at first sight is a cliché"

Part One: Tristan Thomas (1994)

A little too sensitive for the cruel world of politics? That was always my destiny, ever since attending Rugby School. It was at Rugby, during my time in the sixth form, that I also became interested in drama, the arts movement and economics. I was studying economics for my A Level and my tutor Mr. Revel had a profound effect on me, and the way in which I conducted myself. He was the man who, more than anyone, I looked up to, hanging on his every word.

Economics, and eventually politics, grew to become my passions, with a certain kinship towards the teachings of Adam Smith, the 18th century economist. As my affection for the employee's rights grew, Mr. Revel's economics lessons also expanded my interest in other men, particularly Mr. Revel himself.

I welcomed the chance to spend extra time, out of lectures, with Mr. Revel, and I am sure that he was the first man with whom I actually fell in love, although nothing physical ever happened between us. Too risky, and considered disgusting by many back then within the confines of the school with a master, sexual encounters only began when I exited the gates and walked alongside the high brick wall towards the centre of town. I would wander the streets and pubs and see who I could meet. I was more interested in the company of men than women, and I knew instinctively as soon as I arrived at Rugby that I was homosexual.

Unlike most of the men I would meet there, who made no secret of being gay, I couldn't be certain about Mr. Revel's sexual orientation with as much clarity as my own. I was certain that he enjoyed my company, but he always kept me at arm's length, much to my disappointment. I knew that if I were to continue participating in his private discussions about the Establishment and the Labour Party, I had to be discreet. Eventually my crush on Mr.Revel waned, but I'll always be grateful to him for the brilliant teacher that he was, and I have happy memories of my first, albeit unrequited, love.

Rugby was the ideal place for me to form and develop my political leanings, even though I was outnumbered by at least 70% of the student population. Most of my fellow students were pompous, Tory upper-class snobs, being driven to the school at the beginning of each term in their posh parents' luxury cars, costing as much as some people's houses. During my final year I had developed complete disdain for the whole lot of them, and the outrageous goings on of Thatcher's government just added fuel to the fire when I listened to my colleagues trying to justify or indeed praise her actions.

When I passed my A Level exams with flying colours - an A in Economics, English, Politics and Art, those results gained me a place at Leeds University to study Economics and Politics. While I was there, I joined the local Labour Party and volunteered to help them on a part-time basis. I would go to their headquarters two, or sometimes three, times a week and assist them with things such as designing their campaign leaflets. Determined to change the world, I became quite heavily involved, and soon found myself having meetings with members of various university Students Union groups, which were excellent places to recruit new members to the Party.

My enthusiasm soon came to the attention of Labour MP David Southall, and he invited me to take on some of the secretarial duties that were associated with his position. It was inevitable, bearing in mind the strength of my views, that my career would take a diversion away from what my parents had originally wanted for me. When I told them that I wouldn't be pursuing a career as an accountant in the City Of London, and that instead I would be working in the offices of a Labour MP in his Leeds constituency, at first they were, shall we say, less than pleased. My father was particularly opposed to the idea.

"Firstly son, you know what your mother's and my views are about the government. They're all on the take and they're all as bad as each other, and you'll end up just like the rest of them if you're not careful. And secondly, what sort of job is a secretary? That's a woman's job isn't it? And you're never going to earn much by typing up letters and answering the telephone. What's more son, there's always a need for an accountant in this day and age, whether a firm is in profit or loss - the money still has to be added up and written down, so in counting money you'd have job security for life," he reasoned.

Their simplified view on my world of employment annoyed me, but I didn't wish to upset them, so I decided not to argue and simply go ahead with what I wanted to do anyway but without causing a scene.

My involvement with the Art and Drama studies group certainly put me in contact with several like-minded lovers of the male physique and I had no shortage of friends who were prepared to lead me astray, sexually speaking, if I may put it that way. I became busy in love and busy in work.

After graduating with a First, I was offered full-time employment. My secretarial skills had been recognised at David Southall's office, along with my undoubted passion for the Labour Party, and he outlined my central task, which was to coordinate the campaign in the lead-up to the general election, due to take place the following year. It was during this period of time that I had cause to visit Leeds town hall where I came across Stanley Markland, who was accompanying his father on some planning matter.

As I was walking across that town hall foyer I couldn't help but notice the loud boom of an angry voice as the elder of two men was arguing with an official about one of the details of his application. His words were carried by the echo of the cavernous building, and I turned to see what the fuss was all about. At that same instant the eyes of the younger man met with mine, and immediately there was a spark of interest and curiosity between us. I walked over to see if there was anything I could do to assist, but as I did so the younger man walked towards me, preventing my progress.

"You'd better not interrupt my father while he's in mid-flow," the young man said humorously. "He doesn't like dealing with bureaucracy at the best of times, so the right thing to do in these circumstances is to let him have his say and get whatever it is off his chest. Any intervention, however best intended, will only fuel the fire that's inside him. By the way, my name is Stanley Markland, and my father there is George Markland. You may have heard of him. He owns the Markland Estate over by Saxton."

As it happened, I had indeed heard of him. I had learned back at HQ that the local Tory party had received quite a substantial donation to their cause by George Markland, so my natural reaction was to associate his son with what I considered to be 'the enemy'.

However, I couldn't bring myself to dislike Markland junior, especially with those gorgeous eyes of his. I felt an undeniable attraction towards him, regardless of his or his father's political stance.

As if he were reading my mind, Stanley Markland went on to explain that even though his father was a Conservative with a capital 'C', he had no particular political persuasions of his own. "I'm not really into that kind of thing," he said, brushing his hand through the air as if waiving a wand. I took my cue.

"So what kind of thing are you into then Stanley?" I asked without any thought of disguising my double entendre. It was his turn to flirt with me, still amid the heated discussion going on between his father and the planning officer.

"Wouldn't you like to know!" he responded brightly. "Why don't we meet up for a cocktail sometime so that you can find out?"

And that was it. I know that love at first sight is a cliché, but I romantically believed that it could indeed be possible. My encounter with this delicious man went on to change the course of my life forever.

"What a lucky girl I thought I was"

Part Two: Constance Markland

I could excuse Stanley anything: he was such a kind man. When he disappeared for a few days here and a few days there to go fishing with his friends I believed it only right and correct that he had his male bonding time. After all, I didn't want to become the classic nagging wife, demanding to know the whereabouts of her husband every waking minute of the day.

When we first met in the summer of 1990, he swept me off my feet with his generous manner, and I don't only mean generous with his cash. I can't say that money was ever all that important to me, anyway. Despite my reasonably middle-class upbringing, there was in fact a fair deal of wealth in my own family and that was down to my mother's sister, to be precise. My lovely Aunt Mimi had been married into a very well-to-do dynasty of sorts. Her late husband, Thomas Cranbury was his name if I remember correctly, owned several factories making pottery. "I never knew there could be so much money in cups and saucers," my mother used to say. When Uncle Thomas was killed in a plane crash one December day, and Aunt Mimi received his life assurance fund, we discovered just how wealthy the family had become.

Mimi was thrilled when she learned I was getting married and expecting twins – she couldn't have children of her own on account of her enormous size. And poor, dear Aunt Mimi had taken great pleasure in setting aside a small part of her substantial fortune for when I ever had children of my own, as I'm sure she wanted to experience motherhood vicariously through me. That made me financially independent of Stanley – at least independent enough for me to afford clothes and shoes and hairstyling without having to go cap in hand to him for the 'loose change' as I joked to Stanley. The 'notes' were safely deposited in our bank, and I had no reason to keep them separate from the rest of our money.

That was something that I later came to regret, especially when I found out about Stanley and *that* man.

Aside from the flowers and clothes Stanley loved to buy me, it was his generous nature and kind demeanour that mattered most to me. No one had ever shown me that type of attention before. After all, I wasn't exactly a beauty queen, even though he told me many times over that I was his own Miss World, bless him.

I suppose you could say that I was actually quite plain and not terribly feminine. More often than not I chose to dress in a trouser suit rather than a dress, in dungarees rather than in a skirt, and certainly I had a preference for wearing mens' white shirts with the sleeves rolled up instead of a conventional ladies' polyester blouse. My hair was usually straight and parted to one side, and I was quite pleased that it wasn't curly or particularly long. In my younger years at school my friends would tease me and call me "Lesbo" but I wasn't that way inclined in any way - I just simply preferred the individual look, instead of following them to the same fashion shops and hairdressers.

I adored Stanley and couldn't wait for the weekends when he would collect me in his car and take me to the pictures. I never cared what we would be going to see, it was enough just being with him. He had his funny ways, but don't we all? He seemed to get a thrill when I went over the top with the masculine attire that I chose to wear along with my minimal makeup and boyish hairstyle. We'd walk along the street arm in arm with him hoping that someone he'd know would bump in to us so that he could introduce me and show me off. I was sure he'd had many girlfriends in the past but I felt I was someone special to him. What a lucky girl I thought I was.

It wasn't long before he took me home to meet his family. My friends, particularly Anna Hennings and Carol Duggan, who I'd spent most of my early teenage years with, teased me about being a gold-digger. I didn't know what they had meant until Carol explained to me who Stanley Markland was. Anyway, I most certainly was not any such thing, and I wouldn't have cared one dot whether he was from a well-to-do background or a sweeper of the city streets. Though I have to admit it did make things even more exciting for me when I got to meet his folks at his family home, and discovered that I wouldn't have to worry much about what we could or couldn't afford if we ever got married one day.

I wasn't too impressed with his dad, though. He was abrupt and harsh, although I dare say he was friendly enough to me on our first meeting. But his mum was a completely different kettle of fish, friendly and warm, but with an air of anxiety etched on her face. I liked her, I really did, but I could tell that she was always keeping the peace in that house between Stanley and his brother Leslie, and also between Leslie and his father. My old dad would often use the expressions 'there's nowt stranger than folk', and: 'families - you can't live with 'em and you can't live without 'em.' I'd say both sayings summed up The Markland family perfectly.

I only really met Leslie a couple of times, and it struck me how different he and my Stanley were, in all ways, and not just in looks. Their temperaments were different for sure. Stanley was confident and almost bullish, a bit like his father, whereas Leslie was quiet and reserved. I thought he was sad although I couldn't put my finger on it. As I said, I only met him once or twice so I couldn't really tell. Besides, Stanley was my man and he was all I cared about.

We didn't want a big deal, so Stanley and I eloped to Gretna Green to get married. His dad knew that we were planning on going and why, and we had his blessing, but his mum didn't have a clue and I felt some guilt about us going off and not telling her. My own mum and dad were long passed, so I didn't have to worry about my side of the family. I only had my Aunt Mimi to be concerned about and I sent her a card as soon as we'd arrived in Gretna. I knew she wouldn't mind what I did. "You go off and do whatever makes you happy, my dear," she would always say to me, bless her.

So we were married, Stanley and me, and not before time as I was already showing. I must have been four months gone already and that was one of the reasons why we went off when we did. Stanley said that if we had planned a big wedding at his home it would have taken ages to arrange and the baby would have popped out at the alter. He was so funny - another of his endearing qualities. He often made me laugh. They say you can fall in love with someone if they have a sense of humour, and that was the case with me alright. His dad knew that I was expecting before we got married, and I had been worried that he'd be angry if he found out. "Don't worry about my father. He'll understand," Stanley assured me. In later years I learned that his dad knew all about getting a woman pregnant before marriage.

We moved in to a modern house with a nice garden that Stanley's dad bought us in Pudsey soon after our honeymoon. We had driven to the lakes directly after the wedding service and rented a cottage by Buttermere that was so gorgeous it could have rained all week and I wouldn't have cared. If I recall rightly, it did more or less rain the whole time, but I didn't mind. I was so blissfully happy to have married the man of my dreams. After the week was up and we returned to Yorkshire, we settled comfortably into our new house, with me choosing various pieces of furniture to turn the house into a home. He was always working so hard that it was the least I could do for him.

I did my very best to please my man, inside as well as outside of the bedroom. When we weren't playing intimate games to satisfy his sometimes overactive sexual appetite I always made sure I looked my best for him, and paid attention to every word that he spoke. I took pride in looking after his every want and need – doing his laundry, keeping the house nice for him, cooking him perfect dinners and generally taking care of him. I did none of this under duress – I was in love.

By the time I was five months pregnant I could hardly get up the stairs, I was so huge. Once when Anna and Carol came round to visit they joked about me having twins inside of me, and it turned out that they were blinking well right. I couldn't wait to tell Stanley the good news after I'd been for my scan, and the ultrasound technician at the hospital showed me the image on the screen. To be honest she could have told me anything on that day and I would have believed her. She printed off a photograph for me to show Stanley after he finished his day's work.

He'd been with his dad sorting out some building plans over at the council in town. "Well, I can't tell head from tail," he joked when he got home, as I pointed out the contents of the grainy image, and he smiled at me. "Twins, eh? Who would have thought I could be so clever?"

Who indeed would have thought that he could have been so clever as to deceive me so well for all that time that we were married?

Part Three: Stanley Markland (1994)

"There was only one problem"

Even all those years ago when I was at my last term at Franklin House school I knew that, following my first 'gay' experience with Philip Mennotsy in the medical room, I was forming an interest in both men and women. I dared not let on to Father that I had even the slightest tendencies in any direction other than the full-blooded heterosexual type, so I decided to stay in the closet - a term that I had come to learn during my days at senior school. When I was about 14 there was one particular lesson that I looked forward to each week where Jonathan Sanders and I used to sit next to each other, and while the master was droning on about the Earth's plates and rock formation we would take it in turns to 'play spiders' with each other. Playing spiders was where we would run our fingers over each other's legs under the desk, moving ever closer upwards. The thrill of what we were doing was indescribable, what with being so exposed in the class and yet so hidden from everyone's sight. Whenever the master looked over to us we would bow our heads down and look as if we were attentively taking notes about his boring subject matter.

I was confused, though. There were plenty of girls that I also had a liking for as well as Jonathan. I recall there was one particular girl, Danni Bernard was her name, and she was fancied by just about every other boy in the school. She had a dark complexion, having come from the Bahamas or somewhere exotic like that. Quite what she and her family were doing at Cromer Road Secondary School on the outskirts of Leeds, I had no idea, but I wasn't really interested in that. All I was interested in was having some 'private time' with her in the printing room. I'd been privileged to have been given the key by Mr. Nathan, who looked after the photography and graphics class. Under the pretext of Danni helping me clean the ink off the machine plates, we would sneak in there during lunch break, close the door behind us and lock it. She made no attempt to stop me when we snogged and my hand went up underneath her skirt so I could feel her womanly warmth, if you get my drift.

They say that school days can be the best years of your life, and I wouldn't argue with that. I had a good time. I was bright enough to do quite well in my tests every year, and I found school to be a very social place, often joking and larking around with the many friends I had there. But as I was developing more and more of a curiosity about my sexuality I assumed that any feelings I had towards boys must be very wrong, so I hid them well by being openly flirtatious with the girls.

Yes, I was somewhat confused about my orientation, but life was never dull. It was definitely exciting compared to the life of my brother Leslie, who was as dull as dishwater. He never seemed to actually do anything except stay in his room listening to his record collection. He loved his music, particularly that American singer Harry Nilsson, ever since he heard Mother playing one of his LPs over and over on the radiogram at home.

After leaving school I went to work with Father, helping him on the estate. It wasn't for me to go to university. I daresay I could have done so if I had I been bothered to work harder for my exams, but it simply wasn't a path I wanted to pursue, and to be quite honest I was lazy. I know that Leslie called me 'Stanlazy' behind my back, and the truth of the matter is that he was correct. So when Father gave me the option to learn the ropes looking after the various properties on the land I considered it to be the easiest option for me.

I can't say that I was much good with the practical things to do with property maintenance - that was more Leslie's forte, and that's what he went on to make his living from when he left home. No, my strengths lay in the administration side of things, looking at the various contracts relating to the farm business and the property tenants, planning applications for alterations to the buildings, and capital purchases like the plant and machinery. I found it all quite interesting actually, and it wasn't too long before I was taking responsibility for some of the estate's affairs.

On one such occasion I accompanied Father to Leeds Town Hall for a meeting with the application officer regarding the building of a livestock feed storage unit next to the cow sheds. It should have been an easy box-ticking exercise but we came up against some jobs-worth who seemed to take pleasure in making life difficult for us. Father was arguing his point in the way he always did, while I stood aside and observed the progress, taking notes along the way. Voices were becoming raised, particularly Father's, and that's when we met Tristan.

Tristan Thomas was a handsome devil, tall and muscular with piercingly blue eyes and an authoritative air about him that almost took my breath away. He tried to intervene with the ongoing 'discussion' that was taking place between the planning officer and Father, but I persuaded him to keep a wide berth and let Father have his say, unhindered. He introduced himself to me and I'll never forget that voice of his. It was oh so seductive without him meaning it to be. Or perhaps he did mean. Whatever his intentions, there was no doubt that Tristan's deep, rounded, smooth tone, with a slightly, I would say, posh accent really entranced me.

Instantly, I wanted to see more of him somewhere other than a public foyer of a town hall, and it filled me with anticipation when he suggested we should meet again for drinks, or rather cocktails as he put it. That suited me. I was never a beer drinking man, and much preferred a Cockburns port or a delicious Amontillado. It was in fact the story of *The Cask of Amontillado* by Edgar Allen Poe that first intrigued me to give the sherry a try when I was 15, and ever since then it's been my tipple of choice. But I digress from my main point - the point at which I predicted Tristan would become the most important person in my life.

There was only one problem. Well two actually. No three in fact. I was married to Constance and she told me that she was expecting twins in less than four months.

CHAPTER 12

Wivenhoe

"My lucky stars had definitely been shining on me that day"

Leslie Markland

I t's funny, isn't it, how split second events can sometimes change the course of your life forever? I'd say in my case that was certainly true. I really ought to thank my lucky stars that I'm only in here for a sentence of one year and five months, and if I'm lucky and with good behaviour, I hope the term will be reduced to precisely a year. That's more or less what the parole board told me. They desperately need those prison beds, and they'd like to see me gone as much as I'd like to leave. So, there's now only three months, one week and four days to go, which should be just enough time for me to complete writing this. It will also be only three months, one week and four days before I can become properly reunited with Oliver, my son.

But I'm getting ahead of myself thinking about the future. First I should look to the past and explain how I ended up living in Wivenhoe after leaving the oppressive and disparaging George Markland and how I ended up living on a boat in Essex, miles from my family home in Yorkshire.

Helping me leave Yorkshire was the best and worst of cars, my old Fiat Sport I liked to call Alfonso. It was the worst because it wasn't exactly reliable, but it was the best because of what it represented to me. Freedom: Freedom to get up and go, and freedom to be in control of my own destiny. I hadn't really had a clear idea of where I wanted to go, but I instinctively wanted to head south: south, but not London. I wanted somewhere I could make an average living doing bits and pieces for local folks, using the practical skills I'd accumulated during my years growing up on the estate. I was attracted to the town of Colchester because I knew that it was the oldest recorded town in England, and I had always been intrigued to discover what it was like there. So Colchester was where I headed.

When I arrived in the town and took a look around, I remember initially not being terribly impressed with what I saw. While sitting on a park bench having a sandwich and about to move on, maybe to Kent or Sussex, I overheard a couple of ladies strolling along the path in front of me. They were discussing their forthcoming luncheon appointment due to take place in a place called Wivenhoe, and I noticed them checking their watches. I was not one to eavesdrop under normal circumstances, but there was something about the enthusiasm in their voices that kept me listening. Where was this Wivenhoe, I wondered? It couldn't be far, as I overheard the ladies discussing being due there at one o'clock and it was already twelve-fifteen. Nothing ventured, nothing gained, I thought to myself, and I decided to investigate where this village or town was. I walked back to Alfonso and got my AA atlas from the boot. At first I couldn't find Wivenhoe on the map - I had been looking in the wrong direction, towards London - but then, ah, I found it, just outside Colchester in the direction of Clacton, down by a river.

After spending some of the afternoon exploring Colchester's busy shopping streets, I returned to Alfonso and drove along the A133 with some huge ugly tower blocks on the horizon. They were enough to put me off, and they very nearly did, but I kept going, knowing that I'd be turning off soon and heading down to the River Colne, according to my map. Up until then I hadn't considered living near a river, but the prospect rather appealed to me. By the time I reached the village at the end of the road my mind was made up. I parked the car and wandered around. Normally it would take me a while to mull things over in my head before making a decision, but not this time. Without a moment's hesitation I knew it was my destiny to remain here in this very convivial spot. All I had to do was find somewhere to stay that suited my relatively shallow pockets.

As I was on a roll and acting uncharacteristically impulsively, I decided to check out one of the village pubs and see if I could pick up any tips for where I might get a room. Perhaps there was a hotel or bed & breakfast nearby. I had parked in the train station car park, and immediately opposite was The Station public house, and in I went. It was early evening but already it was busy with many suited and booted commuters who'd endured a hard day's work somewhere down the line. I could see from my AA atlas that there was a connection directly to London, so I assumed that many of these people were City workers.

I sat at the traditional 'L' shaped bar and glanced around, taking in what I instinctively knew would become my local just as soon as I became settled here. It felt good. There was a relaxed atmosphere and nothing pretentious about the place. I ordered a Guinness and stared at it blankly when it was placed in front of me. Having consumed about half the contents I turned towards the girl collecting empty glasses and began my search for a roof over my head.

"I don't suppose you know of any accommodation around here, do you?" I asked. Before she could reply, a voice next to me answered my question with another.

"You're not from round here, are you? Welcome anyway. How long are you looking to stay?" A good-looking young man in his early twenties was sitting next to me and extended his hand, which I instinctively shook. Goodness! I thought the people of Yorkshire could be friendly, but this was an unexpectedly pleasant and swift greeting.

"I'm not sure yet," I responded. "I guess just a couple of weeks or so to begin with until I get myself sorted out with some odd jobs here and there – I'm a bit handy with a few tools and paint brushes, you see. Then I can start looking for somewhere more permanent."

"You could try Lynne," he said helpfully. "She's a friend of mine and has an old steel barge that needs some work doing to it. You never know, she might be able to help, and she may even be there at the moment. If she is, you can say Neil sent you."

Was this a stitch-up or a con, I wondered? I hadn't expected this kind of assistance, but nevertheless I gratefully followed his tip and asked Neil to show me the way. After hurriedly finishing my Guinness, I collected my bag from the car and walked from the pub towards the river, following the directions I'd been given. Soon I reached the water, and what I saw was quite breath-taking, with unspoiled views of fields and greenery on the opposite bank and sailing boats bobbing up and down on a tide that was clearly in. Along the quay I went, soaking up the atmosphere of people sitting and chatting in the sunshine outside the riverside Rose & Crown pub, while I headed further along towards the location where I hoped to find Lynne and her barge.

I did find her and I introduced myself, explaining why Neil at the pub had sent me in her direction. My lucky stars had definitely been shining on me that day, and I was delighted by the outcome of our conversation that must have lasted less than five minutes flat.

"It's not a luxury hotel by any means," Lynne began. "But you can stay on here for a few pounds a week and do some work to help me get this old wreck up to scratch," she concluded. "This could work for both of us, and if Neil suggested that you should come and find me, then I don't mind taking a punt. So that's my deal if you fancy it. Come inside and take a look."

I needed no persuading. At last, I thought! After years of unhappiness up in Yorkshire things may be about to take a better turn for me, as I walked the gangplank from the quayside and onto the smelly, dark and damp old vessel. And that's how I came to live in Wivenhoe, where apart from this year in prison I've lived ever since.

CHAPTER 13

Responsible Adult

"The next time I saw him he was thankfully inside a wooden box"

Leslie Markland

S ince I moved to Wivenhoe when I was 20, I kept my head down and worked. I became responsible, reliable and dependable, and soon the word got round. I worked and worked and worked, doing whatever jobs came my way. And being handy with tools and brushes, I never had any shortage of assignments. I had some business cards printed and handed them out to anyone who asked.

LESLIE MARKLAND
PAINTING, DECORATING, FIXING, MAKING.
LOCAL, FRIENDLY, RELIABLE SERVICE
JUST FIND ME AROUND WIVENHOE
AND ASK ME FOR A FREE QUOTE

I didn't have a telephone on the barge, which I nicknamed 'Barnacle Barge', and mobile telephones were only imagined on *Star Trek* back then. 'Find me around Wivenhoe' is exactly what people did, and I was always busy. Before long I'd saved enough money for a small van that was much better at lugging things around than Alfonso ever was, although I kept the old Fiat. And talking of money, I never trusted the banks, so cash – always stashed in bundles of notes around the barge - was always king for me.

My life on the Markland Estate became a distant memory. Apart from the odd legal letter from Roger Ainsworth during the eighties and early nineties, I hardly kept in touch with anyone from the family, which suited me right down to the ground. I did get to hear about my brother's wedding and mother moving away, but that was about it. I was reasonably content with the world, until my father died in the mid-nineties and left that will.

Do you recall the will reading when I left Roger Ainsworth's offices in Leeds? I was pretty distraught. It took me years to find out the reasons for his callousness towards me. Prison has given me time to reflect and calm down a bit, but at the time I became determined to scupper George Markland's final wishes. How dare he cause me even more grief than when he was alive? I remember how my mind had been working; I'd bloody well have my own child, and that would teach the bugger a lesson, even though he was dead. It would also knock Stanley off his conceited perch too. And as for those dreadful twin girls, who had been left pretty much everything, well! I could hardly bring myself to think of them inheriting so much at my expense.

In late 1995, when I reluctantly visited Stanley and Constance to attend the girls' christening, I was asked to fulfil the role of godparent, or Responsible Adult, to be strictly accurate. After much thought I declined, which didn't go down well with Stanley or my father, and Roger Ainsworth stepped in to the breach. Even then I thought there was something odd about those girls. Although I couldn't put my finger on what it was, their eyes caused me to feel uncomfortable and unnerved. And they were only a year old, for goodness sake. No wonder Constance did what she did. But again I'm rather jumping the gun – I'll tell you about Constance later.

That was the last time I visited the estate, and the last time I ever saw my father alive. He passed away early the following year, so the next time I saw him he was, thankfully, inside a wooden box.

CHAPTER 14

Letters from America

"Come on Mother, I'm a grown man now"

Leslie Markland

Remember that 'smelly, dark and damp old vessel' I told you I'd rented from Lynne? By 1996 it had become fresh, bright and airy after I'd saved up hard and purchased it from her in the late eighties, with cash, of course.

After a tedious train journey home from my ordeal in Mayfair, once inside 'Barnacle Barge' I was completely drained, and very much in need of a stiff drink or three. I reached for the ornate whisky decanter from the fiddle. Seafarers out there will know that the fiddle is the shelf-type contraption with raised wooden edges, used on boats to prevent things from falling off when out on the water. My boat never tilted as it was permanently tied to its moorings, but it did go up and down with the tide twice a day. After wearily discarding my jacket on the bed, I opened the rear shutters that looked out on to the river, from where I could admire my smaller wooden fishing boat tied up against my barge's no-longer-rusty steel hull. The light from the evening sun flooded into the cabin and I glanced at the letter I'd just collected from the American-style mailbox that I'd erected next to the barge's gangplank on the quay. The letter was from America, from Indiana to be precise, and it was fitting that the letter had been posted to the mailbox. Both the letter and the mailbox had come from the same source - the mailbox being a gift. It had been brought one day by a gruff sounding delivery-man. "Are you Mr. Markland?" he'd asked. "How am I s'posed to find you when all this address says on this label is 'Barnacle Barge, Wivenhoe Quay, Essex'?" Thank goodness my mother had kept her sense of humour, I chuckled to myself.

I sat down in my comfy chair. In fact it was my only chair, with space being at a premium within the barge's cabin. My chair was high backed and covered with a grotesque deep red velvet material, well-worn at the edges and quite thread-bare on the right arm. It was rather unsightly and not at all suited to being on a boat, but I liked it. Anyway, who was going to see it, except Harry and me? I sank back in it with my drink perched on the small mahogany side table next to the chair, as I proceeded to cut the envelope with the silver letter-opener, also a present from my mother. I took a sip of whisky and began to unfold the three thin sheets of writing paper she had no doubt bought on one of her weekly expeditions to Walmart.

Plainfield,
Indiana
Dearest Leslie,

I hope this letter finds you well and that you are still enjoying life on board your boat. I wish I could be there to see how you have settled in Essex and to see for myself the village you are living in. It sounds almost too good to be true, and it's a blessing you have made such a good life for yourself there.

Have you heard anything about your father's will yet? It came as such a shock when I heard of his passing, but in hindsight I'm not so surprised now, knowing how highly strung he was and not keeping himself healthy.

I used to tell him off for all those rich dinners.

I bet you never miss living on the Markland Estate? I certainly don't.

I hope one day you can come out to visit me. Have you got that passport yet? My job at the store is still going well. Mr. Dellinger says that I'll be up for promotion soon if I carry on at the rate I'm going. It would be nice to move off the tills, but I do get to meet the customers as they pay for their groceries. They always ask me how I'm doing, and they listen to what I have to say. I think it's because they like my English accent. I am getting a little tired of being asked whether I've met the Queen though, but I know they only mean well.

Well, I mentioned Mr. Dellinger, and that's the news I have to tell you. We have become 'an item', as they say here. I know that you and he would get on just fine and I've told him so much about you, he can't wait to meet you. I'm sure we could find you all sorts of jobs around the store if you ever felt like coming, and even more in my condo. The fly screen is falling off the front door for a start, but I wouldn't want you to think you should come out here just for that. The truth is that I miss you like crazy and I hope you can one day forgive your late father for how he treated you. I believe I have managed to find forgiveness in my own heart and move on.

In the end it was his constant lying to me that drove me away. I knew he enjoyed the company of other women and I could forgive him even that, if only he'd been truthful about it.

One day I will be brave enough to tell you all about your past, as I believe you should know why he was so unkind to you. I can't bring myself to write it down in words just now, but one day I will, and perhaps you'll then understand why he behaved like he did towards you.

Have you heard from Stanley recently? How is he doing? He doesn't write to me like you do, but I know he has his hands full with looking after Constance and the twins. Those twins, I don't know.

I've heard from Roger Ainsworth that they're becoming quite a handful for Constance. Dear old Roger Ainsworth. I always liked him, but I'm not so sure about his son who must be getting ready to take over the firm soon. I know that Roger has his reservations, but he's getting on now and can't keep going forever. I guess you'll see him soon if you go up there for the will-reading.

Anyway dearest Leslie, it's been nice 'talking' with you. Get that passport sorted and don't forget your mother's fly-screen, ya hear! That's how they talk over here. Let me know what you come out with from the will. I hope it will be enough to settle you and then you can come on over.

I miss you.

With much love and fondness,

Mother x

PS Is that rusty old car still going for you? I still have the letter you wrote years ago and told me it got you all that way south.

I took a deep sigh, stood up and walked over to a box resting on top of a pile of antiques magazines. It was one of those wooden filing boxes with a spring clip inside. I opened it, lifted the spring and placed the letter in among the others. Unusually that was only the second she'd sent to Wivenhoe that year. I glanced sadly at one of the others – the one I kept at the top of the pile that she'd sent me after she'd left Father.

16th March 1983

Darling Leslie,

It was a very difficult decision for me to leave you and Stanley and I know that I don't deserve your forgiveness, but I pray that you at least will understand a little. I'm afraid it simply became intolerable, especially as I could see how unpleasant things at home were becoming. And what with those affairs on the side it just all became too much for me to stay, so I had to go. I'm so proud that you had the courage to leave the Markland Estate as soon as you were able.

I read no more, as I took a large mouthful of whisky and tried to get drunk in order to dull the mental anguish I felt.

How ironic that I should receive Mother's letter enquiring about the will, on the very same day that I was returning from London after attempting to change my life because of it. And what did she mean about my past? What does she know that I don't? I thought Roger Ainsworth would have written to her about the will, but maybe he hadn't. Surely she would have become a beneficiary, wouldn't she? There were more questions than answers. I decided to break out of my sombre mood and put on some music, choosing something from my collection of old tapes. I know I should have moved forward with technology, but I had so many cassettes and there was something comforting about them. I put Neil Young's *Harvest* into the Philips machine and pressed the 'play' button upwards.

Usually I would have left replying to Mother's letter for a few days, but on this occasion I had too many thoughts milling around my head. So, I replenished my glass and pulled my Montblanc fountain pen from my top pocket while searching for some Basildon Bond to write on. I am a tad sad, I admit, but I do like these old 'proper' things. So much better than a biro and some cheap A4.

With my large *Times Atlas* to rest on my lap as a table, I began my reply.

Dear Mother,

Thank you so much for your letter.

I am so pleased to hear that you have found friendship with Mr. Dellinger. You deserve to find some comfort and happiness, and I hope he treats you well.

You know, one day I may well surprise you and come out to meet him in person, and fix your fly screen while I'm there. How about that?

It is obvious from your letter that you don't yet know about the will. The property was left to Father's grandchildren, but with the grandchildren's parents having the income from the estate until any grandsons reach 18-years of age, or 21 in the case of granddaughters. So, as I don't have any children of my own, I'm afraid I'm out of it. And if you yourself haven't been notified by now, I guess you are too. I suppose that since becoming divorced you wouldn't automatically become a beneficiary. So you and I have something in common, Mother – we've both come out with nothing. Diddly squat, as they say!

You never know though. Things could always change, and if I ever did father a child of my own that would teach the old man to be so presumptuous, wouldn't it? And that smug expression would also be wiped off Stanley's face, for sure!

I paused to catch my breath. I was writing as quickly as I could, as if I were having an imaginary conversation with my mother there and then. I could feel my hurt and anger building. Calm down Leslie, calm down, I told myself. Have another drink. Turn the cassette over. I took a deep breath, got up and went to the 'heads'. That's the toilet to you and me. I opened the lid and the stench soon brought me back to earth. I made a mental note that I really ought to empty its container that night when everyone around was asleep. My bladder emptied, I sat back and continued to put pen to paper, deciding to end on a positive note.

In the meantime, Mother, I must tell you about my new friend, Harry. He's adorable and I know you'd love him. I have finally fallen madly head over heels! But don't get the wrong idea. This boy is the cutest little terrier you've ever come across. He just jumped into the back of my car recently - in fact it was after Roger's reading of Father's will. Harry and I are an item! So that's the both of us becoming items, eh?

I must finish now. I don't know what Father had been thinking when he made his will, but what do you mean about telling me about my past? What are you keeping from me? Come on Mother, I'm a grown man now and I can take whatever it is that's thrown at me.

You take care of yourself and remember that I love you and think of you daily. Write back soon – don't leave it so long next time. YA HEAR!

With fondest love

Your son Leslie

xxxxxx

CHAPTER 15

Attack of the Heart

"I assumed it was meant to be for my pleasure, not his!"

Constance Markland (1995)

My marriage to Stanley Markland was the best thing that could have ever happened to me at the time. I was amazed. He saw something in me that other men who'd previously been in my life, if that's what you could call them, hadn't. No, they weren't men that swept me off my feet and treated me the way I wanted to be treated. Basically, without being too crude, they tended to shag me and leave me. I always tried to give them my undivided attention and to take care of them, wash and iron their clothes, clean their flats or houses for them, but it was never enough. They would lose interest in me soon after I let them in my bed, or soon after I made it into theirs, and I could never really understand why.

And then I met Stanley and thankfully he was different. I adored him and he appeared to feel the same way about me. The news that I was pregnant with his child made me overjoyed, until I discovered that I was actually having twins. At that point I became ecstatic!

At last my life was really taking a turn for the better and I was sure that

I would be living happily ever after with my man and our two children.

But around two or three months before the girls were born I began to notice a slight change in Stan. He seemed a little distant towards me. I was so huge, so I couldn't really blame him for going off the idea of sleeping with me. For one thing, he told me that I snored. Can you believe that? Well, I could, because I had no choice but to sleep on my back and sometimes I would even wake myself up with my own noise!

The poor lamb. He needed his sleep for the busy day ahead working with his father on the estate, and so I suggested one morning after a restless night that he slept in the spare room.

"It will only be until I have these babies, my darling, and then we'll be back to normal and we can be together again for the whole night."

I suppose I wanted him to protest, but instead he agreed a little too immediately for my liking, and the rest of the day I felt so low. Silly, stupid me. How pathetic I was being. It had been a perfectly sensible and practical suggestion of mine, and surely he had only been agreeing simply to keep me happy, but I was sad nonetheless. I sat in the kitchen and made myself a coffee as I wiped the tears from my eyes. I reached for my new Nokia phone and smiled gloomily as I remembered having unwrapped it on my birthday the previous month. It had been a gift from Stanley. It must have cost a fortune and I just loved the way it flipped up. He'd always been so thoughtful and loving towards me. I pressed the buttons and called my friend Anna.

"Hey Chuck," she began. My initial hello must have sounded down in the mouth. "What's up? Haven't you dropped them little 'uns yet?"

Anna was always so direct. She never seemed to get fed up, unlike moody old me. I answered her first question and ignored the second. "I just don't know, Anna." And I proceeded to explain my irrational thoughts to her. As I had expected she told me not to be so daft.

"He'll probably come home this evening with a big bunch of flowers for you and you'll wonder what all those tears were about. Well I'll tell you Connie, it's just them hormones inside you. Just remember tomorrow who told you that, and I'll come round for a coffee just as soon as our Jake's been packed off to nursery, and you can cut me a big piece of your cake, okay?"

And sure enough, Stanley did come home later with a big bunch of flowers for me as I was making the dinner - spaghetti bolognese, his favourite. And sure enough, Anna did come round the next morning to get her piece of cake. She had bundles of self-confidence, did Anna. I guess that's why I considered her to be my best friend. Why couldn't I be more carefree like her? Instead, I was constantly worrying about how to keep Stanley happy and content enough to stay in love with me.

Our first night in separate beds felt odd. I woke up having had a really good sleep, the first for ages, so maybe it was actually a good idea of mine after all. It was one of those times where you wake up and drift back, wake up and drift back again, over and over. Had I been dreaming or had I been awake? I couldn't be sure. Eventually I had to get up to go to the loo and make a cup of tea. I pushed open the door of the spare room and called out.

"Good morning my darling, would you like a cuppa?" It was odd that there had been no reply, so I went in to discover that he'd obviously left for work earlier than usual that morning.

At ten o'clock Anna came round for a coffee and we chatted about how stupid I'd been to feel the way I had, and that I should be grateful to have a bed to myself without having him crawl all over me. That sort of comfort would have been the last thing on my mind, and she did have a point. I ought to let him get on with his business and be grateful that he'd been willing to sleep in the spare room so readily. A week went by and I became used to finding him already off to work by the time I got up in the mornings. In fact I was seeing him less and less as he would often come home at around seven in the evening, take a quick shower, grab something to eat, and then around nine o'clock I'd have to go off to bed myself, I was that tired.

One particular night I got up to go to the loo at around two in the morning. That wasn't anything unusual as my bladder was becoming weaker by the day and it seemed that those babies were pushing against my insides more and more. Unusually though, on this occasion, I needed some company from my husband and I hoped he wouldn't mind me waking him for a few minutes for a cup of tea together.

He wasn't there. He'd been there earlier though, when I saw him trying on some new trousers he said he'd bought for a forthcoming business meeting. Looking back, I realised he'd been spending a while longer in the bathroom than usual those last few weeks, and his appearance was becoming more smartly groomed than I was used to seeing.

It suddenly dawned on me that he must be seeing another woman. My head span. My heart stopped as the realisation of what had been happening sank in. I was devastated.

I didn't know what to do except call Anna who came round as soon as she could. She listened attentively to my semi-coherent words in between my wails and sobs. After I'd calmed down I reminisced about our earlier courting days, and how funny it was that Stanley always liked going out with me being dressed up in 'the works', as he liked to call it. The brogues, the dark blue suit with white shirt, the pink tie and my hair parted and quiffed to one side. He loved that look. Those had been the days when we were having fun, well before I became my larger pregnant self. I'd heard that some men liked a bit of what I'd call 'kinky sex', and I had been happy to oblige him in bringing his fantasies to life. After all, I loved him and that was what a good marriage was all about, so I had no qualms about using his adult toys on him that were, I suppose, a little unusual. When he'd excitedly brought home a LoveHoney Sixinch, I assumed it was meant to be for my pleasure, not his!

And now, after all that special attention I used to give him, he's gone and found another woman to satisfy his whims. Well, we would see about that. I'll not be letting go of my man that easily, I remember telling Anna.

I knew some people would have thought me naive, but I imagined I was being rather clever to be so forgiving. I'd only just read a piece in the previous weekend's Sunday paper about how common it was that some husbands left the marital bedroom during and shortly after their wives' pregnancy in order to satisfy their own sexual needs elsewhere. Stanley was only doing what any red-blooded male would do under similar circumstances, wasn't he? I would find a way to entice him back to me in a way in which he couldn't resist, I decided.

After Anna had finished listening to my rant, she calmly suggested I was surely jumping to the wrong conclusions about my suspicion of his affair. But I wasn't convinced that she was right. I pretended to Stanley that I hadn't noticed his extra-marital behaviour. I didn't want to nag him, and after all I wanted him around for when the babies were born, which came sooner than I had expected.

It was around 11 o'clock one evening when I knew that would be *the* night. A mother instinctively knows these things, and I was already packed and ready to go to Leeds hospital when Stanley hurriedly returned home to take me there, after receiving my text message. *'baby! now! get here!'*, was all I'd said. He pulled up outside the front door with a screech of tyres and rushed in. My, he did look handsome, I remember thinking, and so smartly dressed. His other woman, must have been so disappointed about their evening together being prematurely cut short.

"I came as quick as I could, love," he said anxiously. "There are some real problems with one of the cottages and I had to meet with the roofing contractor at The Albion to work out the repair schedule."

I'll say one thing for him, I thought, - he's got an active imagination. As if he believed I could be so daft. But I let him continue thinking I was clueless about his affair.

"Never mind darling," I replied with false calm. "You're here now, that's the main thing. We'd better get going to the hospital straight away please. You can carry on dealing with the builders another time - once you are a daddy."

Thirty minutes later I was in the delivery room, with me screaming blue murder, according to the midwife.

Apparently, it had been a tense time at the point the forceps went in.

But in fact I don't recall too much about it. I was in and out of my mind, using gas and air as much as I could. I think I had been administered an epidural to relieve the pain which was like something out of a horror story. I can't believe I made such a fuss, silly old me, but it did leave me feeling extremely tender down below. They had to place the forceps to literally pull the babies' heads out with all the strength that they could muster. Hilary came out first, followed by Sophie a few moments later, or so I was informed by Betty, the very caring and lovely midwife.

During the quiet times following the birth, Betty would come round to make regular checks on me and the twins. She was from Trinidad and had a big beaming smile and large round face that matched her size. She made me feel so safe and comfortable. I wished she could stay with me all day, but sadly she could only spare a few minutes, during which time she'd write a few things on her clipboard and move on to another ward. She joked with me about how my husband had to be taken out of the delivery room before he fainted at the sight of all the blood spewing from my 'business end,' as she called it. I made a mental note to find Betty later to thank her with a card and a small present for all her smiles. I did send her a nice tea towel that had a picture of the Markland Chapel printed on it from the gift shop near the estate next to the Post Office. The card was signed 'thank you for everything, from Stanley and Constance Markland', although, of course, it had been I who had written it, as Stanley was always so busy with everything else. Of course he was.

I was in that hospital bed for three days and three nights while my stitches healed sufficiently and until I was deemed safe to leave. During that time I had the children in a see-through crib next to me at the same level as my head, so that I could always keep a watchful eye on the little cherubs. I called them my children rather than my babies, because they already seemed to be so mature. I gazed at them, dreamily wondering what would become of them and how they would turn out. Already they appeared so well-natured and in harmony with one another, although I have to admit they only looked well-natured when they were sleeping.

The rest of the time when they were awake they were literally painful to be with. Betty had taught me a way in which I could balance them together in both arms, so that they could suckle on my breasts for a full protein dinner at my expense. Of course I was tremendously proud that I was able to offer them this most natural of functions, but bloody hell they hurt me! I could have sworn that they had teeth already. There were times I almost wished that they were back in the comfort of my womb - comfort for my sake, not theirs!

Stanley was kind to me, of course he was, but over the coming days, weeks and months he became gradually more patronising and distant towards me. I assumed that it was because I didn't yet want to play his sex games, and who could blame him for becoming frustrated and going off to his bit on the side? Sometimes I wondered who she might be, but I didn't really care to find out, the coward that I was.

However, it was his reluctance to accept what I was telling him about the twins that really upset me the most.

It was probably my overactive imagination again, but ever since those first days in the hospital I felt that it was like two against one. I could imagine them somehow communicating with each other about the precise time they'd fall asleep, the exact moment when they'd both wake up, poo their nappies in unison and appear to bite me at exactly the same time until my breasts hurt so bad. I did tell Stanley all this, and I only wanted some sympathy, that was all. But he just didn't seem to understand like another woman would. He just told me I must be imagining things because the babies were far too young to know what they were doing.

Anna understood though, thank goodness, and she also seemed to understand when I told her that although Stanley had another woman on the side I preferred not to confront him. I knew that would only push him away further and possibly for good, and that was not what I wanted. No, I wanted him back where he belonged, with me, Sophie and Hilary in our home, together as a happy family. I wasn't being stupid or naive, just practical, sensible and loving. Anyone could see that, couldn't they? Well, Anna could, and that was what mattered to me.

More weeks and months went by. Stanley always provided for whatever I wanted or needed, or at least what could be bought with money. We settled into a routine. He would stay at home three evenings a week, and for the rest of the time would come up with some convoluted story about why he had to visit this or that contractor, or call at the estate to see his father about something or other, or simply that he was going fishing with his mates at the weekend. He must have thought I was completely stupid, as I knew he didn't know the first thing about fishing. Fish fingers at the Co-op was the extent of his angling knowledge! However, I naively adored him and they do say that love makes you blind, and that was how it was for me. I loved him, and that was that.

We were coming up to nine months or so after the twins had been born before we got round to discussing their christening. Stanley didn't want to have one, as he was not into religion at all. My mam had been though, God rest her soul, and I wished she could have been around to witness what would surely have been a tremendously proud moment for her. So it was for her sake that I pleaded with Stanley that we have some sort of service - some kind of acknowledgement of the twins' existence in the eyes of our Lord.

We finally compromised by agreeing to have a civil service. We had firstly asked Stanley's brother Leslie to play the role of 'responsible adult', but he backed out. So we settled on solicitor Roger Ainsworth. In my opinion that was like a second-rate God-parent if ever there was one. Nothing against Roger Ainsworth, but really it should have been kept in the family, don't you think? But Stanley knew best of course, and so that was what we'd arranged. And although Leslie had declined his official role he did at least attend the ceremony. I do believe that was the last time he ever saw his and Stanley's father, George, alive.

Stanley and Leslie's father died of a heart attack a few weeks after the ceremony. I'm not usually one to feel sorry for myself but on one hand I had a grieving husband so distraught that he wasn't able to string two words together, and on the other I had to deal with two babies who appeared to have a personal vendetta against me.

Get over it, I told myself, and with Anna's help I believe that I very nearly did. At least that was until things really became unbearable for me when Roger Ainsworth's son Brian started to take over at the solicitor's office. What a complete bastard - and that's not a word I'd use loosely.

CHAPTER 16

Plan of Deception

"If only I'd picked up on Connie's throw-away comment"

Anna Hennings (1996)

I had known Constance, or Connie as I called her, for quite a few years. We were at school together but we didn't really hang out back then. We both had our own circle of friends, although I should rephrase that. I had my circle of friends, but she didn't seem to belong in one. She was something of a loner, I used to think, and I hadn't been that keen on her if truth be told. But I was fascinated by her style. It was so unique. While everyone else, including me I have to admit, was wearing whatever was in fashion at the time - dungarees, tank tops, hot pants, bell bottoms - there she was coming into the sixth form common room looking like a female David Bowie in a suit. And just as David Bowie changed his style like the weather, so did Connie. I doubt whether she deliberately tried to copy him. It wouldn't have surprised me if she hadn't known who he was. She was in her own cocooned existence, doing her very own thing. I admired her for having the courage to stand out, especially as she appeared so lacking in confidence in all other ways. She was quietly spoken and often had difficulty making people hear what she had to say. But the more I gradually got to know her, the more I liked her. She allowed me into her personal world, and for that I was very grateful. I'm glad I was able to help her, although I'm riddled with the guilt that it may have been my actions that eventually contributed to her tragic downfall. I'll never forget that day when I discovered her hanging like a rag doll behind her bedroom door. Anyone would have been under enormous strain if they had to go through what she did. She just hadn't had the strength to cope, the poor darling.

Things had been looking so promising for her back at college. That was when I would say we became proper friends. The fact that, later, we both went on and had one thing in common made our bond even stronger; we both had husbands whose jobs afforded us lots of free time to spend together. I was fortunate enough to be given a generous allowance by my husband every week from his not unsubstantial salary. Charlie had joined Warne's Farm Supplies on leaving school, and had worked his way up the ranks to becoming Senior Regional Sales Manager, for Yorkshire, no less, and I was very proud of him. Warne's was no tuppeny-ha'penny concern by any reckoning either. They were the national leaders in their field – selling products all over the country to the farming industry, particularly with anything to do with pigs. Pig feed, pigpens, even pig fertility equipment. And there are an awful lot of pigs around our county, and Charles Hennings was doing very well out of them, thank you very much. He was certainly bringing home the bacon, ha ha!

Anyway, Connie seemed to let her guard down with me and felt comfortable in my presence. My other good pal, Carol, said it was because with me being kind of a larger than life character it helped to make Connie feel more confident. From where I was standing, I could usually only see the good in people, and in my book Connie had a lot of good in her.

I ought to explain to you what happened, and hope that you can see that I only meant well for her. If only I'd known how things would eventually turn out, I'm sure I would never have made those phone calls in the first place.

She came to me right at the beginning, when she first told me in 1994 that she was thinking about getting married, and wanted to ask my advice. That was my first mistake. I should have told her straight there and then that I thought something was not all there with her Stan, but I couldn't really say anything, could I? She was so besotted with him and if I'd told her back then what I had thought, it would have broken her heart. She was so loved up. I didn't want to be the one to do that to her, so I suppose I was the coward, wasn't I, not wanting to confront the situation on her behalf? I could see a mile off that he was swinging both ways, if you know what I mean. Sure, he was happy to be with Connie, and I do believe his affection for her was genuine alright. But it was all a pretence, obviously to me. But then I didn't really need to analyse things all the time like Connie did - I just had a sixth sense about matters of the heart.

I so miss Connie's quirky ways and her soft nervous laugh, and I so miss the times we spent together pouring over the articles in the tabloids, with our cups of coffee at her kitchen table. Sometimes she would literally pull me indoors by my sleeves when she opened the door. She would be so excited to show me the latest 'Top Five How-To' section in the paper.

How to keep your man interested in you… How to glam up your sex life… How to spot if your man is being unfaithful… I used to tell her to stop being so gullible, and she would look up at me forlornly, with her reading glasses perched on the end of her nose, before breaking out into a nervous giggle, and I couldn't help but join in.

I had been so delighted for her when she broke the news to me that she was pregnant. "How on earth did that happen?" I teased, remembering from previous conversations when she confessed they rarely made love in the usual way. It certainly hadn't been that way for Charlie and me. I mean, we were at it like rabbits all the time. He told me, and still does, that he loves me for my inner self and not just the size of my breasts, which are pretty large I have to say. "Of course you do darling", I'd say, squeezing them in front of him. And then we'd fall about laughing.

"We still hardly ever have full intercourse sex," Connie told me. Apparently she had rarely managed to get him to actually ever 'do it' - even in those early loved-up days, and that it must have been God's will that she fell pregnant with her twins so easily. "Either I was very fertile, or he had exceptionally strong swimmers," she joked during one of our heart-to-hearts.

We often used to chat over coffee, and the conversation would come around to her sex life. I remember one such occasion, probably about two years after she'd had the twins.

"Anna, I've got something I need to ask you," she began. Even though we were alone in her kitchen, she still lowered her voice to a whisper. I had to lean forwards, as I could hardly hear her. "Anna, do you think there's something wrong with me? Stanley's very kind and gentle with me, but he still doesn't want to, you know..." And at that point she slowly mouthed the words "PUT-IT-IN", pointing down there, and not looking me in the eye, as if she were ashamed.

"There's nowt wrong with you, my girl," I tried to reassure her, as I got up to get the bottle of Cava I knew she had in her fridge. "Come on girl. Let's have a glass of this together and you can tell me all about what's on your mind. No need to be shy with me, you know that." Before we knew it, the bottle of Cava was empty and we had to break open a second.

Connie told me some pretty personal stuff that afternoon, and normally I would never repeat that sort of information to anyone, but I was asked to disclose some of it at the inquest, so I suppose it's in the public domain now anyway. She adored Stan, as we all knew, but she discovered that he was bisexual and was in fact carrying on with some fellow. She only found that out much later on. To begin with she thought he was having an affair with a woman, and she'd been blaming herself for not being receptive enough to him in the bedroom following the birth of the twins. That scenario was even semi-acceptable to her, broken hearted though she was, thinking that Stan was your normal, red-blooded male. But in the bedroom apparently all he wanted was – well, I can't actually bring myself to say it, it's so disgusting, but I'm sure you can work out what I mean. She told me about the dildos he would bring home for her to use on him. Yuck! The dirty bugger. I didn't mention that bit at the inquest, but I did describe how those twins used to drive her to distraction sometimes and I was sure that couldn't have helped her at a time when she was already terribly depressed on account of Stan's homosexual carryings on.

But it had been her pleading with me to help her get pregnant and have another child that set the chain reaction off good and proper. I should have told her a straight "no" there and then, but I must admit I had also been intrigued and excited to help her with her plan, however misguided it was. She even offered to pay me, but I declined that. I didn't need the money. So, what she meant about getting pregnant was that it would be pretty unlikely to happen with Stan under normal circumstances. For him to believe that he was to become a father again, she planned to get him so drunk that he wouldn't remember what had happened. Or rather what hadn't happened. She'd planned to pretend that she'd leapt upon him with wild abandon at the crucial moment. Of course it wouldn't be true, but she was betting on the chances of her conceiving with another man were actually quite high, and as it turned out, she was right.

Connie needed another baby and was becoming more and more desperate every time I saw her. She thought it would be the end of all her problems, when in fact it would only lead to more, and tragic ones at that. She wanted to get Stan focused on her and their family. After all, Stan adored the twins and he was very good with them. They didn't play him up like they did her. That was the other reason she craved another child: I think she felt she was outnumbered. The twins tormented her but Stan just couldn't see it, and so poor Connie never got the emotional support she so wanted from him.

To cut a long story short, she wanted to get pregnant by another man but pretend to Stan that it was in fact his child. She was convinced he would then see the light, leave the person she thought was his mistress and return to her, bring up the three kids together and go on to live happily ever after. I did try to put her off the whole idea, but she practically begged me to help her go through with it until I eventually agreed.

"Look here Connie. This is never going to work, and it's all going to end in tears," I reasoned. "Besides, how do you know that he's going to want to leave his bit on the side for good after you fall pregnant? I did try to dissuade her, honest I did, but the thrill of all this undercover extra marital business got me right excited. It beat doing the housework, that was for sure, and I found myself waking in the middle of the night planning and plotting every twist and turn in this tale of deception.

"He'll come back properly and for good, I'm sure of it," she argued with me. "Look, I've been reading up all these things in the paper about how I can be a great wife and how I can make my man never look at another woman again. You'll see Anna, I just need you to help me. Pleeeease say you'll help me."

What could I do but say yes to her? "Alright Connie my darling, I'll help you." I sighed. "It's obviously not going to be easy and it's a bit unorthodox but I know quite a few single men and I'm sure they'll be queuing up to have a quick fling with you, so long as they never know that they are being used as a baby-maker. You've just got to promise me that this will be kept between you and me - and the chosen candidate must never know, okay? Promise me?"

Well, I'd got completely the wrong end of the stick, because as soon as I uttered those words Connie went ghostly white. Actually, she looked like she was a ghost, poor thing.

I was confused to begin with, until she regained her composure and went on to explain. "No Anna, I couldn't go to bed with another man, now that I'm married to Stanley. Just because he's being unfaithful to me, it's probably my fault anyway because I'm not looking after him properly like a wife should. No, I don't want to be with anyone else."

"Well, my darling," I began. "I think I'd better tell you all about the birds and the bees. As far as I know it was only Mother Mary that had an immaculate conception, and if I'm not mistaken, my darling, you're not her. Let's finish off this bubbly and forget about the whole thing, eh?" I was pleased with my little joke and expected to see her laugh, but the expression on her face couldn't have been more serious if she'd tried. This was clearly no laughing matter for her.

"I'm well aware that I'm not Mother Mary, Anna. But I am a mother and I want to become a mother again. You know, there are other ways of becoming pregnant, don't you, other than the normal sex way? I've been reading about it in the paper. There was an article only the other day about sperm banks where you can get what you need from the bank and insert it 'down there' all by yourself. She mouthed the words 'down there' and pointed. "I just want someone to go to the bank for me." By now I thought she must have been joking, but then I realised she clearly wasn't going to let this go.

"Jesus H, Connie. Have you gone stark staring bonkers or something? You can't go down the local Barclays and ask over the counter for the means to have a bloody baby, you know." I don't know whether it was the Cava that was getting me hot and bothered or simply the bizarreness of the way this conversation was going.

"Anna, believe me, I'm being serious," she retorted. "You've got a computer, haven't you? I've read up all about it. You can connect up to the internet and you type things on it and you can find all sorts of things on the world wide web, you know. Look, wait here and I'll show you." She got up quickly and staggered over to a pile of newspapers stacked up neatly on the worktop in her utility room. She must have been feeling very tipsy by now, I knew I was, but she managed to find what she was looking for, bring it back and open the paper at the relevant page.

LESBIAN COUPLE HAVE LOVE CHILD WITHOUT A MAN was the headline she put in front of me.

"You may dress and look like a man sometimes Connie darling, but you're no lesbo," I said, or rather I slurred.

"Read it please Anna," she demanded, rather assertively I thought by her standards, and I began to sober up the more I read and the more I realised she really was serious.

With my glass of Cava in one hand I pulled the paper towards me and began to read with a growing fascination...

A lesbian couple has surprised their family and friends by having a baby - without having a man about the house. Amanda Robinson, 31, and Gwen Keith, 29, both from Watford, Hertfordshire, have been in a lesbian relationship with each other for the past four years and had almost everything they ever wanted. Their high-powered City jobs earn them a combined £200,000. Amanda drives a Porsche while Gwen has a new Mercedes SLK. They are members of an exclusive golf club costing thousands to join, and they frequently holiday in Richard Branson's luxury hotel in Mallorca. But there was one thing missing from their lives - a baby! Being in a lesbian love affair could have been problematic for most, but not for Amanda and Gwen. They found that it can now be possible to conceive a child in a very unconventional way when they discovered a unique London clinic offering 'sperm for sale' to wealthy clients just like them. "We were over the moon when we realised our dreams of becoming parents could come true," said Gwen in our exclusive interview with the couple. Amanda went on to explain: "Although there is nothing new about couples having fertility treatment, for a gay couple like Gwen and me, we didn't want a man near us in a sexual way and that proved to be more difficult, as you can imagine". But thanks to the internet and an 'underground network' of lesbian friends they found the help they were looking for in London. Money wasn't a problem for Amanda and Gwen, and that was lucky because they needed plenty of it. "It cost thousands just to register with the clinic and an additional sum for every sample from them, but it was worth every penny."

I ploughed on reading the article, skipping some stuff about the Church leaders being "up in arms" and where the law stood on test tube babies, gay marriages and something called 'alternative structures' before getting down to the juicy bit about how Gwen and Amanda 'got it together.'

When we put it to Gwen that some people may consider the whole practice abhorrent, she defended her position robustly. "What could be more natural than having a baby? The only part that's different is that we are receiving the man's sperm in a somewhat mechanical way, instead of with the man himself. If we had wished to meet the donor at the agency we could have, but in our case we preferred to receive the sperm from an anonymous donor."

Amanda explained how the couple received their life-making consignment. "We didn't even need to visit the clinic in person, except for our initial consultation. After we had registered with them, all we had to do was to tell them what type of donor we were looking for, in our case Caucasian, and then wait. Gwen and I chose myself to be impregnated and we told the clinic the dates of my cycle. I had an optimum window of opportunity for conception to be successful, so when the time was right the clinic took the donor's sample from the freezer storage facility and couriered it round to us and we did the rest. They even supplied the pipettes. We weren't successful on the first try, and having to wait for the next cycle the following month was very frustrating, not to mention expensive. That said, it was just the same as for any normal heterosexual couple eagerly trying for a baby. After the third attempt it was bingo for us and we hit the jackpot nine months later with the birth of our fabulous little Sebastian. It may be that one day Sebastian will want to discover who his biological father is, and of course we won't prevent him from doing that, but for now Gwen and I are his mum and his dad."

A spokesperson from the London clinic that supplies the sperm samples declined a full interview with this newspaper, except to say "we cannot discuss individual cases for ethical reasons and our clients' confidence and faith in us, but we are delighted to work closely with a leading surrogacy agency successfully playing a small but crucial role in bringing together fathers with mothers in this way."

I looked up from the newspaper and saw Connie eagerly awaiting my reaction. I had been taken aback by what I'd read and it took me a while to gather my thoughts.

"So what exactly do you want me to do, Connie darling? I'm not really sure how I can help, and if you want me to go sticking a basting tube up you, I'm afraid you're asking the wrong girl!"

"No Anna," she replied solemnly, I can do that myself. Look... you see it says you don't even need to meet the man if you don't want to. As long as I carefully select a white man, Stanley will never know that he's not the real father. I've already chosen a name for the baby - Oliver if it's a boy and Anna, after you, if it's a girl. Stanley will be surprised to be sure, but he's bound to be over the moon when he finds out we're having another child; he's so good with the twins. You can tell he loves being a dad. All I want you to do is track down this place in London for me. I haven't got a computer and even if I did, I wouldn't know how to use it. I don't think they're going to be in the telephone book but it must be possible for someone like you to find them - you're so clever. Oh, and I would only want Oliver or Anna to ever be told about this if anything really bad happened to me. You know what I mean? Only if I died. There should always be a way for them finding who their real father is if a record of all this is kept somewhere, but apart from if I died then Mum's the word, okay?"

Christ! She already had names for her third child, and I must say I was flattered that she'd want to name a daughter after me! God, I could tell she was serious now, and Connie always had a way of getting me to do things I wasn't quite sure about. Also, I had to admit I was actually intrigued by this whole sordid affair. I've always fancied myself as a bit of a Sherlock Holmes. And like I said, it was more exciting than doing the washing up. If only I'd picked up on Connie's throw-away comment, I could have helped her in a very different way than her getting pregnant and having Oliver. I wasn't as clever as she thought I was, the poor darling. I wasn't clever at all.

CHAPTER 17

My 'Highly Irregular'
Business Meeting

"Had I imagined it or did she really give me a small peck of a kiss?"

Leslie Markland

Writing this down keeps me occupied, and the other inmates tend to be actually quite friendly, especially as they know I'm writing this book. Some of them even come over to sit with me at meal times and ask me if they can be included in the story. I haven't told anyone that this is actually a true account of the events that led me to being here, so it would be difficult to include any of these likely lads in my story - not unless I invented things about them, weaving them into the tale somehow. Maybe I could try. For example there's old Mark Mantis - a unique individual if ever there was one, always walking around pretending to be on the telephone and talking to God, telling 'The Almighty One' how he wants to pray for his forgiveness. I've caught him, when he thought no one was looking, sitting cross legged on the floor with his hands clasped together, whispering a load of tosh. You'll know by now how I like to make up names: Harry the dog after

Harry Nilsson, Alfonso the Fiat, Barnacle Barge, and now I've dubbed my fellow inmate Mark as 'The Praying Mantis'. He wasn't the sort you'd want to quiz about why he'd ended up in prison, but he'd tell anyone who'd listen "I used to be in banking". But the word inside was that he'd been a carpet and flooring fitter, managing to secure a contract fitting out several NatWest banks, until one day he actually robbed one!

Anyway, enough about the Praying Mantis. I need to return to the crucial part of my story and an important letter from the Angelpride agency in London, telling me that they had the results back from the clinic's laboratory. They were delighted to inform me that the quality of my sperm was excellent, and that they could now proceed to match the next sample with a potential recipient. The letter went on to request that I please telephone Miss Silvie Tosgiev at the agency to make arrangements for providing that sample.

Well, I was beside myself, I don't mind telling you. My emotions were all shaken up: Excitement about the prospect of meeting Silvie again - and anxiety about my moral ethics. I recalled the mini lecture given to me by Miss Pinchbeck when I last went to Mayfair, and I also remembered vividly the encounter I had with Silvie. How could I forget? It never occurred to me during that humiliating day that I'd be keen to go back for more of the same. But Miss Tosgiev had clearly brought out some inner feelings that had lain dormant up to now.

Standing on the quayside next to my US Mail box, letter in my hand, I was oblivious to anything and everyone nearby. I hadn't noticed Andy Stollery coming up to my side.

"A penny for your thoughts, Leslie. How are we this bright and sunny morning?" he enquired cheerfully. Andy would engage anyone he met on the quay in conversation. He was just that sort of man and was one of the most popular folks around the village.

I decided to divert the conversation away from anything to do with the envelope and letter I was clutching in my hand.

"Andy, there's something I've been meaning to ask you. Your boat that's tied up behind my barge there," I said, pointing to his old wooden fishing boat, attached with one line to the jetty and another to the barge. "It doesn't ever go anywhere, and I've been wondering if you've ever thought of selling her. I've always fancied having a boat that I could actually take out on the river, so I wouldn't mind making you an offer for it."

It had certainly seen better days and was in need of some attention but I'd often watched enviously as other boats travelled past my permanently moored old barge with its seized engine.

"I'll give it a ponder Leslie," Andy replied, rubbing his chin. "It hadn't crossed my mind to sell her, but I suppose it does seem a shame that she doesn't get used as much as she ought. We can have a chat in The Station on Sunday if you like. But now I'd best be getting on. You have a good day, okay?"

Bidding goodbye to Andy, my thoughts immediately returned to the Angelpride letter. It was at times like those that I wished I possessed a mobile telephone so that I could respond immediately to Silvie's correspondence. No matter. I would go up the High Street as soon as I was ready and use the kiosk there. Thirty minutes later I was holding the receiver in one hand, with a number of coins in the other, ready to feed the slot.

I was surprised at how quickly the telephone was answered. Silvie's unmistakable Swedish accent seemed even more pronounced than when I'd met her in person.

"It's Leslie Markland here and I've just received your letter," I began hesitantly, until she cut in and relaxed me by her response. How did she manage to do that so easily, I wondered?

"Ah, Leslie, I'm so glad you called, I've been looking forward to hearing from you and making further arrangements."

Oh my goodness... I couldn't distinguish the difference between my eager anticipation and my nervousness about the next stage of this potentially life-changing journey I'd embarked upon.

"Er, hello Silvie," I replied awkwardly. And then, without quite knowing what I was saying I continued with a question: "Silvie, I've been wondering whether it's necessary for me to actually come all the way to London to bring my, er, you know. Maybe *you* could visit *me* and collect it, you know, in person? You could get the train, and obviously I'd be more than happy to pay the fare."

Had I really just said that? I didn't know where my courage had suddenly come from. The fact was, I had originally dreaded having to repeat that humiliating experience at Angelpride, but now here I was instigating a repeat performance at my place in Wivenhoe! I didn't know what on earth had come over me.

Before any embarrassing silence could develop, Silvie responded. "That is highly irregular, Mr. Markland," she said, this time with a very serious and stern tone.

Damn! Realising I'd overstepped the mark I hesitated, not knowing how to apologise until she continued, this time in a softer voice.

"Yes, highly irregular, Leslie," she repeated. "But it would be kind of interesting to combine my official work with a day out from London. Although I love it here in Mayfair, I can say it would be nice to make a, how do you say, change of scenery for a day. I will have to check with Miss Pinchbeck of course, but yes Leslie, that could be a nice idea. I cannot leave the agency during the week, but I could come on a weekend. Shall we say Sunday?"

Goodness me! Before I had time to think too deeply, we'd finished the conversation with provisional arrangements about where and at what time to meet, subject to permission being granted by Silvie's boss, and I slowly put the telephone back on its cradle. Pushing the door to the kiosk open, I stepped out into the sunshine in a daze. That had surely been a dream, hadn't it? And yet I looked down at the notes I had written and the proof was there in front of me. Sunday: 1pm, Wivenhoe station. I had also scribbled down the words 'official work', and I reminded myself that this was merely that for Silvie. Wasn't it? Sunday was only four days away, and all I could think about was Silvie coming here for our next 'business' meeting. I was petrified. I went back to the barge and made myself a cup of tea.

Sunday came. Needing some Dutch courage, (or should that be Swedish courage?), I called in at The Station pub opposite the rail station at midday as soon as the doors were unlocked. After the telephone conversation with Silvie, the rest of the week passed without a letter either confirming or cancelling our 'business meeting'. So I could only assume, and hope, that Miss Pinchbeck had given her blessing to the unusual work arrangement Silvie had proposed to her. I sat at the L shaped bar and ordered a Guinness. Andy Stollery walked in, beaming as usual. In all my excitement I'd clean forgotten I was due to meet him to discuss his boat. At least a nautical chat with him would preoccupy my thoughts for an hour. I welcomed his company, especially as it concluded with an agreement for him to sell me his lovely old boat for a reasonable price, so long as I promised to look after it and bring it up to scratch in the same way as I had restored Lynne's barge.

Shaking hands with Andy, I looked down at my Omega watch - I do like nice things, I thought to myself - and then my nerves came rushing back. There were only ten minutes until the 11.32 from Liverpool Street would be arriving on Platform Two. Would Silvie be on it? I hoped she would be, but I equally hoped she wouldn't.

The Black Buoy was another fine Wivenhoe hostelry, serving the best pub grub for miles around. It also had the advantage of being very close to my home, and I'd already decided that this was where we should first go for some refreshment and to give her a good impression of my village – assuming of course that she was on that train.

Well, she did arrive at Platform 2 and I suppose at this point I ought to recount how good Silvie was at her job, if I can bring myself to actually write about something so private. Before conducting our 'official work', 'business meeting', or whatever we agreed to called it, we went for a spot of lunch at the Black Buoy before going to my barge where earlier in the morning I had been frantically tidying up. I'd even bought some fresh flowers, made the bed and opened all the windows to let out Harry's doggy smell.

The atmosphere between Silvie and me was warm enough, helped by the fact that the food in the pub was served quickly, so there were no awkward silences. Also, there were plenty of people I knew who stopped at our table to say hello to us, probably out of curiosity. After all, I'd never been seen in the company of a woman in all the years I'd lived in Wivenhoe, not least one as attractive as Silvie, so I guess everyone was curious to know more. I must admit I was quite proud to show her off, and took pleasure in introducing her simply as 'Silvie, my friend from London'. Less is more, I decided, and thankfully out of politeness no one asked me to elaborate, but I could sense their tongues wagging immediately after they moved on up to the bar. "You certainly seem to know a lot of people here, Leslie", she remarked. And I suppose she was right, I'd just never really given it much thought.

We finished our food, left the Black Buoy and meandered down the lane to the barge that was currently sitting on its mud berth, with the tide out. Silvie appeared genuinely intrigued by my unusual home, but I was naturally nervous of what was expected to follow. I needn't have been, as no sooner had we walked across the plank she took complete control of the whole situation - but not before she went all gooey at the sight of little Harry. I'd say he won her affection the moment he first tilted his little head at her. If I hadn't know better I'd have sworn he was playing extra cute for my benefit, as if he knew what was about to happen.

Maybe it was because we were now on my territory that I felt so much more relaxed than when I was at the Angelpride agency. There were no X-rated videos or magazines here, only the sound of the incoming tide lapping up against the steel hull of the barge. "Do you have any music we can put on?" asked Silvie. Of course I did, and pointed to the shelves containing all my CDs. She glanced quickly at the spines and pulled one out and handed it to me. "This one should do," she said, and seconds later one of Chopin's Etudes was playing on my stereo system. She appeared to go into a trance as she moved and cavorted her slim body in time with the music, provocatively swaying her hips and arms, only inches from me. "Don't forget, Leslie, no touching," she said. "Except if we dance. There are no rules about dancing."

She outstretched one hand, inviting me to stand next to her, which I did. With the other hand she softly caressed the material of my trousers, gently touching my bottom, pulling me closer to her so that our legs became intertwined. Goodness me, I'd never heard Opus 10 in F Minor that way before. Her hand moved from my posterior around to the front of me and she teasingly brushed against my rapidly growing bulge.

And then she suddenly backed away from me, leaving me vulnerably exposed. I wanted her to return to hold me. But instead she continued to dance around in front of me, erotically unbuttoning her blouse and exposing the fact she wasn't wearing anything beneath it. Her eyes fixed on me and as she did so she expertly pouted her lips and ran her fingers over her breasts. Her nipples mesmerised me. They were simply perfect, pert and forward pointing. Now, nothing else mattered to me as I moved towards her with an overwhelming urge to touch them. She moved back slowly shaking her forefinger at me.

"No Leslie, you can look but not touch," she reminded me. "But I can tell you are liking what you are seeing," she smiled. "I think you are nearly ready, aren't you? Just a little longer."

And with that she continued her solo dance, this time moving one hand down to the hem of her skirt as the other continued playing with her breasts. She teased me more by gradually lifting the skirt and twisting her body away from me, bending over at the same time so that the smooth round skin of her behind was in full view. Just then a wave lashed against the barge making it gently sway from side to side as a motor cruiser chugged its way up the river causing a large wake. Until then I hadn't noticed we were now at high tide and were floating, and why would I? – I had far more interesting things to think about right in front of me.

Silvie clearly knew exactly what she was doing. She reached into her handbag that was hung on the back of my red chair and handed me a container. "I think you're about ready now. You know what to do, don't you?" she asked. I did know, and I took the container with me to the small washroom. This time I wanted to be private and free from any embarrassing humiliation. But I do believe I noticed an expression of disappointment on Silvie's face as I closed the door behind me.

Her visit was certainly fruitful. Having arrived empty handed, she returned to London a few short hours later carrying a very important consignment that she had so expertly helped me to produce. When it was time for her to leave I hoped that this wouldn't be the last time I'd be enjoying her company; I liked her, and I don't just mean her physical attributes, as pleasing on the eye as they undeniably were.

Perhaps she might show me some little sign that there was more to her business trip here than merely sample collecting. Sure enough she did. At the platform while I was waiting to say goodbye to her, she stood on tip-toes, leant towards me and whispered some words softly in my ear: "I enjoyed being with you very much Leslie. Let's do that again. Next time it will not be for work." And then she was gone in a flash as she jumped into the train carriage that now had one of its doors open in front of us.

Had I imagined it or did she really give me a small peck of a kiss? Perhaps it was merely an accidental touching of her smooth lips against my cheek, but nevertheless I wouldn't forget her words in a hurry. I walked dreamily back to the barge where Harry greeted me with his usual wild enthusiasm, indicating that he really needed me to take him out for a little business trip of his own.

Meanwhile, Silvie was speeding back to London with a polystyrene insulated box containing a small plastic jar and a very precious substance of mine inside it. I had no idea where it would eventually end up.

CHAPTER 18

Perfect Day

"Things felt so right between us"

Part One: Silvie Tosgiev (1997)

I am very happy to say that a few months after my first visit to Wivenhoe, Leslie and I did indeed have another shared encounter. And this time it was all pleasure and no 'business'. Leslie certainly had a quality and handsomeness about him like no man I had ever met, with his attractive beard, and fair, ruffled hair and rather wonderful physique. But more than his physical looks I loved his calm nature, even though I did recognise that it masked some sadness. He told me that he felt some of his pain beginning to recede, thanks to me. Too deep for me to understand what he meant, but what I did know was that I was liking him more and more. Having made love that night - properly this time - on his boat, things felt so right between us.

While we were lying in bed together in the morning, I'm afraid I rather let my professional guard down. Although stopping short of disclosing where Angelpride had dispatched his sperm sample to, I did inform him how the agency had received four enquiries already that month for a Caucasian sperm donation. Two from London, one from Wales and another from somewhere up in the north of England, Yorkshire to be precise. Leslie laughed when I told him that. "Of all the places in the world!" he said. He went on to tell me that Yorkshire was originally where he was from. He said that his father had died late 1995 and that while he was up there for the funeral, he could have just driven round and dropped his pot through the letterbox and saved himself a fortune! I was shocked, and I told him that of course that would not have been possible because he would have had no idea who the recipient was or where they lived. He just smiled at me and I then understood that this was an example of the renowned British sense of humour that I was still getting used to.

Naturally enough, he wanted to know where his sample had been sent, but I regained my composure and only said that a woman wanted to bring up a baby with her same-sex partner, that her first name was Anna, and that was all I could tell him. I explained if the matching were to prove successful, and this woman did eventually have a baby as a result of his sperm, he could officially apply in writing to the agency for the mother's details a year after the birth. That was what Anna had ticked on her form, and I told him that we all had a moral duty to abide by her wishes. He said it all seemed so cold and matter-of-fact, but I told him that was the way things had to be done, and I reminded him that Miss Pinchbeck had gone over all that during his initial consultation at her office last year. At that, he sighed, laid back and pulled me on top of him yet again. I didn't mind him taking command of me in bed, and I told him so.

Part Two: Leslie Markland

"I wondered whether I may have been falling in love"

I'd actually made love to a woman, a beautiful understanding woman! Our third liason was as Silvie had promised, not a meeting at all, and certainly not involving any business or work. After she had gone, I reflected on our fantastic weekend together. I sat in my special chair inside Barnacle Barge with my devoted furry friend curled up in his basket, where he'd chosen to stay the whole time Silvie and I had been making love. The rear doors were open so that I could look out at the fishing boat I'd recently acquired from Andy, and as the sun was lowering itself in the sky, with its rays glistening upon the muddy water of the river, I replayed in my head over and over the special words that Silvie had said to me: "I love the way you make love to me, Leslie." In my wildest dreams I could never have imagined anyone ever saying that to me.

I got up and walked over to the shelves where I kept all my Nilsson CDs. I'd become obsessed by the music of Harry Nilsson. You may have heard of him, and I did say previously that my mother used to play one of his LPs, Nilsson Schmilsson, over and over. That triggered something in me, making me search for his entire past catalogue of recordings way back to the late sixties. I became so consumed by my interest in him that I even grew a beard just like he'd done. I would scour every record and tape shop in Leeds for anything Nilsson related, and I'd eventually collected his entire set of albums, all on cassette tape, popping them into my trusty tiny Philips transistor player. Now, I'd upgraded them all to CD and the sound was so much clearer.

Actually, if it hadn't been for Harry Nilsson, I might never have met and become friends with Silvie in the first place. In a wonderful twist of fate I'd discovered that the Angelpride agency was close to Curzon Place in London's Mayfair, the address where my hero had lived and worked. Not only did Cass Elliot of the Mamas and The Papas die in his apartment, but it was also where Keith Moon of The Who breathed his last breath. As a music fan, I'd always wanted to visit the place and I did, in a bit of a daze admittedly, after my consultation at Miss Pinchbeck's that day. That may well have been the catalyst for me braving the consultation at all. So, thanks Harry!

My eye moved along the CD spines that were proudly displayed in chronological order. I pulled out the last one on the right and put the silver disc into my new stereo system. I played 'Perfect Day' with its beautifully haunting choral arrangement, and sat back. It hadn't only been a perfect day, I can tell you. It had been a perfect night, and a perfect morning as well. Silvie had actually slept in my bed with me! As Silvie and I were lying intertwined earlier that morning I wondered whether I may have been falling in love with her. Later, after she'd gone home to London and I was on my own again, I was sure of it.

CHAPTER 19

The Family Way

"I always knew I had brains"

Part One: Constance Markland (1997)

Anna was such a sweetheart to help me in the way she had, without question. On my behalf, she spent an awful lot of time on her computer at home. How she managed to do it I don't know, but she said she had to contact the newspaper and ask them about that article I'd shown her. She had the patience of a saint, that was for sure, calling back time and again. She was like a dog with a bone, not letting go until getting what she wanted. Eventually, after a lot of effort the woman at the paper relented and gave Anna a number to ring, and she got through to a place called Angelpride, somewhere in central London. I'd never been to London before and it scared me to think I might have to travel down there all that way on my own to collect sperm samples. Also, what would I tell Stanley? It wasn't like I could say

I was going down to do some shopping, even though I suppose I would be in a way. By that time though I had really set my heart on having another baby, and I was determined to see this through. Anna found out that I could register my name and address and have all the relevant documents sent by post, and even the actual samples of sperm could be sent in an insulated box by next-day special delivery. That way I could get them to coincide with the best time of my monthly cycle, without the worry or hassle of having to travel to London.

All I had to do was pay the money to the agency, confirm the date of my next period and they would do the rest. Angelpride did warn me that I shouldn't expect to get pregnant on the first attempt and that it might actually take several tries. It all depended on the strength of the donor's specimen, my own fertility and of course God's will. There was no guarantee that it would ever work and it could all be a complete waste of effort, time and money. But to me it was all worth trying. I had the money saved up, thanks to my auntie, and I just needed to get Stanley excited, so that he believed he'd done the deed under his own steam, so to speak. He enjoyed his drink, so I figured if I got all glammed up for him, did my hair and makeup like David Bowie singing 'The Jean Genie', made him a nice dinner with all the trimmings and lots of wine, then trapped him so he couldn't go out that night, he'd be none the wiser. He still thought I was oblivious to his affair. Sadly he must have thought me really dim.

My carefully arranged plan would unfold in the bedroom, where I'd give him some extra special treatment with the toy that he liked me using on him, or rather in him I should say. I'd get him so drunk and excited that he wouldn't be able to remember what had or hadn't taken place. Then, when he'd fallen asleep, I'd go into the bathroom and do my own private business with the pipette. I'd have the small pot of the anonymous man's sperm ready and waiting in our bathroom cabinet. I'd even concocted a story to explain that little pot if Stanley found it by mistake. It was my new anti-wrinkle cream with a special pipette applicator, was what I'd tell him, not that I could imagine him asking. In that respect I'd say he was a typical man, not having a clue about how much effort us girls go through to keep our men happy. Obviously in my case it wasn't working terribly well, otherwise I wouldn't have to be going to all this trouble to hold on to him. Well, we would see about that, wouldn't we?

That was my plan, and Anna and I had a right giggle when we talked about it over coffee one morning after the twins had gone to pre-school and her Jake was at playgroup.

"You're bloody loopy, you are Connie," she told me. "I never knew you could be so conniving, but I love you all the same. Although what's your Stan going to say when he sees all these letters and packages suddenly coming through the letterbox with your name on? You hadn't thought of that had you?"

Well actually I had, but I let her continue.

"Won't he get a bit suspicious?" she pointed out. "The only post you normally get are those readers' offers you send away for from the newspaper. I don't think you'll be able to get these agency people down in London to send the bloody jizz in a packet with bloody 'Daily Mail' stamped on it!"

We were in hysterics at that and giggled away the rest of the morning, but the more I thought about it the more I realised Anna was right. I couldn't risk Stanley asking awkward questions if he saw the postman suddenly delivering unusual items to me.

At our next coffee morning together I plucked up the courage to ask Anna to go even further to help me. Further than I had the right to ask really.

"Anna, you know what you said about the post coming here and Stanley maybe seeing it and asking questions like?" She stopped me mid-sentence.

"I know what you're going to ask me," she cut in, and then proceeded to stand up and put on a deep voice like that bloke on the telly. "And who are you going to be for us today, Constance Markland?" Then in a mock high voice she continued, "Well tonight Matthew, I'm going to be Anna Hennings" and sauntered around the kitchen pretending to be her, pretending to be me. I laughed, but was very relieved that she instinctively knew what I needed her to do for me without me actually asking her directly. I had to say she really was taking the whole project in great spirit.

"Don't fret pet." Anna loved saying that whenever things got sticky. All excited, she continued, "I'll apply to this Angelpride lot under my own name, and I can send them one of my own gas bills and a phone bill to give them the proof of address that they want - they're in my name here - and hey presto, before you know it Anna Hennings will be having another baby. Except for one small detail - Anna Hennings will really be you. Besides, they won't check too carefully so long as they get the money. But that's *all* I'll be doing, okay? Don't go asking me to wait in the bathroom ready with the plunger. I love you Connie, but not quite that much!" We laughed even louder at that.

It's not terribly often in my life that things have gone completely according to plan. There's usually been some kind of hiccup along the ways, but I'm proud to say that on this occasion - my life-changing big one - and with the help from Anna that made it all possible, my scheme worked brilliantly. I always knew I had brains. After only the first attempt, having received the parcel brought round by Anna at my body's most fertile time, I became pregnant for the second time in my life. Stanley didn't know what had hit him, neither in the mock 'production meeting' as I called it under my breath, nor when I announced the wonderful news to him a few weeks later that he was going to be a father again.

He did look a bit shocked, bless him, but I felt sure my announcement would completely bring him back to me. As soon as he saw sense and left his bit on the side, we'd go on to live happily ever after. Family life would indeed be getting even better for us. After the news of my pregnancy had sunk in, Stanley said he'd decided we should move to the Manor house on the estate where his father and mother used to live. He said he couldn't see the point in leaving it empty any longer, not now that his father was no longer alive and his mother was settled in the USA and hardly likely to ever be coming back. What a wonderful house for the twins and our new baby to be brought up in! Perhaps we wouldn't now all be quite so much on top of each other. The girls could create quite an oppressive atmosphere at times, and I was so looking forward to us all having the extra space. Perhaps that would encourage the girls to behave better towards me. I certainly hoped so.

I didn't know who my donor was, but I liked to imagine he must have been some stud, particularly as I fell pregnant so easily after that first attempt. I silently thanked whoever he was from the bottom of my heart. I thanked Anna even more so. I couldn't have done any of it without her.

Part Two: Stanley Markland

"I just didn't remember how I got her pregnant"

"Jesus Christ, Stanley, how in God's name did that happen?" were the words that greeted me when I broke the news to Tristan that Constance was expecting. It had come as just as much of a shock when she'd told me, I don't mind saying.

"I had been dreading telling you, Tristan, but I had to let you know. I'm so sorry, I can't quite remember too well how it happened myself - but I do need to still have marital relations with Constance once in a while so that she doesn't suspect anything. As far as she's concerned I'm so busy with work and she thinks that's the reason I'm sometimes not at home. Much better that we enjoy each other's company without any suspicion from her don't you think?"

Tristan's eyes said it all. I knew he could be a fiery old so and so sometimes, so it was no surprise that he flew off the handle at me. There was anger and annoyance, but more than that I saw disappointment and jealousy, and that hurt me so much. I had never wanted to cause him pain, and I was so scared that he wouldn't want to be with me anymore.

At long last I had found happiness, true happiness, with another human being, and I didn't want to lose that.

His career, as secretary to David Southall the MP, meant a lot to him and I knew he had aspirations to become an MP himself one day. He did love his job and was very protective of his position, and I'm sure that was why he sometimes had a short fuse if he felt threatened in any way. Protecting his corner was one of his most endearing qualities. But I didn't like being at the receiving end of his temper when it was directed at me. All I could think of saying was "I'm sorry", and reassure him with a cuddle. That was a mistake. "Please, Stanley. Do take your arms off me, you are stifling me," he said coldly. "I don't know how you can still be with her in *that* way! I find it disgusting. It's appalling that you could want to still do things like that with that woman as well as me."

I decided not to argue with him for fear of upsetting the situation further, and I also didn't like him referring to Constance as 'that woman'. After all, she was still my wife and the mother of my little darling twin girls, and even though I had found true love with Tristan, I still had feelings and respect for her. I just didn't remember how I got her pregnant, and so I was just as surprised when I learned that I was to become a dad again. I must have been so drunk, but at least Father would have been proud of me. I took my arms away from Tristan and sat in the chair he had next to the fireplace. I didn't say anything but instead stared into space waiting for him to calm down.

"Well, what are we going to do, Stanley?" he asked after his temper had receeeded. He always called me by my full name when he was worked up about anything. Feeling insecure, I sat there like a naughty schoolboy being told off. Then my hand felt something sharp down the side of the cushion, and I hoped my discovery could diffuse the tense situation before it escalated.

"Look Tristan, you really ought to take more care where you leave these lying around." I held a jagged fingernail clipping in the air for his inspection.

He tried not to laugh, but eventually gave in and as I stood up to embrace him he whispered in my ear. "You know I'm only upset because I love you so much, don't you?"

With tensions relaxed we sat and chatted about what the future had in store for us. There was one real advantage for Tristan that came out of my revelation. At least Constance and me having another child together would help throw the outside world off any scent of our homosexual affair, which could have been somewhat damaging to his career if found out.

Of course the arrival of a new family member could have had an effect on how the income and property from the estate would be divided up. But there was enough money coming in from the rents and farmland for that not to be of any concern for many a year, if indeed forever. Whether the estate was to be inherited by Sophie and Hilary, or Sophie, Hilary and one other sibling: that would be of little consequence, as there would still be plenty to go round between the three of them. Besides, it wouldn't be until the girls reached 21, or three years younger if a boy were born, that it would make any real difference anyway. Until that time I could continue benefitting from the income that the land and the estate created.

However, Tristan, being much more clued up about these things than me, understood all there was to know about my late father's estate and how his will had been set up.

"You realise, don't you," he began "that as the twins are not even two years old yet, if you and your wife were to have a son, then he would receive his share of the estate before the girls would. That might be a little unfair, wouldn't you think?"

I suppose he had a point, but the twins were so young that I couldn't imagine any problems. "Come on Tristan, they're only toddlers. They're too young to know the first thing about money and the estate and their inheritance. Besides, I'm sure they're going to love having someone else to play with at home."

Tristan tapped the side of his nose like a wise old man. "I saw how those girls were at their naming ceremony, and I can assure you they know a lot more than you think they do," he said, only partly joking. "Haven't you seen how they act together? The farm and the properties on the Markland Estate are worth a tidy sum already, and in the future an absolute fortune will be at stake. They're not going to take too kindly to sharing anything with anyone else, and they're going to be a formidable handful the older they get, you mark my words."

Part Three: Tristan Thomas
"I had no choice but to make allowances for his behaviour"

That was a complete bolt out of the blue when Stanley dropped the little bombshell about his wife expecting another child with him. And there I was, previously thinking that he was mine and mine alone. How selfish of me to forget that he occasionally still had to perform his marital duty. He was right, of course. His wife could have become suspicious if he were to entirely cease having sexual intercourse with her, but if I'm honest it did rather turn my stomach to think that he could be with me one night and her the next. It may have been true that his times with her were very infrequent, according to him, but still! I wasn't best pleased with the situation, as well you can imagine.

At the beginning of our affair just over three years previously, Stanley had promised me that he would stop going 'all the way' with his wife, so he clearly must have broken that promise on at least one occasion, what with a new addition to the family arriving in eight months or so – April next year to be precise. I'm sorry that I struggle to refer to his wife by name, but I suppose jealousy has always been one of my weaknesses.

While I preferred not to visualise him keeping things 'up' in *their* bedroom as well as at mine, disgusting though it was to me, I had no choice but to make allowances for his actions, and under the circumstances I decided to just throw myself into my work. If he and I really did have a strong bond with each other, and I believed we did, I was sure that this temporary blip would just be that - temporary. True love would prevail.

I really was such a romantic old chap, wasn't I? If I wanted to continue being with the man I loved, then I had no choice but to accept the status quo and simply accept the situation as best as I could.

As it was, my career in politics was certainly occupying a great deal of my time anyway, and David Southall was relying on me more and more to take the reins at his office, now that he was moving in ever-higher circles. Following his re-election as an MP, and with a greater majority than even he had expected, he was invited to join the Cabinet, which of course he accepted with relish. This meant that I was scurrying back and forth with him from Yorkshire to the Houses of Parliament, and as a consequence my whole life was changing rapidly.

Never unfaithful to my dear Stanley, I did nevertheless encounter many temptations that needed resisting with diligence. I had never realised that there was so much homosexual activity going on in and around Westminster. There were clubs for this, committees for that, and a lot else in between. Being also involved with the arts, I was often invited to join cross-party groups where I met many interesting people. I couldn't believe how many of the men were gay, hiding behind the veils of 'normal' marriages. Marriages of convenience were how I'd far better describe them.

I joined a body down in London dealing with the promotion of the arts through funding by local councils. Who received what was discussed, decided upon, and grants distributed by this committee. And, there were many weird and whacky applications coming across my desk, I can tell you. I was definitely going up in the world of politics, as by then I actually had my very own desk, with my name on it too. Granted, it was a desk placed in a cubbyhole at the foot of a staircase, but being positioned in such a place so close to the Commons, I soon got to meet a number of friendly characters from the gay community. I would often enjoy a social drink or two with them before accompanying David back to our constituency headquarters in Leeds.

I soon discovered that one of the benefits of becoming part of the political establishment was that I could enjoy first-class train travel paid by someone other than myself. Another benefit was that I could join up to three London clubs where the membership fees - and those fees could cost a pretty penny – drinks included, were all on my expense account, which was settled once a month. All I needed to do was confirm that I was present 'on official business' related to Her Majesty's Government, write out a chitty and get it approved by the lady upstairs. And that was that. I never did find out that lady's name, and I wish I had. She was certainly very helpful in the way she occasionally turned a blind eye before bringing her rubber stamp down with a thud three times over my triplicated expenses book.

Recalling what my old dad had said about politicians being on the take, here I was taking full advantage of the system myself. One could really go to town if one wanted to, but luckily my morals were at least high enough not to go too far down that path. I never overstepped the mark with what I claimed for. The odd luncheon at Groucho's in Soho was a little pricey I admit, but I always kept within the hundred pound threshold so as not to raise any eyebrows, particularly those of the lady upstairs with the rubber stamp!

One club, known as Abacco's - although there was no sign of its name anywhere - was introduced to me by a wonderful Member of Parliament fairly high up in the Labour Party. Discretion on my part would prevent me from naming him, so for the purposes of my account, I will simply refer to him as Mr. B. Very ambitious, very astute and actually very likeable, Mr. B. taught me that in politics, as well as life in general, it was often the case of not what but who you knew that could make all the difference. He advised me to continue frequenting Abacco's. "You will always find someone in that place who can help you with anything. And if they can't, they will know someone who can."

Those were wise words that I never forgot. One day, several years later, when my own career as an MP was in full swing, I would come to want something that I thought would be impossible to arrange.

It was then that I discovered how this little cavernous cluster of four basement rooms that could only be reached from the unlikeliest of East London streets certainly provided me with the contacts I was looking for. An acquaintance with a fellow I only knew as 'Grasshopper', on account of him looking ever so slightly like David Carradine in the old *Kung Fu* TV shows, was what very nearly led to my downfall and political obliteration.

CHAPTER 20

Handover

"I needed something stronger than Ovaltine on this occasion"

Part One: Roger Ainsworth (1998)

I wasn't normally late into the office. The reason was nothing too serious, and in fact it was becoming quite regular for me to need to see the doctor about some ailment or other back then. There wasn't anything majorly wrong with me and Doctor Mahood assured me that everything was functioning just as it should. Blood pressure was fine; cholesterol could be slightly lower but nothing to be alarmed about. "Just eat some more vegetables and fewer steaks," were the doctor's words of advice. Sometimes I thought he must consider me to be something of a hypochondriac as this was the third time I'd paid a visit to his practice in as many weeks. No, there was nothing seriously wrong with me, just various aches and pains that I suppose come with getting old. After all I was approaching 65, an age when most folk were slowing down or retiring.

Walking into our solicitor's reception area I said good morning to

Hatty as I went through to my office. Hatty had been with us for many years now and was one of a kind, as I'm sure I mentioned before. Despite putting her through law school for some conveyancing examinations, which incidentally she'd passed with first-class grades many years ago, she was content to keep her position in the firm as our receptionist. Possibly the highest paid legal secretary in the country, she was much more than merely a receptionist. She ran the whole place like clockwork and did the same workload as two or even three employees. And I'll let you into a little secret: she not only ran the office with ultra-efficiency, she also ran me likewise and we'd become a couple. I always did have a soft spot for her and, thankfully, she eventually reacted positively to my less than subtle advances after a suitably sensitive period of time following my wife's passing.

"Did everything go alright at the surgery, Mr. Ainsworth?" she asked, genuinely concerned for my wellbeing, but always keeping our working relationship on a professional footing. I told her it was just me being silly about my aching hip and leg and arm and that it was nothing that couldn't be cured with a total body transplant. Hatty could always be relied upon to laugh at my jokes. After all these years, she would still call me 'Mr. Ainsworth' when in the public reception area, and 'Roger' only when within the privacy of my office.

My physical aches and pains weren't helped by the ricochet effect from pulling the rifle trigger on the old clay pigeon shoots that I used to love attending, but sadly have now given up. I just wasn't able to hit anything anymore and it was time to pack it in and rest up. Not only had I locked away the old Beretta rifle, more importantly I'd now decided to hand over the reins of the firm to Brian.

My son had certainly worked hard at the firm, and was brilliant at pulling in new business. We were by far and away the largest firm in Leeds now, possibly even in the whole of West Yorkshire, and it was thanks mostly to Brian. To be frank, I don't quite know how he did it, but I suppose it must have in part been down to all those boring dinners he seemed to relish attending. Whenever there was some association function or other, he would be happy to go along, mixing with the delegates, drumming up new clients. I'm afraid I couldn't bring myself to be bothered with all that, which is why the firm would probably have remained as it was until he came into it. If he was happy to attend the gala evenings of the Galvanised Steel Manufacturer's Association, or the National Conference for Pig Husbandry and Handling, to name but two, then he was very welcome to them. The only dinner I wanted to attend was one sat in front of a television, watching the shouting matches on *Coronation Street*. Although I could see he wasn't quite as diligent as I would have liked, I decided it was high time for me to gradually retire and make Brian the senior partner of Ainsworth and Company, the firm that I renamed after my partner Philip Stephens left for pastures new - to become a barrister in Dublin of all places. The time came for me to stop looking over Brian's shoulders and let him continue to run the firm as he saw fit. My body ached and I was tired. I wanted to rest and enjoy the remaining years of my life living comfortably.

There! A momentous decision had been made, and I hadn't even had my Ovaltine yet. When Hatty did come in with my hot drink and copy of *The Times*, I was already feeling better. I felt an air of excitement and anticipation come over me. I could begin a new chapter in my life, take a holiday: maybe a cruise across to New York. I had always wanted to do that, but never had the time: Or, Australia perhaps. I could even go on one of those tours that I saw advertised in the Sunday supplements that I always assumed were for people other than myself.

But first, of course, I would need to wrap things up here thoroughly and correctly, finish off all the cases and files I was currently involved with, and generally bring things to a proper conclusion. I would begin today, I decided, but I shouldn't yet tell anyone except Brian. No need to be hasty. I would just gradually delegate new matters over to the other partners and let Brian oversee them, work through the current files until concluded, to the point when they finally reached my 'out' tray. Cross the t's and dot the i's and my work here would be done. I'd give it six months. Nine months tops.

It was time to acknowledge my positive decision, but I pressed the intercom buzzer on the desk phone with a little too much enthusiasm, nearly knocking over the green plastic 'in', 'pending' and 'out' tray next to it. I really ought to get a new one, I thought. There had been a piece missing that made it wobbly for years. Why had I never replaced it, I wondered? It was because I had become stuck in my ways, but now there were going to be some big changes around here, and I decided to celebrate.

"Dear Ms. Palmerstone," I said with the emphasis on her name title becoming our private joke, "would you bring me another Ovaltine when you have a moment? And bring in the biscuits as well, would you please?" "Yes of course, Mister Ainsworth. Right away *sir*," she flirted. Hatty Palmerstone was very good at making my Ovaltine.

When she returned, she dropped a letter on my desk from the tray of biscuits and Ovaltine she was carrying. It wasn't the kind of letter any solicitor who was planning to slow down to take it easy would want to receive.

My first reaction was to query whether the letter was even genuine. At the top of the letterhead in silver embossed lettering were the words 'ANGELPRIDE - MAKING FAMILY DREAMS COME TRUE' above a PO Box address in London. The letter began in a straightforward fashion addressed to our Leeds office, but then began to get stranger and stranger.

April 26th 1998

Sir or Madam,

We have been asked by our donor client to inform you of his arrangement to make regular maintenance payments of £300 (three hundred pounds) on the 1st of every month, increasing by £10 (ten pounds) per month each year until the child born 7th April 1998 reaches the age of 16 (sixteen) years old, on the 7th April, 2014 (seventh April, two thousand and fourteen).

Name of beneficiary recipient: Surrogate mother Mrs. Anna Hennings, Leeds

Name of donor: Mr. Leslie Markland, Wivenhoe, Colchester

Child gender: Male

At Angelpride we pride ourselves on our discretion and confidentiality and we hope you can appreciate that no further notifications will be forthcoming from ourselves. We cannot enter into any correspondence relating to this matter, but our client has requested you be informed of the above information so that appropriate actions can be instigated by your estates team. Mr. Markland will soon be contacting you under separate cover.

Yours faithfully
Silvie Tosgiev
On behalf of Penelope Elizabeth Pinchbeck (Ms)
Angelpride, London

I read the letter twice, turned it over to see if anything was on the reverse, and laid it flat on the desk. I had never seen anything like it before in all my professional life. Then I read it a third time. Was it some kind of practical joke? I couldn't throw it in the waste paper basket even if I had wanted to, just in case. In case of what, I wondered? A real document about a real situation? I doubted it, but nevertheless all paperwork had to be fastidiously kept – that was my golden rule. And if there was a grain of truth in it I would have to take my hat off to Leslie Markland. I guessed that he must have been very cut up about the contents of old George's will, but I hadn't seen him nor heard from him since the reading of the will. That must have been two or three years ago, and I recalled how I'd felt so very sorry for Leslie that afternoon, as much about his father's treatment of him as the actual inheritance itself, or lack of it, the poor fellow.

I never thought in a million years that Leslie would go and do something like this. Surely it couldn't be true that he'd had a son through some kind of broker? How did that work, I wondered? We were in a different world to the one I grew up in, that was for sure. Not only that, I didn't think he had it in him. What a rascal. This would clearly throw a legal spanner in the works with Stanley, Constance, Hilary and Sophie, and now their latest addition to the family, whose name I was ashamed to say I couldn't remember.

If this letter was true, and Leslie really did have a son of his own, this could and would change everything. The twins and their new baby brother would no longer be the only beneficiaries when they came of age. That wasn't all. Stanley and Constance would have to share the estate income with Leslie from then on. This could turn out to be quite a difficult muddle to sort out. But I was intrigued. I was going to have to hang on to this case-file and see it through before handing it over to Brian. I had a feeling he might not grasp the delicate nature of this letter's potential consequences.

I slumped back and pondered what I needed to do. Firstly I'd pour the Ovaltine into one of the potplants so as not to offend, and then I'd ask Hatty to bring me a cup of coffee. I needed something stronger than Ovaltine on this occasion. I sat there, staring into space until she brought it in.

"Are you alright Roger?" she asked, "You look kind of pale."

"Just a little tired, thank you Hatty. Something's cropped up that I need to have a think about and I may leave early after I've had my coffee. Thank you Hatty, I'll see you in the morning. Have a good evening, won't you?" Hatty hadn't been due to come over for dinner that evening, so our conversation was kept very businesslike.

Slowly sipping my coffee, I thought to myself that if I was honest I didn't really like it. I couldn't for the life of me see why all these new coffee shops that were popping up all over the place could be so popular. Having been so busy recently, what with the Leyland takeover and my visits to the doctors, I hadn't even had the time to personally call in to congratulate Constance and Stanley since their new baby had been born. Now what was its name? It was a boy I think, but I couldn't be sure. I looked around for the card they sent me. I realised at the time I'd first heard their news that it would probably mean more work for me concerning George's will, but since George had passed away I'd not seen the family as much as I ought. And I hadn't been much of a 'responsible adult' to the twins lately. I hadn't even taken the Easter eggs I'd bought for them. In fact, since the twins' christening-naming ceremony, I hadn't seen them hardly at all, and that was well over a year ago now. Where did all that time go? I asked myself. As they were my 'goddaughters', I should have been keeping an eye on them.

Reluctantly I'd agreed to Stanley and Constance when they practically begged me to be the girls' 'responsible adult'. They certainly weren't the most loveable of toddlers but as I'd not set eyes on them for a while, I wondered if they had begun to improve with age.

Just as I was about to give up my search I found the card Constance and Stanley had sent me about their newborn baby. Oliver Markland was the little fellow's name. A pang of guilt came over me as it dawned on me that I hadn't paid much attention to their news. I'd even asked Hatty to send a gift and a congratulations card on my behalf. Blowed if I could remember what the gift was, I buzzed her to remind me. Ah, it was a silver spoon. "Well done Ms. Palmerstone," I thanked her. Trust Hatty to have chosen something appropriate.

I drove the long way to Saxton, through the country lanes instead of the motorway, to the Manor house on the estate, recalling the first time I'd been there all those years ago to see George when he asked me to deal with that Chris Dickinson tenancy problem.

And now, all these years later, here I am again two more generations of Marklands later. It was another reminder to me of my own age and that my decision to retire was the right one. It occurred to me that not only had I been feeling increasingly tired recently, but my memory wasn't nearly as sharp as it once was. Fancy me forgetting the name of their son so soon after his birth.

Stanley wasn't at home when I arrived at the estate. Perhaps I should have phoned ahead. He was out working somewhere, although goodness knows he didn't need the money. Constance seemed ecstatically happy as she proudly showed off baby Oliver to me as he lay sleeping peacefully in his cot. That was until those wretched girls came into the nursery screaming their heads off, both at the same time. They'd been asked nicely by their mother to keep their noise down after baby Oliver had only just got off sleep, but they had the devil in them. My God, their screams almost pierced my eardrums. How Constance was going to cope with them as they grew older was anyone's guess. Spiteful, disobedient and very strong willed, was how I would have described them. And if that letter was true and they faced sharing the Markland fortune with two other siblings, what kind of a can of worms might that create in the years ahead?

Later that evening I laid back with a tumbler of Malt resting on the wicker chair at the side of my bath, thinking about my visit to see the Marklands. I got out of the bath and towelled myself down, put on a robe and wandered into the kitchen. Uh, hum, I'll have one of the ready meals tonight that I've got in the fridge, I decided. Uh, hum, here we are - pasta and meatballs in a rich tomato sauce.

As I waited for the microwave to ping, I put my suit away in the bedroom wardrobe, brushing it down carefully as I did so. Just as I was closing the door I noticed the Markland's card poking out of the jacket pocket. I took it with me into the lounge to put on the mantelpiece next to the clock with the rotating ball weights. As I placed it there, half open, I glanced at the words inside.

"Constance and Stanley Markland are delighted to announce the birth of baby Oliver, weighing 7lb 2oz, born at 6.20 am on 7th April, 1998." That date rang a bell, but I couldn't for the life of me remember why.

I ate my pasta and meatballs in a rich tomato sauce, watched the latest shouting matches on *Coronation Street*, and fell asleep.

"Senior Partner, eh? I couldn't say it wasn't before time"

Part Two: Brian Ainsworth

Somewhat the worse for wear was how I would describe my state that afternoon when Dad popped his head round my door and asked if he could have a word. Whenever he asked to 'have a word' it usually meant he wanted to talk about something using hundreds of words, not one. I'd been noticing recently how tired he'd been looking, but on that occasion he appeared to have a spring in his step about something, and we fixed a time for four o'clock that afternoon, by which time a few strong coffees should have done the trick in perking me up. The previous evening I had been out at the Small Brewers Awards dinner at the Fighting Cocks Brew House down on the Keighly Road, where naturally I was invited to sample just about every different type of beer available to mankind, or at least Yorkshire mankind. There were many jokes floating around about them not being able to organise a piss-up in a brewery, but I can assure you that if last night had been anything to go by, they bloody well could. It was a damn good evening, and I even managed to persuade old Tom Yates at Croftons to come and see us about their little lease problem that would be coming up soon. If we won their account for even just looking after their pub chain that could be worth at least twenty five grand a year, I reckoned. If he'd sobered up in time to come in today I was praying he'd bring that delicious secretary of his along too. I wouldn't mind letting her continue where we left off in the toilets just before the presentations were being announced last night. She was some woman.

At four o'clock I went in to see Dad. We had a mutual respect for each other's timekeeping. That was one thing he'd taught me that I particularly did admire about him.

"Time is, uh hum, money, Son, and being late on someone is no different than stealing money from them," he used to say to me. I may not have always agreed with his fastidious ways in some other aspects of his work but timekeeping was one area in which we were in total agreement. So, if ever a client was even a minute late for an appointment with me at an agreed time, then they would be charged accordingly. And with our fees at £150 an hour, those minutes added up over the months and probably went half way to paying my BMW's petrol bill.

Dad and I didn't always see eye to eye though. I mentioned his fastidiousness. Well, that would drive me mad on occasions. Rules were there to be broken sometimes, weren't they? So long as nobody gets hurt then what's the problem with having a little 'creative thinking'? No one else is one hundred percent squeaky clean, so our firm would have been left behind long ago if we hadn't looked for ways to bring in a little extra here and there, wouldn't you agree?

Dad was basically a sound old boy, but I was worried about him. He looked exhausted at times. My silly old father – he had been pretty much on the go non-stop for years, hardly taking any holidays unlike the rest of us. So when he informed me of his future plans for the business I was both surprised and pleased. When he told me that afternoon that he wanted to wind down and take retirement by the end of the second financial quarter, I assured him I'd work with him to see things through for a smooth handover. Finally, it appeared that he was coming to his senses before it was too late. There were a few outstanding files to deal with, such as the completion on the Jones' bungalow coming up on Friday and Mrs. Briggs' death certificate that she needed for her husband's probate. There was Leyland's new engine plant that required the Council's planning permission, beginning in two months. The accounts that were in the current file would be finished off by him, he said, and any new matters coming in would be spread out among the other partners, with me overseeing the more important or longest standing clients' affairs. I said it wouldn't really matter which partner dealt with which client, but he was adamant that he wanted me to personally look after and give specific attention to certain special cases such as Leylands, who he'd worked with for more years than I could remember. Another client on his 'special' list was the Markland family estate over at Saxton, and as it happened there was some new 'activity', as I liked to call it, that had come in only that day. He said he'd hang on to that one.

"Dad, if you're going to hand things over, you may as well start as you mean to go on," I argued, but he insisted on keeping hold of the Markland business for the time being, although he did reluctantly show me a letter concerning Leslie Markland he'd just received. It was from an outfit called Angelpride and I quickly scanned the contents before tossing it back to him. He was clearly unsettled by the letter. Leslie Markland was a father? I couldn't make head nor tale of what Dad was going on about. Angelpride agency? Donor client? Maintenance payments? "Best of luck with that one Dad," I responded.

As I imagined he was going to find it hard to let go, I didn't argue when he said he'd take care of it. But I knew the Markland file was one of our largest, and was always being worked on concerning some matter or other. I was certainly looking forward to taking it over. The potential growth in that business could wait. Until then I would be happy to raise a couple of glasses of Scotch with him and congratulate him on his 'decision momentous', as he put it. After he'd gone home, I returned to my office and put both feet up on the desk, looked around at the certificates on the wall, and poured myself another Scotch. Hmm, Senior Partner, eh? I couldn't say it wasn't before time, but I was pleased with myself for having waited so patiently for the moment to come. I pulled the desk-drawer open and began thumbing through the glossy brochure of the new BMW Seven series.

It was about time I rewarded myself, I decided.

CHAPTER 21

Relations and Revelations

"Father was now getting the comeuppance he deserved, the old sod"

Part One: Leslie Markland

The moments I have with pen in hand are what I live for each day. Sometimes I even sit up in bed during the early hours of the morning when everyone else is asleep, just to get a few more paragraphs down. I'm rather enjoying it especially now that I've arrived at the bit where my life was improving. Let me get on with the next episode of my tale. As I keep telling myself, I couldn't have made it up!

I walked up the High Street with a pocket full of coins: fifty pence pieces and one pound coins mostly, though I was sure there were a couple of twenty pence pieces tucked in the seams as well. This could end up being quite a long conversation, so I had better be well prepared, I'd thought.

I wanted to instruct Mr. Ainsworth to legally set my new financial affairs in place, now that I'd become a father. By now I had purchased a mobile telephone, but sometimes the signal wasn't too good, especially from inside the barge, what with all the surrounding steel around the cabin. The phone could sometimes get more bars from outside The Station or The Black Buoy, but usually anywhere in Wivenhoe I ran the risk of it cutting out mid-conversation. I definitely didn't want anyone eavesdropping, so the telephone box was the best place to be.

Having dialed the number I waited for several moments. No, I didn't know what extension number I wanted, and option five seemed the best bet, since I wasn't wanting conveyancing, human resources, whatever that meant, nor probate or family matters, which I guessed meant divorce. Why didn't it just say 'divorce' then? So 'any other business' on option five was the one for me, and I waited a few more moments until an efficient, female voice answered. I requested Mr. Roger Ainsworth, and when asked "who's calling please?" I was informed that Roger Ainsworth was out of the office that morning.

The voice went on to say that "Mr. Ainsworth possibly won't be in the office for quite a while Mr. Markland, but I'll put you through to the acting Senior Partner, Mr. Brian Ainsworth."

Before I could say "not to worry thank you" and that I would call back the following day, I heard a series of clicks until someone else picked up their receiver.

"Mr. Markland, good morning. It's Brian Ainsworth here. My father did mention to me that you might be calling at some point about some family business concerning the Markland estate. I'm afraid he's not here today and possibly won't be for a few days while he takes a short rest, but I hope I can help you instead. I can assure you that you can discuss any business with me just as you would with him. We are one and the same."

Rather thrown off course by his introduction, I said I'd be happy to wait a few days until Roger was back. But Mr. Ainsworth Junior was quite insistent that Mr. Ainsworth Senior's return date wasn't exactly certain and that to save me the trouble of waiting indefinitely I really could talk with him.

I had never met Brian. In my younger years I had overheard Roger Ainsworth being asked by Father how his boy was getting along on the occasions when Roger would call in at the Manor for a pigeon shoot or something. Now that he was in a senior position at the family firm, I ought to be able to discuss delicate and confidential topics with him, I concluded. However, I was still disappointed that I wouldn't be speaking with Roger as I'd been looking forward to catching up with him after so long.

Brian was certainly very attentive. I could almost hear his pen going ten to the dozen, trying to keep up with the details I described surrounding disclosures about my son - my son and heir, in part, to the Markland estate.

"I'm fully aware Mr. Markland that all this could have quite a significant impact upon how the respective parts of the inheritance will be affected and divided, and of course we will do our utmost to bring this matter to a satisfactory legal conclusion." Reassuringly, after a slight pause, he then began to give me the impression that he already knew quite a bit about my current situation.

"My father did show me a letter that he'd received from a London agency. Although it's an unusual business, I'm sure the surrogate mother of your child, this, - er, Mrs. Hennings is it? - will do a fine job bringing up the boy, especially with your financial support. I'll make certain that things are all put in place for you Mr. Markland, and of course put in place for the new young Mr. Markland. No doubt you are aware that your brother and his wife have also recently had a new baby boy and our firm has already been dealing with matters arising from that new arrival. The next sixteen or so years will no doubt fly by and I'm glad you called us to act for you and your son today, sooner rather than later."

Shocked by this new revelation, after the courteous thankyous and goodbyes had been finished with, I hung up the receiver and stepped out of the telephone box, dazed to learn that I now had a nephew. I suppose I should really have given Stanley my address at the barge at least, or my mobile telephone number, so that he could have given me the news himself. What Brian Ainsworth had told me was rather too much for me to take in. Momentarily my thoughts were diverted. It had begun raining during the time I'd been inside the telephone box, so plans to paint Mr. Poulson's exterior windows later that day were obviously out of the question. Just as well, I remember thinking, I wouldn't have been able to concentrate anyway, as I had far too much on my mind.

Instead, I went back to the barge to think things over. During the conversation Mr. Ainsworth had asked me to repeat the main details to him, and so now he had all the information he needed to do his work. Names, addresses and dates. Hmm, dates…that was a point. I wondered which of the two recent newborn boys had actually been born first, and whether that would have any significant consequences. I decided to leave that question for another day and concentrate on the consequences of me having my son. Thanks to Father's will, I'd soon be receiving a boost in my income, income that Stanley and Constance had, until then, been enjoying all to themselves. That'll upset the old apple cart, I remember thinking.

How satisfying. Even more satisfying was that this was all in compliance of Father's will. My son would become a wealthy man in the future, I would have quite a few extra pounds to live on, and the twin girls' share of the Markland fortune would now be much reduced. I couldn't deny that wiping the smug smile off Stanley's face would be very rewarding.

Father was now getting the comeuppance he deserved, the old sod, and I almost wished he were still alive to see it for himself. Perhaps he might have even been a little bit proud of me for being so clever.

Part Two: Brian Ainsworth

"I certainly wasn't averse to a bit of roly-poly action"

Despite the Markland Estate account being big business for our firm, it hadn't been occupying very much of my time until something happened to dramatically change all that. It occurred at one of the many business functions I enjoyed attending. Those lunches and dinners were an excellent way of networking while eating superb food at the expense of someone else, with the added enjoyment of a free bar for an entire evening. There was usually the chance to enjoy some female company as well. I don't think I can remember an event when there hadn't been some bored glamorous wife or girlfriend of one of the delegates simply gagging for the chance to exclude herself from the group she was stuck with. Discussions about sales figures, production processes or customer portfolios would not be of the slightest interest to them. And you wouldn't believe how horny they could become once they'd had a few glasses of bubbly poured down their necks!

As a partner in the largest firm of solicitors in the area I was often invited to such dinners. It would have been rude to refuse wouldn't it, I'd chuckled to myself one morning when going through my post. I opened an envelope containing an invitation to none other than The Yorkshire Farmers' Exhibition of Pig Husbandry and Handling Equipment. What the...?! I simply had to go to that one. It could well turn out to be the event of the year, and was not to be missed under any circumstances. Sarcasm could sometimes get the better of me but I nevertheless filled out the acceptance form. There would no doubt be bountiful free booze and canapés galore, I thought, not to mention a million women at the bar just waiting for someone interesting like me to come along and talk to them.

When the evening came I wasn't disappointed. After an hour or so, wandering around the various stands and dipping in and out of a few of their presentations about this or that new piece of machinery designed to hugely improve a pig's life, I strolled over to one of the bars. Seated there was a group of three rather attractive ladies, and separately, a woman with beautiful eyes and the prettiest face you could imagine. I certainly didn't object that she was so - how should I say this without sounding sexist - amply breasted. I certainly wasn't averse to a bit of roly-poly action, if you get my meaning. But, with this lady, I'd found myself naturally drawn to her for some other reason, not only because of the size of her bosom. I walked over and introduced myself to her, and she did to me. Anna Hennings was her name.

I knew that name, I was sure I did. Had we met before? My brain slowly clicked into gear and I had my answer. No, we hadn't actually met, but I remembered where I'd seen the name previously. But of course it couldn't have been the same 'Anna Hennings', the same Anna Hennings that I'd recently seen named in correspondence concerning Leslie Markland. It couldn't have been, could it? By that point I'd already downed quite a few pints, and my tongue was wagging as freely as the beer was flowing. I probably shouldn't have blurted it out in the way I did as I'd only been making small talk. I mean, all I'd said was something along the lines of 'how's the surrogate mum doing?' and 'I guess you're not the Anna Hennings I've been reading about recently?' Unprofessionally, and in my drunken stupor, I'd thought it had been a brilliant chat-up line. I'd assumed that she'd engage me in jovial conversation, followed by a mock apology from me for the mistaken identity, she would laugh, and BINGO! I'd be on my way to scoring with her! But instead, that pretty face of hers went deathly white in seconds, and all I scored was an own goal.

Her eyes looked like they were going to pop out of their sockets, and tears formed around them in seconds. She got up off her stool, her legs unsteady on high heels as she went running off without saying another word to me. The commotion caused the other girls at the bar to stare in my direction as if I were the devil himself. I didn't understand. I'd hardly said more than a few words to her. In my embarrassment, I also decided to beat a hasty retreat, watched by the three other girls at the bar. Then I noticed that the woman, Anna Hennings, who I'd inadvertently upset, had left her mobile on the counter. Sheepishly picking up the phone I nodded in the direction of the departed woman, trying to indicate to the three startled onlookers that I'd better go and return the woman's property to her.

I went in search of her, but couldn't see her anywhere. Systematically checking each exhibition stand, I drew a blank. She was nowhere to be found. I was about to give up and allow myself to be enticed onto a stand that was offering some rather delicious looking plates of smoked salmon and caviar blinis, when I spotted the woman grabbing a man in a suit. The man was clearly in mid flow talking with another man - a customer of his I presumed - and the woman was practically frog-marching him out of the exhibition hall. Almost film noir, the plot was thickening. I stood there mystified, looking down at the mobile phone I had in my hands. Perhaps it would give me a clue and help me solve the 'mystery of the woman that ran away'. I decided to leave it until returning home later that evening before investigating the phone further. Meanwhile there were more pressing issues to deal with. Having always had a soft spot for caviar, I thought I might as well raise my standards from beer to the Champagne that was on offer. I loved those events, I truly did.

I really shouldn't have driven home after the exhibition closed, but I did anyway. Live dangerously, I thought. Actually I had a knack of being able to sober myself up by quickly drinking hot water and strong coffee, so I did just that before leaving the exhibition hall, and it worked. At least, that's what I stupidly told myself. I got home and changed into my casuals, made myself comfortable on the sofa and then turned on the woman's mobile phone. I was hoping to find some clue to who she was and why she had run off in such a distraught manner. I found the clue alright. There was message after message that I simply could not believe I was reading, as I scrolled down the history of texts between this Anna Hennings and the actual Constance Markland of the Markland Estate. No wonder she had run away from me!

By now I had completely sobered up, even though I'd poured myself a huge glass of red wine. My heart was pumping and adrenalin flowing as I worked out what had been going on between the two women. Text after text gradually gave me all the information I needed to know. I was shocked! It appeared that Anna Hennings had pretended to be the surrogate mother of a baby born from a sperm donor, but she was passing the sperm sample on to Constance Markland who then used the donation to become the true mother. A boy had been born as a result. So it appeared from those text messages that Constance's new baby wasn't actually her husband's but someone else's.

What a revelation! What a bizarre situation. Did Stanley Markland know about this? No, of course he didn't. That was clear from one of Constance's messages.

"WATEVR HPPNS WE CNT EVR LET STAN FND OUT ABT THS." she'd texted.

Well you silly bitch, I thought, he wouldn't need to, would he, if you hadn't written it down in black and white for all and sundry to see? Well okay, not exactly all and sundry, just anyone who might find her phone. Why hadn't Anna Hennings deleted those texts as soon as reading or writing them, I wondered? Anyone could use them for a bit of fun if this phone ever found its way into the wrong hands - my hands for example.

With knowledge, one gains power.

I was intrigued to find out the full story. Anna Hennings clearly didn't know the identity of the donor, and nor therefore would Constance Markland, but perhaps there would be more clues within all the messages, so I scrolled through them again. These girls had been plotting over some time it appeared, and many of the messages seemed hurriedly written, using abbreviations and the new 'text-speak' that had become all the rage.

One of the earliest messages read "ANGELP SNDNG PAPERS 2 SIGN" and another one, a few weeks later said, "ANGELP SAY SAMPLE CMNG SAT. USE IN 48HRS. U BETR GET STAN PSSED & READY." Then there was: "SAMPLE JST ARIVD FRM ANGELP"

How could anyone abuse our English language so appallingly? Fathoming out what most of the messages meant wasn't too difficult but it was this ANGELP that stumped me. It had been a long day, my large glass of red wine had become empty and I decided to sleep on it. Words of wisdom that Dad had taught me: "Brian," he would advise, "whatever's bothering you at night, by the morning you will see it with a fresh pair of eyes and the solution will usually present itself."

I put the cat out, turned off the lights and went off upstairs to bed.

Dad was right, the solution did present itself, as soon as I awoke in fact. Of course! ANGELPRIDE had been the word shortened on the texts, and I instantly remembered where I'd seen that name before. It had been on that unusual letter Dad had shown me from the Markland file. And of course: Leslie Markland talked about an Angelpride agency when he'd phoned me the other day. How intriguing, I thought: what on earth was going on?

Excited, I skipped breakfast, shaved and dressed as quickly as possible, jumped into the BMW and arrived at the office earlier than I'd done for months. In fact, I was the first one there that morning. Never before having arrived ahead of Hatty Palmerstone, who would usually open up first thing, I struggled to remember the security code on the door. Ah yes, Dad's date of birth: 7832. I went into his office and pulled all the Markland files off the shelf, and began going through them in close detail, one by one. We'd just been working on the Markland Will and Testament concerning how the estate would be divided and separated for the new benefactor, Oliver Markland, born on 7th April 1997 to Constance and Stanley Markland. Well, that was a farce, if ever there was one. Additionally there was now the work to be done on behalf of Leslie Markland's offspring – a plan made, in my opinion, to scupper his old man's wishes, with 'made' being the operative word. That had undoubtedly been my impression when Leslie had phoned and spoken to me. I looked again at the details he'd given me, and then I looked again at the letter Dad had received from that Angelpride Agency in London. "Making family dreams come true." You could say that alright. I carried on reading. "...each year until the child born 7th April 1997..." It's the same bloody date! Everything I was reading here, and what the Hennings woman's mobile phone texts had revealed, were forming a clear picture of the whole affair. Leslie bloody Markland has tossed out his bloody spunk to this sham of a place in London and they've only gone and sent it to that Anna Hennings woman. The same

Anna Hennings that I'd met at the exhibition hall. And she'd passed it on to Constance bloody Markland, who then went and got herself up the duff with it and had his bloody kid. It's the same bloody kid, one and the same. Shit! I don't effing believe it. So Leslie Markland's had a kid with his own sister-in-law, and he doesn't know it, and Constance Markland has given birth to her brother-in-law's kid and she doesn't know it, and Stanley Markland thinks the kid's his. Jesus Christ, what a bloody mess!

As I went over the whole scenario in my mind, it began to dawn on me that I was probably the only person who had connected all the pieces of this jigsaw puzzle together. Let's not be hasty, I thought. I must take my time and think things through before acting.

By now Hatty had arrived for work, so I buzzed her to get me a coffee, very strong and very black, while I pondered what I should, or rather what I could do. With knowledge, one gains power, I repeated to myself. And now with power can come money. I needed to work this through properly.

Okay, I knew it was wrong and maybe my hangover was clouding my judgment, but I couldn't resist hatching a cunning plan. Some may have called it blackmail, but I preferred to describe it as 'information management'. I could earn myself a tidy bonus if I planned things cleverly.

CHAPTER 22

Disclosure

"A feeling of cold terror came over me"

Constance Markland (1998)

My flip-up mobile phone vibrated on the kitchen worktop, indicating that a text was coming through. I hadn't long been home from taking Sophie and Hilary to their pre-school nursery and I was worn out already. It was such a palaver getting them dressed and ready in time, whilst seeing to Oliver and giving him his bottle at the same time as the girls' breakfasts. Maybe I was making a rod for my own back by being too lenient with the girls, but try as I might they just didn't take any notice of what I told them to do. I tried the 'wait till your father gets home' approach, without any effect whatsoever. Anna suggested I bribe them with sweets. That worked until they got the sweets, and then they went back to how they had been before. I tried being nice to them and I tried being strict. I shouted, I talked calmly, I raised my voice, I whispered. It made no difference whatever I did, except when I gave them the silent treatment and ignored them. That really wound them up, so much so that they would just stand there and hold their breath until they looked like they were going to pass out. So, of course, I gave in. They would look slyly at each other, with a wry smile as if to say 'there you are mummy, we've won again'. Of course I loved them, but being a mother in charge of two such difficult girls was taking its toll. Sometimes my confidence was so shattered I imagined they were in control, not me.

They were mean to their new brother too. The little darling was only a few weeks old and they could not bear him to be comfortable and content. They'd snatch his dummy out of his mouth and hide it somewhere when I wasn't looking. Their new trick was to get Oliver's comfort flannel and soak it in the milk from the bottle so that it was wet and smelly. Worse still, one morning I even caught Sophie peeing on it and putting it back in his cot next to his face.

When Stanley came home, they were all sweetness and light, and he simply would not believe me when I told him how horrid they were while he was at work. That of course was on the occasions when he did come home at all. He was working away more and more frequently, always busy with something. The girls doted on him and vice versa, but they seemed to have some personal vendetta against me. I found myself living for the moment when I'd drop them off at nursery. At least I could come home and have a few hours respite until it was time for me to collect them again.

But Oliver was a joy. He was so cute and well behaved, and pretty much perfect in every way, so his goodness countered the girls' badness, if that's the right word to use for them. How could I possibly think that way about any of my own children? But the truth of the matter was that the girls were beginning to make me dislike them. I loved them, of course, but they weren't exactly pleasant company.

One morning Oliver was settled in his pushchair, and the kettle had just boiled. While breathing a sigh of relief and enjoying a bit of 'me' time, I picked up the paper from the doormat and sat at the kitchen table. I was immediately interrupted by Anna's text message. "URGNT. MUST TALK. CMNG RND NOW. R U IN?"

"YES. KETTLE ON. C U IN 10", I quickly replied. Whatever could she be wanting to see me about that was so urgent, I wondered? Within 15 minutes I found out, as she described her chance meeting with our family's solicitor, or rather the son of our family's solicitor to be more accurate. I had heard that dear Roger Ainsworth hadn't been too well recently and so it was Brian who was now in charge at the firm. I wasn't so keen on him, but it was Stanley who usually dealt with most of our legal matters. I was aware that there'd been some necessary paperwork recently after Oliver had been born but to be honest, Ainsworth & Co's business didn't really concern me. That all changed that morning, when I found myself listening to Anna's tale of horror about her chance meeting with Mr. Ainsworth junior, while being bored out of her mind at one of the events that her husband's company had exhibited at. When Anna called round she was shaking, and by the time she left I was shaking too. She had only gone and left her phone behind at the exhibition - the phone with all our private messages about the surrogacy business. That could potentially be disastrous if it fell into the wrong hands. As it turned out, that was exactly what had happened.

I just sat there, shocked to the core by what Anna went on to tell me. She'd received a call on the house phone, out of the blue, from Brian Ainsworth about the child maintenance payments she'd been receiving from the donor father for Oliver's maintenance. But quite why Brian and not Roger Ainsworth had anything to do with all that I had no idea, until she went on to tell me what he'd said.

It had been at the end of Ainsworth's conversation with Anna that he'd dropped his bombshell.

"I know everything about what you and Constance Markland have been up to," was what he'd said to her. She told me how she'd gone cold at that point. When she asked him what he meant, he wouldn't elaborate except to say something about 'solicitor confidentiality – for now', and that he had something important belonging to her and she'd be getting it in the post soon. And then he'd hung up.

Anna, still shaking like a leaf, continued to explain how that very morning she'd received a package in the post. Initially, when she'd opened up the Jiffy bag she was delighted, as inside was her mobile phone that she'd thought was lost for good. For the past few days she'd been looking for it everywhere and couldn't remember where she'd last had it. Her delight quickly turned to horror as she'd then noticed the accompanying business card from Brian Ainsworth.

"The little slime-ball must have read all our messages and added two and two together to make four. He's worked everything out", she stuttered to me.

A feeling of cold terror had come over me as I ran through the potential consequences if Ainsworth ever decided to spill the beans to Stanley.

I looked across at Oliver sleeping peacefully. How could my emotions alter so abruptly? Happy and proud at ten o'clock, I was paralysed by worry and fear by eleven.

"Oh Anna, why hadn't you deleted those messages?" I cried. But to be fair, I hadn't done so either. I couldn't blame Anna.

After a lengthy hug, and when Anna had gone home, I spent the next hour or so going through the same series of communications between us on my own phone. I pressed the delete button after each and every message, feeling numb as I read over what we'd been texting to one another, realising that unfortunately it was now too late. I hoped to God that Ainsworth could be trusted to keep all this to himself. If Stanley were to find out, well, I didn't know what I'd do.

But it wasn't only Ainsworth's 'I know everything' statement that resonated. It was also a more specific disclosure to Anna that she'd related to me. Ainsworth had told her that he also knew who the real father was. He went on to say to Anna that neither I nor anyone else would want to know the truth. What he'd meant by that, God only knows.

CHAPTER 23

Monkey Business at the Zoo

"This was only his second job of the whole year – he wasn't exactly Lawrence Olivier!"

Tristan Thomas (1999)

S tanley and I had become settled into some kind of routine, and I would say that I had been enjoying life very much. My career was going in the right direction by leaps and bounds and it had been made clear to me by the party whip that I would receive much support were I to ever stand for Parliament when a safe seat became available. I could imagine my parents eating their words about how they wished I'd become an accountant when seeing me on TV being cheered and clapped at the Labour Party constituency headquarters.

I knew that Stanley was in an awkward position, and I respected that. I believed that I was his true love and that when the time was right he would leave Constance and come to live with me permanently. Having met his wife on several occasions, I'd successfully managed to control my feelings of jealousy towards her. At the end of the day, she had only been doing her best to bring up those children, and Stanley was being a good dad to them. I wouldn't have wanted it any other way. He tended to split his time pretty much equally between them and me, but of course I was quite often down in Westminster and so we had to take that into account when we planned our 'together' time. He even came down with me to London on a few occasions where I introduced him to my friends at the Abacco club and he appeared to be very comfortable in their company, although I teased him about not becoming too comfortable!

My observation of his wife was that she was constantly on edge about something. I wouldn't describe her as a person with much confidence, and it was as though she was always looking over her shoulder and expecting something to go wrong. I guess some people are just naturally anxious, while others are naturally relaxed. Stanley told me that she had become progressively more like that since having their son Oliver, or Oli as they sometimes called him. He was a nice enough little boy, and would no doubt grow up to be a success in whatever he chose to do. Oliver was well behaved and likeable, and if you are liked in the world, opportunities open up for you: at least, that's my experience. I wouldn't have got where I was in life if I hadn't been popular. I know that sounds terribly big-headed of me, but it's the truth. And even as a baby, I could see that Oli was going to turn into a good looking chap one day, that was for sure. He bore little resemblance to his dad though, but I guessed that would come with time.

Their girls were more of a problem. They appeared to be getting progressively more difficult and there wasn't a week that went by when their school didn't report some mischief they've been up to, causing upset and chaos with other children. Stanley told me that sometimes he'd go home only to find his wife crying with despair and frustration after receiving yet another summons by the headmistress about a problem they'd caused. It wouldn't have surprised me to hear from Stanley that they had been expelled. No wonder their poor mother was constantly uptight.

I had to keep my distance though, and not get involved within

Stanley's family life. Painful as it was, sharing my man with them was what I had to do, and to compensate for that I simply concentrated on my ambitions with my career in politics. I made sure I kept my private life very separate from my professional life as I didn't want myself mixed up in any scandal that would upset my future plans, especially if I were to become an MP. There was enough scandal within the Government without me adding to it. It's funny sometimes how your life can actually turn out as you imagine it to. Even back in those days at Rugby School I'd visualised working my way up to the House of Commons.

The relative calm of our relationship got a jolt one day. I had been working away in my 'cupboard', as I called it, one day in Westminster, when I took a rather strange and unpleasant phone call. My desk had been moved some time previously from under the stairs to my very own tiny office situated in one of the corridors of the Houses of Parliament. Of course it wasn't really a cupboard, but it was certainly no larger than one, and the dark wood paneling only emphasised the feeling of claustrophobia when I was working there.

The phone call was from a man claiming that he knew all about my affair with Stanley, and that he had "certain other information" that wouldn't do me much good if it ever found its way in to the public domain. Well, I wasn't going to take any nonsense like that, and I told the fellow straight there and then that if the world found out I was gay, then the world wouldn't be learning anything the world didn't already suspect, and that I couldn't care less if I were 'outed'. Half the Government were closet gays anyway. I told him I was sure the world wouldn't be in the least bit interested about one more. But the phone call didn't end there. He went on to say something about me becoming embroiled in a sex scandal involving a love child. I took more notice then. I had no idea what he was talking about but any personal connection involving a combination of the words "child" and "sex" were to be avoided at all costs, so I reluctantly agreed to meet with him. In hindsight I should have just told him to bugger off. That was my first major error.

Anyway, I didn't tell him to bugger off, and instead we arranged to meet somewhere no one would overhear us. His chosen rendezvous location was bizarre to say the least. Despite my fear of what was to come, I felt weirdly excited by the whole James Bond-like scenario. Granted, it was more Peter Sellers in *Casino Royale* than Sean Connery in *Dr. No* but, nonetheless, I felt like a spy in a film when I agreed to his demand for a meeting outside the gorilla enclosure at London Zoo. I really ought to have told the fellow, emphatically, to piss off.

Four days after the phone call I was down in London on Labour Party business and I excused myself from my colleagues to take the tube from Westminster to Regents Park and paid the entrance charge at the zoo turnstiles. I obtained a guide map and found my way to the gorilla enclosure where I sat and waited on the conveniently positioned bench. The green paint was peeling and one of the wooden slats was beginning to rot and I questioned myself for having noticed such trivial detail. I also questioned what I was doing there on a cold spring day when I could have been in the warmth of the Members' Tea Room back at the Houses of Parliament. I was early for our appointment and maybe that was another error of judgement on my part - showing myself to be too keen. But I suppose I actually was keen. Two o'clock had been our agreed meeting time, and when I had asked how I would recognise the man during our phone conversation I was told that it wouldn't be an issue. I waited, and two o'clock was nearly up when a large Rastafarian chap with a brightly coloured woollen hat sat at the other end of the bench. I was about to get up and walk away when a very high pitched and squeaky voice told me not to move. It was Rasta-man's voice and he continued to sit there, looking straight ahead and didn't turn his head to me once. During my political career thus far I had become involved in some pretty strange situations and conversations, but this wasn't just strange, it was surreal.

The man spoke in a kind of squawk. "Name is Bob Wasa, and I here to tell you how to avoid gettin' in big mess and trouble, ya hear?"

How could such a large black man have such a high-pitched voice, I thought to myself?

"Ya hear me?" he repeated, still looking straight ahead.

"Now look here," I said to the fellow. "I am here to meet someone, so if you don't mind, please be moving on." Then he turned to me, rather menacingly, and I saw his face was scarred on his left cheek, and his eyes' whites weren't white at all - more like cream coloured.

His voice suddenly changed and became much deeper. "Sit down, man, shut up, listen. These are my words of advice to you, my friend, you understand me?" Before waiting for me to answer, he continued. "I have a message for you from the chief, so listen to me carefully..."

I did listen to him carefully, I didn't really have much choice after he hinted to me that he could 'have a little violence,' as he put it, with people who didn't take him seriously on account of his rather unusual vocal characteristics. Afterwards, the craziness of the meeting went round and round in my head as I tubed it back to Westminster, but it was the content, rather than the nature, of his narrative that bothered me the most.

Bob Wasa was apparently the messenger for 'The Chief'. Wasa himself turned out to be actually quite a nice man once he'd dropped his ridiculously false act. And an act was certainly what it had been. Although he wouldn't disclose who The Chief was, he did let me in on the fact that he himself was an out-of-work actor who had got his first job of the year working at a conference promoting tourism and trade for the Caribbean in Harrogate. He'd been paid £65 plus hotel accommodation, his train fare from London, and as much food as he could eat, just to walk around the exhibition hall inviting people to go visit the 'I Love Jamaica' stand, whilst strumming a guitar and posing for photographs. It was at the Harrogate Conference Centre that he had met someone who had offered 'dis gig', as he described it, to come and meet me. On occasions I had to stifle a laugh at the ridiculousness of the whole situation. Mr. Wasa needed to keep referring to a crumpled up piece of paper with some notes written on it. You simply couldn't have made it up. At the end of our highly unusual conversation, he stood up and almost handed me a bundle of ten pound notes held together with an elastic band, initially mistaking it for an envelope that he was obviously supposed to be giving me instead. I could see why this was only his second job of the whole year – he wasn't exactly Lawrence Olivier!

Although I found it almost impossible to take the fellow seriously, he did end up passing me that envelope. I opened it once I'd got a seat on my return tube to Westminster, and had a few moments to myself. The note caused me great concern. In a nutshell, it gave me the shocking news that Stanley hadn't in fact been the biological father of Oliver, but instead his wife had become pregnant via a sperm donor! Well, thinking about it, I suppose that did make sense, remembering Stanley's complete and seemingly genuine surprise on learning she was expecting 'his' child. In some ways, to me, that was actually good news, but the news that followed certainly was not. As I read on it became clear that, incredibly, the sperm donor had been her own brother-in-law, Leslie Markland. So, young Master Oliver's uncle was also his dad: The poor little fellow. And via some twist of fate, both Leslie and my Stanley weren't aware of the fact - not yet, so long as I could prevent it.

How devastating that news would be for Stanley. I knew him well enough to appreciate how distraught he would be if he ever found out. I also knew how damaging all this could have been to my career if the papers ever got hold of the story. Imagine the headlines! If my name were to be associated in any way, the support that I had thus far enjoyed from my party colleagues would soon be transferred elsewhere. Whoever 'The Chief' was, as Bob Wasa described him, he was remarkably well informed, even knowing the details of Leslie Markland's maintenance payments of £300 a month, rising by £10 a month each year, to a woman called Anna Hennings - who apparently was in turn saving it for Oliver until he reached 16-years-old. I remember totting up the figures in my mind, concluding that a sizeable chunk of money would be accumulating in the years to come.

As I finished reading the contents of the neatly typed note I wondered whether Stanley might also have access to that money. At the bottom of the thick parchment paper I was being 'cordially invited to make an initial lump sum payment of £5,000', and as well as that, 'transfer £300 each month, rising by £10 per month each year thereafter'. This 'cordial invitation' was completed with the numbers of an offshore bank account in the Channel Islands.

I was well aware from my chats with colleagues in the House that I wouldn't be able to trace who the account belonged to. Initially, I contemplated ignoring the whole situation, but after I'd fully digested what I'd read I concluded that I really needed to contain this information at all cost. I began to work out how I could possibly pay that kind of money. I could see plainly how and from where I could get the monthly payments - I would have to work on Stanley for that - but that initial lump sum was more problematic. On my salary I simply didn't have sufficient funds lying around. Hmm, maybe one of my pals at Abacco's would see me through with a loan for now. At least until I became an MP with an MP's expense account. Hmm.

So deep in thought was I, on my tube journey back from the zoo, that I nearly failed to get off at my station. At the last second I jumped up and squeezed through the doors as they were sliding closed. I would have to find a way of coming up with that lump sum, and that would buy me some time. I didn't like the situation I found myself in. I didn't like being boxed into a corner.

CHAPTER 24

Breakdown

"My heart is broken. There's lasagne in the fridge for your tea tonight"

Constance Markland (1999)

Depression is a terrible thing. It is an illness of the mind in much the same way as a physical illness like breast cancer is an affliction of the body. Some people associate depression with 'having a screw loose,' and mistakenly believe that all the sufferer needs to do is simply get on with things and they will get better. Well, I can tell you from first-hand experience that nothing could be further from reality.

At first I was able to control it a little by ensuring I got a good night's sleep, using off-the-shelf anti-stress pills from Tesco. Then after a while I found myself waking up at two or three in the morning, just lying there waiting for the day to break, thinking about my guilty secret. Eventually, when it was time to get up and dressed, I'd be so tired that I'd spend most of the day in a complete daze. Anna was a star, helping out whenever she could, looking after Oli so that I could rest a little. If I managed to get even ten minutes sleep during a day I was then at least able to get Stanley's dinner ready when he came home from work. I say when, but I should really say if. How could I have been so stupid about him working away on business and seeing another woman? I can't believe that I thought I'd win back his heart by following Top 10 Tips from a tabloid newspaper.

My depression grew and eventually I decided to seek help from my doctor. No stranger to the surgery, another symptom of my illness was anxiety about pretty much everything, including Oli's health, and so I would be taking him there every time he as much as sneezed or coughed or had a temperature. I'm sure any young mother would recognise that trait. It was during one such visit, I think it was when Oli had tripped over his pedal-tractor and badly gashed his knee on the gravel, that Doctor Singleton asked me if I was feeling alright myself, as I looked like I needed a bit of a pick-me-up. Well, without any warning I broke down there and then in front of her, and it took her at least ten minutes just to calm me down to a state in which I could talk again with any coherence. I vaguely remember hearing her calling reception to say she couldn't take any more patients for the time being and also asking if they would hold any phone calls as well.

Eventually I was able to describe some of my difficulties to her, namely the lack of sleep, my worry about Oli's health problems, me not being a good enough mother to him or the girls, the way the girls' behaviour was becoming worse and worse - oh, and the matter of my husband's affair. What I couldn't bring myself to tell the doctor were the two things that really sickened me. The first thing literally did make me sick when I'd first found out, and the second thing kept me feeling sick with worry.

I will explain. Doctor Singleton was actually very good to me. She was very sympathetic and understanding, and reassured me that she would certainly be able to cure the lack of sleep by prescribing some proper drugs instead of what I had been buying amongst the carrots and the toothpaste with the weekly shop. That was her little joke to try and lighten my mood, but although I was too upset to appreciate it at the time, it did help me to loosen up a little. Also, I felt a good deal better when she convinced me that young Oliver didn't in fact have any health problems and that he was just a normal little boy getting a few things wrong with him from time to time. She was also sure that I was being a perfect mother, and that it was my lack of sleep that was clouding my judgment. She dismissed my comments about the girls' behaviour with a brush of her hand through the air, which I guess was understandable on account of me not disclosing any of the terrible things I'd been catching them doing. Although she couldn't actually help me with the situation regarding my husband's affair, she did say that it was, sadly, all too common nowadays, and that there were counselling sessions we could attend that might help us.

I considered the counselling sessions, as in an ideal world I would have loved to turn things around positively between Stanley and me. But on reflection, I decided that in our particular case what had become broken by then could never actually be fixed. How on earth could it, when he confessed to me that he preferred another man's company to that of his wife's? I'd been assuming that he'd been having an affair with another woman, when in fact all along he was being screwed by a bloke!

Ironically, I thought we were really becoming close again following the birth of Oliver. It was true that for a while he was being a real sweetheart to me, being very attentive and kind and caring, and simply nice to be with. How stupid of me to believe that those times when I thought he was working away he was in fact with his man friend. The moment I found out, I threw up there and then. I'm not homophobic, but there is a limit to how much anyone can take in a relationship and I had reached that limit.

His confession came about one evening when we had been having a heart to heart. You see, I had been letting off steam about yet another difficult incident involving the girls. This time they had gone too far, and I was seriously becoming concerned about what was going on inside their heads. The flooding of the school toilets or their placing of a spider in a lunch box belonging to one of their classmates were mere pranks in comparison to the latest incident. This time the twins had shown a much crueller side of themselves.

Unusually for Stanley, he was actually listening to me as I told him how Miss Mernaham, the class teacher, came up to me in the playground as I was waiting to collect Sophie and Hilary, and asked if she could see me in the school office, along with the Head Mistress, Mrs. Evans. Apparently the girls had caused an enormous amount of upset and distress to all the other children, not to mention Miss Mernaham herself. They had sneaked the class hamster out of its cage, took it to the rear of the classroom behind the screen, and held it down on the desk to see how many books it could carry on its back before something cracked. The shame I felt on that occasion was simply awful. The other children were in tears when they discovered what had happened. Miss Mernaham herself was in a state of shock as she had to deal with removing and finishing off the almost dead animal as humanely as she could, before burying it in the school nature garden.

The tears were streaming down my cheeks when I described all this to Stanley. He listened patiently while I added how uncomfortable I had felt facing the other mums in the school playground afterwards. The whispering and the pointing directed at me were bad enough, but when one mother came and started shouting at me, spitting with anger as she did so, I didn't know what to do or where to turn.

Naturally he was sympathetic and upset on hearing what our daughters had done, and the emotion of the moment led him to tell me some news of his own which turned our heart to heart into what felt to me like some kind of slow motion car crash.

He might have been my husband, but when he told me about his affair he was no longer a man, in my eyes. He was a man to someone else, and I told him so. As I imagined what my husband had been doing under the sheets with that other man, and then on another night sleeping with me, that's when I spewed up in front of him. After cleaning up the mess, he quietly said that we should separate. Why he fancied me with my masculine clothes and hairstyle all began to make sense. He tried to explain everything by saying that his favourite record had been Bowie's Aladdin Sane, as if that was a good enough excuse! No wonder he'd enjoyed so much pleasure when I'd used my bedroom toys on him.

I was at breaking point. His big secret was now out in the open but I also had a big secret of my own. I was sick with worry that he might learn what I'd done in giving birth to Oliver. Stanley's son wasn't his own flesh and blood, and I was terrified that one day he would find out. I just wouldn't want to be around in this world if he ever did.

Needing to calm my nerves I took another Prozac. After the trauma of our heart to heart had subsided slightly with the help of the pill, Stanley disclosed something else that made me wonder whether he did know something about my terrible secret. It was probably just my imagination running away with me but in my depressed mind I still wondered. He told me he had been paying some money to 'a good friend of his who was in a spot of bother', as he put it. Now, one thing that I admired about Stanley was that he was very good with money and he was good at sharing with me everything that was going on with income from the estate, and being open and honest with our bank accounts. At least, that was what I had thought until that evening.

I should explain something: Anna had been receiving the maintenance payments from the sperm donor, but as I hadn't needed that money myself I'd asked Anna just to set up a standing order to my bank savings account. It was the same account that my Aunt Mimi had paid some money into for Oli's future. Because Stanley was never likely to actually meet Aunt Mimi, I felt it was the most convincing tale I could come up with that wouldn't arouse too much suspicion if he saw the money accumulating there and asked questions. I would simply say that Aunt Mimi was generously sending me some of her fortune to go towards Oli's future education. So, I'd been building up a tidy little nest egg from my anonymous sperm donor at a rate of £300 a month, plus the £10 a month after Oli had had his first birthday in April. And there was Stanley, openly admitting to me that he'd been giving some money to his 'special friend' who had found himself to be in some 'spot of bother'. The sum in question? £300 a month to begin with, but now with an added £10 a month! This was more than my simple little head could take. Since taking the Prozac that Doctor Singleton had prescribed, I'm afraid that my mind wasn't as sharp as it used to be, but it was sharp enough to know that all this was making me sick with worry. "He must be a very good friend," was all I said quietly, before taking myself up to bed and without saying goodnight.

I was still very tearful and upset the following morning after a restless night, and I deliberated over how I should best deal with all the worry, angst and heartache. I decided to write an emotional but, strangely, calm letter to Anna. She was soon due to come round to pick up little Oli for an hour, supposedly so that I could get some sleep. What I had to tell her was too big to be said face to face. In my best handwriting I wrote:

"My dearest friend Anna, I'm so sorry to have to do this to you. You have been a wonderful friend to me over the years, but particularly recently. Thank you, thank you, thank you. I couldn't have had the joy of having Oli without your help and I'm going to miss him so much from wherever it is that we go to.

Stanley told me he didn't love me last night. He'd been in love with someone else, and his lover was in fact a man. I'm afraid that as much as I want to I can't forgive him his deceit and lying to me, even though I'm still in love with him. Don't ask me why. My head is in such a muddle now. I've tried a couple of days of not taking my pills but I can't see me ever feeling better now, not after Stanley told me he was going to have to leave me…for him!

I know I could manage to just about bring up Oli. He is such a darling little boy, bless him, but I just can't cope with the twins. They run me ragged and the thought of them tormenting me without Stanley being around is just too much for me to bear.

Please can you do me one last big favour? Can you find out who Oli's real father is and let him know how much I love his son.

I hope he's a good and kind man. He deserves to see his son one day, and

*he needs to know that I thanked him from the bottom of my heart for what
he did.*

*And now my dearest friend, I am going to end this all now. My mind is in
a jumble and I can't see the wood for the trees, as you used to say. I am so
sorry to do this but I can't think of any alternative. Please don't be upset for
me and don't cry for me either. You mustn't show this note to Stanley. I'm
sure they will all be looking for a suicide note but you mustn't show this to
anyone, please. I am going to write another letter to Stanley. They can all
see that one.*

*I am quite calm about this and I am not afraid. Please forgive me for what
I am going to do. I love you Anna, you are my best friend, and I thank you
for everything.*

*I want Oli to know that I love him so much, and the girls as well in a
different way.*

*Please somehow find who Oli's father is and let him know that I love his
son. If anyone can find out who he is, I know you can, Miss Marple!*

I'm sorry. xxxxx"

I folded the note neatly and placed it lengthways in an envelope and
on it I wrote Anna's name and address, licked a first class stamp that I
had in my purse and stuck it very precisely on the top right hand corner,
trying to make it as square-on as I could. As I did so I found my mind
wandering, wondering why we put stamps on the top right hand corners
of envelopes. Then I walked briskly to the end of the drive of the Manor
house and dropped the letter into the bright red post box set into the
wall with its 'GR' raised markings. Now what on earth did that mean, I
wondered as I dropped Anna's letter through the slot.

I walked back to the house, more slowly this time as I played through
in my mind how I would tie the scarf around my neck and whether the
coat hooks on the door would be strong enough to hold my weight. I was
sure they would be. Those doors must be three inches thick. What would
Oli think of me if he ever learned that Stanley wasn't his father? What
should I wear? How would the girls react when they returned home

from school? Should I put on high heels or sandals? Will Stanley stay now to bring up the girls and Oli, and will he do a good job? Will he do them the lasagne that's in the fridge for their tea tonight?

Once Oli had been collected, back in the Manor house kitchen I wrote my second letter of the day and folded it neatly and placed it lengthways in another envelope. I attached it, with the words 'LASAGNE RECIPE' clearly written on the outside, to the door of the fridge, using one of those magnets that they sell at the gift shop. That done, I climbed the stairs and headed for the bedroom wardrobe, before carefully selecting my favourite scarf. The blue one with white spots was more of a neck-tie and I'd bought it because it looked like one that I'd seen David Bowie wearing in a picture once. It was long enough and easy to knot. All I'd written on the note inside the envelope was:

Dear Stanley. Please always look after Oliver, Sophie and Hilary. My heart is broken. There's lasagne in the fridge for your tea tonight.

CHAPTER 25

Coincidences and Consequences

"Something clearly hadn't been right"

Part One: Silvie Tosgiev (2000)

The last occasion I had seen Leslie we had enjoyed such a great time on his big boat. It had been my second time of going to the quaint Wivenhoe village where he lived, and that time my visit had been purely for pleasure, with no business strings attached. No collection of sperm samples in a jar on that occasion! I had found him quite endearing. I'd watched this man fumble around, not really knowing what to do with me once we had become naked. Should he try to seduce me? He was, how do you say, in my favourite British expression, like a rabbit caught in the headlights; not knowing for the life of him what to do.

I decided to put him out of his misery that night and I took over proceedings, and that's all I am going to tell at this time, except to say that I remember the following morning was very different. A new, confident, Leslie took control of our situation, and the rest I leave to your imagination. But I will tell you this: I hadn't anticipated I'd be having more than only sexual encounters with Leslie. I hadn't anticipated having encounters of the heart.

I recall how later that evening, after I'd left Wivenhoe to return to London, the train's motion had sent me into a sleepy daze. And it was then, as I drifted in and out of consciousness that I suddenly felt some alarm bells ringing inside my head. The Swedish word 'älskar' wouldn't go away.

An altogether alien word to me. Could I have been falling in love? Could that have been possible? I didn't want to be falling in love with Leslie. By the time the train had slowly lurched and screeched its way into the darkness of London's Liverpool Street station, I'd decided that London and my lifestyle were too precious for me to give up. I needed to take a step back from Leslie and keep my distance, regardless of how much I'd come to enjoy his company – and his delicious body. I felt that in some ways it may already be too late. In my heart I wanted to be with him again, but my head said otherwise. That was not the right time for me to get all soppy and sentimental about a man, any man. I was going to have to be strong and forget about Leslie Markland so that I could continue with my life in London just like it had been before. No älskar, thank you very much.

Six months later, I had to make a very serious phone call to Leslie about a very serious matter. Miss Pinchbeck had instructed me to do so as a matter of urgency, following a very distressing phone call from one of our clients by the name of Anna Hennings. Something clearly hadn't been right.

Miss Pinchbeck had called me into her office late one afternoon - her usually pale complexion having turned a few degrees brighter. Anna Hennings had confessed that she had in fact been acting on behalf of a friend, by the name of Mrs. Constance Markland, and that Mrs. Markland had been the true recipient of the self-insemination sperm sample that we'd supplied.

That was bad enough, but there was worse: Constance Markland had recently taken her own life by hanging herself on the back of her bedroom door. How ghastly. How upsetting. How sad. But why? Miss Pinchbeck continued, taking frequent and hurried drags on her cigarette, filling the room with a thick fog that engulfed her entire office. Between gasps on yet another cigarette she explained quickly what she wanted me to find out.

She was unusually passionate as she spoke, and I looked directly at her face as she was talking to me. "Silvie, I want you to use your discretion here, and I know it may be particularly stressful for you to contact Leslie Markland again, but please put your professional hat on and discard your emotional one," she began. "Please find out what the connection is between Leslie and Constance Markland, if there is one at all. Surely, hopefully, I pray it's all just a strange coincidence that their names are the same. Remember, we're dealing with real people here, real lives, and we must not forget that there is now a small young boy at the centre of all this."

Her eyes were bloodshot and the mascara that she rarely wore was half way down her cheeks, combined with the tears that were streaming from her eyes. I really had no idea that she could be so emotional about her work. She went on: "When Anna Hennings phoned me she was extremely insistent that we inform the donor how much the boy means, I mean meant, to her friend, the real mother."

We both knew this was no coincidence, and feared the worst. So I was trembling as I picked up the phone and, with little introduction, made a very difficult call with a very awkward question: "Leslie," I asked him, tentatively, picturing him outside The Station pub near where we last parted with a kiss and an embrace six months previously. "Leslie, does the name Constance Markland mean anything to you?"

"Yes of course," he replied. "Whatever's the matter? She's my sister-in-law. She's married to my brother Stanley, and is the mother of my twin nieces, Hilary and Sophie. They've also recently had a new baby boy called Oliver", he answered, confirming just what I, and Miss Pinchbeck, did not want to hear.

"Leslie," I whispered, taking a deep breath. "I'm afraid I have two pieces of rather disturbing news to tell you. One of them involves your sister-in-law, and the other involves your son."

My mind raced ahead, nervously thinking about how poor Leslie was going to cope with the revelation I was just about to tell him.

Part Two: Leslie Markland

"Where family nightmares come true"

Serving 'time' in prison certainly gave me the opportunity to write this story down and even form quite a good friendship with The Praying Mantis of all people. But, more often than not, my thoughts would turn to the boy I was increasingly beginning to think of as my son.

By the turn of the millennium he'd been getting on for two years old, and I'd been sending money to an account every month to help towards his upbringing. I knew nothing about the lesbian couple in Yorkshire who I believed were bringing the boy up, but I often thought about them and hoped they were doing a good job. The identity of the mother was a complete mystery to me. Although I could have perhaps requested more information, I'd chosen not to, so I only knew, from what Silvie had told me previously, that her name was Anna. And she was bringing up the boy in a same-sex partnership, somewhere in Yorkshire.

Did the boy resemble me? How would he do at school? Hopefully, my financial contribution to his education would help in that respect. Would he have the same interests as me? What would he do when he grows up? Will he ever want to meet me? These were all questions that increasingly began to occupy my thoughts. One thing was for sure: I hoped he would have a happier start in life than I did.

I'd often spend time at The Black Buoy pub, or at The Station's L-shaped bar, nursing a pint of Guinness or enjoying a glass of Merlot, just thinking. Thinking about the little boy who I'd helped to 'create' for this same-sex couple. One day he would become quite a rich young man, thanks to the way my father had drawn up his will. Hah, Father! He'd never seen that coming had he?! Not only that, but I was by then receiving an income enabling me to live very comfortably as well. Thanks Father!

That said, I still believed in having a work ethic, so I continued to paint windows, fix up boats, put up shelves and generally make use of my handyman skills around the village. Work is good for the soul, I always told myself. Not all my time at The Station or The Black Buoy was spent thinking and drinking on my own, though. Sometimes someone would come in and I'd have a chat. Maybe Andy, from whom I'd bought the boat that I'd been gradually working on, and then there was Neil. Neil was the chap who I met when I first arrived in Wivenhoe, who kindly suggested I should find Lynne to see if she'd rent out the barge to me. I liked to buy him a drink whenever I got the chance, and like me, he had a fondness for the red wine. If he wasn't in The Station you could spot him on the quay outside the Rose & Crown, or more likely on his boat that was moored there. Like my barge, his boat never went anywhere, only up and down with the tide. He did have a rather quirky collection of plants and flowers on the deck of his boat, and some would say he was a little eccentric. But the longer I lived in Wivenhoe, the more I realised that many of its inhabitants were indeed a little radical, often influenced by alcohol. Sometimes the place is described as a small drinking village with a large fishing problem. I'd drink to that!

Life wasn't half bad back then. All that changed one evening after I'd finished work. I'd reached the end of a large decorating job. I never minded doing the actual decorating, but I hated doing all the clearing up afterwards. So, after loading the last of my brushes and tools into the back of my small white van and taking an admiring final glance at the work I'd completed, I decided to treat myself to a celebratory drink and a packet of pork scratchings at The Station.

Once there, my mobile telephone vibrated inside my pocket just as I was about to bring the glass to my lips. Damn. This will probably be someone asking when I can go round to look at painting their soffits, or their shed roof that needs re-felting. I saved that first sip of Merlot and stepped outside, keen not to impose my working life on any of the other locals enjoying their first drink of the evening. There's nothing worse than people loudly talking into their mobile telephones in pubs, is there?

"Hello? Hello?" I shouted, trying to compete with the noise of a train as it went through on its way to Clacton-on-Sea. "Hello Leslie, it is Silvie here, calling you from London, from Miss Pinchbeck's Angelpride agency. Remember me? I'm sorry I haven't been to see you again but I thought it best not to do so."

Remember her? Only almost every night since she'd last been here half a year ago! Hearing Silvie's voice again definitely caused some excitement in my heart department. Or was it the loins department? I had tried telephoning her on a few occasions. But sadly she'd always been too busy to take my calls. I knew how to take a hint and eventually ceased trying. However, I was very pleased to hear her voice again one more time. I guess I was still very fond of her.

"Of course I remember you, Silvie. But whatever's the matter? You sound upset," I replied, with genuine concern. And I do mean genuine concern. But there was an abruptness about her voice, mixed with a tinge of anxiety and some sadness too. "Whatever's the matter Silvie?" I asked for a second time.

Then, she went on to say that she wasn't making a personal call, and that she was ringing on behalf of the Angelpride agency. The agency whose motto was 'Where family dreams come true'. Where family nightmares come true was more the case, as it would eventually turn out. Questions about my sister-in-law? What on earth was she trying to tell me?

At that moment all I could hear was the thunderous roar of a train, as I battled to hear what she was trying to say to me.

"You'll have to shout, Silvie, I can't hear you. What did you just say?" I bellowed down the phone line. But it was too late. The phone line finally gave up its weak signal and cut out.

CHAPTER 26

The Arrival of Miss Baudet

"All these years I'd been drinking tea without sugar"

Part One: Stanley Markland (2000)

It had already been a peculiar day by the time I came home to find that Constance had killed herself. The previous night she and I had had a real heart-to-heart, and I'd confessed to her about my extra-marital affair. Understandably upset after I'd suggested we think about separating, she calmly went to bed, and I'd gone round to get some comfort from Tristan, after what had become quite an emotionally draining conversation. At breakfast the following morning Tristan and I had been discussing our future plans together, now that Constance knew all about our relationship. The subject of Oliver had come up. Tristan, who was quite astute, pointed out something that I had been a little slow to recognise. "You do realise that he's going to inherit his share of the estate before your twins get theirs, don't you?"

The following day I drove back home and turned into the gravelled drive that led up to the Manor house, and even from the road I could make out the flashing of blue lights reflecting against the walls of the house in the distance. Clearly something was very wrong, and as I approached the building I counted no fewer than six vehicles, including one ambulance and two police cars. I wasn't sure who the other three cars belonged to, but it wasn't long before it became obvious. One belonged to a reporter from the local Gazette, who immediately started to approach me, until a policewoman stood in his way. The second, an old Corsa, I recognised as being Constance's friend Anna's. I didn't know whose the third was.

My heart began pounding and my head began to spin. It was as if I were watching a film in slow motion and I began wondering why on earth all the vehicles were parked randomly in all kinds of positions, so that they were boxed in by each other - just like they are in American police TV dramas. It was funny, in a peculiar sort of way, how the mind reacts to unusual and stressful situations: it was totally illogical for me to be thinking certain thoughts, and yet logical at the same time. As I walked towards my front door in a daze with my heart thumping, the ambulance reversed to manoeuvre out of its boxed-in position and began setting off down the drive. It was being driven quite slowly, and its flashing lights were turned off half way towards the gates. Why was that? Surely, if someone had been taken ill or had had an accident, they should be racing away as quickly as possible. The woman police officer came up to me and asked me to confirm my name, and she then proceeded to tell me that she had some bad news for me, and that I should come inside the house.

I will always remember that awful evening. The policewoman sat me down in the hallway and quietly told me that Constance was dead. "How?" I blurted out in shock. She hesitated at first before going on to explain that my wife had killed herself by attaching one of her scarves to the hook on the back of the bedroom door, allowing herself to hang from it until she had passed out and died from asphyxiation. Thank goodness it hadn't been me making the grisly discovery, as I know the image would have haunted me forever. Anna had been the one to find her there. Anna Hennings had probably been Constance's best friend for a number of years, and she was understandably distraught when I was led into the kitchen where she was sitting at the dining table.

Apparently, Anna had come to the house to return Oliver from toddler group. This had been a regular arrangement for a while, enabling Constance to catch up on some much needed sleep while the twins were at school. I knew that Constance had been a bit down recently, but this? What a fool I'd been, so wrapped up in my own life with Tristan, never realising what she had been going through. The feeling of guilt is a strange emotion if you are inflicted with it. It's impossible to relieve yourself of it, and I knew I never would.

There had been so much to take in. So many random thoughts, all at the same time. Where was the journalist from the Gazette? His car was no longer there, so he must have left. Where were the twins? Apparently they were upstairs in their room being taken care of by a specialist bereavement counsellor. I was told that this lady was an expert when a parent had committed suicide. I hadn't realised there even existed such a person. She would be staying at the house to take care of things for me until they settled down. And what about Oliver? Where was he? As it turned out, he was fast asleep in his bedroom, thankfully oblivious to all that was going on around him. There had been one other thing – another random thought. What I was going to have for dinner later? I'd hardly eaten all day, and I couldn't help feeling faint with hunger, believe it or not.

I wanted to call Tristan so much, but I knew he was on his way to London. I'd have to wait and call him later in private. I so wanted him to be with me and make everything better.

I finished my cup of tea that had been made for Anna and me by the policewoman, and I remember thinking how much I enjoyed it. All these years I'd been drinking tea without sugar, and now with the policewoman putting in two spoonfuls without asking, it transformed it entirely. So much so that I even asked for another one. There! That was another random thought strangely manifesting itself under the duress of those terrible circumstances.

But thoughts about sugar in my tea quickly came to an abrupt and sudden end. Anna had been sitting opposite me saying nothing up to that point, obviously in a state of understandable shock. And then she looked up from the cup of tea she had been clutching tightly with both hands, and began to speak with a shaky voice. Not about discovering Constance's body, but something equally shocking.

"Oliver is not your son," Anna said softly. She looked down and repeated her words. "Oliver is not your son."

I thought she had gone completely mad, until she calmly and quietly continued, describing all the details of what she and Constance had done, and how I'd been tricked into believing that I'd fathered Oliver. It was all too much for me to take in, and I felt an additional emotion on top of all the others. On top of the guilt, the confusion, the sadness, the worry, I was now angry, and I told the woman in no uncertain terms to leave the house before my anger got the better of me.

She began sobbing, and the policewoman accompanied her to her car. I could see through the kitchen window that they were talking together next to her Corsa before she got in and drove off down the graveled drive. It was dark by then, and I remembered noticing that one of her brake lights wasn't working and that she ought to get it fixed soon. Another random thought. I suppose my brain was compensating for such a massive blow to the system by focusing on such a trivial thing.

Initially that evening I didn't believe what Anna had told me about Oliver. I really did think that she had lost the plot. But she had explained everything so matter-of-factly that I couldn't deny her story was plausible. It wasn't until several weeks later that the true identity of Oliver's real father was proven. That was after the inquest had taken place, and the funeral too.

Pulling myself together, I realised I needed to concentrate on the immediate crisis at hand. I went upstairs to see the twins and Oliver.

First I looked in at Oliver as he lay sleeping soundly in his small bed that we'd bought from Ikea. Despite their reputation, if you follow the instructions and prepare all the parts exactly as they're shown on the drawings, putting the furniture together is plain sailing, or 'a piece of cake' as my father would have said. Why was I thinking about flat-pack furniture at such a time, or Anna's brake light, or sugar in tea? Oh, how I wished I could have had Tristan with me to make some sense of it all. Instead, I had a policewoman who made nice tea, and a temporary nanny to help look after the children. And by now, on top of everything, I was starving.

As I entered the twins' bedroom, I was greeted silently by a lady in her sixties who immediately put her forefinger to her lips, and whose eyes directed me to the twins' beds. The girls' eyes were closed but they briefly opened as I leant over to kiss them lightly on their heads.

"Daddy, we're glad you're home now. Mummy did a very stupid thing didn't she?" whispered Sophie. I didn't answer, but turned to Hilary to kiss her as well.

"You're better off without her now, aren't you?" she mumbled as sleep finally won the battle that she'd been fighting.

Shocked and surprised, I nevertheless whispered back under my breath so I couldn't be heard: "Yes, I guess I am Hilary. I guess I am."

As I exited the room, along with the counsellor, closing the door quietly behind me, I experienced yet another powerful emotion - shame.

Miss Alberta Louise Baudet introduced herself to me after we'd quietly tip-toed downstairs. The policewoman was still there but was ready to leave, and we both said goodbye to her. It occurred to me that she probably earned as much in a month doing her very demanding job as I do in some days. I thanked her, and she told me that she would probably see me again at the inquest if not before. Apparently an inquest is quite normal under such circumstances, and I knew it would be an uncomfortable day to endure.

"Nobody can die in this country without it being formally recorded, Mr.

Markland," she said as she opened the door to leave. "That's something we all have to be thankful for."

What an odd thing to say, I thought to myself, but I suppose she was right.

Miss Baudet sat down at the table. I liked her immediately. Guessing she was in her late fifties, I could tell that she took great pride in her appearance. Immaculately turned out, her fine fair hair was tied up neatly in a bun and her woollen dress-suit gave her a distinct air of respectability. She had a calming quality and I was grateful that she was there to help look after the children.

I don't think I could have managed on my own and I hoped that she could stay for more than just that night. She told me that she'd already made herself comfortable in one of the spare bedrooms, that I wasn't to worry about anything, and that it was her job to do the worrying for me. Yes, I did like her and I felt safe in her company. Perhaps she could stay beyond tomorrow.

On the cream-coloured American-style refrigerator door I noticed there was an envelope with 'LASAGNE RECIPE' written on it in Constance's handwriting. That was odd, I thought, as she never follows cooking instructions, preferring to make things up as she goes along – usually, I have to say, with excellent results. I was expecting to find something describing how to make béchamel sauce.

Shockingly, a suicide note was not what I expected. I quickly read the contents before returning the letter to its envelope and into my back pocket.

"Would you like some lasagne, Miss Baudet?" I asked. "I believe we have some in here that my wife prepared earlier."

"What I saw chilled me to the core"

Part Two: Alberta Louise Baudet

"My mummy's dead", said the first girl.

"My mummy's dead too," added the second girl, straight away, as if competing for the attention and concern that I was showing.

I'd been a qualified child minder with many years' experience, but for the past 18 months I had a particular specialisation in looking after bereaved children, especially where suicide of a parent was involved.

When called by the police I'd been asked to go as soon as possible to the Markland Estate at Saxton, to take care of two young children who had returned home after school, with 'home' being the scene of their mother's suicide. It was something I had to take in my stride as, unfortunately, I had dealt with quite a few similar cases during my career. My credentials for such a job? Capable and formidable, I'd like to think that I possessed a no-nonsense presence but with an extremely kind and compassionate side. My friends always encouraged the mischievous and fun side of my personality, an important trait when you remember some of the traumatic cases I sometimes had to deal with.

When I drove up to the Markland Estate that day, a place I had driven past many times before but never imagined would become one of my call-outs, I hadn't yet been informed of all the facts. All the police had told me was that I was to take care of a young boy and twin girls about five years old who had been dropped off at home by one of the other mothers from their school. The seriousness of the situation hit me soon after I arrived. What had been more than unusual was the fact that the girls had been found playing in their bedroom while their mother had been hanging on the back of the door just across the landing. They must have realised that their mother was there, as the mother's bedroom door was open and there was a full length mirror on the opposite wall, clearly reflecting the whole grizzly sight to anyone who went past.

I had noticed that Hilary tended to have an instinctive dominance over her sister, with Sophie never questioning her sibling. My knowledge of twin behavioural characteristics led me to assume that Hilary had been the first out of the womb. I later learned that my assumption had been correct. Sophie was indeed younger than Hilary by all of two and a half minutes, but those seconds were enough for them to form their specific relationship with each other.

After being briefed by the policewoman who was already in the house, I went upstairs to the girls' bedroom, expecting to find an emotionally draining scene. I might have expected to discover two children wailing and screaming, or at the very least, simply crying their little hearts out. But no, it was as if they weren't at all bothered by what had happened. I was very surprised at just how quiet they were, except for their giggling and chuckling as I entered the room. That was most odd.

They say young children can be very resilient and can take almost anything in their stride. These twins appeared to be no exception. Sophie and Hilary simply continued playing on the floor over at the far side of the room, next to the large dolls house. They looked up at me as I said hello, gave a false smile, and went back to playing their game. Their bedroom was larger than the entire area of an average semi-detached house. The size of the room meant that I wasn't quite able to see what toys the girls were playing with until I walked across the room and got closer. What I saw chilled me to the core. Both the girls were holding Barbie dolls, with tiny scarves wrapped around the dolls' necks. The other ends had been tied around the chimney pots on the rooftop of the model house. They were taking it in turns to hold the dolls up against the side of the wall and then dropping them to watch how they dangled and bounced around. This clearly amused them immensely, judging by the little giggles that were coming from both of them. At the time I didn't know them well enough to distinguish one twin from the other, but I remember every moment of my first meeting with them with horror.

"My mummy's dead now," said Hilary, without looking up. "So's my mummy too," said Sophie, who slowly turned to me with a broad grin across her face.

CHAPTER 27

Silvie Drops a Bombshell

*"It would have made a decent black comedy if it
hadn't all been so tragic"*

Leslie Markland

I'd tried telephoning Silvie back straight away after we'd been cut off yesterday, but the signal for my mobile telephone was too weak. As a result I had even tried the public box in the High Street to make a land-line call to her office, only to discover a blue notice stuck to one of the glass panes: '*This call-box no longer accepts coins and is operated by payment cards only*'. That's progress for you. I didn't possess a bank card, and I hoped I never would. I still don't trust the banks to look after my money at the best of times. It wasn't until the next day that all was revealed.

Sometimes I took Harry with me on my jobs, especially if I was working locally and could easily pop back to the barge during the day. Harry enjoyed scampering around in front of me as I trundled along with my teak tool-chest-on-wheels to the premises of whichever customer was employing me for that day. He would leap up and down like a yo-yo during the short journey, but then settle down and be happy to lay in the sunshine as I proceeded with the task in hand. It was the day after I'd received that telephone call from Silvie: The one that I couldn't hear properly.

During that troublesome telephone call I thought I'd heard Silvie saying something about news concerning my sister-in-law, but I couldn't have heard her correctly, could I? I mean, why on earth would Silvie, of all people, have anything to do with Constance? Surely, I must have misheard her, but it did lead me to wonder how Stanley, the girls and the new baby Oliver were getting along. It made me think that perhaps I ought to go and visit them at some point, maybe when I was less busy.

It was around midday and Harry and I went back to the boat, as we would often do, for our snacks, with me collecting the post before climbing aboard. I would usually make a sandwich, and he would have some scraps left over from my previous evening's meal, mixed in with some Winalot biscuits. He really liked those, and used to bounce around with eager anticipation as I'd fill up his bowl and place it on the floor next to my chair. I sat down with my sandwich on a plate, tea at my side and Harry at my feet, and opened the mail.

There was a letter from the bank offering me a credit card. No thanks. There was one from a company offering me decorative stone cladding for the side of my house. Why didn't they research these things before wasting their stamps? There was one from my mobile telephone company informing me that I owed them £15.19. And then there was one from Ainsworth & Co.

My mouth dropped open in complete shock. It informed me of the sudden death of my sister-in-law Constance Markland. Even though I'd hardly known the woman, having met her only when I'd been up to the Manor house for the twin girls' naming thing, and of course Father's funeral, I was very saddened by this bad news. She was, at the end of the day, a family member, and she was also my brother's wife, and mother to three young children, what with Oliver being their latest addition.

And then I remembered again about Silvie's telephone call to me the previous day. I was highly confused. I couldn't for the life of me work out what the connection was, if any, but I knew I had to find out.

It was hard to think who to try calling first. Over the years I'd become quite content to hear any family news from either my mother in America, or through Ainsworth & Co if it was something of a legal nature. Should I telephone Brian Ainsworth, who had written me the letter? No I decided, I didn't like him and didn't want to talk to him. If the news had come from his father Roger it would have been an entirely different matter and I would have picked up the telephone to call him instantly. Stanley? No, I was embarrassed to talk with Stanley for the time being, not knowing really what I should or could say to him under those awkward circumstances. Granted, he hadn't been my favourite person in the world, but when all was said and done he was my brother, wasn't he, and he had just lost his wife. For a brief moment, I even contemplated telephoning my mother over in America. Whenever I'd previously called, usually when it was her birthday, I really enjoyed talking to her. However, I was aware that she'd be seven or eight hours behind our time, so it would have been too early in the morning for her to get an unsettling telephone call from me. So I settled on telephoning Silvie for now; to find out what she'd been trying to tell me the previous day.

My mobile telephone connection was thankfully better today, and the signal was good. Four bars! The direct number I had for her got me straight through and she answered in a cheerful voice, which immediately changed tone the moment she heard who was calling.

"Hello Silvie, it's me, Leslie," I began nervously. "I'm so sorry about the mess up with the telephone signal yesterday. How are you? What's going on? What had you been trying to tell me yesterday before the line cut out?"

Calmly and quietly, she responded to my barrage of questions. "Leslie, I need to tell you of a terrible mistake that has occurred that affects you very directly."

I listened numbly as Silvie continued. She went on to tell me how the Angelpride agency had indirectly and unknowingly supplied my sperm sample to Constance Markland. Incredibly, it had been my brother's wife who had received my sperm donation, and not Anna Hennings as had been thought by the agency. Anna, she told me, was Constance's best friend, and had passed on my sample to her, and Constance was the one who got pregnant with it. And now she was dead. Constance had decided to kill herself when things all became too much.

What? How? My head was in a spin. This was all too much to take in. My mobile telephone fell from my hand and landed in Harry's Winalot, where it remained for at least an hour. I just sat there, completely still and frozen in my chair, going over what Silvie had told me. She'd said the boy's name was Oliver. Stanley and Constance's new addition was called Oliver. So, it was my brother Stanley who was now bringing up *my* son as *his*, and as far as I knew he was none the wiser about me being the biological father. Bloody hell! What a mess! What a complete farce. It would have made a decent black comedy if it hadn't all been so tragic.

Despite that devastating conversation with Silvie, I couldn't be angry with her or, for that matter, Miss Pinchbeck's agency, or Anna Hennings, or Constance. It was a bizarre set of circumstances that could have happened to anyone, couldn't it? Well, no, I suppose it probably couldn't, but who could I blame? Me! I was just as guilty as the rest. I should never have embarked on this ridiculous quest for revenge against Father. I recalled Mr. Brennan, my old physics O'level teacher, lecturing me at school. "*For every action, there is an equal and opposite reaction*". How right he was.

Having gathered my thoughts together and wiping the remnants of Harry's dinner off the telephone, I called Silvie back.

This time she offered me some words of comfort. Firstly, she emphasised what Constance had said in a letter to her friend Anna; asking Anna to ensure that Oliver's real father understood and appreciated how much she loved her son, and that secondly Constance was very grateful to whoever the sperm donor was for what he'd done. That was why Anna had phoned Miss Pinchbeck and why Silvie had then tried to call me. It was all beginning to make some sense to me. Well, sort of.

I took the plunge and asked Silvie if I could see her again. No one knew my predicament better than Silvie, and I could imagine what comfort it would be to have her wrap her arms around me.

There was a pause before she responded. "I often think about you Leslie, and I would be, how do you say, tickled pink. However..." She paused again and I recall thinking that she needed some guidance on the use of English expressions. "...However, I am sorry to say that I can't. Something has happened and I will be going back to spend time with my family in Sweden soon. I don't know if I'll ever be coming back." She then clearly tried her best to end things on a positive note. "But I will always be thinking of you Leslie, I promise you that." I thought I detected a wobble in her voice and I wondered whether I meant as much to her as she did to me. I got my answer. "I love you," she said, before hanging up.

Oh my goodness. I slumped back in my chair again. How much more emotional trauma could a man take?

After stunned reflection following Silvie's declaration of love, the next telephone call I made was to Stanley. I wasn't looking forward to it, but I knew that I must speak to him. Unsurprisingly, it was initially a very uncomfortable experience. We hadn't seen or spoken to each other for around five years, and he received my call coldly. After offering my condolences for his loss, with trepidation I began to repeat to him what Silvie had told me about Oliver.

To say he didn't take it too well was an understatement: "Look, you conniving little fucking liar. I don't know what your game is, but for fuck's sake, I've just lost my wife and now you're giving me this crap. What have I done to you to deserve this? Huh? Why are you twisting the knife like this? What you're telling me is horrific. I don't know how you've got the gall. I don't believe a word of it. Go to hell!" he yelled at the top of his voice.

And with that he slammed the phone down. And yet he hadn't actually cut us off. In his anger he must have thought he'd rested the phone back on its cradle properly, but instead I could still hear everything that was going on there. To begin with I could hear him making a noise like an elephant in labour. If it wasn't all so serious it would have been funny. Then I heard him shouting and swearing with a string of every expletive I knew existed. I suppose I shouldn't have been surprised by his reaction. After all, he must have been mortified by the news I'd just given him, on top of his raw bereavement as well.

But then I heard what sounded like a door opening, followed by footsteps on a hard floor and then a woman's voice. "Stanley, why don't you sit down my dear, and I'll bring you a nice cup of tea?" She spoke in a soothing voice. Who was she, I wondered? "Alright, Louise, that's a good idea", Stanley said. "That was my f-ing brother, trying to get his own back on me"

Who on earth was Louise? A couple of minutes went by and all I could hear were a few knocks and bangs. And then there were more footsteps, when presumably 'Louise' re-entered the room with Stanley's cup of tea. "Why don't you call your brother back now and talk things through with him?" she said. "But drink this first. It will calm you down." Whoever this 'Louise' was, she was certainly doing a remarkable job of bringing Stanley off the ceiling.

I heard the sound of crockery clanging, and then footsteps becoming louder. "Oh shit!" I heard, followed by "Leslie? Are you there?" as the telephone was picked up again.

Luckily, Stanley listened again to my story, this time calmly enough for us to have a rational conversation. Although I fell short of making an apology for what had happened, I agreed with him that it was a ridiculous scenario, and I told him that I wished it wasn't true. I also agreed with him that I couldn't offer any proof that in fact it was true – it was only what I'd been told by Silvie. While he was digesting the facts an idea popped into my head. Although he initially resisted my suggestion of having a DNA test, he eventually conceded that it would be a way of establishing beyond doubt who Oliver's biological father was. He finally agreed, and thank goodness he did.

That test would go on to prove I was indeed Oliver's father. Thank goodness Stanley and I were able to come to an agreement about Oliver's upbringing. It could so easily have become so very, very nasty between him and me, and I was so very, very grateful that it hadn't.

CHAPTER 28

If Truth Be Told

"The shit, as they say, well and truly stuck to the fan"

Part One: Stanley Markland (2000)

Constance had only been dead for a day. The situation was all so surreal. Miss Baudet and I consumed Constance's lasagne in a silence, only broken when we respectfully raised our glasses of Sandemans Port in memory of her. I instinctively knew that I felt comfortable in Miss Baudet's presence and hoped she could stay on longer. After dinner we were so exhausted that we both excused ourselves from each other's company and headed off to our respective bedrooms. I rested my head on the pillow before I'd even washed or cleaned my teeth and fell into an instant deep sleep.

Incidentally, the lasagne dinner - the one that Constance had so thoughtfully left in the fridge for me before taking her own life - was incredibly delicious. It had been a heartbreaking last gesture of hers.

The following morning we were both up at the crack of dawn and found ourselves together again in the kitchen. Despite the events of the previous day, I was alert and refreshed and had a proposal: "May I ask you Miss Baudet, or may I please call you Alberta, how much you would normally expect to earn as a registered child-minder specialising in this type of work?" I knew it was an impertinent question, but it was one that I needed to ask.

"Please, Stanley, call me by my middle name, Louise," she began, before obligingly informing me that she only made a bare living, amounting to less than a couple of hundred pounds a week if she were lucky. By her own admission, she was constantly juggling her credit cards and swapping between various interest-free transfer offers, if she could find them. I then made her an offer she couldn't refuse.

Having already seen enough of her capability in dealing with my crisis, I took the plunge. Out of necessity, and a degree of desperation, I set out my hastily arranged plan: "Louise, how about you come and be here, full-time - at least until things settle down - to take care of the twins and Oliver, and become their nanny and my housekeeper?" Without hesitating I continued, "I will pay you five times what you're currently earning, you can live here rent-free, and I will also pay off your card debts."

Despite the big upheaval this would mean in her life, I hoped she wouldn't say no. Thankfully she didn't. We shook hands, and that was the end of the shortest job interview I'd ever given.

Next I called Tristan to explain why I wouldn't be able to meet him for lunch in London, as had been previously arranged. If his brain had been a clock, I could have heard it ticking all the way down the phone line as he digested the contents of my conversation about what had happened yesterday after I'd gone home from his place. He was wonderfully sympathetic, and I couldn't wait to see him again as soon as possible, but I knew that would have to wait for the time being while I sorted some things out at home.

No sooner had I put the phone down from him than I received an extraordinary phone call from my brother Leslie. He'd heard about Constance's death and he began with his condolences. But then he went on to say some things that were so unbelievably hurtful that I'm afraid I blew my top with him.

With the help of Miss Baudet's cup of tea, I eventually managed to calm down and agree I should do something with Leslie. I wanted to put him in his place once and for all, and I was positive that the results from a DNA test would show Leslie to be the liar that I was by then convinced he was. But I couldn't understand his motive for claiming that he had a son in the first place. Let alone that it was Oliver.

A few days later we met at the place that would show Leslie's ridiculous claims to be unfounded. I arrived at the hospital with a tiny lock of Oliver's hair in a small polythene bag. During the tests, Leslie and I hardly spoke a word, rather like the time when we had met at Roger Ainsworth's office for our father's will reading. And then it dawned on me. Of course! This was all to do with that will!

The nurse who took our blood said we'd get the results during the following week. We left the hospital and parted company, attempting to be as cordial to each other as we could.

Then, six days later, I simply couldn't believe it! The results came through from the tests, and the shit, as they say, had well and truly hit the fan. Unbelievably, Oliver as it turned out, was in fact Leslie's son! My brother's ludicrous story was true.

But Oli, as I called him, was part of the family. My family. He was coming along very well, and now with the help of Alberta Louise Baudet as his nanny, I had high expectations that he would continue to grow up happily at the Manor house. With dread, I then second-guessed that Leslie's next move would be to suggest Oli go and live with him, and initially that was exactly what happened.

I couldn't let him go, could I? What sort of life could my brother offer him, living on board a boat in Essex? Apart from whatever was going on between Tristan and me, Oliver would surely be far better off being brought up properly instead of living like a gipsy on a floating caravan.

To my surprise, for the sake of the little boy, good sense eventually prevailed and Leslie dropped any further talk about the custody of, shall we say, 'our' son, and we agreed that I would look after him as if he were mine. Well, that was, at least until he reached the age of 15, by which time 'our' boy would be old enough to decide for himself where he wanted to live and what he'd like to do with his life.

We agreed that, for the time being, Leslie would remain 'Uncle Leslie' to Oliver on birthday and Christmas cards and at any subsequent family gatherings, unlikely as they were to occur. Leslie and I would do our best to remain civil to one another, although as you can imagine we were not the best of buddies. Thankfully however, we were both thinking about how we should do what was best for Oli. We decided, rightly or wrongly, to let him continue believing that I was his dad, Leslie was his uncle, and Hilary and Sophie were his sisters.

In the aftermath of her tragic death, I missed Constance terribly. Despite my affair with Tristan, Constance had been my wife, the mother of my gorgeous twin girls, and the mother of my, er, stepson. Of course I worried how things would work out with three children losing their mother, but I couldn't help having a feeling of cautious optimism about the future, whatever that future would hold in store for me - for Tristan and me. The children presented the biggest concern.

How would the relationship between the girls and Oliver develop? Even at Oli's young age I could tell they were clearly worlds apart in their mannerisms and temperament. I would simply have to wait and see.

Part Two: Tristan Thomas
"All this was enough to make anyone's head spin"

For some time now I had been paying over £300 a month to an offshore bank account somewhere, belonging to a person or persons who had known about what Stanley had only just found out. I had been paying the money, along with a one-off initial sum that I had to borrow from a friend from the London club Abacco's that I frequented, in order to protect both me, and Stanley. The last thing I needed was to be associated with a situation involving surrogate mothers, sperm donors, mixed up pregnancies and mistaken identities. The very slightest hint that I was involved in some sex scandal involving a child would have meant the end of my political career. At the same time I cared deeply about how Stanley may have been affected if he ever became aware of what I knew.

I had already known about Stanley not being Oliver's real father when he phoned to tell me about Constance's suicide. I'd always prayed that Stanley would never find out the truth about Oliver's parentage. I thought it could destroy him, especially as I could see how his relationship with Oliver had been developing. Stanley had been oblivious to the fact that he wasn't the natural father of the little boy. The truth, I thought, would have been hard enough for him to stomach, but if he ever discovered who the real father was, well, I simply didn't want to think about that. I imagined what his reaction would have been, thinking that his brother had had intimate relations with Constance. But of course, at least that part hadn't been the case.

How on earth a London agency dealing in such matters could have messed up so badly astonished me. This type of thing really needed regulating and governing more strictly, I thought, and perhaps it was an area I could look into in the future, if I were ever in a political position to do so. However, for now I was being forced to deal with the whole business a lot closer to home than I would have liked.

Stanley's Constance had killed herself, and that was tragic news for Stanley and the children, and bad news for me. I dare say that the state of her mind must have been affected when Stanley confessed to her about our relationship. Perhaps she'd been convinced that Stanley was eventually going to leave her for me, and that might have tipped her over the edge, especially, I guess, if her mind was already unstable. What with that, and how those twin girls were misbehaving towards her, according to Stanley, it must have been awful for her. But to feel bad enough to hang herself in her own bedroom? That had played very heavily on my mind.

I predicted then that the secret I'd been keeping from Stanley about him not being Oliver's father was bound to come out one day. I didn't know what was going to be worse - the actual fact of the matter, or that I had also known the truth but had chosen to keep quiet about it. I hoped that if Stanley did ever find out that I knew, he would forgive me because of the tremendous pressure I found myself under to avoid being mixed up in such a scandal.

After Constance had died, Stanley told me about the call he'd received from his brother Leslie. I decided to play it cool and act surprised. I mustered up all my acting skills and responded in a suitably shocked manner. Stanley, the dear love, had his head spinning in a whirl as it was, and he didn't need to further discover that I'd already known about everything all along. I opted for damage limitation, and simply listened and comforted him in the way I knew best.

It was eventually proven who Oliver's real biological father was. With the help of the live-in nanny, who by all accounts was turning into a real godsend, the two brothers agreed that the youngster was better off growing up at the Manor house. Leslie insisted on continuing to pay maintenance for the boy - even though Stanley had made it clear it wasn't necessary. I'd been convinced that his motive for having a surrogate child was so that he would come into some money. How disgraceful, I'd thought, creating another human life for that reason! But maybe Stanley's brother was a conscientious man after all.

And speaking of money, now that the whole story had come out into the open, there was less pressure on me to keep paying three hundred-odd pounds every month to the offshore bank account. I had told Stanley that I needed that money for some 'personal reasons' and he, bless him, had been willing to help me without asking for further details.

I decided that I would continue to pay the blackmail money for now, so as not to rock any boats unnecessarily. I needed time to work out my strategy and what was going to be for the best. But it did occur to me how bizarre and ironic the whole farce had become: Leslie had been paying child maintenance to a friend of Constance, who was in turn paying it into Constance's and Stanley's joint account, and Stanley was in turn lending it to me so that I could keep my anonymous blackmailer quiet about Stanley's brother being Oliver's real father! All this was enough to make anyone's head spin. It certainly did mine.

Thankfully, and perhaps surprisingly, things settled down into a routine and my relationship with Stanley became stronger than ever over the months and years following Constance's death. We were clearly meant for each other, and I believed we would always be together. But while my career was on the up and up, I didn't really wish for all and sundry to know my business and my connections with The Markland Affair, as I called it, so I kept my head down and carried on as best as I could.

CHAPTER 29

Giving it All Away

"It had been as if a light bulb had suddenly been switched on inside my head"

Leslie Markland

The first part of my story is just about done. Checking my watch, I see that Oliver will be visiting soon, and I am enormously looking forward to seeing him, as usual.

When Oliver had been growing up thinking that Stanley was his real father, of course I was worried that he may not want to associate with me if and when he learned the truth, which I knew he would inevitably do at some point during his life. I hoped that he'd forgive me, in the same way in which I'd forgiven my mother for having upped and left to live in America. I wouldn't have blamed him if he hadn't though, but I always hoped for the best, and luckily the best happened.

There had been many occasions when I'd be sitting at The Black Buoy or The Station's L-shaped bar, mulling over what I'd done; being responsible for bringing a new life into this world and into the Markland family, and wrestling with my conscience. I often tried drowning out my remorseful emotions with a whole bottle of The Station's rather good Merlot. In his teens, when he eventually visited me in Wivenhoe for the first time, Oliver accepted things for what they were with a degree of understanding that was mature far beyond his young years. And I don't like to use the word 'drowning' too loosely, as it had been the drowning of the twins that got me in here, in prison, in the first place.

My cellmate, The Praying Mantis - dear Mark Mantis - has been a tremendous sounding board for me. Sitting on the floor, cross-legged and with his hands clasped together, he'd listen while I read him my latest few pages each evening prior to lights out. I tried telling him to keep his voice down when he asked me to read. I was afraid one of the warders might overhear and demand to read what I'd written. After all, I was afraid that some of what I'd scribbled down so far could incriminate me, just like in that old black and white movie *Kind Hearts and Coronets* starring Alec Guinness. Remember the movie's main character? He had been writing a book in prison, explaining how he'd gotten away with murder. When he'd been let off on some technicality, the film ended with the look of horror on his face as he walked away as a free man, only to remember that he'd left his manuscript behind. Those confessions would have been enough to have had him hanged.

Well, I'm not going to do anything as stupid as that, not that I'm in here for murder, you understand. But I nearly could have been, had it not been for Roger Ainsworth's help.

Dear old Roger. He'd been the family solicitor since I was a child, until he retired and the firm Ainsworth & Co was then being run by his son Brian. Brian was a dodgy character if ever there was one, and apart from those early years after Oliver had been born, I decided to have no further contact with him. He was not like his father, who was genuinely concerned for his clients. No, with Brian he always looked on his clients as people he would try to extract the maximum amount of money from.

I'm sure that he was somehow mixed up in the business involving myself, Stanley and 'our' son Oliver, and my maintenance payments. Had he been operating beyond the scope of legitimate legalities involving our affairs? I will make it my business to get some answers after I get out of here and settle back into normal life.

Can my life ever be normal again? As I said, it was thankfully due to Roger Ainsworth that I can even consider that question. Had it not been for him agreeing to come out of retirement for one last case - mine - then I'm sure I would have been looking at a much longer sentence than the one that was eventually handed down to me. I was convinced that it was only Roger, with his full knowledge of the whole Markland history and, in particular, my position in it, who could help me, and I know that Roger went to considerable efforts on my behalf. For one thing, his background had been in conveyancing, probate and employment law, not criminal defence of a man suspected of manslaughter. Why he agreed to help me I don't know, but I am very grateful that he did. Perhaps he had a guilty conscience, suspecting that his son was a bit of a dodgy dealer, and he wanted to make amends as far as the Marklands were concerned. Everything could so easily have turned out very differently, but for Roger's involvement.

While I'm waiting for Oliver I still have enough time to fill in some gaps. Let me quickly let you know how I turned my life around in Wivenhoe, with the help of Paul McCartney – yes Paul McCartney. It was one of life's eureka moments.

I had been sitting silently in my chair on my boat Barnacle when Harry had jumped up onto my lap as if to comfort me. He could tell I needed some company. As well as enjoying his presence, I put some music on. Not wishing to let go of him I carried him over to where the stereo was, and randomly selected Paul McCartney and Wings' *Band On The Run*. I returned to slump in the chair feeling a concoction of various emotions and a feeling of emptiness and lack of direction about my own life. I hadn't found religion, unlike my present day cellmate Praying Mantis. I hadn't found my meaning to life. I was feeling mixed up. I was drifting: until the music began. Great lyrics, I thought. Then it dawned on me that maybe I could copy the sentiments expressed in the song, now that some of the income from the Markland estate was by then winging its way to me, if you'll excuse the pun!

So, when I heard the words *"If I ever get out of here"* being sung by arguably the most successful and famous musician on the planet, I was inspired to consider putting some of my new-found wealth to good use, to help others less fortunate than myself.

"Thought of giving it all away" - well maybe not quite all of it, as I ought to be prudent about the future oughtn't I? But I could at least afford to give a fair chunk of it away - that was for sure.

'All I need is a pint a day': That pretty well summed me up, I'd say. Father would never in a million years have even considered doing anything so noble.

Giving some of his money away *'to a registered charity'*? For him it was always about keeping it for himself, to pay for his fast cars and fast women, the selfish, greedy, old bastard.

The music had enormously improved my mood. "Thanks for the inspiration Paul," I said out loud.

I was by then receiving a percentage of the Estate's wealth, with money from the farmland being transferred monthly into my bank by the estate's accountants. Despite distrusting banks, every now and again I would venture into Colchester town centre to my local branch and check out my balance. Although I'd insisted on paying regularly towards Oliver's maintenance and education, I was still accruing thousands of pounds that in practice I didn't really need. After all, I was very comfortable living on the Barnacle barge, and that hardly cost me a lot - only a small amount in mooring fees to the chap who I referred to as Del Boy. I always had a few bills to pay on keeping Alfonso going, my old Fiat, as well as the tiny van I used for my handyman jobs, but they didn't amount to much.

Basically, as long as I had enough cash left over at the end of the week for my Guinness or Merlot at the Black Buoy or the L-shaped bar in The Station, I was feeling pretty content at long last. Life was finally beginning to feel not so bad, on the financial front at least. The wounds from my earlier life growing up on the Markland estate were finally beginning to heal. It was only my conscience about Oliver that sometimes got me down.

Back then, when I was living freely on the barge and listening to Band On The Run, I could never have predicted how the words 'If I ever get out of here' could have ended up becoming so profound and relevant to my subsequent position, here in prison.

As I now glance out of the cell window at a cloudless sky, I can clearly remember the morning on the barge when, with a fresh feeling of enthusiasm following my decision to give to charity, I had woken up feeling much more positive than I'd ever felt before. From that moment onwards I decided I would look positively to the future and stop reflecting on the past. It had been as if a light bulb had suddenly been switched on inside my head. I decided that I would try to find a way of doing some good with my life and my money, and I would certainly try to be a good father to Oliver. He deserved only the best from me, and I just hoped that my efforts wouldn't be too little too late. I remember hoping that maybe one day he might even become proud of me.

Up until that day my mind and life had been cloudy and without a clear focus. It was a eureka moment, if ever there was one! I had family. Firstly, of course, there was Oliver, who only knew of me as his uncle, but I certainly knew of him as my son, and I thought about him daily. Secondly there was my mother, who was living across there in America. I tried visualising her from the few photographs she'd sent me over the years. I would definitely visit her one day and maybe mend her broken fly-screen, if indeed it still needed fixing. I decided I should write her a letter and tell her all about Oliver. I decided she had a right, as the boy's grandmother, to know the whole truth about how he came to be born. I knew Stanley hadn't had anything to do with her since she'd left Father, so he certainly wouldn't have told her.

And then there was Stanley himself. Despite our differences back then, he was bringing up Oliver as if he were his own son. I'd had no problem with his 'coming out', as they refer to it these days, so long as he was happy and it didn't affect Oliver's upbringing. Of course it had always been in the back of my mind whether Constance's suicide had been because she had found out about Stanley's gay relationship and simply couldn't cope with it.

Not 'family' but also on my list of very important people, there was Silvie, the girl who had taught me all I knew about real intimacy, something that I had never previously or since experienced. I had hoped that she may have had some special feelings towards me, and that I wasn't just another of her casual adventures. I liked to think that I represented a little more than just another flirtation to her. I dared not imagine that there could be any future for me where she was concerned. Still, there was no harm in hoping, was there? Goodness me. Perhaps that was simply too much to dream for, but 'dreams are nothing more than wishes, and a wish is just a dream you wish to come true'. More musical inspiration... Thanks Harry Nilsson, for those words of wisdom. Incidentally, David Cassidy recorded a version of Harry's 'The Puppy Song' and, believe it or not, made a pretty good job of it.

Yes, I'd say that my life at that time in Wivenhoe was becoming pretty good. But I was completely unprepared and oblivious to the potentially devastating news that I was about to learn. It all began to unfold following that letter I'd decided to write to my mother.

But I'll have to dash now as the bell has just rung for visiting time and I don't want to keep Oliver waiting.

CHAPTER 30

Iris's Secret

"So that had been the reason for Father's disdain for me!"

Leslie Markland

What a boost Oli's visits give me. I look forward to the day when we can share a conversation again outside these prison walls. Anyway, with more time on my hands I can get on with explaining about that letter I wrote to my mother. It turned out to be more important and valuable than I ever could have imagined when I wrote it.

It was my good fortune and luck that Roger Ainsworth had had the foresight to keep all the emails that went back and forth between Mother and Stanley and him. And luckily, I'd also kept Mother's letters to me and she'd kept mine. If I hadn't been able to produce these as evidence at my trial, the sentence handed down to me may well have been vastly different to the one given. Someone from above must surely have been looking down and taking care of me. But, it wouldn't have been Father, that was for sure.

With some diligence and patience Roger had been able to compile a dossier of all the correspondence for the court to see. He was worth his weight in gold, and his agreement to help me quite possibly saved my life, or at the very least gave me the will to carry on with it.

Roger's file contained a series of letters and emails each printed out or photocopied in precise date order and labelled with his spidery handwriting. At the top of the first one he had scrawled in capital letters:-

'LETTER FROM LESLIE MARKLAND TO IRIS IN AMERICA'

Barnacle Barge

Wivenhoe Quay

Essex

October 1st, 2000

Dearest Mother

I thought it was about time I sat down and wrote to you with some rather exciting news. I kept putting it off for fear that your reaction might not be too positive. But I can't hold back any longer, and I do hope that you can find it in your heart to be happy for me.

You are a grandmother again!!! So not only to Hilary and Sophie: You will hardly believe what I am about to tell you, but I am in fact the father of a little boy called Oliver.

It's taken some while for me to summon up the courage to tell you about Oliver, and I don't know whether you had heard that Constance and Stanley had had a new baby boy too, before Constance's sad and untimely passing. I understand that Stanley doesn't keep in touch with you very much, so that news, in itself, may be a bit of a shock and surprise to you. Whether you have heard or not, you may think it a coincidence that their child was also named Oliver.

Mother, I hope you are sitting down while you read this, so that you don't fall over. Stanley's Oliver and my Oliver are in fact one and the same! Don't be confused too greatly Mother, as I will try to explain.

You know that I was devastated by Father's will when I learned, once and for all, what he truly thought of me. He knew that I didn't have any children of my own and that Stanley did. He knew I was hardly ever likely to have a relationship with a woman, not in the normal sense at least, and it was clear to me that he always favoured Stanley over me. To this day I don't know what I ever did to make him be like that. It simply wasn't fair, was it Mother?

Rightly or wrongly, I wanted revenge against Father and the way he'd treated me. I decided to make arrangements with one of these new surrogacy agencies and have a baby with an anonymous mother. I won't embarrass either of us by describing any more detail than that, but suffice to say nine months later, after making these arrangements, I became a dad. I bet you never thought I had it in me, did you??!!

Well, there had been a bit of a catastrophic mix-up at the agency. It wasn't really their fault, but what happened was that at around the same time Constance was also wanting another baby, and she ended up becoming pregnant with the very same sample that I'd provided to the agency.

I know it's possibly a bit confusing, so I will just say that her baby, Oliver, wasn't Stanley's, but mine! And after a lot of soul-searching I can say that after the initial alarm I'm now very happy and comfortable about it.

It's all very bizarre Mother, but it would mean so much to me if I knew you were happy for me too.

And I do hope you believe me when I tell you that what I did was never about the money as such. To be sure, it's great to have a bit of spare cash for me from the estate's income, but the really great thing is that, not only is there a male heir to continue the line of ownership of Father's estate, but that Oliver will still one day inherit a share of all the property. And that would have happened whether he was my son or Stanley's - so there's no harm done is there?

I never imagined I would ever become a dad, and I must say I really quite like the idea, even though, right now, Oliver is growing up at the Manor. Stanley and I have come to an agreement that suits us all for the time being. After his initial negative reaction to learning about Oliver, I must say how good he's now being.

It had been such a sad affair when Constance couldn't cope with her life anymore, but maybe something good can come from all of that. I'm assuming you may not have heard about her suicide if you haven't heard about Oliver either. I don't feel I should be the one to give you details on her tragic death and hope that Stanley will do that at some point. He's been coping well and has a live-in nanny there now, who apparently is doing marvels at looking after the house and the children, thank goodness.

Now that I have some extra money, thanks to Father, I may even be able to come out to America and stay with you for a while. I would love to meet your partner if you are still with him. Forgive me, I don't recall his name, but I'm hoping that this letter finds you well and enjoying life.

Please be happy for me, and don't be cross with me. In bringing Oliver into this world I was seeking revenge against Father initially, but in doing so I think I may have found some love for a very special little boy.

Do please write and tell me that you can accept what I've told you. And do also please write and tell me what it was you meant when you wrote previously that 'One day I will be brave enough to tell you all about your past.'

By the way, whatever secret you have about my past, I'm sure I'll be able to cope with it. I'm much stronger now than I've ever felt before, so please Mother, spill the beans. Whatever it is, it can't be all that bad!

With much love, your son
Leslie
xxx

The next piece of Roger's 'evidence' was an email, printed out and marked 'FROM IRIS TO ME'

From: Iris Dellinger [iris.dellinger@lemon.com]
Sent: 14 October 2000 09:21
To: rogainsworth@tb.co.uk
Subject: Leslie

Hi Roger
Hoping you are well and enjoying your retirement. There is something I

have to ask you to do please. This isn't in the capacity of being our family solicitor, and I appreciate since your previous email to me that it's now Brian who's taken over dealing with Markland affairs. I am asking you this as a friend.

I have just received a letter from Leslie. He obviously doesn't realise that you and I are occasionally still in touch with each other as he told me about Constance's suicide, not knowing for sure that I knew. But he also told me some unbelievable news about Stanley and Connie's boy Oliver actually being Leslie's and not theirs. Apparently there was some mix up with a surrogacy agency that Leslie got involved with as he wanted to have a child without being in a 'normal' relationship. His child would become one of the heirs to the estate.

The trouble is that there is something Leslie ought to know, and I can't find the courage to tell him. It's a secret I've been carrying around with me since before Leslie was born, and as far as I can work out there is only myself - and now you - who knows this. George clearly knew, but he took the secret with him to his grave. With me being here in America, it helped that I was thousands of miles away, and I never could face up to it. But now I must.

Do you remember Chris Dickinson with whom I used to live on the estate before George got you to evict him for rent arrears? Well, that hadn't been the real reason why George wanted him gone. It was because at that time I had been pregnant with Chris's child. Leslie was in fact that child, and that was why there was never any bonding between him and George, and why George was so much kinder to Stanley when he was born three years later.

Leslie isn't, and never has been a true Markland, and I don't know what to do. I have to let Leslie know, but I simply can't after all these years of silence about it. Does it mean that his inheritance will be affected? And what about Oliver's?

I know you have a much cleverer brain than me, and I hope you can guide me in doing what's right.

It's a good job that Leslie doesn't have email, otherwise I may have emailed back to him in haste and without thinking through the consequences.

Could you to find it in your good nature to inform Leslie (and Stanley?)

on my behalf, in a sort of legal capacity? Please don't do that until you've emailed me back to tell me what you think should be done.

Sorry, but you are the only person who now knows my guilty secret. Even Chris Dickinson hadn't known, and I don't want him to know now.

Best wishes to you, as always

Iris

PS Do you still keep in touch with that secretary of yours? What was her name? Hatty? If so, please give her my regards. I liked her.

PPS You may notice from my email address that I am now a Dellinger. Adam asked me for my hand in marriage in May and I said yes. We had a fabulous honeymoon on the Florida Keys.

There followed another email that Roger had printed off and marked 'FROM ME TO IRIS'

From: Roger Ainsworth (rogainsworth@tb.co.uk)

Sent: 15 October 2000 07:21

To: Iris Dellinger [iris.dellinger@lemon.com]

Subject: Leslie

My Dear Iris

Firstly, I congratulate you on your wonderful news. If you ever visit England I hope you will come to see us. You will always be welcome. I say 'us' as my ex-assistant Hatty eventually became my wife! Despite the obvious age difference we are extremely happy.

Your email sent a shockwave through my system, and now that I have had time to digest it I can see how stupid I had been all those years ago when I was orchestrating the eviction of Mr. Dickinson from the estate on your late husband's instructions.

Your news can, and probably will, have far-reaching consequences that will affect Leslie and Oliver. If Leslie isn't a Markland by true blood-line, then that explains why George was always so hostile towards him and always more loving and caring towards Stanley. It also explains how and why Stanley and Leslie are so different in their looks and demeanour. How could I have missed such an obvious situation? That poor Mr. Dickinson: I had him evicted on some technicality concerning his rent when all along George wanted him gone for an entirely different reason. And there was me thinking I was being astute.

Although I am no longer acting in any formal legal capacity for you or anyone else in the Markland family, I feel I am duty-bound to act accordingly based on your news. But this will mean that Leslie will cease to have an interest in the estate and will cease to receive an income from it. It will mean that Oliver will have no claim either. Of course if he were actually Stanley's and poor Constance's child then he would eventually inherit a third of the estate and the twins would receive the other two thirds between them. But if it's proven that Leslie is Oliver's father and that Leslie is in fact Mr. Dickinson's son, then I'm afraid he has no claim at all, and nor will Oliver.

I don't wish my actions to cause any more distress for poor Leslie. It will upset me too greatly my dear, and yet I am torn between doing what I know is right and not doing anything at all. I may be older but I don't think I'm any wiser, since we last met. I can't tell any untruths Iris, but I could let sleeping dogs lie for the time being if you prefer. Please let me know what you would wish me to do. For once in my life I really need someone's guidance, and that someone has to be you. On this occasion I am not thinking in an official capacity with my legal hat on, but purely as a friend.

With kindest regards

Roger

If Roger had been shocked by Mother's news, imagine how I'd felt when she did actually pluck up the courage to tell me. I remember shuddering when I first found out.

It was then my mother's turn to respond, and once again Roger had kept a copy upon which he'd written 'EMAIL FROM IRIS TO ME'

From: Iris Dellinger [iris.dellinger@lemon.com]

Sent: 15 October 2000 13.01

To: rogainsworth@tb.co.uk

Subject: Leslie

Hi Roger

Thanks for your email of this morning. How lovely that Hatty and you got married. We really will have to get together some day and have double celebrations!

Now I must turn to the unfortunate business at hand. Of course! Everything is now becoming clear to me! I have mulled this over and over and have decided that I must tell Leslie the truth and I will point out to him that it will mean he and Oliver will no longer have a claim on the estate. I can't bear to phone Leslie even though it is quite urgent, but in any case, I don't have a number for him, so I will write to him instead. The letter will take a few days to reach him by airmail and I will tell him that you are the only other person who knows about this twist of circumstances, so it will give you a little while to make some preparations with the paperwork, assuming of course that you won't mind doing this. I'd be terribly grateful, Roger. Will it mean that your son Brian will have to be involved? If that's to be the case, I know I can't stop that, but I would so much appreciate if this affair could just be kept between ourselves, if at all possible.

I do hope Leslie's not going to be too angry with me, although he will have every right to be furious. Oh dear, Roger. I really should have told him about all this a long time ago. Wish me luck in finding the right words for him.

Best wishes

Iris

Roger soon emailed back to Mother, this time simply marking the printed copy 'R.A. - I.D.'

From: Roger Ainsworth (rogainsworth@tb.co.uk)

Sent: 15 October 2000 18.24

To: Iris Dellinger [iris.dellinger@lemon.com]

Subject: Leslie

My Dear Iris,

That is a very good idea. Of course I will deal with the paperwork, but I suspect it may be necessary for Brian to become involved, as he is running the firm now and he will need access to all the documents. I'm sure he will be discreet over such delicate matters. For now I will await the outcome following your disclosure to Leslie.

Good luck!

Roger

And then 'I.D - R.A.'

From: Iris Dellinger [iris.dellinger@lemon.com]

Sent: 15 October 2000 18.52

To: rogainsworth@tb.co.uk

Subject: Leslie

Dear Roger

Thanks.

We shall see.

Iris x

And then there was THAT letter I'd been sent by Mother from America. It was rather long, and took up three sheets of paper, neatly folded together. Luckily I'd kept it safely, and later handed it to Roger so that he could include it in his dossier. He labelled it: 'IRIS'S LETTER TO LESLIE'

Plainfield, Indiana

October 16th 2000

Dearest Leslie

First of all, I must say sorry for my delay in replying to your letter. I am delighted by the news you sent me about Oliver and I am so proud of you, and so happy that finally things are working out for you.

I am writing this to you with such a very heavy heart, but I know it's what I must do. You will have every right to be angry with me and I know I should have told you this a very long time ago but I just was never brave enough until now.

It is time for me to 'spill the beans', as you put it. You always had a funny way with words Leslie. The secret that I've been carrying around with me all this time is that George wasn't your real father. I was expecting you whilst

I was a tenant on the estate with the man I was living with at the time. You won't remember him because he left before you were born. Please, you mustn't have any anger towards him - he was actually a good and honest man, and he never knew I was pregnant with you. In those days it was frowned upon to be living together out of wedlock, and when I discovered I was pregnant I didn't know what to do as I didn't love him and I was seeing George with whom, at the time, I had much more affection. I'm afraid it was George who had him evicted on some rent technicality, and I never saw or heard of him again. How strange it must appear, me writing to you about your father but calling him George.

You see, George found himself to be boxed into rather a tight corner, and he didn't like it, and I'm afraid I was partly to blame. I'd led him to believe that the child I was expecting - that was you – was his. I was blinded by his affection and attention at the time, and I was too young to really know what I was doing. It wasn't until you'd been born that George had been able to calculate the relevant dates and conclude that he couldn't have been your father. But by then it was too late. We were married and he had no choice but to proceed with the pretence that you were the child we'd made together. Only he and I knew the actual truth, and he never forgave me from then on, nor could he love you. But you see he was too proud a man to admit that he was bringing up someone else's boy, and so he took you on as his son – at least as far as the outside world was concerned.

I really should have been stronger at the time and stopped George from getting his own way like he always did, but you have to understand that at the time I was only just turned 20, and didn't know anything about the way the world works, and I suppose I was guilty of being somewhat whisked off my feet by George's wealth and power. Of course I am older and wiser now and realise that those things are far less important than love and honour. It's a cliché, but it's true. I am sure that you will share those sentiments with me, as I know that your heart has always been in the right place. I know that young Oliver will grow up good and strong, just like you.

However, despite all this, you are going to have to make an important decision that will affect you and Oliver for the rest of your lives, and it is only you who can make this decision. I'm sure you've already figured out that what I've just written will have consequences for your inheritance. There's no easy way of putting it. If you are not a Markland, then nor is Oliver, and neither of you are entitled to continue receiving any money from the estate.

There is only one other living person who knows my secret about your real father's identity - Roger Ainsworth, and I asked him to sit tight on the information unless you decide to contact him. He no longer acts professionally for our somewhat disjointed family, as I'm sure you know, but he has agreed to make this one exception on our behalf if you ask him to.

So, you see, that had been what I had meant in that old letter to you when I had said 'One day I will be brave enough to tell you all about your past.'

It's going to be a lot for you to take in. I hope and pray that you can understand and not be too angry with me. I only did what I thought was right at the time. Please write back and tell me what I need so desperately to hear; that you can forgive me. I hope that your good and kind nature will prevail, and even one day possibly that you can see the humorous side to all this - somewhat dark humour, I must admit. With this in mind, please don't worry about that old fly screen as I got a new one fitted now, but I would love it if you could ever come over here to see me and Adam, and even bring young Oliver too, perhaps. I bet he grows up a handsome man just like his father.

With much love and hope from

Your Mother X

PS Adam and I got married, but that's small-beans news compared to the ones I've just spilled to you!

Even now, remembering this letter again, I find it hard to hold back the tears. My life, which had taken a turn for the better had been flipped upside down in the few minutes it took to read Mother's confession.

The letters and emails were about to become even more emotional and this was the point at which dear old Roger Ainsworth began to really get involved.

CHAPTER 31

Back to Work Again

"I made a mental note to tick Stanley off"

Part One: Roger Ainsworth (2000)

I hadn't anticipated prising myself out of retirement because of the Marklands, but in view of my fondness for Iris and particularly Leslie, I had decided to do so. It had always been my fastidious way to keep any documentation together in a file in date order, and with Hatty's assistance I made up a dossier of all the emails and letters exchanged between the parties involved, once Iris had sent hers over to me. I marked them all clearly at the top of each letter or printed-out email. What foresight! At the time I'd thought this was only going to be used with regard to the inheritance issues. Little did I know how relevant this file would later become in Leslie's subsequent hour of need...

In the dossier there were already the letters between Leslie and his mother, and the emails between her and me. Clearly, judging by the following letter that he hastily sent to Iris, he was very upset when he found out about his mother keeping such a big secret from him.

It's never a good idea, in my opinion, to write anything fueled by strong emotion, and his letter is a classic example of why I hold that belief. Despite Leslie later asking Iris to tear it up, for some reason she kept it:

'LETTER LESLIE TO IRIS'

22/10

Mother, or are you in fact not really my mother after all? Is that something else you hadn't told me?

I trust this letter finds you well, and things are going well for you and your new American husband! Congratulations on getting married again.

I don't know how you could have kept that secret about my father not being my father from me all this time. No wonder George (I can no longer refer to him as Father) hated me like he did. Why didn't you ever tell me? I know I shouldn't say this Mother, but it's a good job we are 4,000 miles apart right now.

Leslie

Next in my pile was Iris's email to me which I headed 'EMAIL FROM IRIS TO R.A.

From: Iris Dellinger [iris.dellinger@lemon.com]

Sent: 27 October 2000 12.13

To: rogainsworth@tb.co.uk

Subject: Leslie

Dear Roger

I have just received Leslie's reply in the post. He is very angry and upset with me. I suppose I shouldn't have expected anything else. Oh dear. What have I done?

He didn't mention anything about contacting you, so please will you leave things as they are for now. I've clearly caused him enough upset without making matters worse.

Love from Iris x

Then, I was glad to see that Leslie retracted what he'd previously sent to his mother...

'LETTER FROM LESLIE TO IRIS'
Barnacle Barge
Wivenhoe
23rd October 2000
Dear Mother
I am so sorry I sent you the letter that you probably would have received yesterday. After receiving yours, I was torn up with various emotions - shock, surprise, hurt, upset, and admittedly anger. I had read your letter and hurriedly written back without taking it in too well at the time. Before I knew it I had stormed up to the post box and put the letter through the slot and then it was too late. That will teach me a lesson! Never to write something in anger, especially after a few glasses of wine!

Of course I forgive you. You are my mother and that's that (sorry I wrote those cruel words at the beginning of my letter). I can indeed see a funny side to things, although sadly not much at the moment. At least I can understand now why George acted the way he did towards me, with him knowing all along that I wasn't his real son and Stanley was. Mind you, I don't dislike him any less for the way he treated me, but at least it does make things a little clearer. It also explains why Stanley and I are worlds apart in mind and appearance, something that always puzzled me. Does Stanley know about all this? Does he know that I am his half-brother?

I appreciate that this is all going to affect my present income and Oliver's future inheritance, but to be honest I'm not too bothered about it now that I've had a little time to think things through. I had actually been planning to give a large proportion of the income away to charity anyway. I hadn't finally decided which one, or ones, to help yet, but I guess that idea will all have to be shelved now. Maybe one of them would have been a mental health charity, or The Samaritans, in view of what happened to poor Constance. She couldn't have been in sound mind when she killed herself, and there are well-meaning organisations out there desperate for funding who would perhaps have helped her with what she was going through. If only she had asked for help, or even just talked things through with someone.

I'm comfortable enough here Mother, and what I did was never about the money for the sake of it. It was more about getting one over on him, who I must now call my step-father George, and finally winning my struggles that have stretched back to when he was alive.

I will get in touch with Roger and ask him to set things straight. I guess Stanley won't be too disappointed when he learns that he'll become even wealthier than he is already. And of course his girls will be getting the entire estate when they are 21, and not have to share a penny with Oliver after all. What a pity!

Anyway, for now Mother, please tear up my letter of yesterday. I would still like to visit you in America and bring Oliver one day. Now I have an extra reason to visit - to meet Adam and congratulate him in person for being so lucky to have married you.

With fondest love

Your son, Leslie

xxx

I was so pleased that Leslie had the good sense to write that straight away. The next correspondence in the dossier was...

'EMAIL FROM IRIS TO R.A.

From: Iris Dellinger [iris.dellinger@lemon.com]

Sent: 28 October 2000 11.52

To: rogainsworth@tb.co.uk

Subject: Leslie

Oh Roger. I have received the best news from Leslie. I am so relieved and my heavy heart has been lifted - I can't tell you how much! His letter of yesterday, which I'm sending you a copy of just for the record, had been written in haste and anger, and he didn't mean what he'd said. He's not bothered about the money and he's going to contact you about settling everything correctly. I bet that's a relief to you. It had been unfair of me to ask you to keep things secret, and I'm sorry for that. I know you like to do things properly and ethically. Leslie was actually going to donate some of his income to a mental health charity in memory of Stanley's Constance. I'm so proud of him. I think I should tell Stanley about that.

Do you have his email address please?

With fond regards, Iris xxx

And then there was my reply back to Iris...

'EMAIL FROM R.A. TO IRIS'

From: Roger Ainsworth (rogainsworth@tb.co.uk)

Sent: 29 October 2000 18.24

To: Iris Dellinger [iris.dellinger@lemon.com]

Subject: Leslie

Dear Iris

I am indeed pleased to hear that Leslie has in fact taken things so well and his idea to give some of his money to charity is very noble of him. It will be up to Stanley to decide what's best to do, but he could, if he wanted, make a special arrangement to enable Leslie to continue receiving a share of the income from the estate and then Leslie will be free to set up a charitable donation if he so chooses. It will even be tax efficient, but the actual transfer of the property deeds will still need to be executed to the twins when they reach 21.

It was proven with the DNA testing that Oliver is Leslie's son and not Stanley's, and it will be impossible to revoke the will on that count, but it won't hurt the twins to believe that they'll be sharing some of the property with Oliver until such a time when it is deemed appropriate to inform them - perhaps when they do reach the age when they are due to inherit.

While remembering that you are their Grandmother, may I offer an opinion as their 'Responsible Adult' and your friend? They are rather too spoiled already and have all the advantages so it wouldn't hurt for them to be brought down a peg or two.

From a personal perspective, I am really very pleased and relieved for you that things are beginning to take a better course. I will wait to hear from Leslie before taking any action.

Stanley's email address is markland1@mailhot.co.uk
Yours
Roger

Iris certainly demonstrated her newfound assertiveness with the email that followed, and that she'd blind-copied me in on...

'EMAIL FROM IRIS TO STANLEY'
From: Iris Dellinger [iris.dellinger@lemon.com]
Sent: 28 October 2000 11.52
To: Stanley Markland (markland1@mailhot.co.uk)
Bcc: Roger Ainsworth (rogainsworth@tb.co.uk)
Subject: Leslie and Oliver
Dear Stanley

We haven't been too close over the years since I left your father but I was so sorry to hear all about Constance. I know you are in a male relationship, and although it took me by surprise when I first heard, I have a free and open mind about such things. You have my blessing as I just want the best for both my sons, and it's with Leslie and you in mind that I am sending this email.

This is tough to write but I will come straight to the point, and the bottom line is this: Your father was not Leslie's father. I won't go into details here except to say that I have been carrying this secret around with me for far too long and it's time that it was out in the open. It means Leslie is not a Markland, which in turn means that he will have his income from the estate stopped and Oliver will not inherit a share of the property. He had thought he and Oliver would be receiving a part of the Markland fortune, but that now won't be the case.

I would like you to contact Roger Ainsworth (not Brian), and it would be my sincere wish that you find it in your heart to allow Leslie to continue receiving his original share of the estate's income for the foreseeable future. The twins will now continue to inherit the entire estate when they reach the age decreed in your father's will, but for now they perhaps don't need to *know that. You never know, when they get older they might want to share some of their good fortune with Oliver, which would be wonderful, wouldn't it?*

For now though, please get in touch with Roger so that he can deal with the paperwork. I cannot demand this, but I am asking you as your mother to be compassionate about Leslie's plight.

Poor Constance must have been going through hell and could not have been in sound mind to have taken her own life, knowing that she would be leaving behind the twins and Oliver. I recently found out that Leslie, thinking that he'd be receiving payments from the estate, was planning to donate some of that money to a mental health charity in her memory. It would be nice if your actions enabled him to still do this.

Love from your mother

x

I was very pleased to see that Stanley quickly reacted positively...
'EMAIL FROM STANLEY TO IRIS'
From: Stanley (markland1@mailhot.co.uk)
Sent: 29 October 2000 14.06
To: Iris Dellinger [iris.dellinger@lemon.com]
Subject: Leslie and Oliver
Hi Mother

It's good to be back in contact after all this time. As you can imagine, life has not been easy lately. You are right about me being in a gay relationship, and I hope that one day you will be able to meet and welcome Tristan as part of our estranged family. I am doing my best to juggle my life between being with him, bringing up the twins, and of course Oliver, and still managing the estate. There is always so much to be done, but I feel like I'm coping quite well, thanks to a wonderful live-in nanny by the name of Miss Baudet (pronounced Bo-day - I think her family stemmed from France), and thanks to Tristan's loyal and loving support. I am bringing up Oliver as if he were my own, until such time in the future when he can decide what he wants to do with himself. For the time being Leslie and I have come to an amicable agreement about Oliver living with Miss Baudet and me at the Manor house. You can imagine how things were when Leslie dropped his bombshell about him being Oliver's real father because of a mix up with the surrogacy agency he was using. The whole episode was like watching a TV soap opera unfolding.

As far as I can see, things are working reasonably well here with Miss Baudet taking charge of the children in her caring but firm style. The girls are adorable and growing up so fast, although I don't see them as often as I'd like, what with me being so busy, and them being at school. Oliver does seem a little shy and withdrawn at times, especially compared to the girls who are so confident. But with Miss Baudet's help, I am sure everything will work out fine.

To get to the point Mother, yes I am happy to let Leslie continue receiving an income from the estate until the girls reach the age of 21, which is when they will be due to inherit the whole property portfolio. Leslie has been quite honorable in that he has insisted on making a financial contribution towards Oliver's future schooling costs, and the news about him wanting to donate money to a mental health charity is a wonderful gesture to Constance's memory.

I will get on to old Roger, like you've asked me to, and instruct him to put the necessary paperwork in order. I've realised that it's not until we get older that we appreciate the importance of our families, and despite the news that Leslie is my half-brother, we still grew up together didn't we? I know that we didn't always see eye to eye on things and I used to tease him something rotten. But we can't turn the clock back now, can we?

Don't worry, Mother. Things will all be okay for Leslie and Oliver, you'll see.

Stanley

I wasn't sure that I liked being referred to as 'old Roger', and I made a mental note to tick Stanley off if ever the opportunity arose! In the meantime, I then received his request for me to get back to 'proper work' on behalf of the Markland family...

'EMAIL FROM STANLEY TO ROGER'

From: Stanley (markland1@mailhot.co.uk)

Sent: 29 October 2000 15.31

To: rogainsworth@tb.co.uk

Subject: Leslie and Oliver

Dear Roger,

My mother has disclosed to me the fact that my brother Leslie is in fact my half-brother, and not of the Markland heritage. I'm sure you are aware of this if you have been in contact with her. I have decided that Leslie's financial arrangements should carry on as they have been, and that this should continue until my daughters Hilary and Sophie reach the age of 21, at which point they will inherit the Markland estate, as set out in the will of my father.

I would be very grateful if you could personally take care of these arrangements on our behalf.

I am aware that you are enjoying retirement, but I am hoping that you will make a special concession to act for us for one last time. We all really appreciate the dedication, loyalty and discretion you have offered and shown us over the years, and I do hope that, even though I assume much of the paperwork will be dealt with by Brian and his staff, it will be you who will personally oversee things. I know that Mother would be pleased and relieved to hear that you are working once again on behalf of the Markland estate.

With kind regards

Stanley Markland

The following day I replied to all three members of the family...

'EMAIL FROM R.A. TO STANLEY AND IRIS, WITH COPY BY LETTER TO LESLIE'

From: Roger Ainsworth (rogainsworth@tb.co.uk)

Sent: 30 October 2000 08.09

To: Iris Dellinger [iris.dellinger@lemon.com], Stanley Markland (markland1@mailhot.co.uk)

Subject: Markland estate

Dear Iris, Stanley and Leslie,

As dictated by the will of the late George Markland, the property known as The Manor, all tenanted buildings, farm buildings and all other properties on the land will be put in trust for Hilary and Sophie Markland until they reach the age of 21.

This is to confirm that, at Stanley's request, I will set out the appropriate documents in order that income from the estate will continue to be paid to Leslie and Stanley Markland.

It should be noted that the monies continuing to be transferred to Leslie Markland are a goodwill gesture and are not legally binding.

Yours truly

Roger Ainsworth

And that was that! I knew that there would be a lot of legal paperwork to be completed, but despite my senior years, I came to the conclusion that it wouldn't do me any harm to stimulate the old grey matter once again. And besides, I was becoming bored with doing the *Daily Telegraph* crossword day in, day out.

I rather relished the idea of putting my slippers away and getting back to work once again.

Part Two: Leslie Markland

"Finally I was doing something really worthwhile with my life"

So, after much to-ing and fro-ing of emails and letters and our various family confessions, Roger Ainsworth had helped us all to reach a happy and settled conclusion. Finally I was doing something really worthwhile with my life and I felt good about my decision to donate half my monthly trust allowance to MIND, the mental health charity, as well as The Samaritans. Thanks to Stanley I was still able to honour the name of my son's late mother.

"Come on Harry," I called as I put on my jacket. "Let's walk round to the post box before I change my mind." By the way he looked at me with his little head cocked to one side I could have sworn that he understood every word I said. Off the gangplank of the Barnacle barge we went, with me marching round to the Post Office box in the High Street, and Harry scampering behind. As soon as I'd dropped the envelope containing my bank standing order forms through the slot I felt a great sense of euphoria. I would be keeping a look out for other worthy causes to benefit from my estate money, but for the time being those charities, I thought, were a good start.

"Okay Harry. Let's go round to The Station for a little celebration," I said to my companion, and three minutes later Harry had a bowl of water on the floor and I had a lovely glass of Merlot in my hand as I sat contentedly at the L-shaped bar.

CHAPTER 32

Changes

"Stanley let me rule the roost"

Alberta Louise Baudet (2001)

S ome people that I meet think I'm a little too posh for their liking, but one can't help the way one talks, can one? I was brought up 'correctly' and sent off by my parents to finishing school in Switzerland and that was where I learnt how things ought to be done. After I returned home - a rather grand house in Devon – I'd say I rather went off the rails when I met and fell in love with a chap by the name of Peter Pritchard, who was by all accounts a bit of a local scoundrel. I now think of him as Peter The Prick, but really I shouldn't let my bitterness get the better of me. As my dear mother used to say: "if you haven't got anything nice to say about someone, then don't say anything at all."

It was good advice: I followed it – moved on and let go.

After a couple of years floundering, supported by the generosity of my parents, I came to my senses. After all, there were only so many parties one could become the centre of attention at, and to be fair I would say that after a while the Champagne lifestyle at someone else's expense became a little boring. So I decided to sober up, get a job and in doing so, get a life.

My parents both died within six months of each other, leaving me with less than nothing. They loved each other so much, and couldn't bear to tell me the truth about their finances, for fear of upsetting me. You see they doted on me, their only child, and constantly wanted my approval. They were my parents, you know, and it shouldn't have been that way round, should it?

Anyway, they died owing more than they owned, and so I had no choice but to buckle down and get to work. The trouble was that I didn't really know what I wanted to do, until a friend of mine asked me to cover for her at the Ousthwaite's home. My friend looked after the children there while their parents earned a small fortune in one of the big banks in London. The problem with my friend was that she was kind of up the duff, and had to have time off to go to some private clinic in Ealing. She told the Ousthwaites that she had a family matter to attend to and that I would be covering for her until she returned - which was in fact never. She never went through with the abortion and ended up with a baby at the tender age of only 18.

So that was how I fell into the world of nannying and childminding. And, much to my surprise, I discovered that I was really rather good at it. I can think of more ghastly ways in which to earn a living, and at least it kept a rather sumptuous roof over my head, and there was never a shortage of smoked salmon in the refrigerator to which I had been explicitly instructed to help myself. But I was always struggling, tirelessly struggling, to keep those damned credit card companies at bay. You see, my parents always told me to use them when times became a little difficult for me, and I had no idea that they didn't have the wherewithal to settle my monthly expenses. Why should I? But then they'd died, and as the cards were in my name, I had to pay up, didn't I?

One day, my dear friend Fiona O'Brien-Smith, with whom I had shared my room in Basel, came to visit when I was feeling rather down, and confronted me with a proposition: "Now come on Louise, buck yourself up and get a grip. You see this advertisement here that I placed in *The Times* yesterday?"

She unfolded the newspaper and shoved the page of classified ads under my nose, before continuing. "There's no need to apply through the normal procedure. If you want the job, it's yours."

Fiona was such a dear. It had been after we'd returned to England from Switzerland that I went my way and she went hers – with hers being vastly more lucrative. She was now the owner of a very successful recruitment agency, and I daresay that if it hadn't been for her, I don't know what I'd have done. You see, I really had an enormous amount of money owing, and with the wages that the Ousthwaites paid me I had no hope in hell of ever paying it off. But Fiona had professional connections with the police forces and occasionally got asked to provide someone when there was a sudden death in a family - where children needed instant supervision due to the loss of a mother or father. The pay she was offering was more than I would earn from the Ousthwaites and so I said yes, and found myself on her register. Thank goodness for Fiona, because with the interest on interest on interest, those credit cards always had the better of me. With Fiona's help, at least I had a fighting chance of pulling myself out of the financial mire.

I always had belief in myself and I always thought that I was someone 'special', but not knowing how to define that word I just continued in my own sweet way, waiting for the time when life's circumstances would change in my favour. And they did, the day I went to the Markland's house.

"When you have a problem, something will always turn up when you least expect it," was what my dear old Dad used to say. That 'something' happened, when answering a call from Fiona's agency to take care of three children suffering the aftermath of their mum's suicide. For me, there was nothing particularly unusual about that, as I had been well trained and experienced in dealing with such unfortunate circumstances.

You wouldn't believe how many suicides take place among mothers who can't take things any more. All very sad, I must say, but it gave me a job.

But this job was different. For a start it was at a house that was not your average three-bed semi on a council estate. It was very large, very grand, and clearly money was in abundance. Secondly, I was aware there had been rumours going round about the master of the house being mixed up in a gay affair. Thirdly, there were the children: twin girls, about six years old and their brother, three years younger, who I was drafted in to look after until their dad came home on that tragic day. The little boy was lovely and sweet, but those girls were like something out of a horror movie, I tell no lies. They gave me the shivers from the very first moment I cast eyes on them, but that gave me an interesting challenge. Could I tame them?

But the fourth, and most important, element in this saga that stood out for me was the dad - Stanley Markland. There was something very intriguing and, dare I say, attractive about him. I can't really explain the ripples of excitement he sent through my body when I met him on that first night. Not a very appropriate feeling directly after his wife had been found hanging from the back of her bedroom door, but there you are.

After that long day when I first attended the scene, and when all the authorities had departed, we had sat down at his kitchen table, eating his sadly departed wife's lasagne and drinking his port. Gosh, there was something about his hair, his eyes and the manner in which he conducted himself. His voice was very commanding. He had a certain gravitas from day one, despite the unhappy circumstances, of someone who forces everyone to feel his presence when entering a room. Golly gosh, I was all of a quiver, and when he popped the question I had no hesitation in saying yes. I don't mean a marriage proposal, although if it had been that on our very first meeting, I would probably have said yes! No, sadly, it was only a proposal of employment looking after Oliver and Oliver's sisters Sophie and Hilary, the twins. I would probably have said yes anyway, but when Stanley offered to pay me handsomely as well as settling my card debts as part of the package, I would have been a fool to say no. He was obviously desperate for my help, the poor thing, and it was, at that stage, to be only a short-term arrangement. I knew the chances of anything other than an employee/employer relationship was never going to happen, more's the pity, but hey-ho.

My professional training and experience looking after traumatised children led me to expect classic bereavement behaviour. In some ways children are more resilient than adults. Initially, there would normally be the shock of discovering that someone had died, followed by disbelief, anguish, sobbing, deep sadness and then a period of either constant chatting or quiet reflection. But in the case of these girls it was as if nothing had happened, as they simply continued playing in their bedroom with their Barbie dolls. Oliver had displayed more 'normal', if that is the right word, behaviour and I made a mental note to myself that I ought to keep a look out for him. I could tell right away that, if left unchecked, those twins could be capable of either isolating him completely, or teasing him, or ganging up on him. Of course I needed to make certain allowances for the twins' unusual behaviour, as I was well aware that some children can deal with trauma in all sorts of different ways. But I felt that Oliver was particularly vulnerable already, and being such a young little boy I was determined to keep an especially watchful eye on him.

Poor Mr. Markland, he had come home from work to discover that his wife had committed suicide. Before even meeting him I had already decided to stay the night at the house and had found one of the bedrooms in which to put my overnight things. Little did I know at that time that it would remain my bedroom for years to come.

The bedroom itself was very comfortable, although I have to say a little sparse of home comforts. The ceiling was at least nine feet high, and the size of the room, with its large sash windows overlooking the acres of land, not to mention the lake near to the house, was almost the same size as my entire flat in Leeds. I thought I could easily make that room very comfortable with a few of my personal possessions and a few cushions scattered here and there. The en suite bathroom was a luxury I hadn't had since I was living at home with my parents, and it was jolly nice to have one again, I can tell you. I couldn't help congratulating myself for rather landing on my feet when dear Stanley Markland had asked me to stay on, and I couldn't quite extinguish the fantasy of somehow one day becoming more than just a nanny and housekeeper to his family. I'd never be able to admit my feelings to him but if love at first sight existed, it was exactly what I had felt for Stanley.

During the period of time following that traumatic first day on the Markland Estate I was able to nip back and forth to my flat in town to collect more and more of my personal belongings, and I made myself properly at home. The days turned to weeks, weeks to months, and before I knew it a whole year had gone by. We as a 'family' settled down into a kind of routine. I say 'family' very loosely - it was certainly an estranged one, what with Stanley flitting between his life at the estate and being with his man-friend. What a waste, I thought! I remember the first occasion when Tristan, his partner, had been introduced to me. It had been one evening when Stanley had invited him to dinner at the Manor. He had asked me to prepare 'something special' for them, and I later found out that it was to celebrate the seventh anniversary of their first 'date' together. Generously, he had asked me to join them at the dinner table. The children had gone off to bed, and I brought out the special 'Snaffles Salmon Mousse' that I had prepared the previous day, along with some extremely delicious port wine jelly that went down superbly well. Rather too well I would say, as its alcohol content made us all become rather tiddly, if I'm honest. But it provided a good opportunity for us all to get to know each other. I was jealously only too aware how much Tristan meant to Stanley, but with me feeling the way I did, at least I was able to learn a little more about Mr. Stanley Markland. If it had been a woman with whom Stanley was so deeply infatuated I would have been terribly forlorn. But as it was another man, and in a gay world that I had no knowledge of, somehow that didn't seem to matter to me. In fact it made me even more determined to protect him from the trials and tribulations of the sometimes harsh world we all have to live in. Rather than being jealous of Tristan himself, or competitive with him for Stanley's affections, I found myself rather liking the man. Perhaps it was the power thing that I admired. He was clearly well connected in the political world, and he had an attractive quality about him that I could appreciate, just in the same way that Stanley did. Well, not exactly in the same way, if you get my drift, but I'm sure you understand what I mean.

Occasionally, Stanley would show his gratitude for what I did around the house or with the children, with a gentle little peck on the cheek, and a soft but well-meant 'thank you'. I lived for those moments. The slightest physical contact between us, like a fleeting brush of his hand on my shoulder, or even just eye contact with his cute curled up smile took me back to being a hormonal schoolgirl again. Surely it was unmistakably a wink of his eye, wasn't it? Surely I wasn't imagining it? Whether I was right or not, I simply wanted to take care of him for just as long as I could.

I had well and truly settled in to my new life at the Manor house on the Markland estate. Most days went by rather routinely, but increasingly the children's behaviour would surprise me. Well, the twins' behaviour, to be more precise. I had to keep my wits about me to keep their little tricks from bothering me. Luckily I had had plenty of professional training in the past, and so I knew what to do and how to handle them, but I have to say that in all my experience as a trained nanny and professional child-minder, our Hilary and Sophie did stretch my capabilities to the limit. But they weren't a match for me, thank heaven, despite the cruelty they would dish out to little Oliver, the sweet little mite.

Our daily routine would go something like this: up at seven, breakfast at the table at seven thirty. In the early days, the girls would come down late, but they soon learned that under Miss Baudet's rules 'no show' meant 'no go', and off to school they went the first day they tried it with nothing in their little tummies. That taught them that I was a force to be reckoned with. Fortunately, Stanley was often away otherwise I'm sure he would have given in to their crocodile tears, and my tactics wouldn't have worked. After breakfast, the girls would get their satchels ready and walk with me down to the bottom of the drive while they waited for the school bus to arrive. Even if it were raining cats and dogs we would do this. I didn't care how much they stamped their feet and screwed up their faces at me, pleading with me to get the car out, I just told them that they should put their waterproof coats on and carry an umbrella for the few hundred yards down to the bus shelter. Gosh, I nearly gave in once or twice when it was cold as well as raining, but I knew that if I did it would be a big mistake for me.

Oliver, while he was too young to go to school, would watch some cartoons in the TV room, sprawled out on the beanbags situated around the white-washed wooden floor boards. After the girls had gone off to school, I would make myself a cup of Nescafe and bring it into the room and watch Scooby Doo or Thomas The Tank with him. It was always a joy to hear him chuckling away to himself as I approached the door, a sound that I noted usually ceased when the girls were also present. When they were there with him he tended to go into a little insular world of his own.

For the rest of the day, we would go around together with me doing whatever chores I had on my list for that day. Monday was washing day, so I'd pull the sheets off the beds, occasionally discovering, at best, melted chocolate bars under the girls' pillows or, at worst, some stain or other. Tuesday was ironing. Wednesday was shopping, although a lot of the produce items like eggs, milk, meat and vegetables could be phoned in to old Tom at the farm-shop and he'd bring them over. But usually I'd need to go off to the supermarket as well for whatever – toilet rolls, tinned tomatoes and suchlike. Thursday would be 'my' day, and was a chance for me to nip into town with Oliver to put my wages into the bank, buy myself a magazine or two, and to get my hair done. My hair was very important to me, and I liked it to be prim and proper, neat and tidy. It was naturally greying at my age, but I'd regularly get it coloured to look my best for when Stanley would be home - which was usually on a Friday.

Friday was his day at home to take care of estate business in his office that used to be his father's, and his father's father before that. Friday would also be my cleaning day, rinsing the baths, wiping the sinks and doing the dusting, ready for the weekend. At the end of each weekday, during term time, the girls would return from school at four in the afternoon, and I would have their tea prepared for them at five, whether they were ready for it or not. They soon learnt that if they weren't down by a quarter past at the latest, the tea was put away and they would be going to bed hungry. Of course I knew where they had a secret stash of chocolate bars up in their room, and when they discovered the bars to be gone they'd have a fit of temper tantrums. Sometimes they did manage to outwit me, hence the chocolate stains under their pillows, but usually I was one step ahead of them, and that used to rub them up something rotten. I generously supposed that it was all pretty usual behaviour for little girls of their age.

At the weekend, Stanley was usually at home. He was a good dad, doing his best to spend some quality time with the children - and even with me as well. Saturday evening was my favourite time, when we would have what we'd call 'tea-tea', consisting of something like pizzas which we'd all make together, choosing whatever topping we'd want, followed by cakes and all sorts of goodies that I'd picked up from the supermarket on the Thursday. It was the one occasion that I would allow us all to take our plates into the TV room. When I say I allowed it, that was pretty much the truth. Stanley let me rule the roost, so to speak, and he used to say to me that I could make the rules up as I saw fit. And I saw fit that every mealtime should be sat at the dining table in the kitchen, with the one exception, our Saturday evening treat.

Those pizzas! I would prepare a number of different ingredients for the toppings after making the bases and adding the sauce for them. There would be dishes of onion bits, ham, grated mozzarella, spicy chicken pieces, sliced peppers, pineapple chunks, and at least four or five other things of whatever I could rustle up from the fridge. Stanley would help Oliver to choose his toppings and I would do my own, but I noticed that without fail Hilary's and Sophie's were always identical, right down to the order in which the ingredients had been placed on the bases. And then when the pizzas had been taken out of the oven and the rest of us would add a little ketchup or mayonnaise, the girls would literally cover theirs with chili sauce, and it was hot sauce at that - far too hot for my taste. They egged each other on with how much they could each bear. I didn't take too much notice to begin with but after a few tea-tea evenings I tried a slice of their pizza, and it damn well nearly blew my head off. It made me come out in such a sweat that even my hair became damp and I had to suck on an orange - a trick my dear parents had taught me to alleviate the effects of an over-hot curry. Well, all that was okay if it was what they wanted to eat for themselves, but one day when their father wasn't around and I caught them sneakily adding the chili sauce to little Oliver's pizza when his back was turned, my patience snapped. They should have known that at his tender age his little mouth would have become so painful, and I don't know what we would have done had he taken a bite. That was when I first really recognised that those girls had a problem, and that it was time for me to go into battle mode against them.

CHAPTER 33

The Eleven Commandments

"I'd never in my life come across anything like this before"

Alberta Louise Baudet (2012)

It took more than twelve years on the Markland Estate to get to the point where I felt I might be failing in my job. Every once in a while, when I had some free time to myself, I would catch up with my good friend Fiona, who had been instrumental in getting me the job with Stanley Markland in the first place. It was always a pleasure to see her as I was awfully fond of her, and it was also a golden opportunity for me to let off steam whenever things became a little fraught.

Whatever Hilary, Sophie, Oliver or Stanley did would always have an effect on me and my own well-being. Nothing did ever happen between Stanley and me in the romance department, more's the pity. He often showed affection towards me, but not of a heterosexual kind - it was purely platonic. After several false alarms where I thought 'this is it', I realised that in fact it never would be 'it'. Stanley was in a happy relationship with Tristan, and I wasn't ever going to be able to change that. No, instead I buckled down to the business that I was being paid to do - bringing up those children, almost as if they were my own. I had a real soft spot for Oliver. He was so kind-hearted and amenable, in stark contrast to the girls, over whom I had to keep a constant watchful eye. I gradually began to find their behaviour so stressful I would break down, crying. This happened on one particular occasion, memorably during a time when Fiona had called by to pay me a visit. I don't think I'd ever cried in front of anyone in my life before. The tears simply welled up inside me without warning, and she was shocked to see me so upset.

"My dear Louise," she comforted, "Whatever's the matter? I always thought you were so happy with your life here."

Oblivious to my problems up to that point, I found myself describing to Fiona one or two of the chilling things the girls had been up to during the previous months and years that they'd been in my charge. I didn't expect her to be able to put things right, but I knew that just by talking I would perhaps alleviate some of the pressure I was feeling. After all, I couldn't really talk things over with Stanley. I'd developed a fear that he might not believe the stories I wanted to tell him about the twins, and think in some perverse way it was just an attempt to gain his attention. But I can assure you that nothing could have been further from the truth.

"Fiona - I do love it here, and Stanley certainly keeps me well looked after. I've never been so well off financially since he paid off my debts when I first began this job," I explained, "I've been able to save virtually all of my salary, as I hardly have any expenses now. And of course I kept on my little flat in the city that I now rent out, and so that brings in a tidy income too. But it's not just about that, you know. The problem is that I think I'm failing. That's the trouble with me, and it's making me so terribly upset."

I could tell that Fiona was surprised by my outburst, and so I had to elaborate. "You see Fi, I do pride myself on doing a good job with children, really I do, but I fear I'm in danger of gradually losing control over those girls, and that wouldn't be too clever would it? I've been considering offering my resignation to Stanley before he realises that he's employing a nanny who can't nanny and decides to sack me. I'd rather jump than be pushed."

For many years I'd been harbouring my concern that Fiona might have been a little miffed with me when I took the permanent job here. You see, as it had been her employment agency that had got me on the register with the police force, it meant that every temporary placement she'd got me brought in a percentage of revenue for her. So when Stanley had offered me the position full-time, of course she no longer got her cut. Thankfully Fiona rose above all that and wore her 'friend' hat over the top of her 'business' one. She sat back to listen without making any judgement and kept her thoughts to herself - at least until I'd finished. I couldn't help but notice her face becoming a little paler as I proceeded to describe my observations about the twins.

"Fiona. Take it from me - they're not normal. And I will admit to you that I'm even a little scared of them, but I daren't show any weakness. Constantly being boss is wearing me down, Fiona. I know that if they see the first opportunity to gain the upper hand, they'll go for the jugular and bring me down. Just like I'm sure they did all those years ago with their mother. That poor woman. Although I never knew her I'm convinced that those girls contributed to her downfall.

"Go on Louise. I'm here to listen," Fiona said to me, with a kind softness in her voice. She gently encouraged me to continue, even though my voice was trembling.

I did so whilst trying not to lose control of my quivering lips. "They're 15 now, but if you saw them you'd think they were 18 going on 19. Of course there's nothing wrong with that - all girls these days like to flaunt themselves and put make-up on to look older than they are. But it's all a game to them. It wouldn't surprise me if one of them - or even both of them - would trap a young lad to have sex with them and then blow the whistle on him for them being under-age. And I wouldn't put it past them to pull out the old rape card either. Woe betide any poor young lad falling under their spell."

I went on: "They're not beautiful in the classic sense, but they exude a confidence that can only get themselves into trouble - and indeed anyone else that gets caught up with them. I've even overheard lads talking at the bus stop about them. Bragging to their mates about how they'd like to have 'double helpings' with them, and how 'really fit' they are. I should be worried for the girls but, honestly, I actually shouldn't be surprised if they've already seduced some innocent lads to cause trouble. I feel so helpless Fiona. I should be bringing them up properly, shouldn't I?"

Fiona, bless her, did her best to quell my anxiety. "Louise, dear. It's not all your problem or your responsibility," I stopped her short. My worries about the girls' sexual behaviour was just a part of the problem.

"No, it's not just that Fi. I'm constantly worried and afraid for Oliver. He's only 12 and he's not as strong as they are. They bully him, I'm sure of it. Maybe not in a physical way yet, but definitely emotionally and verbally, and it will only be a matter of time before they do inflict some physical harm on him, I'm sure of it. And not only that I wouldn't be surprised if I were in their sights too."

Fiona laughed. As in 'funny ha ha' to begin with, but that soon changed to 'funny oh no!' when she caught a glimpse of how serious my expression was. That was the point at which I decided to tell her about something I'd found in their room under Hilary's bed. It was a sheet of paper that had sent shivers down my spine when I'd read it, and I never did let on to them that I'd discovered it. I don't know what possessed me to do so, but I took it downstairs to Stanley's office and made a copy of it before carefully replacing it. But the following day when I'd gone up to see if it was still there, I discovered it had been obliterated by thick red 'ink', except at the bottom, with what appeared to be the letters 'ALB' – my initials – had been scrawled. I had been so careful to put the paper back in precisely the same position, exactly where I'd found it, and yet they seemed to have discovered that I'd read it. How could they have possibly known? Yes, I was being daft and I knew it, but even Fiona shuddered when I showed her the photocopy of what had been scratchily written on the paper. And what had those red finger-prints dotted around the words been made with? The whole episode had given me the creeps, and finally my friend began to see why I was so alarmed.

Dazed by what I'd read, I'd photocopied and replaced the sheet of paper next to the cheap quill pen-set in a WH Smith bag under Hilary's bed and next to a bottle of red liquid. I had undone the bottle so as to examine the content. Was that blood, I asked myself? Well, it certainly wasn't Quink ink. And don't ask me why I made a photocopy - I just instinctively knew I had to. Thank goodness I had done, otherwise I'm sure Fiona would have dismissed me as being over imaginative. With this proof, at least she could now see where I was coming from.

Fiona read the document, wincing and creasing up her eyes as she came to the last line.

HILARY AND SOPHIE'S ELEVEN COMMANDMENTS
We shall have no other God but one another
We shall make an idol and stick pins in it
We shall indeed misuse the name of God
We shall not keep Sunday holy
We shall respect our father but not our dead mother
We shall one day commit murder
We shall gladly commit adultery when we're old enough
We shall steal what we can
We shall stitch up our idiot brother
We shall damage nice things belonging to others
We shall make ALB sorry for ever being here

"What do you think, 'We shall make ALB sorry...' means?" Fiona asked.

I couldn't answer that. I wanted to dismiss the whole thing as a schoolgirl prank, but it was all so...sinister. I mean, what kind of children came up with stuff like that? I feared that 'ALB' was Alberta Louise Baudet, although I hoped that it wasn't. The whole thing frightened me, especially the sixth 'commandment' mentioning murder. And how could they have said that about their poor mother? Had they no respect or feelings for her? Clearly they had - but not the feelings that normal children felt for a dead parent, that was for sure. I'd never in my life come across anything like this before.

"They're simply not normal, Fi. Do you know, I followed them one late afternoon when they were supposedly out at the shops. Stanley had given them some money for a treat to go and get themselves some new clothes, and he'd told them to get a cab home. It was my free time off and I was in town as well. Anyway, I spotted them and I don't know what it was that aroused my suspicion, but they seemed to be whispering to each other and giggling when they were at the top of Holland Lane. They had no idea that I was anywhere near, but thank goodness I was for the sake of the old lady that I now know lives at number 66. Her house is at the end of the road and around the corner, out of sight from the other houses. You would never believe what they did."

I could tell Fiona had now become as worried as I was. She leaned forward as I continued. "There was a hose-pipe connected to the outside tap at the front of the lady's garden. Hilary only went and pushed the nozzle through the letterbox while Sophie turned the tap on, and then they both ran away giggling uncontrollably. Luckily I had been able to run along and turn the water off before too much damage was done. I helped the old dear mop up the mess, which was quite considerable in only those few short minutes. Who knows what would have happened had I not been there."

I was in full throttle by then, with my friend present to confide in. "And there was another time when I'd caught them at home being utterly spiteful to Oliver."

I needed to let off steam. I had been bottling everything up, and I'm afraid poor Fiona was bearing the brunt of my rant. "Go on," she kindly encouraged me, and so I did.

"Well, the poor little lamb had been given some homework that involved drawing a rather intricate study of a ship that was the subject of a class project to do with transportation through the ages. He'd spent several evenings and pretty much a whole weekend up in his room copying out a drawing all very detailed, showing the positions of the port holes and life-boats and all the other things. He was, quite rightly, very proud of what he'd done, and I knew how much he was looking forward to showing it to Mrs. Bainbridge, his form teacher, on the Monday. You can guess what I'm going to tell you next, can't you? Yes. The twins 'accidentally' spilled their drinks over the picture, on the pretext that they'd tripped. There was no way that it was an accident Fiona. I felt so sorry for Oliver, truly I did, but there wasn't anything I could do. The picture was ruined and he simply didn't have the enthusiasm to do it all over again. Surely, Fiona, those girls can't be normal, can they?"

CHAPTER 34

Dear Uncle

"Writing that letter to him was the best thing I could have done"

Oliver Markland (2013)

f it hadn't been for Nanny Baudet I don't know what I would have done. I'd been pretty confused about my family and where I fitted in right from an early age. One day at school - I must have been only about seven or eight at the time - we had a new mistress and I remember she asked us to stand up one by one in front of all the other pupils to describe our families. I suppose it was her way of getting some idea of who we were and what our social backgrounds were. The boarding school I attended as a day-pupil catered for pupils from fairly well-to-do families, and so coming as I did from the Manor house on the Markland estate, complete with its acres of land and private lake, I didn't feel that my affluent background was anything particularly special. However, when I tried talking about myself to the class I realised, before I'd finished, how different my life was. My mum had died, I had a nanny who acted like my mum, and two sisters who weren't very nice to me, a dad who was sometimes at home and sometimes not, and that he had a special friend who was a man. I sensed my classmates suppressing their giggles when I tried describing all this, and it made me quite upset, so much so that I had to sit down and stop.

My sisters confused and upset me the most. I'd often catch them whispering to each other about their two favourite subjects – me and money. On more than one occasion I asked them to explain but they'd just stop mid-sentence and say in unison something like, "Oh it's nothing that concerns you and you wouldn't understand anyway". Were they so greedy that they hated the idea that their younger brother had come along and deprived them of their share of all of the Markland fortune? I sensed there was something everyone was keeping from me about my inheritance and maybe other stuff as well, and it was so horrible of them. I mean I'm not thick and I'm sure I would have understood if only they would have shared their little secrets. I'd ask dad about it, and he would just shrug and say that he was busy and that I really needn't worry myself.

It wasn't until I was 15, and I felt I maybe had a right to know if something really was being kept from me, that I got at least some answers to the questions that were increasingly worrying me. And it was Nanny Baudet who revealed what my dad had chosen not to tell me, when I confronted her one day. Unusually, she sat me down at the dining table and began an explanation that left me feeling quite numb and shaky. She told me I'd got two 'dads', one of them was my, er, dad, here in Saxton and the other was actually my Uncle Leslie, who lives down south somewhere. I couldn't remember much about him at that moment and my mind began frantically trying to work out what she meant. Had my uncle had an affair with my mum or something, and that liaison resulted in me being born? Sex hadn't been a subject that was a mystery to me, since the age of 11, when one of my friends at school graphically described to me how his parents 'did it'. I'd also become pretty clued up, thanks to our school sex lessons taught by the doddery old Mr. Lumsden. He was rubbish, and we loved to see him so embarrassed; it was really funny watching him squirm when he started talking about penises and vaginas.

But I digress. When I asked Nanny Baudet if my mum had had sex with Uncle Leslie, she looked a bit shocked and said that, "no she absolutely had not."

"Well, not exactly, you dear soul," were, I think, her precise words to me, which left me even more confused.

"Well she either had or hadn't, hadn't she?" I asked rather impatiently, but I got no more out of her then, and the situation seemed even less clear after our little chat. As a result, I decided to take matters into my own hands by writing to Uncle Leslie all by myself. I always received Christmas and birthday cards from him, never without some money in them, usually at least £20. For the most recent Christmas of 2012, and my 15th birthday in April of 2013 he upped that to £50! Dad would always get me to write out a thank-you letter straight away and I'd give it to him to put in an envelope and post it. Dad kept his address book in the left hand drawer of the old American desk in his study. The desk had a dark green leather insert on the surface, surrounded by old mahogany, and the leather was curled up at the edges. As I sat in his swivel office chair and pulled open the drawer to find the address book, my heart was thumping like mad. It felt wrong to be rummaging through my dad's private things. Even though logic told me that I was safe, what with Dad being out, the twins in their room upstairs and Nanny Baudet getting the dinner ready, every little squeak or sound that the house made set me on edge. I wanted to find that address and get out of the room as quickly as I could, so I pulled out the address book, found Uncle Leslie under 'L' and began writing down the address in my red exercise book that I'd taken with me. I hurriedly copied the words 'Leslie Markland, The Barge, Outside Hardings Yard, Wivenhoe, Essex'. What an unusual address. No postcode or house number. There was a phone number too but I didn't want to take too many chances as I kept hearing those house noises, like the creaky sounds that the radiator pipes make when the heating comes on, and I wanted to get out of there as quickly as I could.

I returned the book to the drawer, making sure I put it back precisely as I'd found it, quickly grabbed a stamp and an envelope, and then slowly pushed the drawer in so as not to bang it. I picked up my exercise book and swung the chair round to stand up.

"Caught you!" screamed both the girls at once. How they'd sneaked in and crept up behind me I don't know, but they scared the living daylights out of me. I had to hand over all my pocket money to them for the following four weeks after that. If I hadn't, they said they'd tell Dad all about me going through his private papers, and I didn't want that.

Anyway, having secretly discovered Uncle Leslie's address, if you can say secretly with the twins having caught me, I began writing him a letter. I kept changing it every night because I didn't really know what I wanted to say. And then, as if our English teacher magically knew that I was struggling, one day he set a lesson on how to write a business letter to someone. We were taught how to address the person, make an introduction, say why we were writing, make a CTA, and do a closing paragraph, and sign off with 'yours faithfully' if you were addressing Sir or Madam, or 'yours sincerely' if you are writing to a named person. Oh, by the way, I learned that a CTA was a 'call to action'. It means that you have to state clearly what it is you want the recipient to do, and preferably by when: All very useful.

So, armed with my new-found knowledge, I started again with another clean piece of paper, and in my neatest handwriting, completed what would turn out to be the most important thing I'd ever write.

The Manor House
The Markland Estate
Saxton
Yorkshire

Mr Leslie Markland
The Barge
Outside Hardings Yard
Wivenhoe, Essex

29th April, 2013

Dear Uncle Leslie,

I know I recently wrote to thank you for the money you kindly sent me for my birthday, but I wanted to write again, now that I have your address (usually my dad looks after putting my notes in the post to you). He doesn't know I'm writing to you again, so please can you keep that a secret between us.

There! That was a good start – getting the address in the right way, and then the introduction. Then I went on to say precisely why I was writing:

I was rather hoping that I could visit you some time please. Miss Baudet, the nanny who lives with us here, mentioned some things to me that left me a little puzzled about my family. I've tried to talk to Dad, but he's always very busy as he has a lot of important work to do. I could actually come in the summer holidays if that were convenient for you.

I looked up from the paper and wondered if I should use 'was' or 'were' in that last sentence. I decided on 'were', before continuing.

I've already looked up the train times, and I know how to get there by going to London, getting the underground to Liverpool Street station, and then another train to Wivenhoe. I would be very grateful if you could meet me at Wivenhoe station though, if you didn't mind.

Right! That got the main point out the way. Now it was time for the CTA. That was easy!

Please would you phone me on Thursday at 8pm, when I will be in my bedroom. I have written my number on a small card that I've Sellotaped to the top of this page. I thought you could keep it with you when you are out.

This was coming along quite well, I thought, but when I read it over I decided it was a little too formal, and perhaps even a touch demanding. So I decided to ease the tone. My closing paragraph should be more 'friendly'.

I am so looking forward to seeing you and where you live. I think you live on a boat. Is that true? If it is, I bet that's really fun. You must like it, as I know I would too if I lived on one.

I was really pleased with myself. Now all I had to do was sign off with a neat 'Yours sincerely', followed by my signature. I'd practiced signing my name over and over to make it look as grown-up as I could, then I read the whole letter again to check for any punctuation and spelling mistakes.

Perfect. I couldn't find a single one! So, without further hesitation, I folded up the letter nice and neatly and put it in the envelope upon which I stuck the stamp and copied the address. I then put it in my satchel ready to post at the bottom of the drive the following morning, Monday, on the way to school.

By Wednesday I was wondering whether the letter had arrived, and I imagined Uncle Leslie's reaction if and when he opened it. I felt that, judging by the kind words he always put in my birthday and Christmas cards, he was a nice man. He must have been a bit surprised and I hoped he didn't mind getting it. On Thursday morning I woke up with butterflies in my stomach. Would Uncle Leslie phone me this evening as I'd asked him to in my letter? I couldn't really pay any attention in the lessons at school all day, and in the afternoon and evening at home I guess I was quieter than usual, especially at tea-time. I really like fish finger sandwiches and baked beans, which is what Nanny Baudet made that evening, but I left half my dinner unfinished and quickly dashed up to my room saying that I had a lot of homework to get through. I got myself bathed and into my pyjamas all ready for eight o'clock, and I lay on my bed with my new mobile phone next to me.

Almost exactly on the hour, it rang. I answered it nervously but excitedly, and went on to have a really good chat with Uncle Leslie. Funnily, he said I could just call him Leslie if I liked, and so I did. I found him very easy to talk to, although I thought to begin with he sounded a little nervous. Was he thinking what I was thinking – about him being my 'other' dad? I don't know, as we both skirted around any mention of that, until later on when I asked him a bit about my mum and him. He went quiet and then said he'd tell me all about that in person. Anyway, he went on to say that yes he does live on a boat, and he also has a little dog called Harry. It sounded like the place he lives was great, and he said

I could come down and stay with him in the summer, but I would have to clear it with my dad first.

He said he was already looking forward to it, and we agreed it could be in July, when there is apparently a regatta on in Wivenhoe. Actually, I didn't know what a regatta was, but it sounded like fun anyway, and he said he might take us out on his other boat. He has two! I really couldn't wait to go. Writing that letter to him was the best thing I could have done. The only problem was clearing the whole thing with my dad, and I really didn't want to do that. For one thing Dad would ask how I got in touch with Uncle Leslie, but for now I didn't need to worry about what I'd say.

CHAPTER 35

Moving Forward

"I still couldn't help being reminded about Leslie, pretty much every waking day"

Part One: Silvie Tosgiev (2013)

It must have been 13 years ago since I left London for good and returned to live with my parents in Sweden, and I knew they would welcome me back. Before making the tough decision to go back to Sweden I had been in my own little cuckoo, enjoying the social sexual scenario of the several nightclubs and handsome London men. Or should that be cocoon? Forgive me - I doubt that I will ever master the English language entirely. For quite some time I had been so happy living in Mayfair and working at Miss Pinchbeck's agency. Then of course I met Leslie Markland and, dare I say, for the first time in my life, felt myself falling in love with him, especially after we'd spent that wonderful weekend together on his boat. He was so strong physically, and yet so gentle. I also loved his quirky Wivenhoe home - such a contrast to the hustle bustle of London, and of course I loved his little dog.

Something had clearly happened to me, and I was very much looking forward to spending more of my time with Leslie. But then it all went, how do you say, pear shape.

I had been so distressed when Miss Pinchbeck called me into her office and I first learned about the agency's mix-up concerning Leslie's sperm sample. I was only doing what I'd been told to do at the time, but I couldn't help feeling personally responsible for what had happened. I really ought to have insisted with Miss Pinchbeck that the agency check more stringently about who the end-users of all samples would be - instead of relying on information from a few ticked boxes on forms that anyone could have filled in!

I'm afraid to admit my cowardly reaction when being told of that poor mother's suicide was to run away and distance myself from the whole situation. Despite my growing feelings towards Leslie, and what was happening to me, I had to get as far away as I could from him, and possibly never see him again. I quit my job with the agency, called my parents, and booked a plane home.

After settling back with my family in Stockholm, the enthusiastic sexual appetite that I'd enjoyed so much in my younger years had lessened, but it had not entirely become extinguished. I continued to enjoy men's company, but not quite so obsessively. I was unfulfilled. During one recent liaison, when I was half-heartedly 'walking on the wild side' if you understand my meaning, out of nowhere I had a funny turn. Suddenly I just lost all concentration in what I was doing. The poor frustrated guy: his equipment shrank quicker than it had grown. I got up from my knees, left the job in hand and went to make a cup of tea – a drink habit I'd gained from my time of living in England. He sheepishly got dressed and left.

With my cup of tea finished, I climbed into my bed and pulled the duvet over me. I just lay there for the rest of the afternoon, thinking. I decided there and then that I must do something better than to occupy my spare time having meaningless casual sex with men I didn't care to be with. I had an uncontrollable urge to find out how Leslie was.

Although 13 years and big changes had now gone under the bridge - if that's the way I should say it - since I'd last seen him, I still couldn't help being reminded about Leslie, pretty much every waking day.

Had he been in contact with his son, I wondered? I was also curious as to whether Leslie would ever wish to talk to me again after such a long time? Did he still have his dog? Did he still live on his barge? I wanted to discover the answer to these questions, and others too. I wanted to see him again. I wanted to return to Wivenhoe, to see the river, the boats, the pubs. To breathe in the clean riverside air once again and to discover some inner contentment, something that had been missing from my life. What should I do?

I decided I would get in touch with Leslie one more time.

Part Two: Leslie Markland

"I had a strange feeling of déjà vu"

Out of the blue, at the beginning of May 2013, I received a letter. For some inexplicable reason, only known to him, my son wanted to come and see me, his father - or his uncle, as he called me in his letter. I assumed that meant that he was still unaware of who I really was to him. Quite why I did it I don't know, but I decided to tell him to call me 'Leslie' and told him I would explain more about our estranged family if he did come to see me in Wivenhoe. Judging by his letter he seemed to like the idea of me living on a boat. Maybe I'd already made a positive impression on him. I remember how good that had made me feel.

You see, in his letter he'd asked me to telephone him at a precise time one evening later that week, which I did. To begin with there were mutual jangly nerves and false starts, but then we actually got on famously. Thinking that he was already impressed with me living on a barge I also told him that I had another boat and that we could use it to explore the river. With that he got really quite excited. We arranged that he would make his way to Wivenhoe on the train later in the summer, probably the first weekend of the school holidays, and that I'd meet him at the station. I don't mind admitting that leading up to that date my anxiety grew exponentially. By Oliver getting in touch with me this had been my golden opportunity to make amends, and I was determined not to mess up ever again - for his sake.

As the weeks went by, and the scheduled weekend came closer, my bravado became weaker and weaker, until I got myself into quite a state. I very nearly called Oliver to cancel, making some stupid lame excuse. But thankfully, whilst caressing a bottle of Merlot at the L shaped bar in The Station, my drunken state actually caused me to come to my senses and stopped me being so pathetic. Sitting opposite me, Andy Stollery, from whom I'd bought the little boat that I'd hardly ever used, looked into my eyes trying to fathom me out. "Penny for your thoughts," he prompted.

Andy sat back in amazement when, without taking my gaze away from the old station clock on the wall that kept accurate time twice a day, I said in monotone: "My son's coming here next week".

"I never knew you had a son, you little dark horse tinker you," was the best he could come up with, but it had been sufficient to raise a sense of pride in my heart that I had never previously experienced.

"I very nearly didn't know either, Andy," was all I could offer in reply.

Before starting to elaborate, I took two large gulps of wine from my glass, and when I'd emptied it Andy asked Chelsea from behind the bar to pour me another.

I dare say I could have done with a friendly ear to bend that evening, and I was ready to tell Andy everything. But I'd hardly even begun telling him my story when my telephone vibrated in my pocket. "Hang on a moment, Andy. I'll have to go outside a minute and get this," I said, before continuing. "Probably a customer... The signal's terrible around here so I'll need to move about near the railway."

I climbed down from my stool and pulled out my telephone, looking at the screen as I went out the door. I didn't recognise the number at all, especially as it had an international prefix +46 showing on the screen. Nine times out of ten I wouldn't have accepted a number unknown, but on this occasion it must have been that tenth time.

"Hello?" I said tentatively, and as there was no immediate reply I repeated my "hello."

The caller's first word response sent a rush of excitement through me, just as a train starting screeching to a halt at the platform over the road.

"Leslie!" shouted Silvie down the phone.

Was I dreaming? It had been years since we'd last spoken. After all that business about the agency mix-up she seemed to have disappeared off the face of the earth and I hadn't heard from her since.

There was only one way to find out if I actually was dreaming or not, and so I put the telephone closer to my ear.

"Hello? Silvie?" I shouted back over the sound of the train. "How are you? Where are you?" At that moment the noise of the train brakes increased and the signal decreased. "Hello. Hello. Can you hear me?" We must have both said those same words at the same time, but there was an odd time delay as we tried to communicate, without success.

I had a strange feeling of déjà vu as the line went dead just as it had done once before, in exactly the same spot. I tried to call her back straight away but to no avail. Bad timing: no signal and my telephone's battery had also gone dead. "Bloody mobile telephones - I hate them!" I cursed, under my breath.

I noticed it was getting dark by now as I wandered back to the L-shaped bar, shell-shocked by what had happened. Why, after all this time, had Silvie called me? Andy was no longer anywhere to be seen, which was a shame because I really could have done with someone to talk to, and I knew he would be a good listener. My topped-up glass was still intact on the bar where it had been left. It didn't last very long, nor was it very long before I'd drunk quite a few more. Elated, excited, anxious and happy, I staggered out of the pub, swayed drunkenly along the lamp-lit West Street, turned right into Bath Street and left at the end to go along the quay. The dusky sight of the two swans and their adopted goose gliding gracefully on the river, which was as still as a millpond, made me smile. I passed by the Rose & Crown and chuckled inwardly as I ambled along by Neil's boat, complete with plants growing on its roof and its multi-coloured canopy covered in glowing neon lights that slowly changed colour. That made me feel even more drunk. As I walked along the gravel path I very nearly tripped up over the potholed uneven surface until I reached Barnacle, my barge and my home.

Harry knew I was approaching. I could hear him scampering and running around inside, excited that his master was coming home, as I unlatched the padlock.

"Hello Harry. I'm back," I greeted him as I clambered down the steep steps to the cabin, through to the far end and opened up the rear door looking out to the river.

The red and green flashing lights from the distant flood prevention barrier reflected in the night air against the calm black and muddy water. I bent down to scoop up Harry in my arms. We were companions, both glad of each other's company, one of us sober, one of us not. I began to laugh. A laugh that I stifled to begin with, but the laughter in me grew and grew until I was out of control. Little Harry didn't know what to make of me and he tilted his head first to the left, then to the right, quizzically.

First Oliver, then Silvie: For the first time in ages, drunk or not, I was feeling happy.

Part Three: Oliver Markland

"I did try on one or two occasions to talk to dad"

I couldn't wait to get to the end of term. All of my friends at school were excited because it meant a break from lessons, homework, tests and GCSE's, but for me it was the anticipation of going on my secret journey.

I say secret journey, but in fact it wasn't one hundred percent secret as I confided in Nanny Baudet one day about what I was intending to do. She understood better than anyone else about how I felt about being there at the Manor house. She had observed how my sisters behaved towards me and how I'd taken to hurrying my tea most evenings, then heading up to my room and locking the door. The man I still referred to as 'Dad' wasn't around very often, but when he was at home he didn't see what they could be like. They acted so differently when he was around, and besides, butter wouldn't melt in their mouths as far as he was concerned. Don't get me wrong. He was good to me but blind to how those girls were around me. Nanny Baudet wasn't blind to the twins' bad behaviour though, and I guessed she probably made sure Dad knew about some of the bad stuff they got up to.

They also misbehaved away from the Manor because they quite openly talked about their exploits in front of me. There was the occasion they said they should make a pact between themselves where 'boys will always come second and Hilary and Sophie come first, no matter what'. And their language was terrible. There's no need to constantly be using the 'f' word, let alone the 'c' word, which is quite unnecessary in my opinion. The example of their behaviour that best shows what they were capable of? I should perhaps have told Dad, but what they did was so horrible I felt sure he wouldn't believe his lovely daughters were capable of such a thing.

Sophie and Hilary never do anything spontaneously, and this was no exception. Their latest stunt had been carefully planned to cause the most amount of excitement for them. With me in earshot they described their game of 'chicken' in which they'd coaxed two poor unsuspecting lads in their beaten-up old Mini to play their stupid game. Incredibly, they had persuaded these lads, who were both about 19 and should have known better, to drive to a familiar network of narrow country lanes that crossed a busy main road. The girls blatantly admitted in front of me that they'd promised to have sex with the boys if they completed their dare. They had to drive their Mini at speed down the lane and straight across the main road without stopping or even slowing down, and then turn around and go back and do it again. Of course, on a promise, the boys did what they were told, and the girls fulfilled their part of the bargain afterward in a lay-by. I was pretty disgusted, I can tell you. And of course they were doing their best to embarrass me when they said they bet I wished I had been with them to see how sex was done 'by experts' as they put it.

I did try on one or two occasions to talk to dad about me going to Uncle Leslie's, but it had been a hopeless exercise. He was usually preoccupied with something, or if not we would all be together, including Hilary and Sophie, and they were the last people I wanted to be listening in on that conversation. So in the end I gave up, deciding to go it alone without telling anyone. But the nearer I got to the day - the first Saturday after the end of term, I became more and more nervous about getting into trouble if I left without telling anyone at all. My dad would think I'd run away, and Nanny Baudet might get into trouble herself if it appeared that she also didn't know where I was. So I confided in her and made her promise not to be worried and not to tell dad until well after I'd gone. In fact if he wasn't at home that weekend he needn't be told at all because I was planning to be back by the Monday and he'd be none the wiser anyway. I do love Nanny Baudet. She's so kind. Of course she tried to dissuade me from making my journey, but I think she could see how determined I was to go, and she appreciated my desire to see my 'uncle'.

What I hadn't known at the time, but found out later, was that Uncle Leslie had actually called the Manor and left a message on the answerphone for dad a couple of days prior to my planned visit. That was when everything had to come out in the open during the police investigation that followed 'the incident', and the subsequent inquest. The message from Uncle Leslie was merely reassuring Dad not to worry about anything, that he'd be taking good care of me and that he'd make sure I got on the train safely for my return journey at the end of the weekend. It turned out that the message had never been listened to by the intended recipient, because the twins intercepted it first without telling anyone. In that respect Sophie and Hilary did me a favour without realising. They just continued acting as though they knew nothing of my forthcoming trip, and so I had no idea that they were plotting to do something as a result of what they had heard on that answerphone message.

We finally broke up at the end of term on the Friday, and school closed earlier than usual at one o'clock. I hurried home and pulled out the rucksack from the top of my wardrobe and placed it on the bed. It had a number of side pockets to it, plus two main areas into which I could stuff my overnight pyjamas, my clean vest and pants and two pairs of socks. I'd forgotten to lock my bedroom door but hadn't been too bothered because I thought the girls were out. But I was wrong, and they casually walked in and demanded to know what I was doing. I quickly pulled the rucksack closed so that it was impossible for them to see any of the items I was packing. I made up a story on the spot about sorting out my cupboards, saying that it was end of term and an ideal time to have a good clear-up of my things. I thought that I'd managed to throw them off the scent. The girls looked at each other, and without saying a further word they raised their eyebrows and exited my bedroom. They left me with an uneasy feeling.

Later that afternoon I went down to the kitchen table that was packed high with lovely things that Nanny Baudet had kindly bought for me. There were Penguin biscuits, KitKats, salmon sandwiches and bags of Golden Wonder cheese and onion crisps - my favourite.

"Help yourself to whatever you feel like taking, Oliver dear", she whispered in my ear. "Store them in this plastic container, take them upstairs and put them in your rucksack ready for your adventure. Then come back down here for your dinner. I've made you a nice chicken and mushroom pie and some chips and peas."

I filled myself up that evening, went to bed early and prepared to get a good night's sleep. But before drifting off, I suddenly remembered that I would need money for my train ticket. I pulled the chair over to the wardrobe and reached up for the tin I'd kept hidden there, pulled it down and opened the lid. I counted the notes and coins and I had £132.72 altogether, saved up out of my pocket money and over the previous Christmas and my most recent birthday. I would have had £40 more if my sisters hadn't extorted money from me in return for their silence about me sneaking into my dad's office and opening his desk drawer. I hated Hilary and Sophie, and although I'd miss Nanny Baudet, I would be glad to get away from them, even for a day or two.

Locking my door, I placed my packed rucksack on the chair, put the tin of money under my pillow and felt excited but scared as I drifted off into a deep sleep.

CHAPTER 36

The Following

"Being called 'Sir'– getting taxis – it all made me feel so adult!"

Oliver Markland (2013)

I t was 05.17 precisely when I awoke. The early morning summer sun was not yet in the sky but the dawn was certainly bright enough to wake me. I'd deliberately not lowered the blackout blinds in my bedroom the night before so that I'd wake up nice and early. I lay there, running through the whole scenario of the day's forthcoming adventure in my mind, wondering if it would actually turn out the way I was imagining. I felt excited, I was wide awake, and glad that I'd had a night of good quality sleep.

I looked up at the ceiling. What would Uncle Leslie be like? Would he meet me at the station as we'd arranged? What if he didn't? Would I have enough money for my train ticket and other things that I wanted to get, like a book to read on the journey? How would my bus journey go from here to Leeds station, and what would it be like getting from Kings Cross station in London across to Liverpool Street station? What if I missed the train from there to Wivenhoe? I began to panic, and told myself to stop being so ridiculous and calm down. So long as I could get to Leeds station from the Manor house I would just have to take the rest of my journey one step at a time, and not worry about all the 'what-ifs'.

When I went downstairs for a glass of milk, Nanny Baudet, who was already up, very kindly offered to give me a lift in her car to the station. Relieved, I began to relax and went back upstairs and got dressed, re-packed my rucksack about three times, and then got dressed again after changing my mind about what clothes I should wear. I wanted to create a good first impression when I reached Uncle Leslie's… or Leslie's I suppose I should say. I couldn't wait to see his boat, and I was also looking forward to meeting his dog. I was looking forward to everything.

By seven o'clock I was back downstairs again, eating my bowl of Cheerios. "Are you all packed and ready then, young Oliver?" asked Nanny Baudet. "Because if you are, we may as well set off early just in case we hit the traffic. There's nothing worse than racing against the clock when you need to be somewhere by a certain time and the whole world's against you getting there."

"The twins stayed out last night so I don't have to get their breakfasts or anything," she continued. "And your dad's over at Tristan's, so I've more or less got the whole day to myself. I can park up at the station when I drop you off, see that you get the right train, and then go and have a coffee, get my hair done and do some shopping afterwards. I can use the opportunity to have a 'me' day, as I'd call it. I'd already made an appointment at a posh new hairdressers' that's just opened in Whitehall Road, and apparently they're very good. I'm going to get them to give me a new colour. What do you think I should go for Oliver?" she asked me as she lightly patted her already substantially quaffed bun.

"I honestly don't know, Miss B. I'm not very good on ladies' hairstyles, but I'm very glad that you've got something nice planned for your day. And thanks for saying that you'll help me get on the right train. I think that's the bit I'm most anxious about. I'll go and clean my teeth now and I'll be back down in fifteen minutes."

I'd recently begun calling her 'Miss B' because 'Louise' or 'Alberta' were, she'd decided, too informal and 'Nanny Baudet' rather outdated, now that I was 15. So we'd settled on 'Miss B', which I rather liked. I scraped my chair as I got up from the kitchen table and pushed it back against the wooden floorboards. I wondered whether Leslie would have wooden boards on his boat. Would he even have a kitchen table? I'd be finding out later, but for now I had to get to the station, and so I ran upstairs, did my teeth - remembering to put my toothbrush in with my toiletry bag in the rucksack - checked myself in the mirror, put my jacket on and swung my rucksack on my back. I was ready. Then I very nearly forgot something that would have led to disaster. I went over to my bed, pulled back the pillow and opened the tin containing my £132.72. I left the £2.72 behind ready to start saving up again and put the rest into my Harry Potter wallet.

Within five minutes we were in Miss B's car and scrunching along the gravel drive. As we approached the junction with the road, another car, a brown Nissan Micra was just about to turn into the drive. It was badly dented on its rear wing. Inside I could see a couple of lads in the front, and the unmistakable Sophie and Hilary in the back, all made up and tarty-looking. I guessed they were returning from having sex somewhere last night. God, they really were disgusting. I began to slide down in my seat so that I wouldn't be seen, but I don't think I was quick enough. It was useless trying to continue making myself invisible to them, and as if Miss B could read my mind, she wound down her window as the other car drew up alongside hers, and the lad who was driving wound down his window.

Miss B shouted past him, to the girls in the back. "I'm going to get my hair done, and Oliver's with me to do some shopping. There's some bacon and eggs for you in the pantry. See you later."

"See you later then, Miss Baudet," the twins said in unison. "Goodbye Oliver. Have a good trip won't you... to the shops." They giggled together and the Nissan Micra continued on its way up the drive to the Manor house. The house being empty meant they would probably be indulging

in more sex with their new friends, I predicted. Miss B turned out onto
the main road heading for central Leeds.

Most of the journey to the station was made without us talking to each
other, as we were both intent on listening to the radio. The presenter
was his usual funny self and we chuckled along at his jokes in between
the records. That helped us to calm our nerves – mine about getting the
right train, and Miss B about driving in general. However, despite her
over cautious slow driving, the Swillington Common road works and
the numerous sets of traffic lights in Leeds, we still managed to get to
the station's multi-storey car park in good time for my 9.23 train to
London. Already the car park was filling up with the day's travellers and
shoppers, and we both kept our eyes peeled for a spare gap as we edged
along the fourth floor. As we turned another corner I thought I spotted a
car very similar to the one I'd seen the twins being driven in less than an
hour previously. But brown Nissan Micras weren't exactly uncommon,
and why would those boys be here anyway? Silly me! Paranoid me!
Dismissing the coincidence that this particular Micra also had a large
dent in it, I reasoned with myself that no doubt the young men would be
busily occupied with Sophie and Hilary. They'd be taking advantage of
having the house to themselves, or rather they'd be letting the twins take
advantage of them! And so I returned my attention to more pressing
matters.

Fortunately a vacant parking space presented itself before too long,
and Miss B gently steered in before she locked up and we set about
finding a way down to the station concourse.

Having found the ticket office easily, I joined the queue. In front of me
was a man dressed smartly in a suit carrying a laptop computer, and
in front of him a lady in her seventies or even eighties who must have
only been five feet tall. She was holding one of those portable animal
cages, although I couldn't see what was inside it. At the very front was
a young couple who kept kissing and looking into each other's eyes as

if there were no other people in the world. I made a mental note that if they were going to be on the same London-bound train as me, then I would find a different carriage to theirs. Being stuck in a seat next to them wouldn't be much fun, I thought, but the animal cage lady looked friendly.

When it came to my turn at the kiosk there was by then quite a queue behind me, including a young lad whose face appeared vaguely familiar.

Dear Miss Baudet, bless her, waited with me all the time until it eventually became my turn, and I asked the ticket man for my return fare to Wivenhoe.

Loudly, the man at the counter repeated the destination: "Wivenhoe? That's Platform 11, Sir."

I'd never been addressed as 'Sir' before, and I rather liked it. As I happily grabbed my ticket, I turned and noticed the lad who had been behind me had departed from the line and I saw him scurrying off to the coffee shop opposite to join what looked like a couple of his friends inside. Odd I thought, he must have changed his mind about his journey or something, or felt in urgent need for a hot drink.

I had a while before the train was due to leave - 27 minutes to be precise, but rather than wander around aimlessly I told Miss B that I'd rather get settled and find a good seat, preferably with it facing forwards. So, after a visit to the loo, while she waited outside and held my rucksack we both headed for Platform 11, where I showed my ticket and went through the barrier.

"Thanks, Miss B. I'll be fine now. Thanks for everything, and I hope you have a nice day getting your hair done. And enjoy your shopping as well," I said, relieved that my escapade had so far gone without a hitch. "There's 19 minutes before the train leaves, and there's no need for you to hang around any longer, I'll be fine now. Oh… and I've got more than enough money left over for a taxi back from here to the Manor house on Monday, without troubling you for a lift. I should be home by tea time, so I'll see you then," I added. Gosh – here was I buying train tickets, being called 'Sir', getting taxis – it all made me feel so adult!

Miss B leant over the barrier machine to give me a little kiss and told me to be careful, enjoy the journey, ask for directions to Liverpool Street station, and have a good time in Wivenhoe. She also explained that she would take care of informing Dad if necessary about my trip, but it was more than likely that he'd be away all weekend.

With that I turned and began walking along the platform, choosing the best carriage to sit in, taking account of which forward-facing seats were vacant and, very importantly, who else was sitting nearby. I looked through the windows and saw the lady with the animal cage. She was in the seat facing backwards and at a table. Perfect. I could sit opposite her. I climbed aboard, made my way to the table seat, took off my rucksack and jacket, and got myself comfortable. I placed my book, *Travels with Charley* by John Steinbeck, on the table, hoping that it would become a conversation opener with the lady. She didn't notice though, as she was so engrossed in looking after the contents of her animal cage.

"There, there Baci, you settle down and mummy will look after you," she said placing the cage on the seat next to her. Inside was a black and white cat.

I removed my packed sandwiches from my rucksack, placed them next to my book, and settled back in my seat ready for the train ride to begin.

Part Two: Alberta Louise Baudet

"My hair could wait. This was more serious"

I couldn't help feeling anxious for the young man. Oliver had never been on a long train journey by himself before. Yes, I was aware that there were many 15-year-olds who had done plenty of travelling, but young Master Oliver had been leading a fairly sheltered life on the Markland Estate. The very least I could do - as much to calm my own nerves as his - was to ensure he got on the correct train to London. I almost wanted to go with him all the way to Wivenhoe, just to make sure he coped.

But I realised I was being over protective. Of course he'd be fine, I told myself. After all, he was an intelligent boy and very able when it came to making conversation. If he were to get into difficulty finding his way across London, he was more than capable of asking the way. And there would be several rail staff to assist him in locating the correct platform for the train on to Wivenhoe, where he assured me that Mr. Leslie would be meeting him. He had promised to phone to let me know of his safe arrival.

"So stop fussing Miss B!" I whispered out loud to myself.

As it turned out, I did accompany him to Wivenhoe, but that honestly hadn't been my intention. Well, when I say 'accompany', that wasn't strictly true, as the boy had no idea I was anywhere near.

You see, I had just said goodbye to Oliver at the ticket barrier, giving him a little kiss that I'm sure embarrassed him - I just couldn't help it - and I began walking away towards the station exit. I turned to catch a last glimpse of him as he boarded the carriage, and at that very moment I also noticed, unmistakably, Sophie and Hilary running along the platform, boarding the same train. They had been running together and clutching at each other, which was making it difficult for them to move without drawing attention to themselves, which was why I noticed them from such a distance. Why on earth would they be getting on the train to London? I was absolutely certain it was them. Something was up, and I didn't like it one bit. I needed to make a quick decision, and that was what I did after my initial hesitation.

There were only six minutes left before the train was due to depart, and I could see the queue at the ticket office was at least six people deep, so buying a ticket wasn't an option. Besides, I surely couldn't go with them, could I? I had my own plans for the day, and I'd been really looking forward to getting my hair done. But no, my hair could wait. This was more serious. I ran to the platform barrier.

"Ticket please, Madam," said an insistent railway official. I gave him one of my pleading, helpless looks and breathlessly replied: "It's my nephew - he's only 15, and he's got on the train, but he's forgotten his money. I just need to give it to him."

"Be quick about it then, Madam. The train leaves in three minutes," said the man, who clearly enjoyed being in a position of authority.

A man who likes the sound of his own voice, I thought, as I ran along the platform and jumped inside the first carriage I came to. Once on the train, I moved cautiously along three carriages until I reached the one before where the twins were. I could just about see them through the glass sliding-door. Should I confront them and ask them what they were doing on the train? I sat down in a seat out of their line of vision, while I contemplated what I should do next.

Just then the decision was made for me as I heard the guard's whistle and then the train suddenly lurched forward. The poster hoardings and lamp-posts on the platform began, very slowly at first, to move past my line of sight, as the train gradually gathered speed. I was on my way to London, whether I liked it or not, and all I could do was to sink back in my seat, gather my thoughts and catch my breath. I was following the twins following young Oliver. At least that was what I guessed was happening at the time. The whole crazy scenario was as clear as mud.

CHAPTER 37

Underground, Overground, Undercover

"This was no longer a rehearsal - it was the real thing"

Part One: Oliver Markland (2013)

I felt such a sense of relief as the train finally began its slow acceleration out of the station, and as it gathered speed I looked out at the grim buildings that it passed. Soon we would be hurtling through the countryside on our way to London, and I felt rather pleased with myself to have managed to get out of Leeds without any hitches.

I was hungry already, so I began unwrapping my sandwiches from their foil covering, and I glanced up at the same time to catch the lady opposite watching me. "Would you like one of my sandwiches?" I asked her.

She shook her head. "No dear, that's kind of you, but you enjoy them. Baci and I have already eaten thank you." And that began a conversation where I discovered that the name of her cat in the cage was pronounced 'Barchie', named after an Italian chocolate bar because the cat's distinctive brown chin made it look like it had become stained with chocolate. What peculiar names some people give to their pets, I thought. The lady went on to explain that she used to live near Naples, in Italy, and as a child the Baci chocolate bars were her favourite sweets.

She enquired about my end destination, and my reply was met with a blank expression. When I explained that Wivenhoe was near to Colchester and that I would be getting off one stop after the oldest recorded town in the country, she brightened up.

"Well you have a nice time dear. If you don't mind I'm going to give my eyes a little rest now. It's been a tiring morning, and this thing weighs a ton and my poor arms are rather aching," she sighed, referring to Baci's cage.

With that she put her head to one side and went straight to sleep, before I'd had the opportunity to ask her where she was travelling to. That would give me something to talk about when she awoke.

I ate my sandwiches and read some of my book, but couldn't really concentrate properly. I was simply too excited as I kept looking up and out the window at the changing scenery as it whizzed by. Occasionally there would be an enormously loud bang as we passed a train going the other way, so close to ours that the force of air rattled all the windows and doors at once. The first occasion this happened I nearly jumped out of my seat, but by the third or fourth time I just sat back and took it in my stride. Oh yes, I was now getting used to this train travel business, and I began looking forward to the adventure of my onward journey across the capital on the London Underground. I had planned and rehearsed that section of the journey so many times and now here I was actually carrying out the exercise. This was no longer a rehearsal - it was the real thing. Three days away from the 'terrible twins', as I now called them, and their teasing and bullying - wonderful! Perhaps it might even turn out to be longer if things work out the way I rather hoped they would in future.

I never did discover any more about the lady opposite me, not even her name, although I could see a brass tag attached to her shoulder bag etched with the word 'Lord'. What did that mean, I wondered? Was that the make of bag, or an indication of her faith, or simply her name? I would never know because she didn't wake up until we began trundling slowly and loudly along the tracks as the train snaked its way into Kings Cross station.

As the wheels gave out their horrible screeches, the lady opened her eyes and immediately started a motherly conversation with Baci, asking him, or her, whether he or she had been behaving whilst 'mummy was having sleepy byes'. God, I sincerely hoped that Uncle Leslie wouldn't be talking like that to *his* pet. If that were the case I'd puke within five minutes and have to get off the boat!

"It's been nice meeting you dear", the lady said to me as she stood up to put on her thick maroon coat, which she struggled into, despite the summer heat.

"I hope you have a nice time in, where was it? Wivenhoe - yes, Wivenhoe, I remember dear. Yes, you have a lovely time. Say goodbye to the young man, Baci," she added.

There's nowt stranger than folk, I said to myself, quietly, keeping it under my breath of course, not wishing to be rude in any way. After all, she was only trying to be kind, and when she reached into her bag and pulled out a bar of Baci chocolate that she handed me, I thought how nice my fellow passenger had been. I could have had a lot worse, I concluded.

"There you are dear," she said smiling, "I get these sent over to me by my sister who still lives in Italy. You enjoy it."

A few moments later, after the train came to a halt, she and Baci were gone, as she walked briskly along the platform towards the ticket barrier. I gathered my belongings and, along with everyone else, got off the train and began walking in the same direction. I contemplated catching her up and offering to carry her cat cage - but no, I reasoned, I really had to concentrate one hundred percent on making sure the next leg of my journey went according to plan, without any distractions from Baci.

Part Two: Alberta Louise Baudet
"It dawned on me that the girls had money on their minds"

There wasn't very much I could do on the journey except sit there hoping that a ticket inspector wouldn't be examining my ticket, or rather the lack of one. I'd have some explaining to do and I rehearsed my 'poor, silly old lady' speech that I'd give if the need arose. Fortunately it wasn't necessary, and now that we'd arrived at Kings Cross I worked out what I'd have to do next. I'd been mulling over the various options during the whole journey, and now it was time to put my decision into practice. I couldn't turn round and get on the next train back, not now that I'd come this far. I wouldn't approach Hilary, Sophie, or Oliver, as I was curious as to why the girls were actually on the train, and if I confronted them I was sure that I would probably be fobbed off with some convoluted lie - and I wanted to learn the truth. So my chosen tactic was to follow them if they followed Oliver, but taking care to stay out of view from any of them. That wasn't going to be easy. The station would be packed with people, and I was going to have to keep my wits about me if I wasn't to lose track of them. Fortunately both twins were wearing identical bright lime green tops that thankfully stood out even from quite a distance. Oliver was less distinctive with his jeans and black lightweight rain jacket, but he did have his rucksack on his back and that was orange and red. I would just have to hope that the girls would keep up with him and that I would keep up with them, but as we walked along the platform it occurred to me that there was always the possibility that the twins weren't actually there to follow Oliver and that they may simply have decided to have a day out in London. It was unlikely, but possible, and I guessed I would soon have my answer if they went off in a different direction to Oliver after passing through the ticket barrier.

A sickening thought stopped me in my tracks. Oh no, the barrier! I'd forgotten about that. How would I get through without a ticket? If I stopped and declared my lack of any ticket to the man at the barrier I'd be made to buy one, and that would take up valuable time and I'd probably lose sight of the twins. I'd have to be bold and walk right past the man, and through the open wider section at the end of all the automatic machines.

"Ticket please, Madam," called out the man.

"Shit!" I muttered. I don't often swear, but, believe me, this situation definitely warranted it. Be assertive, I told myself.

"I'm in a hurry. I have to catch a train, and I don't have time to rummage round my bag in search of my ticket. I've already shown it to the inspector on the train," I lied as I continued past him. I hoped he wouldn't cause a scene.

"Madam," he continued slowly, "This is a train station. Everyone is having to catch a train. I need to see your ticket."

"Shit, shit," I thought. The specks of lime green colour were getting further and further away. Just then a party of 15 or so Japanese tourists with cameras dangling from their necks jostled their way past the man. This was my chance to become Japanese for a few seconds as I threw myself into the middle of their group and escaped into the safety of the main concourse. I ran to gain proximity to the lime green colours that were just about still in my line of sight. No railway official appeared to be on my trail but I knew I'd been lucky that time. I'd almost lost sight of the twins, but I would definitely have to get a ticket for the underground and then one to Wivenhoe if the girls really were following Oliver. I prayed they weren't, and that there would be an entirely innocent explanation for their presence here. I was a woman in my late-sixties, and I wasn't built for this kind of excitement at this stage of my life. As the lime green dots went down the steps to the underground I could see that they were a few yards behind the orange and red dot in the further distance, so I could only assume that Oliver was indeed being followed by the twins. What on earth were those girls up to? I sensed that they weren't doing this just to keep a watchful eye over him out of the goodness in their hearts. They had precious little goodness in their hearts as far as I could make out. It was imperative that I didn't lose sight of them so I literally ran as quickly as I could towards them, creating a right old racket with my heels clattering on the hard floor as I manoeuvred myself past the hordes of commuters and travellers along the way. I must have been an undignified sight, as my idea of running was more like a fast walk, especially when my hair became dislodged from its bun and strands of it fell across my face. I reached the area of the concourse where I could just make out the lime green tops disappearing down an escalator. For me to continue I would now surely need to obtain a ticket, and to do so would take more vital minutes. In the chase sequences of movies the hero would jump over the barrier and slide down the central aisle between the up and down sides of the escalator, but alas I was not about to join the ranks of such film stars. I took stock of the situation, accepting that I wouldn't be able to keep up with the others. By the time I'd bought my ticket they would be long gone on whichever tube train they had entered.

I would have to calm down and work out what to do, I told myself. Assuming that the girls were following Oliver to Liverpool Street station and onwards to Wivenhoe, then I would do the same. I would make my way to whichever platform the train to Wivenhoe departed from, keep myself out of sight from them, and go along too. So with my ticket now purchased for the underground journey to Liverpool Street, I proceeded at a much more ladylike pace, managing to catch my breath and slow down my heart rate. I was even able to get a seat on the tube where I could adjust my hair in the small mirror of my compact.

Be calm Alberta Louise - things will be alright as long as you keep your wits about you and don't draw attention to yourself, I told myself. Why was I doing all this undercover secret service stuff instead of simply confronting those girls?

I argued the point backwards and forwards with myself but came to the conclusion that my goal must be to discover the truth. Revealing myself to them wouldn't work.

No, I would have to find a way of staying near enough to them on that train to Wivenhoe so I could maybe eavesdrop their conversation and discover what their game was. If they were indeed following Oliver, I could confront them later.

But how could I remain undercover? The merest glimpse of me anywhere nearby, and the twins would recognise me immediately. Don't worry Alberta, something will present itself, I assured myself, recalling wise words my dear departed mother used to say to me. For now though, I would just concentrate on getting to the station and on that train to Wivenhoe without the others seeing me.

I exited the tube station and entered the main rail station. Walking towards the huge overhead information screens that revealed which platforms were which, I was able to work out that Platform 12 was the one I wanted. The next train to Clacton-on-Sea, calling at a number of stops along the way, including Chelmsford, Colchester and Wivenhoe, would be leaving at 15.37. Ah yes, of course, I remembered Oliver telling me that. Right, that gave me half an hour to buy a ticket and go to the ladies' room, which I was desperate to do by then. Walking back from the ticket office I saw a WHSmith's shop. Great - I would buy a large broad-sheet newspaper to help cover my face. It would help at least. As I queued up at the counter to pay for my *Daily Telegraph* I noticed a pile of special-offer toys, including some fancy dress sets with the most grotesque straight-haired wigs imaginable. Bingo! I knew something would present itself, and as much as I detested the thought of covering my own hair with something so hideous, the point was that it was different. With a straight wig, a large newspaper and some extra lippy and makeup, I would hopefully become a very different Miss Baudet to the one that the twins and Oliver were familiar with. With some dark glasses as well I would be unrecognisable.

Off I went as quickly as I could to the toilets to relieve my bursting bladder and, partially, become Superwoman, with my new long, artificially straight hair. Not bad, I thought to myself, as I then continued doing my theatrical style makeover in front of the large mirror above the washbasins. I noticed a few quizzical glances from some of the other women. "I'm going to a party," I said as an explanation to no one in particular.

One woman actually looked jealous. "Lucky you - It suits you, ya know. It looks like it'll be a lotta fun for ya... Have a nice day now." She had a broad American accent, was probably around 45, and rather glamorous. I'd heard "have a nice day" on the television shows as a parody of American insincerity, but in her case I felt she was being completely genuine.

"Thank you," I responded. "I'll certainly do my best. You have a nice day too." That was something I would normally never say, but as I checked myself in the mirror one last time I found myself easily slipping into character, as I almost didn't recognise my own reflection.

I made a cautious beeline for Platform 12. There! I could see Oliver from quite a way away, with his rucksack standing out like a sore thumb. He was beside the barrier, waiting to be let on to the platform for the train that hadn't yet come in. It must be due in any minute now, I calculated as I checked my watch. Then sure enough, as I looked along the track I could see the engine and carriages snaking their way to a stop. All the doors opened in unison, as the travellers alighted and massed their way towards the barriers. So many people, I thought, all with their own individual reasons for being where they were. Just like Oliver having his reason, me having mine, and the twins having theirs. But where were the twins? I ducked behind an information counter in case they saw me, forgetting that I was incognito. My eyes scanned the whole place, searching for two lime green tops. Then I spotted them. They were over by the adjacent platform, appearing to keep a watch over Oliver's movements. When the railway official allowed the small crowd of people on to the platform, including Oliver, I saw the twins also make their move, following a few moments behind. Okay, this is either going to work or it's not. Walking casually in the open, I followed the girls to the carriage that they entered. Watching through the window, I waited for a while until they took their seats. Then I entered the train through the next door along. Heart thumping, I moved down towards them, and sat in the seat directly behind theirs, with my back to them. Perfect. If they did happen to get up and take a walk past me in the carriage, by now I felt confident that they would only see a somewhat eccentric old lady with tinted reading glasses, buried in a fully opened copy of the *Daily Telegraph*. I was as anonymous as anyone could be. As I stood up for a brief moment to survey the rest of the carriage I noticed Oliver further down the train and facing towards me. Fortunately he didn't look up and appeared engrossed in a book. Right, I thought, after a move across to the seat out of his line of vision, I could now relax, and settle back for the train journey that was scheduled to take just over an hour to Wivenhoe. What I would do once I arrived I had no idea, but for now I'd just do my best to listen out for anything the girls said behind me. Perhaps they'd say something that would help to throw some light on why they appeared to be following the 15-year-old heir to the Markland Estate. Actually, it was only an assumption on my part that he was the heir to the estate, but eavesdropping on the twins' conversations later confirmed that they assumed that was the case too.

We were off. "This train is for Clacton-on-Sea…", the automated voice over the tannoy announced, "…calling at Stratford, Chelmsford, Colchester and Wivenhoe."

It wasn't until we reached Chelmsford and the two or three passengers seated near them left the train, that the girls said anything at all. But, boy, when they did I couldn't believe my ears, as I overheard a torrent of hatred and evil emanating from that seat behind me. I listened intently to a horrible conversation the girls were having between themselves, with my ear cocked slightly to the left so that I wouldn't miss one single word they were whispering.

Whenever I'd previously heard them talk together it had been easy to distinguish who was who. But now, not being able to actually see them, it was impossible to identify which twin was speaking. It didn't matter. Now, as far as I was concerned, they were acting as a pair, and it became clear to me that the pair shared an equal dislike of the young man who was on his way to meet his real father for the first time.

I knew that fact to be the case, Leslie Markland knew it, Stanley Markland knew it, Oliver was on his way to confirming it, but it soon became obvious that the girls didn't know it, because of what I overheard next.

"Look Sophie. We are on our way here..." I heard Hilary whisper. She sounded as though she was showing a map, possibly on her mobile phone, to her sister. "Daddy told us it's where Uncle Leslie lives, remember? You can see Wivenhoe is near the Essex coast, and it's the next stop along from Colchester. Look...there's the river running alongside the railway line and it looks like the town is right on the river, the River Colne. We'll need to follow him down to Uncle Leslie's place and just see what might 'accidentally' happen to the little brat."

They both giggled. "Yeah, he really is a little piece of shit, isn't he? Fucking hell, how dare he interfere with what should be ours?"

What on earth were they talking about, I wondered? And then it dawned on me that the girls had money on their minds. Money! So that was what all this was about.

They went on: "Yeah, if only he wasn't around to get his grubby little hands on the house and everything. Fuck knows what Daddy must have been thinking when he went and banged up our old cow of a mother one more time. At least she's out of the way, so there is just us and our fuckwit of a brother. . .for now."

Their language! I couldn't believe my ears when I heard them talking so disrespectfully about their deceased mother, God rest her soul. Nor could I believe how nasty they were being about Oliver. It had become increasingly obvious that I couldn't tolerate much more from them - but this! My shock gave way to more immediate questions. I still didn't understand why they had decided to follow Oliver to Wivenhoe. Nor did I understand what they'd meant by 'for now'.

The girls went quiet again, apart from the occasional cackle of laughter that I heard, presumably as they played with their mobile phones. I slumped back and sighed a deep breath as the train gently continued swaying from side to side. I glanced out the window as we ran parallel to a motorway with cars and lorries appearing as though they were being driven in slow motion as we sped past them. My mind drifted back to that time when I first arrived at the Manor house when the girls' mother had been found dead. That poor woman: I could only imagine what she had been going through that led her to take her own life. Well, those girls needed their comeuppance. If only there was a way I could deliver it.

Another shock… I must have dozed off! I awoke as the announcement 'The next station will be Colchester' came over the speaker. And Wivenhoe would be next. I adjusted my wig, checked myself in my compact, and applied some more lipstick.

As the train slowed and approached our destination I could see Oliver get up at the far end of the carriage and go to stand next to the doors, ready to alight. The girls also stood up and walked right past me to the doors at the other end of the carriage. I bowed my head and pretended to rummage around in my handbag. Bugger! I only had one door option left to me, and it was in the middle of the carriage. That meant the girls would have to walk past me along the platform as I got off and held back in order that I could follow them to the station exit.

Bugger! What could I do? I needed to have confidence in my disguise and be plucky. And then I noticed, as the train slowed to a halt, that there was a small waiting room on the platform. Good! I could dash in there while I put on and adjusted my coat, keeping my head down as the girls went by. By good fortune 'my' carriage door stopped almost directly opposite and as soon as the door opened I stepped down from the carriage and darted across and into the waiting area, ahead of the other passengers, including Oliver and the twins.

"Phew"… I let out a sigh of relief as I stood with my back to the platform and played around putting up my collar, fiddling with my handbag and generally brushing myself down as the girls sauntered past me, staying several yards behind Oliver so as not to draw attention to themselves. Luck was on their side too. There was a footbridge over the tracks leading to the station exit. If it hadn't been for the ten or so other passengers walking across that bridge, the girls would have had quite a job to remain inconspicuous in their brightly coloured tops. Somehow they managed it, mingling in with the crowd. I remained where I was until the whole platform was empty before climbing the steps to cross the railway footbridge.

Oliver and the twins were by now out of my sight, but they surely could only be a few yards away outside the station. Then, as I began my decent from the bridge towards the station exit, the sounds of an almighty kerfuffle stopped me dead in my tracks.

CHAPTER 38

Come Together

"I couldn't ask the twins to go home straight away"

Leslie Markland

I was well aware of the significance of this very important day, and as the hour approached when I was due to meet Oliver off his train at Wivenhoe station, I arrived a good thirty minutes early to calm my nerves with a couple of Merlots from my favourite pub opposite. Properly meeting my son for the first time, and treating him as just that and not as my nephew, I would at last get the opportunity to make right out of the wrong that had previously existed.

It was quite a busy day, thanks to the preparations taking place for the following week's Wivenhoe Regatta. Typically, a Wivenhoe resident's normal Saturday afternoon might be spent reading the papers, or simply dozing in front of the TV to recover from the previous evening's over-indulgencies. That could even include a post-funeral wake following a service at St Mary's Church down near the quay. Funerals, weddings, engagements, or simply the end of the working week were all good excuses for the people of the village to raise a few glasses! It was true to say that, if inclined, one could be out partying every night of the week in Wivenhoe, and several local folks did just that - but not me. If truth be told, my preference was to simply sit on my Barnacle barge with a good book, a cup of tea or glass of red wine, depending on whether it was before or after lunchtime, with old Harry at my feet.

I say 'old' Harry, because he really was elderly now, surpassing all doggie-life's expectations. I didn't know his secret of longevity, but whatever it was, I wanted some of it. Harry still managed to scamper around when he accompanied me on my jobs or when I took him for his walks.

I said goodbye to him as he settled down into his basket on the barge, and I set off to the L-shaped bar in The Station to wait for Oliver's 15.37 from London to arrive just before five o'clock in the evening.

Andy Stollery was there as was customary for a Saturday. Beaming broadly, he kindly bought me a drink, enquiring: "Today's your big day, isn't it, Old Matey?" Andy had been the one person with whom I confided about what had been going on.

"Yes it is Andy, and I've got my fingers firmly crossed that things will work out for the best," I responded. "And if it does, and if it turns out that Oliver likes the river, I think we may even go out in your old boat tomorrow for a picnic. It's about time I used it for what it's meant to be used for, and I think high-tide will be at around one o'clock tomorrow. With these current spring tides we should get at least a couple of hours, maybe even three, out on the water. I think I'll have a go at getting past Alresford Creek, maybe we'll even get all the way to Brightlingsea if the weather stays calm."

"Well, I'm glad that the old girl is finally going out," replied Andy. "Can you remember those instructions I gave you about how to start her up really slowly? And don't forget there are those two loose stanchions on the port side bow deck that I told you about. I bet you haven't fixed them yet, you little tinker you."

Periodically, ever since I'd owned the boat, I'd occasionally turn the engine over until it coughed and spluttered into life. I'd leave it running for a few minutes before switching it off, but really I ought to have had it serviced properly. 'If you don't use it, you'll lose it', were words of advice I'd been given, and had duly ignored. Andy had also told me about the loose cables way back when I bought the boat from him, and to be honest, in the 16 years since then I still hadn't gotten around to mending them yet, or even given the old girl so much as a lick of paint in the last two or three years. There had always been something more pressing to be getting on with, and the uprights that the cables were attached to, forming a wire rail running around the deck seemed okay to me, and never reached the top of my priority list. "Don't worry, Andy. I'll be sure to give them a tightening up before we set off anywhere," I promised.

With that, I looked at my watch and saw that the train was due in at any moment. I drank up, shook Andy by the hand, and left the pub. I crossed the road and walked over to the bottom of the footbridge that Oliver was due to walk down shortly. I heard the announcement of the train's imminent arrival over the public address system, and a minute or so later the train came into sight. This was it - this was the moment when he and I would be meeting as father and son for the first time. I wondered if Oliver was feeling as nervous as I was. The train stopped and I heard the sound of doors opening and hissing shut. The alighting passengers were obscured from view by the train, except for one lady with long jet-black hair who remained on the opposite platform, adjusting her makeup and coat as the train then slowly moved off on the rest of its journey. I watched the first ten or so passengers come towards me across the footbridge, none of them yet matching the description of a 15-year-old boy. But then a good-looking teenager with fair, short hair and a rucksack over his shoulder came into view at the top of the stairs that lead down to where I was standing. There he was and there I was, both waving to each other and smiling naturally. "Oliver?" I questioned. "Er, Leslie?" he shyly said in return, as he came down the steps.

He grew nearer and we both laughed as we extended our hands to each other, and then immediately withdrew them and bear-hugged instead.

At that point I looked up and saw two identical young women walking down the steps, arm in arm, trying to look the other way. The bright green tops they were wearing weren't exactly enabling them to be discreet in appearance, but it wasn't what was being worn that surprised me, it was who was wearing them. I recognised them instantly, even though they were several years older than the old picture I'd seen of them that my brother had sent me.

"I didn't realise you were bringing your sisters along," I said, as I nodded towards them.

The look of horror on Oliver's face made it plainly obvious to me that neither did he. He turned to them as they neared the base of the steps.

"WHAT? What are you doing here? How dare you follow me! Can't you leave me alone? How come you're here? I don't want you here. This is my place, not yours." Oliver's voice became more and more shrill with rage.

I was completely confused, and it appeared that the girls were sullen with sadness at their brother's outpouring of vitriol towards them. They were quiet for a moment, giving the impression to me that they were thinking out what to say next.

As they turned towards me, what they did say was spoken with such confidence that they had me believing them.

"It was Dad who made us come," they began, turning to me. "He wanted us to keep an eye out for our younger brother, to make sure he got on the right train and be sure he was okay. We were worried for him."

They then addressed Oliver: "We didn't mean to cramp your style Oliver darling, we just wanted to watch over you. Now that you're here safely we can leave you in peace and go back to London and do some clothes shopping."

They certainly had me fooled with their sincerity, and I felt I had to be courteous and polite to them, at least for the sake of good family relations with my brother. If he'd asked them to look out for Oliver on his journey, he'd be pretty furious with me if he then heard that I'd let them go straight back.

But then Oliver spoke, or rather shouted: "What do you mean? You're lying. Dad, I mean Stanley..." he blurted, turning his head towards me, looking embarrassed that he'd referred to Stanley as his dad, before correcting himself. "...Stanley doesn't even know I'm here. How could he? Only Miss Baudet knows."

"Exactly!" exclaimed both the girls in unison, almost as if they were singing. "You don't think that she could keep a secret do you?"

Well, I'd heard a little about Miss Baudet during that telephone conversation with Oliver and he clearly held her in high esteem. But I guessed that, without knowing her myself, it was perfectly plausible that her loyalty could lay with Stanley, and for her to be his informant. After all, he was her employer.

After the raised voices had receded and a sense of calmness prevailed, I said that we could all at least go back to the barge while we worked out our best course of action. In fact both girls were being as sweet as anything towards Oliver, and I remember thinking that perhaps the bad reports I'd heard about Stanley's girls might have been a little exaggerated. Maybe they had grown out of the adolescent bad behaviour I'd heard so much about.

"Come on Oliver, things will be fine, just wait and see," I said, putting my arm around him, and noticing that, already at the age of 15, he was only a couple of inches shorter than me.

We walked along the road leading to the river, with the girls strolling behind us, with their arms intertwined and smiling. As I turned round to say a few words to them I noticed the lady with the jet-black hair was in the distance. She was adjusting her hair before picking up her handbag from the pavement and making her way along the same road as ours.

I made some small talk, trying to ease the negative atmosphere that Oliver was clearly experiencing. I didn't want things to be like this during his first few minutes in Wivenhoe. I had anticipated that there might be a few awkward moments, but this was a scenario I had never envisaged. The sun was shining, its afternoon glow reflecting brightly on the river that we'd now reached. The gentle ripples of the water moved downstream as the tide went slowly out towards the sea. There was a full complement of tables and chairs on the quay, outside the Rose & Crown pub, occupied by scores of people enjoying the sight of the receding high water. I suggested that we should grab one of the tables and I'd then go inside the pub to get us drinks and some chips while we discussed what arrangements to make.

While I queued inside the pub waiting to place our order for a pint of Guinness, two white wines and a Coke, I looked out the window to where Oliver, Hilary and Sophie were sitting. It was obvious that he was upset, but the girls seemed to be doing their best to console him. They sat either side of him and leant in towards his body, both with an arm around him, looking like a picture of sibling togetherness. I couldn't ask the twins to go home straight away, but I didn't know what else to do. There wasn't enough room on the barge for them to sleep, and the chance of finding accommodation this late in the day would surely be slim, if not impossible.

Just then I saw a woman enter the pub. She was a bit of a stunner and she acknowledged me with a nod of her head and a bright smile. I was sure I recognised her as someone I'd occasionally seen along the quayside while I'd been painting windows for my customers. It was Helen, known locally as 'Helen the Hairdresser'. Helen was in her early 40s and by all accounts worked wonders on ladies' locks from her home studio, while also offering the occasional bed and breakfast accommodation when it suited her. This could be the perfect solution if she had a room vacant. Waiting for my Guinness to be topped up at the pump I went over to her.

A minute or so later and arrangements were all put in place. As luck would have it, Helen the Hairdresser would be at home that evening, but not as had been planned. Apparently, with her husband Jimmy, she had been due to go away on holiday to Dubai just two days earlier, but at the very last minute he'd had a call to go to work, his job being something very high-tech in the world of deep-sea oil-rigging in the North Sea. Whenever he was called to go, he just had to go, Helen explained, so holiday plans needed to be put on hold, and as a result Helen was understandably a little down. The thought of a little unexpected company in her empty house was music to her ears, and she welcomed the opportunity of having the girls stay that night.

With a grin at how I'd managed to pull things together so seamlessly, I stepped out through the pub door and walked to the table, tray of drinks held aloft.

"Right! It's all sorted," I announced. "There's no need for you two girls to go back shopping in London. You can stay with a friend of mine who has a room available tonight. Oliver and I will be staying as planned on the barge, as we have an awful lot of catching up to do. And I suggest we can all meet up tomorrow for a trip out on my boat. It'll be fun and we can drop anchor downriver somewhere and have a picnic on board. What do you say?"

The girls looked at each other with raised eyebrows, and Hilary answered for the both of them, without any need for further discussion between themselves. "That would be absolutely lovely Uncle Leslie. It would be great fun, especially as we've never been out on a boat before. Won't that be wonderful, Oliver?"

Oliver was about to answer, but before he was able to utter a word, Sophie interrupted him. "That's settled then. And don't worry Oliver. We'll be on our way home just as soon as the boat trip's over, and you can spend the rest of the time with Uncle Leslie. We only wanted to make sure you arrived here safely, and now we can see that you're more than capable of travelling alone on the train, we're less worried for you now."

Then Hilary added: "We'll ring Miss Baudet and tell her we'll be home tomorrow night – she'll never believe we're here in Wivenhoe!"

After that, we ate our chips and drank our drinks. Oliver seemed to relax and the girls appeared to be, well, nice actually. Maybe it was the

Wivenhoe air. We finished up and made our way to the barge, which I proudly showed off to them, also pointing out Andy's old boat tied at the rear.

The three of them appeared to have a genuine interest in both the vessels, and of course there was Harry, who stole the show, with Oliver at least. He loved the extra, unexpected attention and rolled over on his back, legs in the air, as if to say 'come on and tickle my tummy, and then tickle me some more!'

"Now look here Harry," I said, wagging my finger at him, "We've got some guests, and they haven't just come here to make a fuss of you, have they?"

I turned to the girls. "Okay then, I'll walk you round to Helen's now. And while I'm gone you can unpack your things and make yourself at home Oliver. I'll only be a few minutes. You can keep an eye on Harry, can't you? Actually, I think he'll be keeping an eye on you if you just make a fuss of him. Come on girls, I'll show you the way. It must have been a very long day for you."

"Yes, Uncle Leslie, it has been a very full-on day," Sophie giggled as she and Hilary stood up together. "We're just happy that Oliver and you can get some quality time together."

She gave the impression that they were all sweetness and light, and I caught a glimpse of Oliver's confused expression. I made a mental note to have a good old talk with him later and get to the bottom of what exactly was going on, but in the meantime I led the twins across the plank at the front of the barge and onto dry land.

"That's a cool mail-box, Uncle Leslie. Where did you get it?" Hilary asked.

"Well, in fact that was from your grandmother in Amer..." I didn't quite finish my sentence, because as I looked up I saw someone sitting on one of the wooden benches situated along the riverbank. It was without doubt the same lady that I'd seen an hour or so ago exiting the railway station.

Was it my imagination, or did she immediately turn her head the opposite way as soon as I caught sight of her? She also quickly raised the newspaper she'd been reading up to her face.

Normally, observation wasn't one of my strongest points, but now that she was closer I could see that this lady's unusually glossy, straight, long black hair looked a shade too glamorous for a woman of her age.

With my attention back on the twins, I led the way to Helen the hairdresser's house that lay in the heart of the newly built development of properties, while I made some small talk along the way.

"You know..." I began addressing the girls. "You know it was rather good of you to take time out to ensure Oliver managed his train journey well. You and I have never got to know each other up till now, and I think that tomorrow's picnic out on the boat may be a good time for all of us to get acquainted. It certainly can't do any harm can it?" They both nodded and smiled in confirmation.

"Here we are then," I said as we arrived at a large detached house. "I'm sure Helen will look after you and give you a good breakfast in the morning. And if you want to take a wander round Wivenhoe this evening before it gets dark, I can recommend a nice walk from here, along past the sailing club to the woods and back. There's a beach up there where the river widens on the way to Alresford Creek, although at low tide you'll only see a lot of mud banks as the river will be quite narrow. But at full tide tomorrow you won't believe how much wider it becomes."

I knocked on the front door and introduced the girls to a welcoming Helen, and then said goodbye, deciding to walk back the long way round so that I could call in at the sailing club. I wanted to pick up some information about the following day's weather and tide times before returning to Oliver for a good old chat.

If I'd gone back the same way as I'd come I would have passed the black-haired lady head-on as she too was on her way to Helen's for the night.

CHAPTER 39

A Long Day for an Old Lady

"Had I really heard that?"

Alberta Louise Baudet (2013)

I stealthily followed the twins, Oliver and the man who I guessed must have been Leslie Markland, and eventually reached a point where I turned a corner and came towards the river. My heart skipped a beat. It was so beautiful, and nothing like I'd ever seen before. Sure, there are many pleasant areas in the countryside near Leeds, but nowhere came close to this.

There were throngs of people chatting away outside a pub on the quayside and the boats tied to the edge were bobbing up and down in time with the small ripples created by the movement of the tide. I heard the low whooshing noise as a very elegant and posh motorboat went slowly past and my eyes were glued to it intently, although I observed that no one else took much notice. And there were dozens of people sitting at tables, eating, laughing, shouting, clinking glasses and jangling cutlery. I guessed they were just used to such a sight. As the boat glided past it created quite a wave that sent the moored-up smaller vessels into spasms of rising and falling.

I was mesmerised by all this, and with the bright sunlight making me feel quite sleepy, I was ready for a sit down and something to eat. I could see Sophie and Hilary sitting at one of the pub tables with Oliver, and they appeared to be getting along quite happily. They didn't have any drink or food in front of them, so I surmised that Mr. Markland had gone into the pub to place an order.

On the go since the early hours of the morning, I didn't now care about getting back up to Leeds, and by this time it was too late in the day anyway - there was only so much excitement that an old woman like me could take. No, I'd have to find somewhere to stay for the night, even though I only had the few things that I had in my handbag along with the outfit that I was wearing. For once I would need to forget my prim and proper ways, and relax about not having a change of clean clothes. I turned to a lady who was sitting on her own at one of the tables, clearly enjoying the convivial atmosphere. Her tight jeans and blouse were perhaps more suited to a younger, and quite frankly less tubby person, but she had a kindly enough face. Her eyes were a little glazed, and I could see by the two glasses in front of her - one full and one empty - she was drinking pints, an activity the womenfolk of Wivenhoe had in common with their counterparts in Leeds.

"Excuse me", I asked her. "Would you know if there is a hotel here in Wivenhoe?"

Her answer was a little slurred and I guessed she wasn't only on her second pint, but she was very friendly, nonetheless. She told me there was no hotel, but there were a few bed and breakfast establishments dotted around the town. She informed me that one landlady, called Helen, was actually down here getting a drink inside the pub, and would surely be out any minute. My inebriated new acquaintance promised to indicate Helen to me when she stepped outside the pub and into the crowd. I saw Mr. Markland come out and make his way to where the girls and Oliver sat, and soon after that the landlady was pointed out to me. I then approached her to inquire about the possibility of a room.

"What's going on here today? Is there a wedding or something?" She laughed before continuing. You're in luck my dear, because I shouldn't even be here this weekend, but thanks to my hubby being away at work, I do actually have a single room available if you want it. The larger double has just been booked, but if you don't mind having to use a separate bathroom instead of en-suite, then the room's all yours for £35."

I nodded with relief and gratitude, and accepted the business card Helen handed me.

"It's along at the end of the gravel lane there," Helen pointed. "Keep going and you'll find me quite easily. The address is on the card here with a small map printed on the other side, and I should be back there myself in about an hour. See you later!"

Well, that was a stroke of luck. I was ready for collapsing. I sat at one of the benches and leant back to soak up the last rays of sun before it slipped behind the clouds that had begun to gather. I started to slowly form a plan of action. I decided that I would follow the others to see where Leslie's boat was kept, and then take myself off to Helen's, call out for a pizza or some such dinner - anything would do - and get some much needed rest, ready for whatever tomorrow might bring.

I prayed Oliver, the twins and Mr. Markland wouldn't stay too long. Thankfully, after about ten minutes, they finished their drinks, stood up and left, heading along the riverside. Keeping my distance, I too walked away from the pub's tables in the same direction and sat by the water's edge about 50 yards or so away from the long old barge that I saw them all get on to. So that was where Leslie Markland lived. It was a far cry from the grandiose Markland Estate, and I wondered what it was like inside.

Leslie, Oliver and the twins were all on board for some while, and I was content to sit on a nearby bench in the mild summer air, even though the sun had now disappeared for good, just taking in the peaceful ambiance. Beginning to feel a little light-headed, probably due to all the excitement of the day, I began to rouse myself ready to head off in search of Helen's house. Just then I saw the girls and Mr. Markland, but no Oliver, emerge from the cabin door and walk across the short plank to the gravel path. I quickly tilted my head away and held my Telegraph up to my face. Curiosity got the better of me, and despite my feeling of nausea I felt compelled to follow them and see where they were going.

Well, well, well... After a few hundred yards, and judging by the map on Helen's business card, it soon became apparent that the twins were going to be staying at the same place as me!

I stopped to consider my next move, as I watched Mr. Markland ring the doorbell. Then the door swung open and Helen welcomed the girls in to the large house with a warm smile.

What exactly should my next move be, I pondered? On one hand I was on tenterhooks, adrenaline pumping at the thought of inevitably having to meet with the girls in that house. On the other hand my body was hurting so badly from the muscular pain that was by now enveloping me. I waited several minutes and then I too approached the door and rang the bell. By now I was so worn out I simply didn't care anymore what happened.

Sensing I was pretty near to collapsing, Helen showed me directly up the stairs to my room and left me to rest. We hardly said a word except when I quietly thanked her for pointing out the whereabouts of a kettle and tea bags, as well as some milk stored in the room's small fridge. A nice cup of tea was just what I needed, but first I prised off my shoes and sat on the bed, rubbing my aching feet. Ah! The relief! Lifting them onto the bed, I pulled the blanket over me and before I got to make that nice cup of tea I was in a deep, deep sleep.

It was dark when I awoke in a daze several hours later. I felt like I had the flu, and I couldn't tell the difference between what I was really hearing and the various other sounds that were milling around in my head. I must have been hallucinating. There were female voices, with one or two words that were recognisable being mixed in with murmurs and other indecipherable sounds. All this was combined with one feeling that was very, very, real. I was simply bursting for a pee.

Struggling out of bed, I wobbled a little while I opened the door and walked down the corridor to the bathroom. The door of the room that was two down from mine was slightly ajar. Although I couldn't actually see them, I recognised the voices as belonging to Sophie and Hilary.

I swear their conversation went something like: "He deserves to get the fright of his life," with the other replying: "Yeah, and if it all goes further then the whole estate will be ours again and we won't need to share a thing with the little shit after all."

And there was worse to come. I leant my head back against the corridor wall not only to support myself, but also so that I could hear their quiet voices better. What I thought I could make out from either Sophie or Hilary sent a shiver down my spine: "You can give him a good hard shove." There was a stifled giggle and then a pause before the other sibling said: "That should do it. Just make it look like he slipped accidentally. We just aren't going to share the estate, and that's why we have to get rid of Oliver once and for all." Had I really heard that?

I still had to have that pee. As I sat on the lavatory I mulled over what I thought I'd heard emanating from the girls' bedroom. Or had I really? I'd still been half asleep, so it was entirely possible that my overactive imagination had been working overtime. As I sat there, trying to make head or tail of what I could piece together, I felt beads of sweat developing on my brow. Feeling very weak I flushed the loo and as I crept along the corridor past the girls' room I listened out for any further words, but all was now silent. Only just managing to stagger back to my bed without fainting, I would have to deal with this problem with some urgency in the morning when I hoped I'd be feeling better. For the time being though the most I could do was to lean across and switch off the bedside lamp, before instantly falling back to sleep.

CHAPTER 40

Pre-Dinner Drinks

"I'm afraid it all went over my head"

Part One: Leslie Markland

I was looking forward to having the promised long chat with my son as I walked back to the barge the long way round, via the sailing club. As usual there were people setting up for a function for later that evening, and I slipped inside to see if anyone had seen tomorrow's forecast and to find out exactly the time of high tide. Excellent! The weather was predicted to be a little windy with only a slight chance of rain. So if we set off at eleven we could get down river towards Alresford Creek against the tide, anchor up for a nice picnic, and then come back with the still-incoming tide. We'd be able to come back using hardly any petrol, and I knew I had enough in the tank to get us to the creek.

It was all going to be perfect, and with some luck the experience of us all being together could well help to put a sticking plaster over past family wounds. If I could pull off this act of diplomacy I was positive it wouldn't do the relationship between Stanley and me any harm either.

That would please Mother for sure.

Just as I was about to walk out of the sailing club I heard someone call my name. West Ham John, as we all knew him, was standing there with a look of surprise on his face.

"Hey Leslie. It's my birthday today," he shouted. "We're just setting up for a party tonight, so come by later," he added.

"Thanks West Ham", I replied. "And happy birthday! But I've got a date with someone very special this evening, and he's waiting for me back on the barge."

West Ham John stood back and raised his eyebrows at me. "You little devil, I never knew you were that way inclined," he smiled.

I realised what I'd said, and laughed. Not that being gay was unusual around Wivenhoe - quite the opposite - but nevertheless I thought I ought to put him straight, if you'll pardon the pun! "No John," I lowered my voice. "It's with my son. I haven't seen him properly before. I'll tell you all about it one of these days."

"Crikey!" exclaimed West Ham, "Then you'd better have a drink with me right now and help me celebrate before the guests arrive." He had a bottle of Scotch in his hand, with its half torn gift-paper still partially wrapped around it. Before I could protest, he'd already poured out two large shots, neat, and handed one of them to me. "Down the hatch then, mate," he said and clinked my glass with his.

Oh well, it was his birthday, and I was feeling quite euphoric anyway, so why not? Steering the subject of conversation away from Oliver, I asked him how his team was doing, not that I knew the remotest thing about football. There could have been a match between England and Scotland going on that night and I wouldn't have had a clue what everyone in the pubs were getting so excited about.

"Well, they're not doing too bad at the moment," John responded, getting into his stride. "They drew with Arsenal and won against Fulham and now they're only fifth from the top of the table and if they can pull off the game with…"

I'm afraid it all went over my head. West Ham John could sense it and laughed loudly, as he poured me a large top-up. "You're not a football man, are you Leslie?"

"Not exactly, John," I smiled back at him. "But I'm pleased for you that West Ham are doing so well." I drank up, patted him on the back and shook him by the hand. "Have a fantastic party tonight, won't you? While you're busy clearing up here in the morning, you may well see us sailing past. We'll give you a wave. Say hello to Ursulla for me."

And with that, and with the warmth of a couple of nice large whiskies inside me, I made my way back to the barge for what I hoped would be an evening of getting to know my son.

Part Two: Oliver Markland

"One thing was for sure: they scared the living daylights out of me"

This really was so cool. I was loving being on Leslie's, my dad's, barge. I didn't quite feel comfortable about addressing him as 'Dad' to his face yet - I hoped that would come in time - and 'Uncle' was clearly out of the question, now that I was sure once and for all that he wasn't my uncle at all. But it was okay for me to refer to him as 'my dad'. Apart from the awkward surprise about Sophie and Hilary following me here, I was really enjoying being in Wivenhoe. I was enjoying the attention, and I have to say that I was also enjoying the love. I know that sounds like a crass thing to say, especially for a boy of my age, but well - so what? He loves me, I can tell. There! I said it, and I'm not ashamed or embarrassed either. I was feeling the love.

And it was funny seeing my dad doing his utmost to talk to me without any slur in his voice, as if he were ashamed of having had a little drink at the sailing club. Apparently he popped in on his way back after showing the twins where their B&B was. It was as if he'd been naughty, and was doing his best to attain my approval, and even forgiveness for his errant way. But I'll let you into a secret: I also had a tipple - at least I think that's what you call it. When he was out I was feeling thirsty and was looking around the kitchen for something to drink. There was a carton of orange juice in the fridge, but also a bottle of red wine already opened on the side, and I just thought 'why not?' Despite being 15 I've never had wine before, but now was a good time to try it, I decided. After all, I was really doing adult stuff now. I only had one small tumbler of it, but that was enough for me to decide I didn't really like it. And besides, it soon made me feel a bit light-headed.

Anyway, when my dad returned, he proclaimed that this was his home and, according to him, also my home just as much. As well as that, I could visit for as long and as often as I wanted! And the way I was now feeling, this was where I did want to live, just like my dad on his barge, with Harry. I had also fallen in love with Harry, and I felt that he also had a connection with me. I only hoped that he'd be around for a good while longer, as I could tell he was well into his old age in dog-years.

The barge was amazing. It was long and narrow, and filled with interesting knick-knacks. There was a kitchen at the front end, a proper bathroom with sink, shower and toilet in the middle, and a big bed at the rear that was the best thing ever. The bed folded on a swivel up against the side of the boat's wall when not in use, enabling you to walk to the end and open the hatch door to the small open deck at the rear. My dad had a sofa bed in the living area near the kitchen that he called 'the galley'. He was going to sleep there so I could have his fold-down bed, with the door open. That way I could lie there looking out at the stars. How brilliant! It was a warm evening but if I became chilly I could just lean out and pull the door closed without even getting up. This was far better than being at the Manor house with its cold dark walls and high ceilings.

It was nearly dark and I looked out the window to see a beautiful golden sunset on the horizon as my dad was busy preparing some dinner for us. There would only be a few more minutes left before the sun went down for the night, and I wanted to experience it more than from inside the boat.

I was feeling great, and I asked if I could take Harry for a quick walk while my dad was doing the cooking.

"Okay, but keep him on the lead, and you'll have to take a poo-bag and pick up after he's been," he responded. "If you walk along past the sailing club you'll see some mud flats by the river, and there'll be some grass for him along there. That's where I normally take him so I expect he'll be the one showing you the way. Don't be long. Dinner will be ready in half an hour, and then we can have a good old chat."

I put my jacket on, attached Harry's long lead with a leather hold-strap to his collar, and stepped off the barge on to the gravel path by the US mail box - another cool thing. Sure enough, Harry tugged me along and he clearly knew where he was going. We walked towards the building where the flood barrier was and I could hear the clinking of the lines as the evening breeze blew them against the masts of the boats moored on the sailing club's jetty. I could see the lights were on at the sailing club and there was the distinctive thud of the bass line of some music being played. The sounds combined with the warm night air were now making me feel a little spaced-out. That must be where my dad had had his 'naughty' drink with his friend. Well, he deserved it - it must have been quite a nerve-wracking day for him too - meeting me as his son for the first time.

Harry pulled me along, his tiny legs scattering the loose stones beneath his feet on the path - the path leading along the causeway towards the wider part of the river. He was looking for a patch of grass to do his business on, and I was concentrating on helping him find one. "How about here, Harry?" I asked. He replied in the negative by scampering ahead some more. Ah...there: This was to be the hallowed spot. It was quite dark now, save for the very last of the sun's haze as its hue shone on the horizon against the clouds, some of them thin and wispy, some of them thick and dark. The evening sky was mesmerising and quite magical in the warm air.

As Harry crouched there, his stubbly tail arched upwards, I gazed around, looking out to the river across the mud flats. My attention was diverted by something in the distance. At first it was just a black blob silhouetted against the glow of the sunset reflecting on the shimmering water. Then as my eyes focused some more, I could tell that it was a person. No, maybe there were two persons. I couldn't be sure until my eyes adjusted further. Yes, there were definitely two figures, just standing there, as still as anything. It was unlikely that they were fishermen, I thought. Harry finished his job, and I fulfilled my responsibility of being a good dog-walker. Plastic bag in one hand, and Harry's lead in the other, we walked slowly and quietly closer to where the figures stood in the distance so I could get a better look at them. They were both dressed in dark or even black clothing, standing side by side facing out to the river, away from me, with their arms behind their backs, and what looked like long dark hair, barely visible in the dusk. From staring at them so much my eyes were watering. I rubbed them and then was able to see that they certainly weren't fishermen. I couldn't even be sure they were real. They just stood there, motionless. Then, slowly, both in unison, they turned their heads to the right, and as their bodies moved around, they both appeared to be raising their right arms, and it really looked like they were both pointing at me. With every second that went by the night became darker and my eyes went in and out of focus. It was impossible to make out the figures in detail before they lowered their arms to hold their hands behind their backs again, as they swiveled their bodies back to face the river. Whoever they were they were far too distant to be identified, but although I couldn't be sure I had a hunch they just might be Sophie and Hilary.

One thing was for sure: they scared the living daylights out of me, and Harry too. He let out a shrill bark and began tugging his lead so forcefully that he pulled the strap right out of my hand. No! Please no! I chased after him, almost losing my balance. Fortunately he was scampering back towards the lights of the sailing club. I called after him but he didn't slow down. I couldn't keep up with him, although I was able to still hear his yelps. Oh no! This was my first walk with him and I've nearly lost him already. I ran in the direction of his barks, and then luckily I could see him as the street lights and built-up housing revealed his whereabouts. He knew exactly where he was headed, and it was straight back to the comfort of the barge. Thank goodness! That was a relief. As I approached the cabin door of the boat, Harry was already there, jumping up and scratching at the wood. My dad opened the door and Harry dashed inside.

"I'm sorry," I panted as I climbed aboard, "He just tugged the lead out of my hand and dashed home. I couldn't keep up with him."

I needed some sign from him that things were okay, hoping that he wasn't cross with me for letting go of Harry.

"Don't worry, Oli." he reassured me. "He often gets a bit spooked out there, especially when the cows are out roaming around the field past the sailing club – I expect that was what happened. Come on, dinner's ready. Leave the poo bag outside for now and come in and wash your hands." He turned, crouched down to tickle Harry's tummy, who was by now cowering in his basket, tongue out and panting. "Did you get scared by those naughty cows again, Harry? Those naughty, naughty cows."

I didn't think that now was the right time to tell my dad about the source of Harry's fright. What on earth could the twins have been doing there? Perhaps it hadn't been them after all and it was all just my imagination. I must admit that I was feeling a tiny bit woozy from the wine. But with all the excitement of the day there was one thing I was absolutely sure of. I needed my bed, and my dad had made it up to perfection, with a fluffed up duvet and two soft pillows. We had our dinner - meatballs and pasta with a token gesture of some salad leaves - and that was about all I was good for. I cleaned my teeth and washed my face, got into my pyjamas, said goodnight and climbed into what turned out to be the most comfortable bed I'd ever slept in.

As I lay there for a few moments I had a funny sensation that things were moving around in my head. But that was hardly surprising was it? What a long day it had been. Miss Baudet driving me to Leeds station, the lady on the train and her cat called Baci, the London Underground and getting the train at Liverpool Street station, the arrival at Wivenhoe, and of course the surprise and dismay of discovering that the twins had followed me. And then there was that strange encounter with the figures on the mudflats. Were they Sophie and Hilary? The closer I came to falling asleep, the more I guessed I was just being silly about what I had or hadn't seen that night. But nonetheless I would confront them in the morning at our picnic. Ah yes, the picnic. That would be a lot of fun and I couldn't wait for that.

Dad and I never did have our promised chat, but it didn't matter. When I asked him, he did quietly confirm that, yes, he was actually my dad. That was enough for me.

I just wished that Miss B could have been with me to experience my new found happiness. How she would love it here in Wivenhoe was my final thought, before dropping off into a deep peaceful sleep.

CHAPTER 41

Before the Deluge

"There was nothing I could do now but hope"

Part One: Alberta Louise Baudet (2013)

I felt very groggy when I woke up. I'd had such a strange night. I was almost delirious, so I figured I must have properly overdone things the day before. It was like having the flu but without any shivers or cold-like symptoms. I lay there in bed, reminding myself where I was and what had happened the previous day - and night. Gradually I acclimatised myself to my unfamiliar surroundings. I stood up and looked around at the pictures on the walls, the books on the shelves and the tasteful decor of the room, and then I caught a glimpse of myself in the mirror. Oh my word, what a state! What I wouldn't give to have my hair done. My hair was usually the first thing I thought about in the morning, and despite me not feeling quite all there, this morning was no exception. I wondered, and hoped, that Helen might be able to fit me in with an appointment and get me sorted out. I put on the white toweling dressing gown that I found hanging on the back of the door and ventured out of my room and downstairs in search of her. Maybe with my hair done I would feel better too.

As I descended the stairs I hesitated on the last step. Were the twins up and about? Should I reveal myself now? What was my plan? I could hear the clinking of plates and cutlery as I headed towards where that sound was coming from.

It was nice to be greeted by Helen's cheery "Good morning" as I entered the dining room. "You certainly needed your sleep last night," Helen commented. "You must have been exhausted, you poor thing. I poked my head around your door at nine this morning and you were still out for the count. I usually put the breakfast things away by ten-thirty, but I made an exception for you today because you looked like you really needed a good rest."

"That was very thoughtful of you, Helen. Thank you. I'm sorry if I've messed up your routine," I apologised. "I think I must be coming down with something because I had the weirdest night."

And then it all came flooding back to me...

"Helen... what time is it? I've left my watch upstairs. I was thinking I'd be having breakfast with those young ladies that are also staying here, but I've clearly overslept. Are they still here?"

Helen shook her head. "No. I heard them say something about going out on the river while they were sitting here having their muesli earlier, but they'll be staying again tonight so you'll get to see them then - that's if you'll be staying too... And the time? It's gone eleven already. Like I said, you've been out for the count."

Gone eleven already! Crikey! Everything suddenly came sharply into focus and I was desperate to find the boat that they were going out on. "I'm sorry Helen. I've got to dash. I would like to stay another night please. Oh, and if there's any chance of you doing my hair this afternoon, that would be fantastic." Helen nodded as I shot upstairs, got dressed quicker than ever before, and came back down in minutes flat.

Even though I still wasn't feeling well, I'd gained some strength from somewhere.

"But you haven't even had your breakfast," I heard Helen yell behind me as I literally ran out the door and hurried in the direction of Mr. Markland's barge. I'd forgotten to put my wig on but I didn't care. What must Helen have thought? It didn't matter anymore - I just wanted to warn Oliver and Mr. Markland not to let those girls join them on the boat. They were up to no good as usual, but this was potentially more serious than merely putting a hosepipe through someone's letterbox.

I was no good at running. My head hurt. My bones ached. And I was no spring chicken anymore. My run soon became a quick walk, and then slowed to a pace barely faster than a lady of my advanced years should be going. I was already way out of breath by the time I turned the corner, just in time to see a motorboat edging its way against the incoming tide out in the middle of the river. I recognised the boat as being the same one that had been tied up at the back of Mr. Markland's barge yesterday evening. I could see two people – Leslie and Oliver Markland - on the rear deck. Oliver appeared to be at the wheel - and sitting out on the front deck were the twins wearing the bright green tops they had worn the day before.

Standing at the river's edge, I waved both my arms frantically and breathlessly shouted out, "Oliver! Mr. Markland! Stop! Come back."

Concentrating on carefully steering the boat downriver, Oliver and Leslie were oblivious to my calls that were shrouded by the noise of their outboard engine. Although disappearing fast into the distance, the girls did react to my waving. Whether they could tell it was me or not, I didn't know, but they just acted like they were being waved at by anyone who does that kind of thing - just like I'd seen children at the pub tables do the day before when the posh boats went by. Having stopped their waving, the twins looked ahead as the boat went further and further downriver towards the tide barrier. I shouted some more, but it was useless. There was nothing I could do now but hope that the horrible things I'd overheard the night before were silly, mindless games, and that with Leslie Markland in charge everything was going to be alright.

Heading back to Helen's house, I hoped she wouldn't mind getting the breakfast things out again. I tried to forget my anxiety and what I thought I'd heard the girls say in the night. Instead I occupied my thoughts with what I should eat - I'd had nothing but a bag of cashew nuts in the Rose & Crown the previous afternoon - and how I should get Helen to style my desperately unkempt hair.

Part Two: Oliver Markland

"I didn't want to upset the delicate situation any further than necessary"

As the old saying goes, I had slept like a log. When I awoke early, with the sun shining through the rear cabin door at six o'clock, I felt alive like I'd never felt before - except for having a slight headache. Thankfully that disappeared as soon as I'd drunk a glass of orange juice from the fridge. Absolutely loving being on the barge, my first thought of the day was that I wanted to leave the Manor house for good and live in Wivenhoe permanently. A lot of difficult arrangements would have to be made, of course, with finding a school at the top of my priority list.

My second thought of the day was what I'd seen, or rather what I thought I'd seen the night before: Had it really been the girls standing there, staring out to the river, and then turning round spookily to point at me? They were fond of tormenting me at home, but if it had been them, then it was downright freaky - but I questioned my own take on the situation. I just couldn't be certain, as the whole day had been an exciting blur. No doubt all would be revealed later when the twins joined us for our picnic out on the river.

Such a cool thing to be doing: a picnic on a boat. I could definitely get used to this river and boat life.

I lay there in bed sipping my orange juice, patiently listening out for any signs of movement, by either my dad or his dog. By a quarter past seven I just had to get up and see what was happening in the outside world. If nothing was occurring then I would instigate something by taking Old Harry, as I now liked to call him, for a morning walk. After all, us humans get up for a wee first thing, and so it must be the same for dogs, I'd reckoned.

Creeping around quietly, I tried to locate Old Harry's lead, so as not to disturb my dad who was snoring blissfully on the sofa bed. There it was. "Come on Old Harry," I said under my breath. I didn't need to say it out loud as my new furry friend needed no encouragement to follow me to the cabin door. We walked around to 'our' spot on the causeway where we had been the previous night. The sun shone brightly and I could see the ripples of the water gently moving upstream, indicating that the tide was beginning to come in. There! I'd only been in Wivenhoe five minutes, and I was already thinking nautically. With the brightness of the sun it was very difficult, impossible in fact, to recount the atmosphere and emotions that I'd experienced the previous evening. This was a new day, and I was determined to make the best of it, with or without the presence of Sophie and Hilary. Now that I had decided I wanted to make a new life in Wivenhoe, I didn't care anymore about those girls. For today though I would treat them with the courtesy that they *didn't* deserve, for the sake of good harmonious relations.

Back on the barge after Old Harry had done his thing - I didn't even mind clearing it up - my dad was by now up and dressed, and was cooking us a small breakfast.

"It's only quick scrambled eggs," he said apologetically. "After this I'll just pop up to the Co-op to do some shopping for later and then we'll soon be ready. Look out for the girls," he continued, "they'll be coming round soon. Now I know you're not too fond of them, but I think they were genuinely looking out for you yesterday, so let's see if we can all have a great time together, eh?"

"Don't worry, I've already worked that out and I'll be okay with them today, Dad, so don't worry about anything. You see, I've decided I don't need to live with them for much longer and it's all going to be just fine," I said, and watched his eyebrows rise quizzically. "I'll talk to you later, okay Dad?" It didn't feel odd at all calling him 'Dad', and I must admit I felt more comfortable than I had ever felt with my 'previous' dad.

While my dad was up at the Co-op there was a knock at the door and I opened it to Sophie and Hilary, who couldn't have been more pleasant. Although it puzzled me, I lapped it up, all this 'sisterly' (or was it now 'half-sisterly'?) love. Perhaps they were actually capable of being nice people all along, and the Wivenhoe atmosphere was having a positive effect on them. Not for a long time had they been so, well, nice when just the three of us were together. But I was still troubled by what I'd seen the night before, and I asked them outright if it had been them that I'd seen out on the mud flats.

"Don't be so silly, lovely boy. We were tucked up in our beds at that time. We'd had quite a day of it yesterday making sure you got here safely, remember?" said Sophie.

"But I'm sure it was you," I argued.

"Oh, wait a minute," Hilary cut in. "You might have seen us doing our exercises before bedtime."

Then Sophie added: "Yes, we were down by the river practicing our tai chi - weren't we, Hilary?"

Hilary paused before answering. "We didn't see you though, Oliver, just someone with a yappy dog. We'd have said hello if we'd seen Oliver, wouldn't we Sophie?"

Although it seemed as if they were making up their answers as they went along, maybe I had been silly to think they had been up to no good. I suppose I could have got it wrong. I suppose it could have been someone making slow and steady tai chi movements. It had felt sinister at the time and I did remember my head being in a bit of a whirl. Anyway, I decided not to take that line of conversation any further. Instead, I switched the topic of conversation to the boat ride and the picnic. Between us we all agreed that it would be really fun to sit up front on the deck as the boat made its way along the river to our destination somewhere near a place called Alresford Creek. Dad had said that once we were there we'd be dropping anchor and eating the loads of nice things that he was getting us from the Co-op. Of course I didn't call him 'Dad' to the twins - I didn't want to upset the delicate situation any further than necessary; as far as they were aware I was still their 'full' brother, Stanley was still my dad and Leslie was still my uncle, and I'd keep it that way for now. To all intents and purposes I was still going to be sharing the Markland estate with them and taking on my responsibilities as set out by my late granddad. Little did they know that I couldn't have cared less about the estate. As far as I was concerned they could have it all.

CHAPTER 42

The Picnic

"I kept quiet, not wishing to draw attention to my ineptitude"

Leslie Markland

I arrived home from the Co-op and the twins were already there. The tide was coming in rapidly and I knew that if we were going to be getting anywhere we ought to be casting off pretty soon, otherwise we'd be trying to come back to Wivenhoe against the outgoing tide, and I wasn't sure that we had enough fuel in the tank for that. So I dumped the provisions down in the galley and went on board my smaller boat tethered up at the rear. Strangely, it was called *The Bow Tie*. I kept meaning to ask Andy Stollery if he knew where that name originated.

Preparing for our excursion, I turned the key to start the engine and there was a loud, shrill whistle that generally indicated that something wasn't quite right. Of course! I hadn't primed the fuel line, meaning that I needed to squeeze a rubber hand pump attached between the tank and the motor. I tried it again, and again, and there! She fired up. I left it running in order to warm up while I jumped back aboard the barge to collect the provisions and tell the others to get ready as we'd be setting off in ten minutes.

No one moved. Typical teenagers, I thought.

"COME ON GUYS - time and tide waits for no man!" I shouted. I was more excited about going out on the river than I could ever remember. Perhaps I was ever so slightly showing off, if I were to be perfectly honest.

Eventually we were all aboard *The Bow Tie*. The engine was purring nicely by now as I untied the ropes attached to the buoy, and then asked Oliver to unhook us at the quayside. He took to it like a duck takes to water and within seconds we were freely moving out to the middle of the river and then heading in the direction of Alresford Creek and Brightlingsea. I asked Oliver if he'd like to take control of the wheel, which he happily did. You should have seen the look of glee on the young lad's face.

As *The Bow Tie*'s engine smoothly propelled us along the river, I believe I noticed someone waving at us from the distant shore. How lovely, I thought, that people still get excited by the sight of a boat chugging along. My thoughts turned to the following weekend's regatta. Perhaps I would join in the fun for once, I considered, as I eased the speed controller forward slightly. The motor responded well, increasing our velocity nicely, even against the incoming tide. At this rate we should be reaching Alresford Creek and the wider river within around 15 minutes, and we could drop anchor there, bring out the goodies and have our picnic. The girls seemed to be happy enough up front and Oliver was actually doing very well at navigating us around the contours of the river. He was clearly a natural at this, I thought to myself, rather proudly.

The sun was bright, and despite there being very little breeze when we set off there were by now the occasional gusts of wind blowing us this way and that, with our rear canopy acting as if it were an unplanned sail. I hadn't been expecting the wind, although the forecast had said that there was a slight chance of rain. Judging by the dark clouds in the distance that were coming towards us, I'd guessed that the chance of rain had risen to more than merely slight. Typical Wivenhoe weather I'd thought - very changeable, but never mind. We would simply need a little more engine power to compensate for the wind that was becoming more aggressive by the minute.

A little later than I'd first thought, we reached the area of Alresford Creek. There were many boats belonging to the local Alresford Creek Boat Owners' Association tied up to buoys, and the way in which they were bobbing up and down gave an indication as to quite how choppy the water had become in such a short time since we'd left Wivenhoe.

But no worries: We had come to have a picnic, and that's exactly what we'd be doing. Passing the other stationary boats until we came to a wider but more shallow section, I told Oliver to cut the engine by turning the key, while I opened up one of the lockers and pulled out the anchor. It was a perfect spot, and I heaved the heavy metal contraption up against the inside of the rear deck and lowered it overboard. Shit! It was heavy, and I can't believe I'm saying this but I had forgotten to attach the end of the chain to the boat. Apparently it's an easy mistake to make, and many experienced sailors still manage to do it, but I just wished that on that occasion it hadn't been me making such an idiotic error. The weight of the falling anchor pulled the chain right through my hands and although I tried desperately to get a grip before it was too late, unfortunately it did become too late, and the chain went overboard and to the bottom of the river. I kept quiet, not wishing to draw attention to my ineptitude.

The tide was rising as it came in and I could see a large 'Romford Navy' boat in the far distance, coming in our direction, presumably from the seaside town of Brightlingsea. It was customary for millionaire owners of such super yachts to show them off to the people sitting at the pub's tables in Wivenhoe on their way past to the village of Rowhedge, further upstream. There, the owners would tie up, have a spot of lunch with

Champagne and then return to Brightlingsea on the then outgoing tide. Often waving their arms at the pub's patrons, the owners, who had more money than sense in my humble opinion, mistakenly thought that the people waving back were showing signs of admiration of such wealth. But I don't think it was ever admiration they were indicating.

We could show this lot that you didn't need stacks of money to have a great time.

"Right, let's get the things out for some lunch, shall we?" I shouted so that the girls could also hear. I thought that if we moved the boat over a little further along I could lean over and hook a rope through the eye on one of the buoys, and no one would be any the wiser about my gaffe with the anchor.

"Oliver," I shouted. "Can you take this rope up front and give it to one of the girls? Then with this pole, when I get the boat close enough, I want you to lean out and get the hook onto that orange buoy over there. But make sure you don't drop the pole. It's easily done, Son."

"Eye, eye, Cap'n," he replied, clearly loving his new responsibility. And judging by his broad smile, he was also clearly pleased to be addressed as 'Son', which to anyone else's ears was merely a figure of speech.

I turned the key to restart the motor. Instead of the gentle purring sound that I should have heard, there was only that shrill high-pitched whistle again. I turned the key a second time. Damn! There must be some grit or something in the carburettor. After a third attempt there was a cough and a splutter as the engine finally fired up, albeit sporadically, before cutting out yet again. I opened the locker where the fuel tank was and picked up the plastic container. Shit! It was, as near as dammit, empty.

What a twit I was. We had to get to the buoy and tie up so that I could think about our next move - maybe we could get a tow from the Romford Navy super-boat, which was still several hundred yards away but rapidly coming towards us.

To make matters worse, the black clouds that had previously been in the distance were by now directly overhead. I could feel a few spots of rain on my face, but fortunately only one or two, so it did seem we might only suffer a slight shower, fingers crossed.

As luck would have it we were drifting towards the buoy, although a couple of feet too far portside. If I steered the rudder just slightly, Oliver might be able to lean over enough to catch it. But, I hadn't noticed the Romford Navy boat coming so close to us - nor so quickly. The helmsman must have been doing at least 15 knots, the stupid sod: much faster than sensible for his size of boat. I waved my arms rapidly at him to slow down, and also to try and indicate that we needed some help, but the fool must have thought I was larking around. He just waved back as he sped past, creating a huge wake behind him, as well as a loud and deep barrage of noise coming from his massive twin engines.

There were so many things all going on at the same time but what happened next was beyond belief. As our smaller vessel lurched violently up and down, battling the high waves created by the much larger one, and with me doing my damnedest to steer us closer to the buoy, I noticed the girls standing up either side of Oliver. Good, they're helping him with the pole and hook, I thought, as my concentration switched back to getting us over to the buoy. But a split second later my attention was diverted back to Oliver.

The noise from the super-boat's engines and the splashing of the wake that it had created prevented me from hearing the commotion up front, but it was plain to see the twins weren't helping at all. They appeared to be having a row with Oliver, who was struggling and trying to push them away. The more he pushed against them, the more they were shoving him. He looked across to me, with terror in his eyes, one hand of his holding on to Sophie's top and his other hand trying to grab hold of the wire rail to steady himself. Shit! The rail! I'd meant to tighten it after Andy Stollery had reminded me, and I'd clean forgotten to.

I shouted out as loudly as I could: "Come away from the rail, all of you! Girls, what are you doing, for God's sake?"

I guessed they could barely hear me and I needed to get over there, and fast. As I clambered out onto the narrow side-deck, which was now wet and slippery from the rain and the wash, the force of a sudden gust of wind took me clean by surprise and I nearly toppled, just managing to grab the windscreen in time to steady myself. The girls were using all their strength in an attempt to push against poor Oliver, and his back was forced hard against the rail. It was surely not going to be able to take much more pressure before the upright holding it would come loose. Just then an enormous wave created by the wake from the departing Romford Navy boat engulfed ours. At that precise moment we all lost our balance. Oliver fell down in the direction he was facing, head first onto the front deck. The girls, who had been pushing him against the rail on the boat's side, lurched forward and they both fell against the wire rail with such force that the upright shot clear out of its mounting. The rail came loose and they both toppled over into the water.

I panicked: Fuck me, this was really getting seriously out of hand...

Without thinking, and acting on impulse, I snatched the pole with the hook from where it was lying on the deck, and shouted at Oliver to hold on to my left hand while I leant over as far as I could with the pole gripped as firmly as I could with my right hand. The girls were flapping around in the water, splashing and panicking as they went under and came up in succession again and again, gasping as they did so. "Grab hold of the pole," I screamed urgently with a voice so highly pitched I didn't even recognise it as being my own.

"We can't swim! Help us!" shouted Sophie. Or was it Hilary? It wasn't the right time for me to admit that neither could I. In the water, thrashing about and both dressed identically, I had no way of telling who was who. This situation was turning into a potential disaster and I tried desperately to turn things around.

"Oliver - pass me that rope QUICK so I can tie it round my body," I yelled. "Well done, that's it. Now tie the other end to the cleat over there."

With my safety harness in place I leaned over as far as I possibly could and managed to get the hook under the material of one of the girl's tops. I couldn't tell whether it was Sophie or Hilary.

"Now hold on to your sister. Grab her hand or just grab at anything... anything," I shouted. There was no time and no way I could instruct either girl individually. The flapping arms in the water made it difficult for any grabbing to be done at all, but just when I thought it was game over, the two sisters became intertwined with their arms locked together. Thank goodness! I caught my breath as Oliver shouted incoherent words, in a frenzy. It looked like the worse was over and I'd be able to pull both girls round to the rear of the boat where the transom, to which the motor was attached, would be low enough for them to clamber back on board.

But just as I was beginning to feel a euphoric sense of relief swelling up and embracing me, there was a sickening "*crack*" and the hook broke off from the pole. By now the wind had turned into a gale, the rain shower had turned into a storm and the girls resumed their position of turmoil and panic as the choppy waves momentarily covered their heads. One of them grabbed at the end of the pole and got a grip, but the other was nowhere to be seen, having dipped below the surface.

"Hold on to the pole," I called as I frantically searched the water for any signs of a lime green top beneath the surface. There it was, drifting slowly downwards. "There she is!" I pointed, "Catch her before she goes down further!"

The remaining sibling, still holding the pole, looked away from me towards the gradually disappearing green shape of her sister. She turned back and looked at me, a grief stricken expression etched across her face. She stopped flapping her other arm, glanced up at me for one final time and smiled. Then just like in the movie *Titanic*, as Leonardo DiCaprio finally gives up to meet his maker - she let go of the pole, and slipped away deeper and deeper into the muddy water below.

CHAPTER 43

A Change of Course

"Maybe this was the time for me to throw those eggs up in the air"

Alberta Louise Baudet (2013)

The helicopter made such a din while I was sitting outside the Rose & Crown on the quay.

Earlier that morning I'm afraid I hadn't succeeded with my attempt to halt the boat's progress while it moved further and further away from me, with Leslie, Oliver and the twins on board. I'd got there just a little too late. All I could do was return to Helen's, completely out of breath, to have my breakfast and a nice cup of tea. I was by that time simply gasping for one. I instantly liked Helen, and as luck would have it she had managed to fit me in for a hair appointment at one o'clock and I was looking forward to it tremendously. She'd kindly agreed to do my highlights, give me a good old trim and maybe even an up-do. Wearing that wig hadn't done my chignon any good at all, and I couldn't wait to restore my head of hair to its former glory.

But before all that I had an hour to kill.

During that hour I decided to have a wander around the village, or was it a town? Certainly there was a village feel about the place down in what Helen told me was known as Lower Wivenhoe. I really enjoyed looking into the lovely delicatessen shop next door to the barber's. The barber looked up at me from cutting a man's hair and said a polite 'good morning' as I walked past and peered in at his door. He even stopped what he was doing and came over to say in an inquisitive tone that he hadn't seen me in Wivenhoe before. How friendly, I thought. I loved the flamboyant shirt he was wearing, and told him so. He responded with a broad beam.

From there I walked down to the quay, the scene of my spying game the previous day. It was again busy with people watching the incoming rising tide, and although there were still a few dark clouds remaining following a recent short storm, the weather looked like it would be fair. I was thankfully feeling so much better than I had done earlier that morning, and I decided to treat myself to a little G&T and sit outside the pub, where the warm sunshine had already dried the tables. Why not join the others in this pastime of gazing at the river, I decided.

As I took a seat at one of the circular tables, the distinct sound of a helicopter in the distance was growing louder as it came our way. As it got closer and closer the noise from its rotor blades became quite deafening, causing all the patrons, including myself, to look up, the sound echoing against the water in the river. Hovering there for a few seconds it then tilted forward and sped off downriver, following the course of the middle of the estuary.

I thought about Oliver and the others, but accepting that there was now simply nothing I could do, I could only hope that Mr. Markland would be making a good job of looking after them all. I relaxed, and toyed with a glass of my favourite tipple, picking it up an inch above the table and then letting it slip from my grasp, listening to it making a satisfying thud as it fell on to the wooden surface.

I did this several times, finding myself in a trance-like state as I stared out at the boats in front of me. My trance was gently interrupted by some words uttered by my recent acquaintance from the barbershop. "A penny for your thoughts," he said, as I watched a man doing some work on one of the boats.

"Oh, hello again. Is this your lunch break?" I asked. "I was just admiring that boat over there with the multi-coloured canopy and the flowers on top of the deck. I don't think I've ever seen a boat like that before."

He introduced himself to me as Alfie, and responded to my observation: "Oh, that's Neil's boat," said Alfie the barber, as if that explained everything.

What a life that Neil must have, I thought. Momentarily I went off into a daydream, thinking about how wonderful it would be to have a boat to tinker with right outside a pub. You could be sitting there with your G&T in private, but still be soaking up the atmosphere and ambiance that goes with the pub. You wouldn't need to pay pub prices, nor would you need to queue up if you had your very own personal bar on board. A tall, beautiful, blond woman - perhaps she was the girlfriend or wife of the boat's owner - then emerged from the cabin and precariously balanced herself as she walked the gangplank connecting the boat to the quayside. I bet she's done that a few times before. If it were my boat I'd have to have a proper rail to hold on to. The woman casually walked towards the pub's entrance, stopping to chat to some people who were standing around in the sunshine.

They were all smiling, laughing and socialising together. That was something I hadn't done in a long while, and suddenly it hit me. It hit me like a ton of bricks that I'd been missing out on so many things, being a serving nanny and housekeeper for more years than I could remember. I'd often dreamt that before reaching my seventies I would happily throw all my eggs up in the air, metaphorically speaking, instead of keeping them all safely in one basket as I had done all my life. It really was time to see just how they all landed, I thought. Some would crack, some would break for sure, but some just might have stayed solid and unbroken.

Poor Alfie. I wasn't being much fun to talk to, was I? He left me alone and walked towards the pub. How rude of me, drifting off again into another trance, but I couldn't help it. Was I being silly to even contemplate giving up my secure life in Yorkshire? It was certainly true that with Oliver now in his mid-teens, the twins older than their years and their father hardly ever present and spending most of his time with Tristan, there was little need for me to stay put up in Yorkshire. Maybe that time had come for me to make some changes.

A moment later Alfie returned to the table carrying a pint in one hand and a gin and tonic in the other. "There!" he said. "If a penny isn't enough for your thoughts, I thought another G&T might be."

How kind of him, I thought: I was a complete stranger in Wivenhoe and already I was being bought a drink! After thanking him sincerely for his very kind gesture, I dreamily returned to my contemplative state and said: "I rather like it, don't you?" nodding towards the boat with the flowers on. "I wonder if you could introduce me to this Neil fellow some time?"

I don't think Alfie heard me properly as I must have spoken too softly. But I heard myself as loud as loud could be. Maybe, just maybe, this was the time for me to throw those eggs of mine up in the air.

If Alfie the barber was indicative of the type of person around Wivenhoe, then it must be a good place to live, I reasoned.

Finishing my G&T, I got up to leave, shaking Alfie's hand and thanking him again for the drink before saying goodbye. As I walked back towards Helen's house I was deep in thought. Having those two G&Ts helped to free my mind. I'd been putting the bulk of my wages away for years now and I'd rarely examined those bank statements when they came through the post - I had no reason to - but perhaps I should take a look at them one day soon.

In the far distance I heard the shrill sound of sirens wailing, but I thought nothing of it.

Twenty minutes later I was sitting in the swivel chair that was in front of a mirror, where there was also a shower attachment above a white porcelain sink. Helen was making headway, if you'll excuse the pun, and I was in heaven watching her create couture art from the basics that I offered. Whilst making small talk, we had to raise our voices to make ourselves heard above the constant drone of the helicopter that had reappeared and could be seen from her salon window over by the river. "I wonder what's going on over there?" Helen said. "Look at that one. It has 'POLICE' on it, and there's a second one now with 'RESCUE' in red letters. Something's definitely up."

Not being local I'd assumed helicopters were commonplace on an estuary like Wivenhoe, being so close to the Garrison I'd heard about in nearby Colchester. It hadn't occurred to me that they could possibly have had anything to do with Leslie's boat. I'd forgotten about the words I'd imagined I'd heard coming from the twins' bedroom the night before. My memory was as fuzzy as I'd felt at the time. I'd known something was wrong but there was nothing I could do now but sit back and let Helen work her magic.

CHAPTER 44

In Custody

"I must admit I was now becoming quite frightened"

Oliver Markland (2013)

It had been a complete nightmare, and it was becoming worse by the second. The girls had fallen in the water, which was something that I was secretly pleased about, although I hadn't wished them to go as far as drowning themselves. They certainly deserved to get wet and cold, there was no doubt about that - it may even have shocked them into realising that they weren't invincible and the experience might have humbled them into becoming nicer human beings. Oh my God though, what a disaster. The look of trauma on my dad's face would be a picture indelibly etched on my mind forever. I could tell that the whole thing had been a terrible accident, although if I were to be more accurate I would say that it had been a preventable accident that the twins had caused themselves. I don't wish to sound childish, but at the end of the day they had tried to push *me* overboard, and in doing so, had got what was due to them. It served them right for being evil, twisted, nasty pieces of work. I hadn't realised how much hatred I had been storing up inside me against them, but it was spewing out now, that was for sure.

Unfortunately though, my dad's position didn't look too good when we got towed back to shore by the police boat, and I guess that, in hindsight, he hadn't acted awfully responsibly by taking out his boat with not enough fuel, no life jackets and, as I found out later, faulty guard rails. It had all been so dramatic, like watching some American disaster movie, except it wasn't American at all - it was taking place near this little Essex village called Wivenhoe - a place that, until recently, I'd never even heard of. There had been two helicopters above and a police boat alongside us, as well as another boat later to recover the bodies. The recovery appeared to have taken place within a very short amount time, but in fact it must have been half an hour since Sophie and Hilary had gone overboard.

As it turned out, we had been watched by the owner of the large posh motorboat that had gone past us - much too fast in my opinion - creating the huge wave that caused us all to lose our balance, with fatal consequences for two of us. The captain of the boat, whose name I later learned was a Mr. David Anderson, had called the coastguard from his radio when he could see we had difficulties. Even though he had been more than half a mile away by that time, he'd reported seeing through his binoculars some of what had happened. The coastguard had scrambled into action and called the air-sea rescue helicopter. The RNLI also launched a rescue craft to come out to us from nearby Mersea Island - and of course there were the police with their own helicopter and speedboat. This was what they called a Serious Incident, which appeared on the local BBC News that same evening.

Thank goodness for Mr. Anderson though, because if he hadn't called the coastguard when he did, I just don't know what I'd have done. I was effectively in charge by the time the RNLI arrived - which was amazingly quickly - because my dad was already in a state of shock, and I felt I wouldn't be too far behind him.

My poor dad; he was so traumatised he wasn't able to utter a word. He just sat there with a blanket wrapped around him that I'd found inside the cabin. It wasn't until a whole day later that he was able to coherently say anything at all, and so it was all down to me to try and recount the sequence of events leading to the deaths of the twins. First, briefly on the boat and then later at the police station in Colchester, I did my best to explain what had happened. The fact that I referred to my dad as 'Dad' and then 'Uncle Leslie' in the same breath, didn't help things. The policewoman who was interviewing me was downright confused, and not just a little annoyed with me, assuming that I was deliberately making up my story as I went along. Then, while my dad was presumably being questioned in one room and I was in another room with the policewoman, Mr. Anderson was brought in to join us, accompanied by a male officer who was dressed smartly in a suit.

"Oliver," the man said to me, in a deep voice, "You know your dad, or your uncle, let's call him Mr. Markland for now shall we, is in serious trouble?" He then turned to the man standing next to him and continued: "…and Mr. Anderson here saw it all happen, didn't you Sir? Let's go over again what you told me earlier and see if it jogs this young man's memory."

I didn't like his condescending tone, as he nodded in my direction, and I was quite surprised at the policeman's seemingly unprofessional attitude towards me. Not only that, I must admit I was now becoming quite frightened. Just because Mr. Anderson was an adult and I wasn't, didn't mean that his description was any more important than mine, did it?

Before I could collect my thoughts he turned back to Mr. Anderson, who then answered. "Well, no not exactly, I couldn't quite see *everything* from where I was, but it looked like, from what I saw through the binoculars, from where I was standing on my boat…"

"Please get to the point about what you did actually see Mr. Anderson. Let's deal with the facts, shall we?" interrupted the man in the suit - rather abruptly and rudely in my opinion.

"Very well," continued Mr. Anderson. "I would say that the fool who was in charge of the boat was doing his best to push those girls under with his pole..."

"That's not true!" I blurted out. "How can you say that? My dad was doing everything he could to save them," I protested.

"The truth will out, young man. The truth will out," repeated Mr. Anderson. The suited policeman nodded in agreement.

What was he talking about? He wasn't there, and he couldn't possibly have seen everything in enough detail to make such a ridiculous accusation, could he? But I suppose, on reflection, I myself couldn't be one hundred percent sure about what actually had happened, because during some of those crucial seconds while my dad was leaning overboard, I was lying face down on the deck. But I did know instinctively that my dad was a good and kind man, incapable of doing what Mr. Anderson had said. The trouble was that the police didn't know that, and I knew I'd have to find a way of convincing them.

It was coming to the end of a long and horrible day, and after the suited officer left the room with Mr. Anderson, the policewoman asked me where I was staying in Wivenhoe so that she could arrange a car to take me back there. At first she was going to get me taken to a supervised hostel in Colchester but I really didn't want that. Following my protests I confirmed that I'd be perfectly okay staying aboard my dad's barge, and that anyway I'd be with 'a responsible adult' called Harry. I just omitted to mention that Harry was a dog and it was in doggie years that his age far exceeded mine. The police lady seemed relieved that she didn't need to fill out loads of additional paperwork, and I promised not to leave Wivenhoe without telling them. They would no doubt be needing to ask me lots of further questions, going over things again and again. Thankfully, before the car was ready to take me 'home' they did allow me to see my dad, who was being kept at the police station for now. I wasn't allowed to be in the same room as him without someone else being present, and he was under arrest for something. Although I asked them what he was being charged with, all they would say in a very patronising tone was that "this is a very serious matter, young man," as if I were a small child. I was 15, damn them!

I repeatedly told my dad not to worry, and that things would be alright as soon as the police got their facts correct and stopped jumping to the wrong conclusions. I have to admit that I was becoming increasingly anxious for him. He could still hardly talk due to shock, and I could sense that his prospects were in fact not too good at all. At the very worst it looked like they could be accusing him of murder, and even at the very best he might be guilty of negligently being in charge of a boat that wasn't safe, resulting in two deaths. Did that amount to manslaughter, I wondered? Whatever the outcome, he was going to need help, and I simply didn't know what to do.

Who could I turn to? This was far beyond what I could ask Miss Baudet to assist me with. Oh yes! Miss B. With all the furor I had completely forgotten about her. I would need to contact her as soon as possible and tell her that I wouldn't be coming back home as arranged, and that there would be no need for her to meet me at Leeds station or for me to get a taxi.

My mind spun with all the awful ramifications this tragedy would have, particularly for the man who had been acting as a father to me, and who was the real father of the twins. He had already lost his wife and my mother - and now both his daughters, also to tragic deaths. Guessing that the police would have quickly tracked him down, I assumed that he must have told Miss Baudet about what had happened by now. I felt so sorry for him, as I knew how much he'd doted on my half-sisters. What a terrible shock this would be for both of them!

I knew there would be an in-depth police investigation and I suppose, as well as David Anderson, I was one of the three key witnesses, my dad being the third. I'd learnt at school doing a project on Law And Order that no deaths in this country can go by without being properly analysed and recorded thoroughly. So there would be a post mortem to confirm the cause of death, a coroner's report and an inquest, and then there would be the funeral. Oh God, this was really terrible! And all this would need to be done while my dad was being scrutinised by the authorities. What could I do to help him? I felt powerless. The answer came to me from my dad himself.

As I was leaving the room in which he was being held, despite him hardly uttering a word the whole time that I'd been with him, he called me over to give me a hug goodbye. He looked despairingly into my eyes, and weakly whispered a name in my ear to me. At first I couldn't hear him so I asked him to repeat it. He softly went on to say that since being a boy the same age as me, there had always been one man who he respected. As I exited the room I felt a great sense of relief and anticipation that I had someone professional I could now call and ask for help, as it was clear that my dad couldn't think straight enough to do it himself.

I remembered overhearing the name of that man many times back at home when I was growing up - it was that of the old family solicitor, Roger Ainsworth.

CHAPTER 45

One Last Case

*"I was very pleased to find that the old grey matter
could still work well"*

Roger Ainsworth (2013)

Hatty was bringing me my usual cup of Ovaltine when I received a rather unusual, unexpected and disturbing phone call from young Oliver Markland. Oliver must have been 15 when I got that call from him, and I recalled that he had once been the subject of much correspondence between myself and his grandmother, as well as Stanley and Leslie Markland. I was amazed when I worked it out that had been as far back as 2000. That was practically the last time I had any dealings in law. My oh my, how time had flown!

With me being almost completely retired and rather enjoying life, my wife Hatty, who for many years had been my devoted and very efficient secretary, had managed to do a great job at keeping me young at heart. Unfortunately, she hadn't been able to keep the ravages of old age away from my tired body, but she did her best to keep me as fit as possible, insisting that I go for a mile-long walk every single day, without fail, come rain or shine. I believe that her regime helped to keep my body in fair shape - and an hour or so with the *Daily Telegraph* crossword every evening was also keeping the old grey cells ticking over nicely.

After I put the phone down from Oliver Markland I was in rather a daze.

"Whatever is it?" Hatty asked.

I tried to explain, but in truth I couldn't do a very coherent job of it, based upon the sketchy details that Master Oliver had given me over the phone.

"You remember Leslie Markland from the estate and all those dealings I had with his mother in the States and all that inheritance business?" Hatty nodded and I continued. "Well, it appears that Leslie Markland has gone and got himself into a rather serious spot of bother. There's been what they are calling a Serious Incident, and he's been accused of killing two members of his estranged family - his brother's twin daughters, no less. He's rather under the impression that I can help him and wants me to go all the way down to the Essex police station where he's being kept in a cell. It all sounds rather ghastly to me, so I'm afraid I promised I'd do what I could to help."

There was a long pause while both of us took in the rather shocking news.

"I wonder if you'd mind accompanying me, please?" I asked Hatty. "It's rather a long drive and I'm not sure if I'm up for doing the journey all in one go on my own?" Hatty pondered the proposition and I went on. "Besides, your memory is probably keener than mine these days, and you may be able to recall some relevant facts about the Marklands better than I can. Would you mind awfully, my dear?"

I was very relieved that Hatty said she would be happy to accompany me. Travelling to Essex was something I felt that I just had to do, especially since the Markland family had meant such a lot to me over the years, but I really didn't want to go alone.

Having quickly called the Essex Police station for confirmation of the whole sorry affair, I next phoned the Ainsworth & Co office to speak to my son. "Brian: Something has come up and I need to have all the files on the Marklands please." I did my best to repeat the sketchy information that Oliver had given me. "I don't know exactly what I'm in need of just yet, but I rather suspect that somehow all this is going to be connected with the way that the estate was handled and divided. Usually in such matters, there are only one or two motives; love or money." On this occasion I didn't think it could be the former.

I continued my call by asking Brian if he would drop off all the Markland files to me on his way home that evening. I thought ahead about all the bedtime reading I'd just set myself up for, and thought I detected some reluctance in Brian's tone when I asked for *all* the files. I'm sure that became even more apparent after I'd mentioned the word 'money'.

"Yes, Brian. I *am* positive that I want to do this," I said when he questioned me. "I *have* to do this. The success of our whole law firm - from which you make a very tidy living, let me remind you - has had a lot to do with us looking after the Markland estate over all these years. It's the right thing to do to offer help, now that help is needed. Make sure you bring *everything* there is, every single file please. I'm planning to make an early start, with Hatty, for Essex in the morning."

Later that evening, Brian arrived with two large boxes crammed with old lever-arch and foolscap files of various colours. They all had that certain smell of having been stored in a damp and dusty old cellar for a long time. Not much legal work had been carried out to do with the Marklands for a few years, and at first sight it was fairly obvious which files I could initially discard. I would find little use for those marked with the various labels such as 'PIG PEN BUILDING APPLICATION', or 'TENANTS A-Z', or even 'FARM VEHICLES MOT AND BILLS'. No, I was looking for a file that would help to jog my memory about George Markland's rather unusual will. I wanted to go over the entailment inheritance of the estate he'd left to his grandchildren. And I was sure that the more recent correspondences between me and Iris Dellinger, formerly Iris Markland, could also be very relevant. Recalling that Iris had disclosed to me how Leslie was not technically a Markland by blood, and therefore neither was Oliver, it appeared that neither of them could have a claim on the Markland estate. At this stage I didn't know why that fact would be important but I knew how the police might view things. I wanted to help rule out any ideas they might be having about Leslie Markland having developed any fiscal motive to want the twins dead.

And there it was! The file I'd been looking for marked 'WILL'. That was easy, I thought, as I blew the dust off. I just hoped that Brian, or his secretary, would have been as meticulous as me, or Hatty, at filing every single associated document. I began flicking through the file slowly, turning the pages one by one. As I did so, a loose piece of paper headed with the logo of a bank in Guernsey fell out. On it was printed the details of a monetary transfer to the tune of £10,000 - to Brian. The paper didn't look like it was meant to be there. There were no holes punched through it for filing; it was more like it had slipped in there accidentally. It raised my suspicion, and I called Brian about it later that night.

At first he acted all innocent with me, but I knew my son sometimes better than he knew himself. He eventually confessed to me about something that had been going on more or less ever since young Oliver Markland had been born. It transpired that Brian had been dabbling in business that was nothing short of blackmail, and I told him that he was bloody lucky not to have been caught. I believe that he was actually relieved to finally disclose what he'd been doing all this time. Thank goodness it was me he told and not some investigating officer.

I may have calmed down now, but I was furious with him. My own son! I forcefully instructed him to make good his mistake and pay back the £10,000 without delay, and that he'd be lucky if that was the end of the matter.

What a scoundrel! Apparently, he'd used that £10,000 towards buying the BMW that he'd had his eyes on, and thereafter felt so guilty that he'd never touched another penny that was accumulating in the account month by month. Fortunately for him, the money was all tied up in the firm's office account, and the car had been in the firm's name and technically wasn't actually for personal gain. This was the only 'deliberate oversight' I had ever been prepared to compromise on in all my years of law practice, and I told Brian in no uncertain terms that he needed to do the right thing, and straight away.

Anxiety about the day ahead and the extra shock of discovering Brian's misdemeanors meant that I slept badly that night. What he did was beyond comprehension, and I knew I wouldn't be able to live with myself if I kept quiet. Of course I would have to report him. My own son! In fact, as it transpired, The Law Society was already looking into his less than above-board activities, and this episode turned out to be the final nail in his vocational coffin. I'm rather too ashamed on this occasion to go into detail about what happened. Brian never worked in the legal profession again, and was extremely lucky to have avoided a prison sentence of his own. And from me the less said about all that the better. Just the thought of it makes me squirm.

Early the following morning, Hatty and I set off for Essex armed with several boxes full of lever-arch folders. During my sleepless night I had done some mental arithmetic and calculated that if Leslie had been paying maintenance for Oliver's upbringing, and that money had been building up in an offshore account without being touched, save for £10,000, there would be, er, quite a lot accumulated by now! I tossed some numbers around in my head. Fifteen years at £300 pounds a month, plus an additional £10 a month every year thereafter, would come to over £68,000, without even thinking about any interest that had accrued! That would definitely help Oliver come to terms with not inheriting any of the estate I thought, but I decided to keep that snippet of news from him or Leslie just for the time being. The less the subjects of inheritance and money were mentioned the better, I decided.

I felt like I was being chauffeur-driven, with Hatty up front doing the driving while I sat behind, reading through the documents as we sped down the A1. I don't think I'd ever used the walnut fold-down tables of my old Vanden Plas Princess. Come to think of it, I don't think I'd ever sat in the back either, and I must admit I rather enjoyed it. But at the same time as admiring how beautifully those tables had been made, I also reflected on how I really had no option but to act for Leslie Markland if the circumstances required it. After all, I had known him ever since he was a young insecure lad, and I was very disappointed by Brian's recently discovered 'activities'. He'd blotted his copybook as far as I was concerned, and he clearly couldn't and shouldn't get involved in Markland business ever again.

I was very pleased to find that the old grey matter could still work well when the law was concerned, and I felt more alive than at any time since my retirement. I was itching to get down to see the Essex police to sort out the mess that young Oliver and Leslie Markland found themselves in. Leslie may have been involved in a terrible accident, and he may have made some stupid mistakes about the operation of his boat, but murder was something I felt sure he was definitely not capable of.

CHAPTER 46

A New Beginning

"My mind was made up, and I think that he eventually understood my reasons"

Oliver Markland (2014)

L ess than a year has gone by since I settled for good on my dad's barge in Wivenhoe and I reached my 16th birthday in April.

Dad did go to prison, but that didn't detract or diminish the love and admiration I had for him. Apart from my regular visits to see him, we'd actually only spent a little over 24 hours together in Wivenhoe. All things considered, it was amazing how our bond had formed so quickly and so firmly. I knew that he was a good man, and I firmly believed that he took all the responsibility for that tragic day on the river for my sake. After all, I was the one who the girls wanted out of their way in order to inherit the entire Markland fortune. If only they'd known that they would have got their hands on the whole lot anyway. It's easy to say 'if only', and to be wise in hindsight.

We can all be wise after the event, can't we?

After my dad was convicted of negligence, resulting in the death of passengers of a boating vessel of which he was in charge, he was sentenced to 15 months in prison. I am certain it would have been a much longer term had it not been for Roger Ainsworth's carefully crafted arguments, and Miss Baudet giving her own evidence too. She told the court how she'd overheard the girls the night before the drowning, hatching a plan to push me in the river, and I think that was what swung the judge's opinion - that and the photocopy of the twins' 'Eleven Commandments'. If it made an impact on the judge, that was nothing to the shiver that went down my spine when Miss B read out the line 'We shall one day commit murder'!

But it was the early intervention from Mr. Ainsworth that set the ball rolling. The day after first arriving in Essex, he did his brilliant job of convincing the police to drop their much more serious charges against my dad. I could just imagine him standing tall in front of them, wagging his finger forcefully. I'd heard he'd argued that the Police would stand a far greater chance of gaining a conviction for negligence, than one for murder or manslaughter. Apparently he stressed the point that it would show up far better on their statistics than a charge that couldn't possibly stick.

Good old Roger Ainsworth. I liked him the first moment we met, and I've since heard a lot about him from my dad. He had a certain way of making me feel safe and at ease in his company.

Of course I was distraught for my dad, but he convinced me not to worry unduly for him. He said he accepted his fate and that he'd survive. He even had some ideas about writing his story down to pass his time productively. During visiting times he would tell me about our unusual family, and he frequently shook his head mid-sentence and interrupted himself with the phrase 'you couldn't make it up'.

In fact it was during one of these heart-to-heart discussions that Dad and I talked quite seriously about the inheritance of the estate.

I remember detecting the sadness in his voice, almost as if it were an apology to me, when he explained how he was not a blood Markland. That meant that I wasn't either, and therefore I wouldn't stand to inherit any part of the estate. Luckily, Mr. Ainsworth was astutely aware of all this, and he emphasised these facts to the judge.

Quite frankly I didn't care one jot - I was glad to be far away from the Manor house. And come to think of it, thank goodness I hadn't been a beneficiary. Because if I were, it could have been argued by the Prosecution that I also had a motive for wanting the twins dead. I could potentially have been in the frame for their demise too.

Miss Baudet's help was just as valuable as Roger's, but in a very different way. Imagine my surprise when I discovered that Miss B had actually followed the twins following me all the way to Wivenhoe, that fateful weekend.

You see, everything changed one day after I'd returned from visiting Dad, soon after he'd been charged. I had taken a taxi back to Wivenhoe, and it was time for Old Harry to be taken out for his regular walk. I thought something wasn't quite right as soon as I put the key into the cabin door padlock. Normally, upon me approaching, there would be his familiar yelps and the sound of scampering and paw scratching from within the cabin even before the door had been opened. Not this time. Opening the door I went aboard and saw Old Harry over in his basket, curled up and not moving a muscle. At first I thought he must be sleeping. I had hoped against all hope that he had only been sleeping, but sadly it wasn't to be. All of a sudden, and without warning, everything became too much for me, and the tense emotions I'd experienced during the previous few days all burst out in one enormous torrent.

I desperately needed to get out and have a walk around and get some air. I wandered along the riverbank to the quay, up the High Street where the barber-shop's pole signalled business as usual. A man with a bright shirt was inside cutting someone's hair and he looked up and began to say something to me. I'm afraid I wasn't in the mood for pleasantries so

I pretended I hadn't noticed him, and continued walking. Head down, I aimlessly drifted back towards the river, going past the Royal British Legion building where there were many people laughing and joking as they sat outside drinking their beer and wine. I was traumatised and in a daze, so much so that at first I didn't hear a familiar voice calling my name. I meandered by until I felt a tap on my shoulder.

"Oliver! It's me." I turned around, my eyes bloodshot and wet with the tears I'd been crying. I couldn't believe that the voice was coming from none other than Miss Alberta Louise Baudet.

"Miss B!" I cried, jolted out of my misery.

"Come on, Oliver. We've got many things to talk about, and I don't think here is the right place," she said insistently as soon as she saw the surprised and tear-stained look on my face.

I followed her in the direction of the edge of the quay, past all the tables and chairs belonging to the Rose & Crown pub, full up with people enjoying the late afternoon sunshine. Where was she taking me? Why was she here? What was she doing? She stepped on a couple of wooden planks joined together and tethered to a wooden frame a few feet out in the mud. There was a sturdy timber rail attached to the planks that she used to steady herself as she walked forward. In front of us was the boat I'd noticed on my very first day in Wivenhoe when I'd enjoyed drinks and chips with my dad and the twins.

"Dry your eyes, Oliver", she said. "Everything's going to be fine, you'll see. Miss B is here and she'll make it all alright for you." She smiled at me, and actually I did then feel better, just like she said I would.

"What do you think?" she asked as she swept her outstretched arms in front of her. "What do you think of my boat? Well, it's not mine quite yet, but it soon will be," she went on.

This was all too much for me to take in. Miss B owning a boat? Had she lost her marbles? Apparently not... She explained how she had fallen in love with this quirky village and within only a few short days of being here had put a deposit on an apartment not far from the river, close to her hairdresser's house where she'd been staying. She went on to tell me how she was giving up her job at the Manor house to live in Wivenhoe permanently, and in the process had made an offer to the owner of the boat that I was now standing on.

The boat, with its bright multi-coloured canopy made from a patchwork of different pieces of material sewn together, was called 'Los Amigos', she explained. "But not for long," she continued.

"I'm going to rename it '*Miss Baudet*'. I've always fancied putting my name to a boat, and now's the time to fulfil that - and many more dreams. It's vanity personified, I know my dear. But then that's me all over."

On learning that Miss B was going to be living in Wivenhoe, my sadness about Old Harry's passing began to lift. I was happy that I'd got to know the little canine rascal, even if it had been only for a few days. We had definitely made a connection with each other and for that I was grateful. And then what Miss B told me had convinced me that my own future should also lie here in Wivenhoe. A rush of euphoria swept over me. Yes, I was sure that Miss B was correct - things *would* turn out alright being here.

After talking things over, we both agreed that it would be a great idea to travel back to Leeds on the train together in order to sort our stuff out. But first we had to bury Old Harry, and we chose a spot that he loved so well out by the grassy area down by the flood barrier. When Miss B and I got chatting, I was so impressed with her when she told me about how she'd jumped on the train and followed the twins who were following me down from Leeds to London. I laughed out loud when she retold the story about the black wig she bought as her disguise. I even felt sorry for her when she went into great detail about how it had completely messed up her beloved hair, but relieved for her that she found a saviour, and a new friend, by the name of Helen, her temporary landlady and excellent hairdresser. Every dark cloud has a silver lining, I thought.

With all the confusion about who my real dad was and how I was related to him, I'm ashamed to say that I didn't know how I ought to behave with my *former* 'dad'. Despite Stanley Markland losing both daughters, my half-sisters, I admit I had been totally miffed with him for keeping such an important secret from me. I couldn't express in words to him how I felt, and as a result I decided not to attend Sophie's and Hilary's funeral held at the chapel on the estate. Besides, it would have been hypocritical of me, wouldn't it? Now, I referred to him as 'Uncle' Stanley. During the lengthy phone call I'd made to him he had tried to explain to me that he'd only learned certain truths relatively recently himself. I'm afraid I'd been pretty cold with him and I didn't want to hear his lame excuses. I was only a 15-year-old then, after all. Okay, I know I am still only 16 now, but in a single year I'd say I've grown up very quickly. All the experiences that I've gone through must have matured me, I guess.

Uncle Stanley and his partner Tristan came over to the Manor house to meet us on our return to Yorkshire. It was by now empty and soulless, despite all that family history over the centuries. Stanley also had an emptiness about his character that I had never seen previously, but Tristan did do his best to bolster him up.

I don't know whether the old adage of time healing would be true for Stanley, but I hoped that it would be so in his case. I could tell he was remorseful about having kept 'the big secret' from me, and he tried to convince me that staying at the Manor would be the best thing for me to do, and that he'd make things better for me. He cited my schooling as the most important factor to consider, but I'd already reasoned that I could study for my A' levels in Essex just as easily as in Yorkshire. My mind was made up, and I think that he eventually understood my reasons for wanting to leave, reluctantly accepting that I had a need to live with, or near to, my real father.

Miss Baudet, who had confessed to me that she'd been completely smitten by Stanley in the early days of her job there, thanked him for his continued support, friendship and employment at the Manor house, and politely tendered her resignation.

"You only need a part-time housekeeper now Stanley, and a cleaner to come in once a week," she said, and he nodded slowly in agreement, reassured that Miss B would also be keeping a watchful eye on me down in Essex.

"You know you can both always come back here if things don't work out for you don't you?", he said softly with a quiver in his voice. I hadn't expected him to be so upset about us moving away, and I sensed awkwardness.

To relieve the situation, I reassured him: "Miss Baudet and I can also come down to London quite easily when you're there with Tristan at his flat in Westminster - and we definitely will. The train to Liverpool Street only takes an hour from Wivenhoe, you know," I continued, trying to offer him some comfort.

"Thank you, Oliver", was the last thing he said before he turned and walked away, with Tristan's comforting arm around him.

While I slept in my old room for the last time, Miss B drove to her flat in Leeds that by chance had been vacated by her current tenants only a couple of weeks before. She was going to gather some personal belongings, some pictures and books and some clothes stacked away in boxes in her loft.

"They may come in handy one day," she explained to me later.

Her plan was to then get a good night's sleep before rising sharply in the morning and going straight to the estate agents in the city to put the flat on the market. She would then collect me and we'd drive off back to Wivenhoe to begin our lives anew.

Ready at eleven o'clock as arranged, I kept an eye out from the window for her rather tired looking Fiesta that somehow managed to still keep going. It was so old now you could almost call it a classic. There she was, unusually a few minutes late, coming up the drive, and it would soon be time to say a final goodbye to the Markland estate.

About 15 minutes out of the gates at the bottom of the drive, Miss B said that there was somewhere she needed to go before properly setting off on the motorway. We pulled into the forecourt of a large modern Ford dealership on the outskirts of town. A man in his thirties, dressed in a sharp dark blue suit, was standing next to a car parked in front of the enormous glass windows.

"Come on Oliver," said Miss B, as she drove to a halt next to the man as he held a key with his outstretched hand. "Give me a help with getting the things out the boot of this old heap. This man has the key to a shiny new one I bought earlier!"

A quarter of an hour later we were heading south down the motorway in a brand spanking new bright red Fiesta, with leather seats and the best stereo system I'd ever heard.

"Out with the old, Oliver," she said triumphantly. "Out with the old, and in with the new. We're both about to embark on a new life adventure, so let's get to it!"

CHAPTER 47

Coming Home

*"As I thought more and more about the irony of the situation, my chuckle
turned into an outright laugh"*

Leslie Markland (2015)

Suffering prison life for nearly a year, I only had just over three
months left of my sentence to serve. My guilt was easing gradually.
The Coroner's report that had been read at the inquest had been
sent to Stanley, and although I hadn't expected him to forgive me for the
terrible accident, the report did go some way to alleviating any blame I
might have had from him for anything more. Thankfully, Miss Baudet's
appearance to give evidence had helped my case no end. The report
had also stated that although it couldn't be proven, there had been the
possibility that one of the girls had taken her own life. It was only Oliver
and I who could know for certain that that was indeed the case, although
of course we would never know which of the twins it had been. Going
by Oliver's description of their behaviour – how Hilary was always the
slightly more dominant of the two – I had my own theory which was

this: Hilary was the one who got into serious difficulty when the pole broke, and it was she who influenced Sophie to give up and drown with her.

As I'd said to Oliver on more than one occasion, this whole sorry tale of the Markland Estate and everything associated with it could fill the pages of a book one day, and I had decided to occupy my time inside my cell wisely and write everything down. But writing down my story hadn't quite been finished when I unexpectedly discovered that I was about to leave prison much earlier than I'd anticipated.

I had been recommended for early release based on my good behaviour, and the parole officer, a very kindly and sympathetic lady, called me to her office only last week to inform me of her decision to let me out early.

"Now you know, Mr. Markland, that you will be under scrutiny and that you will need to report to me once a week, but we have considered everything and believe that you are fit to be released back into the community. You have served your time here, and we wish you well."

Well, I couldn't ask for more than that, could I? Of course I was over the moon, although to be truthful, I had become almost fond of the place and some of the people inside. My cellmate who liked to be known as Praying Mantis, and with whom I'd struck up a friendship, would always be welcome to visit me following his release, although I suspected that that might not be any time soon. In all the months we'd shared a cell together, I never did get to the bottom of what he'd done, and I guessed that now I never would.

During my time 'inside' I was fortunate to have had visits from Oliver who, without fail, came every single week. On at least four occasions he came along with his old nanny, the wonderful Miss Baudet, who played such an important part in Oliver's upbringing. I wonder how things may have turned out had it not been for her evidence presented at my hearing. I was delighted when, soon after I'd been sentenced, I discovered that she had made the decision to move lock, stock and barrel down to Wivenhoe and to keep a watchful eye over Oliver while he lived on the old Barnacle barge. Sadly the old barge wouldn't ever be quite the same again without Harry. I had been deeply saddened when Oliver told me that the little scamp had passed away. Oliver had quickly grown particularly fond of him - who wouldn't? - and my theory is that he actually died of a broken heart as soon as I stopped coming home. My heart was broken too, but I comforted myself in the knowledge that he simply went to sleep in his basket that day and never woke up. At least he hadn't got into a fight with a larger dog, or fallen in the muddy banks of the River Colne, or something similarly unpleasant. God rest his doggie soul - perhaps Oliver and I could get another canine friend one day. We shall see.

And speaking of affairs of the heart, I've had some news that I'm very excited about. You won't fail to recall the special friendship that developed between me and the lovely Silvie Tosgiev, the woman who so expertly taught me some really important 'ways of the world', if you understand my meaning. Technically, she also played a very significant part in Oliver's life, albeit before he was born.

It turned out that Silvie moved back to her native Sweden, and I'd write to her from time to time from prison. It was a way of expressing myself outside of writing this book. Instinctively I felt I could share my innermost thoughts in letters to her, without being judged or looked down upon. We once had a special relationship together and I believe that she had felt equally happy in my company as I did in hers. I would certainly never forget that incredible weekend we had together on the barge when she came up to Wivenhoe, all those years ago. Modesty prevents me from saying it out loud but that was when I discovered that I was actually capable of loving a woman in the way that you're supposed to.

I wrote and told her about everything that had happened to me, using far more words than necessary. It was a cathartic experience and, along with my book-writing, those letters helped to keep me going through my occasional bouts of depression. She would always do me the courtesy of sending a reply, telling me how she had left Miss Pinchbeck's Angelpride agency and moved back to live with her parents in Sweden where they helped her to bring up her daughter. Her daughter? That was a bolt out of the blue for me, and I can't deny I felt a small amount of jealousy. I had absolutely no right to feel that way, but I did. Sylvie was never the prolific writer that I was, and her letters were always less than a page in length. Although skimping on the finer details, she did manage to tell me that her daughter's name was Laura, that she was very pretty, and now a teenager studying art and biology - with the ambition to become a forensic artist. She didn't elaborate, so I could only hope to discover what exactly a forensic artist was, one day in the future. Anyway, the exciting news I'd had was that Silvie had promised that one day soon she would be making a trip back to England, bringing Laura along to see all the London sights she had been so fond of.

During my time in custody I did of course have some worries about Oliver. Any father would, but these were unusual circumstances to say the least, and from a practical point of view I was concerned about money. Without me earning, and with limited and finite funds available, I was concerned that my savings, stashed away around various parts of the barge, would all be used up before I came out. Apart from an initial £200 I'd told Oliver about just after the tragic accident, there were also a number of similar packages containing money dotted around the place – under floor planks, taped inside lockers and stuffed in the engine bay. But I knew that those wouldn't last forever. After all, Oliver needed clothing, school books and food, and nothing was cheap these days. And of course there were also the bills associated with the barge itself; heating, electricity and mooring fees payable to Del Boy, as I called him. Although Oliver was very capable and levelheaded, and Stanley was always financially generous to him, I often pictured him there on my old steel boat, living alone and fending for himself, but without Harry to keep him company. At least he had my collection of Harry Nilsson CDs to play, and I was rather pleased when he told me that he actually liked them too. The boy's got taste.

I needn't have worried about the money though. I telephoned Roger
Ainsworth one Monday, a month or so before I was released, to explain
my financial concerns, and to ask him if there was any way he could lend
me some funds for Oliver and me until I was able to get working again and
begin to repay him. I know that I could or should have asked Stanley, but
I just thought I would be kind of rubbing salt into his wounds. Goodness
knows what he must have been thinking when he learned that Oliver
wanted to swap his life up there at the Manor house for living down here
on my boat. All Roger said to me during our conversation was "Don't
worry yourself Leslie. I've taken care of things in that department", but
he refused to elaborate further. It wasn't until Oliver came to visit me a
week later, just two days after his 16th birthday, that everything became
apparent. It was incredibly good news, and I needed to pinch myself
more than once to convince myself that I wasn't dreaming.

"Dad. Take a look at this!" Oliver yelled, pulling an opened envelope
from his inside jacket pocket. He was bursting with excitement as he
handed me the envelope. I pulled out the five folded pieces of paper
stapled together at the top left corner, and then looked at the small
flimsy dark grey book contained within the folds. At first I read the few
words typed on the top sheet of paper.

Dear Mr. Markland

*Our firm Ainsworth and Company has overseen the investment of funds
put aside for you by your father for your maintenance and well-being until
you reach your sixteenth birthday. I have taken the liberty of closing the
offshore account and transferring the balance to a regular UK bank account
for your easier access. I trust you will find everything in order and to your
satisfaction.*

*If we, or our associate accountants, can be of any further assistance, we
would be pleased if you would simply contact me at your convenience.*

Yours sincerely,

On behalf of

Ainsworth and Company

Solicitors

I turned to the following pages one by one. They showed, in very small writing, the beginning of the ledger dating back 16 years with the very first entry of £300, and the same amount each month thereafter until May the following year, when the sum rose to £310. Then it was £320 the following year and £330 the year after, and so on, until most recently when it was £450 each and every month. And at the end of every year there was a figure representing the interest accrued and added to the balance. Every year the balance went up and up, except for the third year when an amount of £10,000 had been deducted. But when I got to the closing figure I could see that £10,000 had been re-submitted in one lump sum. I was puzzled by that, but, hey what the heck, I thought, who's counting? Well, with a balance like this in his account, Oliver wouldn't need to be counting for quite some time, that was for sure.

So, apparently all the maintenance payments I'd been making were being put aside and invested on behalf of Oliver, and I didn't have a clue. What an enormous boost for Oliver and his future. With interest, the total figure shown at the bottom of the ledger was a staggering £102,465.81. Wow! That would do very nicely for the young man!

———————

I've been out of prison for a few months now, and I've got to say it was fantastic to get back on my Barnacle barge, although as it would eventually turn out, not for too long. It was even better to once again frequent my favourite watering holes, and to reacquaint myself with the good people of the village. The Black Buoy was looking better than I remembered, and The Station pub, with its L-shaped bar, was the same as I'd left it. Sadly, the places were minus one or two regular drinkers who had unfortunately passed on while I'd been absent. That's life, I concluded, rather philosophically. However, there was one larger than life character who, thankfully, was still very much around.

"You little turnip," Andy Stollery teased me. "I told you to get that rail fixed," he said before turning to the beauty behind the bar. "Get this man your finest bottle of Merlot please, Chelsea."

That was all he's ever said on the subject to this very day.

Oliver, with his unexpected fortune, has been studying hard at the local sixth form college, and has also applied for his provisional driving license so he can begin taking lessons as soon as he's 17. Like me, he has a natural interest in cars and I know he can't wait to get his own. I'm sure he'll do well generally in life because everyone likes him. He got himself a weekend and evening job at the Co-op in the High Street - not that he needed the money, but he discovered that work is rather good for the soul. He bought himself a bicycle, and I don't mean just any old bike. Choosing a top of the range Cannondale costing more than £2,000, he can regularly be seen going like the clappers along the Wivenhoe Trail - a path that runs alongside the river between Wivenhoe and Colchester.

One day not so long ago, on one of his cycle rides nearing Colchester, he came a cropper when a large labrador ran out from behind some bushes in front of him. He said he must have been doing at least 20 miles an hour when he swerved to avoid hitting it, but lost control and ended up grazing his skin all down his left side, the poor lad. He could easily have been seriously hurt, but luckily the only thing that needed much attention was the bike itself. He called me to go and help him bring it and him back in my van, which of course I did without delay. On my way to his rescue, while driving down Clingoe Hill towards the town, I chuckled to myself about how different things were between Oli and myself now, compared with me and George Markland back then when I was 16. He wouldn't have lifted a finger to help me, whatever scrapes I got myself into. The memory of that time when I came off my motorbike and he just drove on by still haunts me even after all these years. While waiting at the traffic lights as I thought more and more about the irony of the situation, my chuckle turned into an outright laugh.

Of course I'm wiser now, understanding that George wasn't my father at all. I was very glad that Oliver would never again have those uncertainties about who his own father is.

He and I live apart, but that's only because the barge wasn't designed for long-term two-person occupation, what with its narrow gangway and tiny shower room. It was certainly a great place for hanging out together though. We often sit around listening to music on the new hi-fi system he recently purchased for it, exactly the same as the one he also bought for me to keep at my place.

You see, mulling things over, I'd been thinking that with some of his money Oliver could now put down a hefty deposit on a flat or a house somewhere not too far away. But he then went and completely surprised me by saying that he'd much rather stay living on old Barnacle barge. Another surprise followed when he revealed that he would like to use his money to get a place for me instead! So there really is truth in the old saying that what goes around comes around. I'm getting a lovely terraced cottage in Queens Road, which is just a five-minute walk away from the barge - or 30 seconds for Speedy Gonzalez Oli on his bike!

And there's no prize for guessing whose music we most enjoy listening to on our new stereo systems during our evenings together. It wasn't long before Oli would play a game, quoting me lines from Nilsson's catalogue of great songs that he'd written in his heyday. "I'm awfully glad you came" - a line from 'Mr. Richland's Favorite Song' - he'd jovially say, with a beaming smile when I arrived at the cabin door of his home. Why not check it out if you've never heard it? Oliver recommends it. When I would leave the barge to go back to my home, I'd continue the game by using my own favourite quote, giving particularly gruff emphasis on its last word. I'll tell you what it is when we reach the end of my tale.

The two of us regularly visit Louise Baudet. She's such a lovely lady, still very young at heart and always totally full of beans. Many happy hours are passed, chatting about our new lives now forged in Wivenhoe, as well as the old ones left behind in Yorkshire. I don't think she has a single regret about uprooting herself and coming down here to live. When she's not at her apartment near the river, she can usually be found sitting out on the rear deck of Miss Baudet, the boat with its distinctive multi-coloured canopy that she bought. To this day it's still moored outside the Rose & Crown pub on the quay, where its previous owner,

Neil, used to keep it. In fact, Neil can sometimes be spotted doing a bit of touching up of the paintwork for her every now and then when required. I've heard he rather likes doing it.

And that, dear reader, just about brings my story to its natural conclusion, except to say that I've been saving my best news until last.

One sunny lunchtime, Oliver, Alberta Louise and I all went to the station together. Not The Station pub, but the actual railway station, where a train carrying two very important guests would be arriving shortly. Silvie Tosgiev and her daughter Laura were coming to visit the three of us, having heard from me in one of my letters that Oliver and Miss Baudet were now also living in Wivenhoe. I would like to think that, if modesty allows, Silvie was also keen to see me, if only for old time's sake. Without being presumptuous, I hoped that she shared my curiosity about what might also lie ahead for us. Granted, it was merely a glimmer of hope on my part, but you never know where dreams may lead, however impossible they seem at the time.

The train came to a halt on the other side of the track amid the familiar sound of carriage doors opening and swishing shut. As the train obscured the view of all the passengers walking along the platform to the footbridge, it wasn't until they came down the steps towards us that we first set eyes on our guests.

"Hello!" we all said, almost at exactly at the same time, while jostling and bumping as we greeted one another. Miss Baudet and Silvie kissed each other on the left and right cheeks like they would in France. Silvie's daughter Laura and Oliver shook hands politely, nevertheless seeming to have an instant connection with each other, judging by the way their eyes met. And Silvie and I hugged, rather naturally I'm thankful and pleased to say. And then we did it all over again, this time with different partners like performing an unpracticed dance, again jostling and bumping into each other some more. We all laughed, and then we stood back in silence all looking at each other.

It was Miss Baudet who spotted it before I did.

"My goodness me," she blurted out, breaking the brief period of silence after studying the appearance of Laura's striking features for a moment. "Doesn't Laura look just like Oliver?!"

Silvie moved closer and leaned into me, her eyes flashed a look that indicated she was eager to tell me something. She stood on her tiptoes and whispered softly in my ear: "Leslie, there's something I need to tell you."

THE END

'So thank you, and Goodnight' – Harry Nilsson,
'Oblio's Return', from the LP The Point, 1971

The author in front of one of artist wife Jane Watson's paintings,
'Abstract Seascape'
www.janewatsonart.com

About the Author, by the Author

When I was asked to write a few words about myself for the usual author's biography I was unusually lost for words.

My relatively uneventful working career has consisted of almost two decades in sales and marketing, followed by a life 'in the trade' as a handyman and painter. But life certainly hasn't been mundane: A solo cycle ride across America, publishing a magazine for fellow sales professionals, and 'doing up' a beautiful old house in France as a writer's retreat are three of my most memorable adventures.

And music has always played a big part in my life. When I found myself playing volleyball in Harry Nilsson's son's swimming pool in Los Angeles I remember reflecting in wonderment at how I'd got to that high point in my life. Through a natural excitement, I went on to force my way into the music business by working with the multi-talented Joanna Eden, and later played a tiny role in the development of singer songwriter Sam Smith's huge rise to stardom.

My proudest moment from that era? That had to be when I was asked to select the tracks for *One*, a double CD of my hero Nilsson's songs, released by Sony Records. An illustrious radio career followed, which saw me acting out the character of Barnacle Bill on Mark Wesley's

Radio Essex show, a stunt that culminated in my own *World's Smallest Pirate Radio Station* programme, broadcast from the boat I'd renovated in Wivenhoe. I've dined out on that story many times, along with the other tales I wrote about in my blog A Boat For My Potplants: Those tales included the one about a gorilla sitting on the top of the boat. Seriously! Trust me, living in Wivenhoe, that was nothing terribly unusual!

A chance meeting with Wivenhoe music writer and publisher David Roberts gave me the opportunity to write *Muddy Water*, my first, and hopefully not my last, novel. Many fun moments were had on board my old boat, moored conveniently outside the Rose & Crown, discussing various plotlines and prose for *Muddy Water* as the book took shape. So, thanks to David's professional words of wisdom and expertise, I can now add the job of 'author' to my short CV.

Thanks must also go to David's wife Janet and my wife Jane who worked tirelessly, making notes and valued points, helping me to make *Muddy Water* into something I can be proud to present.

It goes without saying, but I'll say it anyway, how much I appreciate my artist wife Jane's gentle persuasion and encouragement for me to try my hand at writing. She suffered badly though, with me constantly demanding her to put her brush down and "have a listen to this," as I read her my latest thrilling paragraph. I was always keen to hear her comments, but I can't possibly tell you what some of them were, here!

Jane and I divide our time between living very happily in Wivenhoe and Montolieu, France, a beautiful place known as the Village du Livres, on account of its 15 book shops for only 800 inhabitants.

Between us we have three grown-up children who have now all flown the nest; there's 'her' daughter Laura, 'my' daughter Laura, and my son Oliver. It was 'my' Laura who did such an incredible job illustrating the characters who have 'narrated' their chapters within the pages of this book. My favourite illustration? It has to be Harry the dog, of course. What's yours?

Neil Watson, Wivenhoe, 2015
www.aboatformypotplants.blogspot.com

Harry

Leslie Markland

The Young Leslie Markland

George Markland

Silvie Tosgiev

Stanley Markland

Tristan Thomas

Constance Markland

Anna Hennings

Roger Ainsworth

Brian Ainsworth

Alberta Louise Baudet

Oliver Markland

MUDDY
WATER

www.facebook.com/MuddyWaterbook